Girl Crazy

Girl Crazy

RUSSELL SMITH

HarperCollinsPublishers*Ltd*

Published by HarperCollins Publishers Ltd.

First edition

HarperCollins books may be purchased for educational,
business, or sales promotional use through our
Special Markets Department.

HarperCollins Publishers Ltd
2 Bloor Street East, 20th Floor
Toronto, Ontario, Canada
M4W 1A8

www.harpercollins.ca

Library and Archives Canada Cataloguing in Publication

Smith, Russell, 1963–
Girl crazy : a novel / Russell Smith.

ISBN 978-1-55468-534-9

I. Title.
PS8587.M58397G57 2009   C813'.54   C2009-905741-7

Printed in the United States
RRD 9 8 7 6 5 4 3 2 1

For the edification of
HUGO

Girl Crazy

1.

The pool was closed. Justin could see that from across the park. His bike was so heavy he had to stand up in the saddle and pull on the handlebars to heave himself up the street. In the traffic, there was nowhere to stop; he would have to get all the way to the lights before he could turn around. He grabbed at the towel which kept slipping from around his shoulders. His eyes stung from sweat. This was supposed to be easy, relaxing; this was the advantage of living downtown: you grabbed your towel and your bike and there was a pool right there, a public outdoor pool, with Portuguese teenage girls in bikinis glistening on the concrete, totally free, like a free strip club, a free beach holiday, this was the triumph of the welfare state, and yet of course when you looked across the brown bowl of grass, across this park that was a pit, from your perch in the insane traffic you did not see the fluorescent blue water and the bright flashes of coloured towels, of course you saw a concrete slab with a backhoe on it and scaffolding around it and stacks of concrete sewage pipe like op-art sculpture. Justin braked hard

3

as a taxi swerved in front of him. This was what rickshaw drivers in Bombay felt like. Although you were supposed to say Mumbai now. All the radio announcers only said Mumbai now.

"Mumbai," said Justin in the traffic.

At the next intersection he got onto the sidewalk and struggled all the way on the bumpy sidewalk along one ridge of the bowl to get closer to the former pool, to see what was going on. The whole park was deserted, except for a homeless encampment under a tree. It was hard to tell whether the lumps of possessions hid sleeping bodies or not. Two dogs of no colour chewed on things in the shade. It was not clear why all the grass had died and turned brown. Perhaps there had not been enough rain, perhaps the air was finally too toxic for life.

This park was built out of a former quarry. It was a depression in the city. One end, where Justin was, was steep. You could, if you were brave, grab hard onto the handlebars of your bike and let yourself go over the edge, plummet down the walls of the bowl and hope your brakes worked at the bottom. Young guys did it all the time. Justin had never done it. He almost did it now, but did not look forward to pushing his bike back up the hill. His shirt was soaked through.

The pool was non-existent; the concrete had been broken up and stacked in jagged piles. The pool was a construction site. The community centre was padlocked. Justin stopped on the edge of the steep hill and looked back at the city. You could see the towers of the core from here. Except today you couldn't: the haze was too thick. The sky was yellow. It was like a science fiction movie about the future.

Justin wiped his face with his towel and tucked it under the strap of his bag, which held the lump of papers he had brought to mark by the pool. There were thirty-five students in his Intro-duction to Media class, and fifteen had submitted their assign-ments, which was about normal, so he could get them done in an hour or so if he could get away from the construction outside his apartment. The park would have to do. He cycled around the community centre on the sidewalk, then down one side of the park to where there was a parking lot, on the really busy street that ran along the subway line, and a convenience store.

"Mumbai," he said.

The parking lot was black asphalt. There was a big green dumpster outside the store, full of black garbage bags, and right next to it, on the asphalt, a picnic table, in the sun. There were guys in heavy jackets and caps sitting on the picnic table, talk-ing on cellphones. You could smell the dumpster. There was nowhere to lock your bike. Justin got off his and pushed it to the sidewalk on the busy street.

There were two pay phones. He could call Genevieve, tell her about the pool, as if she'd been serious when she said that she might join him, although he knew that there had never been the slightest chance of her taking a whole afternoon off from working on her new apartment, even on a Sunday, and even though he knew it was a little weird that they kept making plans to see each other and pretending to be friends so soon after the breakup. The whole thing was weird but he didn't really want to think about it.

There was a girl in those tight and low-cut sweatpants on one of the phones. Her back was to him. Justin looked at her bare midriff and her buttocks for a moment. He'd always found something quite pornographic about this particular item of cloth-ing. They were not like the sweatpants of his youth. They were possibly for yoga. They were pale blue and clung to her tight little buttocks and thighs like a bathing suit. They had a wide band around the hips, so low on her hips he could see the white strings and triangle of her thong, rising like a tattoo from between her muscles. And there was actually a tattoo, too, in the small of her back, a red and green floral thing. Her skin was very pale. The girl was hardly wearing anything, actually: a matching crop-top with an athletic criss-cross back was all that covered her breasts, which he could not see. Justin hesitated before moving around her to the other phone, because he wanted her to turn around. He noticed her hair, then, too: it was a thick cascade of streaks.

The girl was kicking a running shoe against the post that supported the phone. As he stood beside her and picked up the receiver on the next phone, he heard her say, "I've been here fifteen fucking minutes. I've called twice already."

He glanced over and smiled. She jerked her head towards him and he saw her face, her violently blue eyes. She had full lips, some pale freckles over her nose. And her eye makeup was smudged, as if she had been crying. She did not smile at him. She turned her head away.

He glanced at her breasts as he dialled. They were quite full, and the nipples were clearly visible under the stretchy stuff. And there was a silver stud in her belly button, and maybe another tattoo poking up from her groin.

Genevieve's phone rang and rang and then her perky message came on. He hung up.

"I don't have another quarter," said the girl. "Can you please please promise me it's on its way?" Then she slammed her receiver down and put her face in her hands. She turned away from Justin and leaned against the plastic awning of the phone.

Justin stood there for a while, too. He didn't know where he was going, anyway.

He saw the girl walk to the sidewalk, step into the traffic and peer down the street. The traffic was jammed up and down the road. He could take in her whole body then. It was tight and smooth all over. She was really wearing almost nothing. There did seem to be a little tattoo on the lower part of her belly, but he didn't stare at that. He wanted to look at her crotch, because he knew the fabric was so thin and tight that it might be painfully revealing there, but he didn't want to be seen doing it, and also he was afraid, for some reason, of seeing that. And of course it was embarrassing to acknowledge to himself that he had such a thing for underwear, but there it was. He did.

The girl stepped back to the curb and then sat on it heavily and hunched over her knees.

Her white shoulders shone in the sun.

Justin leaned his bike against the telephone and walked over to her. He bent down. "Excuse me. Are you all right?"

She looked up at him. She had definitely been crying. Her forehead was turning pink in the sun. She said, "Could you do me a favour?"

Justin stood up. If she was going to ask him for money, he would walk away.

"Could you just look down the street and see if there's an ambulance coming?"

"Sure." He stepped out into the road and looked east. The traffic was immobile for as far as he could see. The air over it shimmered. "Not right now, no. Did you call one?"

She had put her head down on her knees again.

"Listen," said Justin, "you're really pale. You should get out of the heat. Get out of the sun. Can I get you some water?"

"I'm hemorrhaging," she said flatly, as if saying, *I'm tired.*

"Oh." Justin wiped his face with the bottom of his T-shirt. "Just a minute." He grabbed his bike and ran it over to the door of the convenience store. He leaned it against the glass and went inside. It was cold inside. He waited for the Korean teenager behind the counter to finish his cellphone conversation, and then he asked for a bottle of water. He saw that there was a coffee pot on a hot plate beside the cash, and he bought a coffee in a styrofoam cup. He poured lots of cream and sugar into it. While he waited for his change, he watched his bike through the glass. The guys sitting on the picnic table had all turned to look at it. One by one, they folded up their cellphones.

Justin was almost afraid the girl would be gone when he came out, but she was still there, sitting on the curb, doubled over. He couldn't hold his bike with his hands full, so he left it there and walked to the curb. He sat with her and looked over his shoulder at his bike and the boys. They seemed to be ignoring it for the moment. He said, "Here, there's cream and sugar in this, you should drink it, and that's plain water."

She took the water and said, "Thank you." Her voice was shaky.

"And you should really get out of the sun. It's air-conditioned inside the store. I'll wait out here."

"Where the fuck *is it.*"

Justin sighed. He had to keep twisting his head around at the bike.

She said, "Do you have a cellphone?"

He shook his head. "I can call from the pay phone again, if you like."

"Never mind. It's not even worth it. Ow."

8

Justin got up again and stepped into the road. He thought that maybe in the distance, one of the trucks stuck a couple of blocks away could have been white. "There might be one stuck in the traffic over there. I don't know. It's not moving." He looked at his watch. It was almost three and he hadn't started his marking. The boys by the store slumped off their picnic table and walked away without touching his bike.

He sat beside her on the curb. "Don't you want the coffee? The sugar might be a good idea."

She shook her head. "The water's fine. Thank you." She produced an elastic from somewhere and put it in her teeth and lifted her arms to wrap her hair up in a ponytail. Without moving his head, Justin was able to get a good look at her breasts, her muscular little arms, her naked underarms, the sweaty back of her neck where there were little blonde curls. There was a tattoo there, too, a little black sun. And one of those barbed wire designs around her bicep.

Her hair was multicoloured, actually, with dark roots and blonde streaks of different shades. Its unnaturalness seemed deliberate.

He asked, "Are you pregnant?"

"I guess so."

Justin exhaled. The traffic was edging forward, so he got up again and peered up the street. "That is an ambulance," he said. "It's coming."

"Jesus," she said. "They could at least turn the fucking siren on."

It took another five minutes to get to them. It was like watching a ship arrive from the horizon.

When it approached, Justin flagged it down, and two middle-aged guys got out. They nodded at him, snapping on rubber

9

gloves, and went over to the girl and leaned over her. Justin hovered.

"Now," one said to her, "what's been going on?"

She told them. And they didn't move. They looked at each other and then at her and kept asking her questions. "What else?" they said. "You been doing any drugs today? You in trouble with anybody?"

"Hey," said Justin. "She needs to get to a hospital."

They ignored him. "Western?" said one.

"I'll have to check the list."

"No way," said the girl. "I'm not going to Western. I'm not waiting all day there. Take me to Sinai."

"We can't just take you anywhere you want, sweetheart."

"Yes you fucking can."

"Hey now. Be nice."

"Hey," said Justin, "how about you be nice to her?"

The two men stood and swung to face him. They both had big bellies. They put their rubbery hands on their belts and looked at him. "You her boyfriend?"

"No," said Justin. "I don't even know her."

"You call the ambulance?"

He shook his head.

"All right then. How are you helping us?"

The passing cars all had their windows open, and people of all ages and races were staring at them as they inched past. They all had dull expressions, as if they were watching TV.

"Listen," said Justin, "I know someone at Sinai. He's a doctor. He's an emergency room doctor. If I can use your phone I can call him now, see if he's working. I think he is."

"I don't even know if Sinai's receiving today."

"Check your list," said Justin. "Just check it. Or let me talk to them."

One of the guys lumbered around to the cab of the ambulance. He moved as if he was extremely tired. He swung the door open and took out a clipboard and a walkie-talkie attached to a curly wire.

"How are you doing?" said Justin to the girl.

"Why the fuck can't we just fucking go?" she said.

"My name's Justin," he said. "I have a friend who can help you. If he's working today. He's a med student. A resident."

"I thought you said he was a doctor."

"He is a doctor. Almost completely. He's a resident now."

She looked up at him. "I really don't want to go to Western."

"Sinai's open," called the medic.

"Let me borrow your phone," said Justin to the other medic. "Please."

"Can we please please please get going?" said the girl.

"You want a gurney?" said one of the guys.

"No," she said, standing up. "Let's go."

"I wasn't talking to you."

The other guy strolled back to help her in. "Sure," he said, "if she's okay to walk. You coming?" He was looking at Justin.

Justin looked at his bicycle. "If you go to Sinai. I can help her find my friend."

"You don't have to," said the girl. "I'll be fine." Then she swayed. She put out a hand and steadied herself on the ambulance door. "Oh, God." She swallowed and closed her eyes. "I think I'm going to faint."

Justin grabbed her arm. He put his other arm around her waist. The skin was hot and taut. He glanced at the groin of her trousers, too. It wasn't tight, as he had expected. There did seem to be a padding of some sort under there, a puffiness. But there was no sign of blood, anywhere on her.

Once they had her into the ambulance and sitting down, he said, "One second," and ran back to his bike. He locked it to a chain link fence and ran back to the ambulance. He climbed in and the doors closed behind him.

Her name was Jenna. She kept wanting to leave the waiting room of Emergency to have a smoke, but Justin wouldn't let her. She looked to be about twenty-four or twenty-five. She mentioned "getting to work" once, but she didn't say where.

There was bulletproof Plexiglas protecting the women in the reception booth. The window was all scratched up, as if someone had attacked it with a salad fork.

Big paramedics kept striding through.

It had turned out that Andrew was on duty, but they hadn't seen him yet. They witnessed a whole series of old ladies arrive on stretchers, wrinkled and bunched like discarded clothes, and get pushed through the swinging doors ahead of them.

Once when the doors swung wide and Justin glanced inside, he caught a glimpse of a flapping white coat and some green trousers on a young man and it looked like Andrew's back. But he was walking in the opposite direction.

Jenna went to the washroom a couple of times and returned saying she was okay, but nothing had changed.

They saw a native woman with her eyes swollen shut stagger down the hallway and collapse right in front of them. It took a few minutes for any of the receptionists or nurses or whatever they were to emerge from behind the glass. A big native guy with a ponytail and a pocked face who could have been the woman's husband or her father knelt next to her and took her hand and waited. The big paramedics arrived and wordlessly heaved her onto a gurney and away. The big guy waited in the waiting room.

Justin was just getting up to go to the bulletproof glass again when Andrew pushed through the doors, unshaven, his hair all messy.

"Hey man," he said. "What's up?"

"This is Jenna," said Justin.

"Hey, Jenna," said Andrew. He knelt by her side in the waiting room.

"You sure took your time," said Jenna.

Andrew looked up at Justin and then back at Jenna. "We had a couple of heart attacks and an overdose," he said gently. "We can see you now." He stood up and said to Justin, "How are you doing? Long time. You okay?"

"Dude," said Justin, "I am so grateful for this. I am going to buy you a crateload of beers."

"Sorry I couldn't get here earlier. We should catch up."

"Yeah, absolutely. How've you been? When was the last time you slept?"

"Ah," Andrew, stretching his neck. "Yesterday. No. Day before."

"Huh. Hey, I'm at level thirteen on Sandstorm. You get to drive a humvee with a flamethrower."

Andrew laughed.

Jenna was standing up, walking towards the swinging doors.

Andrew said, "So how do you guys—"

"Long story," said Justin. "Actually we just met."

"Uh huh. Cas-evac, eh?"

"Roger that."

Andrew looked over at Jenna, who was waiting for him at the open doors, her flat belly pushed forward, her nipples erect in the air conditioning, the thin fabric of her suit gripping her hips like cling film. She pulled her long hair loose from her ponytail and shook it back over her bare shoulders and bit her lower lip.

"Okay," said Andrew. "Are you going to be sticking around?"

"You don't need to," said Jenna. "I'll be fine."

"You sure?" said Justin. "You have somewhere to go, after?"

"Of course I do."

"All right. You're lucky to have Andrew taking care of you. I've known him since I was twelve."

Jenna nodded. "Thanks a lot," she said.

"Okay. Good luck. Andrew," said Justin, "give me a call when you have a few hours off."

"You going to Dorothy Liu's networking dinner thing?" said Andrew.

"Oh," said Justin. "I guess. I should. You going?"

Andrew smiled. "I can't really go out these days."

"Oh. No then."

"Might be good for you," said Andrew.

"You guys take your time," said Jenna.

"Okay," said Justin. "You're going in now."

"Sorry," she said. "Sorry. And thanks. I mean it," said Jenna. "Thanks for helping me. I'm sorry I've been . . . I've been brutal."

"Brutal?"

Andrew was standing beside her now, his hand on her elbow, holding the heavy door open with his body. "Okay," he said.

"We're oscar mike."

"Copy that."

And it could have ended there, with Justin turning and walking out the door, and in fact he couldn't have said why he waited there for a second longer, for her to say something: perhaps because of the breakup, he was a little more open to whatever was going to happen, perhaps he was a little unmoored himself, because of being alone for the past couple of months, perhaps because of everything that had been happening at work, but he stood there and put his hands on his hips and looked into her eyes.

She stepped close to him (Andrew was yawning and looking at his watch) and kissed him on the cheek. She smelled sweet, like candy. She said, "Do you want me to call you?"

"I—sure," said Justin. "Let me know how you . . . how you make out." He pulled out his wallet and extracted a business card. "This is my work, but I'll . . ." He fished a pen out of his knapsack. He didn't look to see how Andrew was taking this. He wrote his home number on the back of the card.

She took it and disappeared.

Andrew said, "Call me," and Justin said, "I so owe you," and then he was outside again, in the dizzying heat, breathing in toxins, and he had to find some way of getting back to his bicycle where he had left it.

His apartment was dim, all the blinds were down, but it was still hot. He needed to do laundry. His phone was flashing. There was a query from Guntar Haus about a poker night, a reminder from Dorothy Liu about the networking dinner that he knew he would end up going to. You had to pay a silly amount of money and sit in a restaurant with strangers and it was supposed to be good for your career, and if you said you didn't have a career then people like Dorothy Liu had a knack of making you feel so childish you had to claim it was a joke and agree to go.

He took off his shirt and sat at his computer and played a quick half-level of Sandstorm III (Sheik Assassin), smoking out a few Republican Guard bunkers with the MK19 grenade launchers and then chasing down and incinerating the fleeing officers with a flamethrower, which wasn't strictly necessary but was visually enthralling and satisfying. It was in fact because he was doing this with too much enthusiasm that he failed to notice an easy 200-point Pashtun with an AK bounce up out of a foxhole almost right under him and pop pop, his screen went red.

He refused to check his e-mails, switched off his computer, took off his remaining clothes and lay on his bed under a fan. He saw Jenna's belly, the elastic of her thong. He was quickly engorged and sensitive. He stroked himself and spurted on his belly. Then he fell asleep.

2.

To get to Constitution College Polytechnical Institute, Justin walked six blocks to the subway, then took the subway to the end of the line, then a bus. The bus went along a road which was like a highway, parallel to the real highway. You could see the real highway from time to time between the factory buildings, a pipeline of cars, glittering. The bus to the college was full at this time of the morning, before nine, and not air-conditioned. It usually smelled as if most people had had curry for breakfast. Perhaps they had. Justin stood at the back, between two girls in hijabs and a woman of indeterminate age and shape in a full burka. She didn't, at least, have one of those horrible masks with holes over her face, like something out of a fetish magazine, but her face was covered by a black scarf except for her eyes.

It was strange that no one had yet sexualized the face mask, though: one could imagine it on a porn site. Perhaps he should have tried photographing it and making millions of dollars from it. He often had thoughts like this, of possible lucrative pornographic sites, but he was always stalled on the question of models, and of paying models. Still, it was a reliable fantasy. He sighed loudly at the thought of asking Genevieve to try modelling the head scarf. And a garter belt, maybe. She'd love that.

He had tried asking her, once, to let him photograph her in her special black underwear, with his little digital camera he had just got from her for Christmas. She had said yes, at first, and then got upset when he had asked her to put on some stay-up stockings. She didn't have any stay-up stockings and she wondered why he was so fixated on images that were so clichéd and so not her. It was as if he wanted her to be someone else, or as if he was in lust with the stockings themselves, and not her, which was a little weird. He had not asked her again.

He moved aside for some big boys and their even bigger clothing. Their uselessly warm team jackets and their knapsacks inflated the bus. Their trousers were so large and so low they were like skirts of the nineteenth century, trains, pools they floated in. Each boy had earpieces lodged in his ears and they shouted at each other over their music.

At his stop, Justin had to push through them. And then he was alone in the cloud of bus gas and the blinding sun, across from the Crossways Plaza. Each of the four corners of this intersection was a parking lot. You could get depressed standing here, particularly on a Monday morning, indeed you usually had to fight against getting depressed, but it was only a fifteen-minute walk from there into the campus. And there was a Tim Hortons on the way, so it was at least more pleasant than the bus, in summer anyway. You could get your coffee at Tim's and that would be a distraction, it would break up the walk along the side of the highway and the parking lots of the strip malls and the auto body shops, and that coffee would take you all the way to the concrete gates of the campus, and then there was another hundred yards or so of parking lots, where pleasant fantasies could be entertained of the destructive power of various weaponry available in Sandstorm III (Sheik Assassin) on the assorted gleaming new student cars, particularly the shoulder-carried single-shot AT-4 antitank weapon, and the bipod-supported squad automatic weapon, more versatile than the belt-fed MG4, and fittable with its awesome yet inaccurate M-203 grenade launcher attachment. (The heavy, 40-cal MK19 would be useless here unless you could commandeer some kind of heavy vehicle to mount it on, as you could in the higher levels of Sandstorm III (Sheik Assassin), but you would have to have done that on the highway, before entering the parking lot.) Imagining that you were seeing all the vehicles through the crosshairs on the head-up display of your screen would get you easily through it, and then you could delve into a stairwell and make the rest of your way to Media and Communications Studies almost entirely underground, through the coffee-and-fried-rice-smelling student centre and its food court, with its walls fluttering with stapled announcements. There were at least people there.

He had the papers with him but they were still unmarked. If the staff meeting didn't last too long he was going to at least get a start on them in the half hour before his class. Justin didn't have an office per se, but there was usually some table space in the staff room, which was where the meeting was being held this morning.

There was a departmental office, a closet really, off one of the wider corridors, with a secretary in it and a set of pigeonholes where Justin could pick up his mail. There was never any mail, since all his students and everyone else communicated with him solely—and constantly and shrilly—electronically. However, the secretary, Janice, was always worth looking at.

Janice was hardly older than the students. She had glossy black hair and brown eyes and an olive skin, for she was some Mediterranean mix that could have been part Arab or part Filipina. It was a modern thing, whatever; she was the same colour as half his students, and he really didn't know where they were from and he didn't ask because one wasn't supposed to. She was as slim as a magazine model, and she wore the stretchy black trousers and the scoop-neck tops that the Portuguese girls of his neighbourhood wore. She managed to have, though, a whole series of armour-plated bras whose cups were so stiff that he had never once, despite the thinness of her clingy tops, perceived even the outline of a nipple, not the mildest bump. This was presumably to discourage the leering of nineteen-year-old students who could, indeed, often be heard discussing the departmental secretary's hotness in the corridor outside. Janice did not encourage flirtation from the inmates. She went out with a fireman; this fact appeared in one's first conversation with Janice, and it penetrated almost all of her subsequent discourse.

Nor, if one thought about it, could one ever discern, as she bent over a photocopier or reached up to a high shelf with her back to one, a trace of panty line, not a seam or a string, not a ridge of thong above the coccyx. Her tiny buttocks were always perfectly outlined and perfectly smooth in their matte black skin. This led, of course, to the speculation and theorizing that could occupy a good portion of Justin's bus ride to the subway at the end of every day. It was possible that instead of choosing the most surgically fine of thongs, she was actually wearing a much larger undergarment, one of those seamless smoothing panties that one could see advertised in lingerie shop windows or, if one were to wander accidentally into the women's underwear section of a large department store, on the boxes that were stacked in bins and so easily examinable by the furtive passerby. These things too—they varied from a sort of high-waisted bikini shape to veritable shorts—were not untitillating, especially if one considered their silky thinness, their high-tech, moisture-absorbing smoothness. They might be black or they might be virginal white or they might be flesh-coloured, since their aim was after all to be invisible, to imitate as closely as possible the surface of the skin. Beige underwear was not usually something one thought of as sexy; indeed one usually associated it with the elderly; but in these new microfibrous fabrics there were definitely startling images to be had in imagining how readily such a pale colour would darken in any contact with moisture, moisture of any kind—the faintest perspiration, for example, or any other moisture.

Janice glanced up when he came in and sang, "Hello, sweetheart," although she was already looking back at her computer screen.

Today she was wearing a soft furry sweater, of something Justin had an idea was called angora, with a V-neck, but quite high, so there was no chance of glimpsing an edge of bra strap or any swellings or depressions. It was too warm for such a sweater outside, and yet she had to sit in air conditioning all day and was probably creating, with it, yet another defence against students' and instructors' nipple-seeking eyes. A jet black cross hung at her throat, against her coppery skin.

And there it was again, the fright of helplessness that he felt when he found himself staring so hard at a woman who was not staring back: the feeling of seeping power, the loss of some kind of agency, that you were the wailing infant, waiting for her to feed you.

"How was your weekend?" she called.

Justin pulled out the curled scraps of paper from his pigeonhole. "Ah, kind of boring." The papers in his pigeonhole were all advertisements or admonishments: they were flyers for fundraisers for sports teams, flyers for computer shops, warnings about parking spaces, vague threats of penalty for non-union staff who worked too many hours without officially joining the union (as Justin did), melancholy pleas for the cessation of theft of departmental objects and stationery. "I tried to go swimming," he said. It would be tiring to recount the encounter, the girl, the tense trip to the hospital. He had been wondering about her the night before but he had not thought of her this morning. She had probably just miscarried and was fine, and he would never see her again, and there was something about that fleeting consciousness of having done something good that gave him the confidence to turn his eyes to Janice's desk and look down, directly at her bulbous, restrained breasts and finish, "but the stupid pool was closed. So I was just hot and frustrated all weekend."

"Poor baby," said Janice, typing. "You have to try to get out of the city on weekends like this. Wasn't it just gorgeous?"

"It was hot. What did you get up to?"

She swung in her rotating chair, throwing her ponytail behind her. She looked up at him. "Brian," she said, beaming. "Took me to Wild Water Kingdom. We had a blast."

"Really. Wild Water Kingdom. Where is that?"

"Up highway seven, then over to the fifty. Near Bolton."

"Ah. And what do you . . . what is it?"

"Oh, it's all water slides and rides and pools and things. It's everything to do with water. It's mostly for kids and families, but whatever. I go on every single slide. I just like spending the whole day in my bikini."

"Right," said Justin. "And Brian, does he, does he—what does he do?"

"Oh, I guess he likes looking at the bikinis too. Not that I let him."

"Sounds like fun."

"Take your girlfriend some time."

"Ah, my girlfriend. She wouldn't really—I don't have a girl-friend any more anyway."

"That's too bad," said Janice, looking back down at her screen. It would not surprise Janice that he would not have a girlfriend, that Justin's sex life would not involve bikinis, or exist at all, because for her to imagine his sex life would be like imagining the sex life of a gerbil. Justin half expected her to pat down his hair, hand him his mittens, dab at his face with a handkerchief.

"Anyway," she said, "then we went back downtown and he took me to Ki. For dinner."

"Ki? Really? That's kind of a big deal."

"I know. It's a little fancy for Brian, but I made him. You can get him to do things like that if you make him think it's his idea. Like most guys. Hi Meredyth."

"Hi Meredyth," said Justin. "I'll get out of your way. We meeting in the staff room?"

"I have absolutely not the faintest idea. Not the first clue."

Justin shifted sideways and tried to squeeze towards the door as Meredyth Solberg-Spencer reached for her pigeonhole. She tended to carry an extremely large bag, and she was carrying it today. It was a leather bag and it could have held years' worth of essays or diaries or ceramic pots or simply earth; one didn't know. It was lugged around with a great deal of sighing. Meredyth's hair and her dress were also voluminous, red and yellow respectively, and they also seemed to weigh her down, to be untameable like the swelling bag, like the spectacles that she just couldn't keep sitting high on her nose; it required more hands than she had to simultaneously keep slipping bag and hair and spectacles in place, and to reach for her handful of paper flyers, which she now did, hitting Justin in the nose with her elbow.

"I'm pretty sure it's in the staff room," said Justin, pressing to the office door.

"I follow the herd," said Meredyth. "I go where I'm told. I get lost anyway. I'll probably end up in a broom closet somewhere. Fine with me."

Mike's voice boomed from the hallway. "Everyone complaining about their classrooms again."

He and Justin faced each other in the doorway. Justin tried to slip sideways again, but Mike went for the wrong side and they collided. Justin's head came up to Mike's chin.

"One oh two," said Mike, "anyway. Two minutes we start."

Justin and Meredyth hauled their respective bags down the corridor to 102. There were no windows in 102. It had once been an office but now had to serve as a meeting room or small seminar room, with one table and chairs around it. There was no blackboard, but one of those big paper tablets on a tripod, on which Mike liked to scrawl out his flow charts ("MANAGEMENT ➡ CREATIVITY ➡ END USER") and his motivational messages ("ACCESS = EDUCATION = PRODUCTIVITY").

And sitting at the end of the table, right beside the paper tablet, as if she were already itching to scrawl circles and arrows on it herself, was Annette the PR idiot.

This was a really very bad sign.

She had her steel-grey power suit on, and her briefcase at her side. Her blouse was grey silk. Her hair was striped with blonde in a style Justin would have once called frosted, although he didn't know if that was what it was still called. It was probably blonde to hide grey, although it wasn't exactly clear how old she was. She could be between thirty-five and forty. It could be fifty. Justin was not good at those estimations. She did have quite large breasts, though, and was not afraid of baring an edge of lace camisole in the gap between her lapels.

Annette smiled brightly at the two teachers, and they slumped into seats like prisoners before the parole board.

If Annette was here, at the departmental level, at this crucial stage in the college's fundraising campaign, it meant that there was something wrong with their department. You did not want the attention of PR people at the best of times. And this was a time at which PR people were all quite stressed. This was going to be, then, a meeting at which they would likely hear the word "optics." And "brand." And possibly "awareness." And maybe even "grassroots level."

He and Meredyth waited, their heads bowed. There was only one thing that Justin wanted out of this meeting, and it was to raise again the possibility of expanding his course load to include a class remotely related to what he was trained to teach, possibly even something literary, even though it was well known to all that Meredyth had always had and always would have exclusive rights to the sole actual literature class taught in the entire department

of Media and Communications. This course was called The
Fiction of Betrayal, and she had taught it every year for the
past twelve years. Since the year of her divorce, in fact.

The presence of Annette the PR idiot was bad news for
Justin's expectations of a discussion of literature.

The other teachers were filing in and scraping the metal
chairs around the table. Linda Knelman had had her hair
cropped especially short over the weekend. Her plastic-framed
spectacles seemed even more absurdly oversized on her bumpy
little head. Joe Montalino looked dapper in his grey beard and
black sport shirt. He was always smiling. Justin suspected that this
was because he was always a little drunk. Justin was okay with
that. He liked Joe Montalino.

Two more Mikes, known as Mike B. and Michael M., arrived
next. They were young guys who had English degrees like Justin.
They stayed pretty quiet. They knew their place. They waited for
Mike, the chair.

Mike made sure he was always last. And he was the only
one to be called Mike, just Mike. The others were Mike B. and
Michael M. You got this quickly; you didn't think about these
things after a while.

Mike always came in shouting. "Hello, hello, hello, people.
How's the team this morning?"

Nobody answered him, except of course Annette the PR
idiot, who said, "Just great, thank you."

Mike was already uncapping a marker, folding over a new
clean sheet on the big noteboard. He checked the pager on his
belt, then the portable e-mail device on the other side. "Okay,"
he said, "I won't keep you all for long. There's some routine
business to get to, before we talk about the big issue, which is

the provincial testing issue, and Annette is here to help us with some optics considerations with that."

Mike was hardly older than Justin. Maybe two or three years. But where Justin had wasted his early and mid-twenties on Renaissance drama, Mike had had the good sense to go into advertising. And Mike let you know that. He was bigger than you and richer than you, and he had a crisp blue shirt and sharp dress slacks, and a bunch of communications devices strapped to his belt, like Batman, and he was your boss.

"So," said Mike, his hands on his hips. "I understand people are not happy with their parking spaces."

There was a chuckle around the table.

"Parking space?" said Joe Montalino. "Who has a parking space?"

"With the parking space situation. Listen. It's very simple. There are four parking spaces for the department. And those spaces are assigned first to administrative staff. So the first two go to Janice and Erna, in the office. The third one goes to me." Mike folded his arms across his chest. "And the fourth is assigned on the basis of seniority."

"I thought we were an autonomous collective," said Justin. Nobody laughed.

"Which means that Meredyth," said Mike, "as our senior instructor, is entitled to it. But as you know, since Meredyth doesn't drive—"

"Nobody gets it," said Joe Montalino.

"Mike," said Annette the PR idiot, "could I make a special request?" She was smiling at him like a spotlight. "I wonder if we could change slightly the order of the agenda for this morning. Just because I'm due in the principal's office in fifteen

minutes. I'm wondering if we could get to the initiative question, and then I'll let you guys get on with—"

"Right. Okay. Here's the thing. The province-wide testing
happens next spring, but there will be a special session at the
end of this term for the students in the summer programs who
happen to be graduating this fall. That means that anyone in
your classes right now . . ."

While Mike spoke, Justin drew in his notebook. He drew
a flower which metamorphosed into a giant communications
tower. Then he drew an ambulance with a big flashing red light
on top. He leafed through the previous pages in his notebook and
saw that many of his doodles had involved the name Genevieve.
He put a line through as many of these as he could find.

"Results," Mike was saying, "are what is going to enable this
department to survive. Anyone who is not interested in results is
not going to make it in this environment. And if anyone's wondering how I got to where I am, standing in front of you here
today—"

"Mike," said Meredyth Solberg-Spencer, "when you say
results, you mean solely those results that are measured by the
provincial tests, am I correct?"

"You are correct. In today's environment—"

"So you mean you are not interested in any other means of
measuring results."

"Such as?" said Mike, checking his watch.

"Such as literacy, such as understanding. Such as having
greater communications skills. Such as having a better chance
at getting a job."

"Such as knowledge," said Linda Knelman mournfully.

Mike looked over at Annette and the two of them smiled

at each other. Mike shook his head apologetically. "And how," said Mike, holding out his hands, "how exactly do we measure results like that?"

"Well, exactly," said Meredyth.

"Exactly my point," said Mike. He turned back to his note-board. "Now, let's try to stay on track here."

There was some sighing around the table, so Mike turned back around and laid his marker down. "Listen," he said. He sat on the edge of the table. He was going to come down to their level now. He was going to listen to their problems. "I know a lot of you feel that we should be training our students to become failed novelists." He stared at Meredyth here. She dropped her head. "And there's certainly room for a little of that. It probably makes them more sensitive or something, I don't know. Like a good mind exercise. An exercise for the mind. But I wonder if any of you here have ever had the experience of getting a new product, say a DVD player, and trying to install it and read the manual, and having a little trouble reading the manual. Anybody here had that happen to them? I'm curious." Mike smiled at Annette.

Everyone around the table had taken out notebooks and begun to draw. Justin drew a series of breast-like blobs. He couldn't make them too lifelike or they would be recognizable. He really wanted to draw nipples on them, but he was sitting right next to Linda Knelman. When the blobs began to look too bulbously breast-like, he turned them into raindrops.

"Why is it, I wonder," said Mike, "that all technical manuals are so badly written? And I wonder why we aren't a little more concerned about that. I mean that is a problem we can all solve. If we are the teachers of the writers of technical manuals, and no one can read those technical manuals, then we are directly to blame. And I think that's a whole lot more of a pressing problem than turning out another generation of failed novelists."

There was a silence, and Mike turned back to the board, but Meredyth said, "So instead we're training them to be failed technical writers?"

Mike swung around. "Why would they fail?"

"Because there simply aren't very many technical writing jobs. They can't all get them."

"Well, all right, if you want to be literal about every—"

"Wouldn't it be more useful," said Linda Knelman, "to teach them how to write than to teach them how to answer these multiple-choice tests about writing?"

"Okay," said Mike, "now listen." He rubbed his face with his hands as if immensely tired and sat on the desk again. He shook his head sadly. "I know some of you would like to go back to a system where people who went to really good schools—like most of you—get to succeed in life. And others don't."

"Oh, Mike," said Meredyth. "Don't be ridiculous. That's not at all what—"

"All I'm saying," said Mike, holding up the large flat palm again like a traffic warden, "all I'm saying is that we can get a little bit romantic about what we're doing here. Tell me if I'm wrong, and please do, correct me if I'm wrong, please, I'd be glad to hear it, but tell me, is our first job here to help people?"

"Mike, there are—"

"Or isn't it? I mean, tell me if I'm wrong. Would you agree that our first job here is to help people?"

There was more sighing around the table. Linda Knelman dropped her pen with a flick of her fingers.

"All right then. If our job is to help people, to give them a head start in life, then how do we do that? We know that we service a lot of underprivileged areas here, a lot of new citizens. If we rely solely on this idea of, I don't know what you call it, unbridled merit or whatever you want to believe in, then the kids who have gone to private schools and public schools in wealthy areas have unfair advantages. Maybe you guys don't know anything about that." He sat up, folded his arms across his chest and frowned at them. "Let's be realistic here. We all know that our primary purpose is to help these kids get a start, get in the door. We know that once you have a job, you learn to do it. There's very little specific training you can give for all jobs; they're all different. We all know it, honestly, really. It's not really an education that helps you do well in the world. If it was, wouldn't you guys all be millionaires?" He threw his head back and barked a laugh. "Well?"

He got a few smiles for this one. There was going to be no more arguing; it was not easy to argue with Mike from this point on.

"Nope. What helps you do well in the world is skill at a particular job, and you learn on the job. Now." He opened his eyes wide, held a finger in the air. "How are you going to do that if you don't have a foot in the door? Hey? We provide that foot in the door. Right? And how do we do that? What's the one thing these kids need? It's some kind of qualification. Am I right? They need one post-secondary diploma or qualification, and it's going to change their lives. Why would we make getting that thing more difficult for them? Because we don't want them to have the advantages that we had—or some of us had, anyway? Hey?" He coughed, looked at his watch, waited for objections. The instructors drew on their notepads. "All right, now, since Annette has to go, let's get back to the issues of the standardized testing. This department has a whole lot to contribute to the image of the College, in terms of the results that we can guarantee, and that's particularly important right now in the middle of this major fundraising drive."

"The capital initiative," said Annette quickly.

"The capital initiative. And this department is really going to stand or fall on the basis of the results that we can guarantee. There are going to be some people who are going to make it and some who don't."

Justin drew blobs as fast as he could. It was clear at this point that this meeting was not going to permit, at any point, a discussion of any change in workload, or the proposal of a new class on any kind of literature other than the Fiction of Betrayal. He'd have to corner Mike one on one some time.

Then Annette got up to make her presentation and Justin was at least distracted for a moment by the back of her trousers, as she wrote her key points on the noteboard. The trousers were quite tight, and quite thin, as women's suits were, and there was the distinct outline of a thong in the small of her back. This impressed Justin, as she was quite old for sex; it even made him consider, for the briefest of seconds, listening to what she had to say.

After the meeting, Justin was on his way down the hall to 113 when Mike caught up with him.

"Justin," he said. "Class this morning?"

"Business communications," said Justin. "The Media first years, and the business students on electives. You know that."

"What you planning to do with them today?"

"Ah." Justin tried to remember. "I gave them a newspaper article."

"The one about suicide? That's always a winner."

"Ah, no. One I found. About drugs."

"Can't go wrong with the suicide one."

"Listen, Mike," said Justin. "I've been meaning to talk to you about a couple of things. Remember we talked, when I first arrived, about me doing a lit course somewhere down the line?"

"Hey, yes, that reminds me, there's something I have to tell you about too."

Justin stopped at the door of his classroom. He looked in. Three girls in headscarves were waiting for him.

Mike said, "You know Linda has to take a health leave."

"She does?"

"Yeah. Looks like she's going to be out for a few months."

"Hell," said Justin. "She all right?"

Mike made a face as if he had eaten something sour. "Not really. Surgery, chemo, all that."

"Wow," said Justin. "Poor Linda. That's terrible. She's never said anything to me."

"Yeah. It's rough. And it means I'm going to have to collapse some of the classes. I'm going to distribute her students to other classes."

"Oh boy," said Justin. "Don't tell me." He stepped aside for some students to enter. They were all black boys twice his size. They didn't look him in the eye.

"Yeah. You're going to take about half of her Writing for Advertising class. Into your Business English."

"That will double my class size."

"It's unfortunate."

"You're going to pay me for another class, then?"

Mike laughed, slapped Justin on the shoulder. He pulled his wireless device off his belt and peered at it. There was a student waiting in the hallway, a white girl with a ponytail in stretchy trousers. She was one of Justin's students, in fact, but she didn't look at Justin. She smiled at Mike and hugged her books to her chest.

"That's way over the mandatory class size limit," said Justin.

"It's only temporary," said Mike. "The summer term's almost over." He smiled at the girl with the books.

"No it isn't. It's just started."

"It's halfway through. Listen, we can talk further about—"

"That doubles my workload," said Justin. He was working on keeping his voice calm and low. "That's completely against the collective agreement."

Mike lowered his machine. He stared at Justin with a little smile. "Collective agreement? What collective agreement?"

"With the union."

"Oh, the union, right. You mean the union you're not in?"

"You still have to—I'm still covered by the terms of the—"

"Right. Any time you want me to talk to the union about your status, you let me know. I'm sure they'd be very interested to know about your irregular situation. They'd probably force me to fire you right away."

"Or hire me as permanent full-time."

"Yeah. No. You know Linda is senior. You know as soon as I get to make one hire it'll be her. The union will be on her side as well. You know why?"

Justin puffed out his cheeks. "Okay."

"That's right. Because she." Mike pointed his fingers like a gun at Justin. "Is in the union."

"Okay. Great. Thank you. Thank you, Mike."

Mike slapped him on the shoulder again and said, "You'll manage." He turned to go and then called back. "That article about drugs? Is fine. But give them the suicide one. The one I chose. I told you, it gets great results. It gets them talking. They go nuts over it. They all know someone who's done it."

3.

"**All right,**" **said Justin,** a couple of days later. "So, we're almost through job applications, then, and I want the final drafts of your letters by Friday. And then—" But this was pointless, because the entire class was on its feet, and the enormous jackets and knapsacks were being hoisted, and earpieces being inserted, and cellphones chiming and rapping to life, and the door was open and they were streaming out.

"Mr. H," said one of the biggest kids, a Jamaican with corn-rows and a Raptors jersey the size of a flag, "you have yourself a hype night."

"Thanks, Dushan," said Justin. "I will endeavour to do that." Which made Dushan smile and encouraged Justin to say, "I hope that my night will be indeed hype, and possibly even live, and not wack. Or flop."

"Ah-ight," said Dushan, shaking his head. And then he was gone too, and Justin erased the board and packed up his brief-case. His throat was a little sore. It was the heat that was doing it, and whatever was in the air.

By the time he had closed his classroom door, the hallway was empty. There were no students waiting to see him. And he was not going to see Genevieve that evening.

They had tried having coffee a couple of times, he and Genevieve, and it had not been relaxing. She seemed angry with him, although it had been her idea to stop sleeping together. They were still talking on the phone, though, for reasons that were unclear to him. Perhaps because he had nothing better to do. The hallway echoed.

He thought then of the student whose name he couldn't remember, the one who had been waiting to see Mike, with her ponytail and her clingy polyester trousers, and he wondered for a second what exactly she had to see Mike about, as he was pretty sure that she was an Online Writing student and not in one of Mike's advertising classes. And it was probably the pants that made him think of the girl Jenna. The fabric in these pants that girls were wearing were what bathing suits used to be made of, or leotards for dancing, things that trapeze artists wore when they were performing.

It was not surprising, of course, that the sick girl had not called him; he had not expected it. But he was curious. He hadn't heard from Andrew either. Of course Andrew couldn't discuss her case, it was confidential. Andrew was very prim about that.

He knew he was going to call Genevieve just to tell her about the encounter and a part of him knew that it was just to piss Genevieve off. Why it would piss Genevieve off he couldn't exactly say, but women like that girl Jenna were very likely to piss Genevieve off just by existing. He would try to avoid a conversation about that.

He was passing the departmental office when he heard Janice call out to him. He ducked into the office with something approaching pleasure. He had not yet seen what she was wearing today. "Janice? Did you call me?"

"Yes, sweetie." It was another scoop-top, with white and pink stripes. Her hair was tightly back. He felt a very vague pang at this. Janice's clothing for some reason in this moment was the most obvious symbol and reminder of why people like Justin could never ask people like her out for a drink. This thin acrylic top would strike Justin's friends, particularly his female friends, as garish and cheap and this, ridiculously, would make Justin feel embarrassment for Janice and then, unfortunately, for himself, and it would remind him of the fact that he would have to work very strenuously to convince someone like Janice to go to see a film with subtitles with him and also that he did not know where Wild Water Kingdom was and would not know how to enjoy himself once he got there. This was due to the fact, a fact that someone like Janice would very quickly discern, that people like Justin were simply not very good at having fun, not to mention the fact that people like Justin would be unable to pay for any fun of the kind people like Janice enjoyed. It was unfair, however, that Justin had to disguise to everyone, even to himself sometimes, particularly when he was with people he had gone to college with, that he found Janice's cheap stripey top extremely feminine and expressive and sexual.

She said, "Did that guy find you?"

"That guy."

"Tee."

"Tee?" Justin managed another peek over the edge of Janice's desk to see what encased her bottom half. A white cotton skirt.

39

This was fruitful indeed. He would have to try to find some way of making her stand up.

"A guy called Tee was looking for you. He looked like one of your students. But I'm not sure I recognized him."

"I don't think I have a Tee. Like the letter T?"

"That's what he said. I don't know how he spelled it. I thought you knew him. He seemed to know you. He asked for you by your first name."

Justin made what he hoped was an entertainingly baffled face. "No idea. I don't think I have a Tee. He's probably one of the new ones, though, who has to transfer. One of Linda's. You can give him my e-mail, if he comes back. I'll give him the prerequisites, whatever." Quickly, he emptied out his pigeonhole of flyers. "You have a nice night," he said to Janice.

Janice was frowning, chewing on the end of her pen. "That's funny, I was sure you knew him. He seemed a bit, I don't know, worried. Like it was urgent. He was in a big rush."

Justin stopped in the doorway. "What did he look like?"

"He was, ah, African-American," she said carefully. Then she leaned forward and said, "He was black. Really black. Big huge guy. In like gangster gear. With the head scarf thing. The head rag."

"The do-rag," said Justin patiently. "He could be a student. They all dress like that."

"Okay," said Janice, leaning back. "I'll give him your e-mail. Have a great night."

Justin took the underground route to get to the parking lot, just because it meant a few minutes longer in the air conditioning.

He passed through the food court, which was already shutting up. They were pulling the metal cages around the counters. There was a black kid with his back to him, sitting at one of the tables, a vast broad back and a black head scarf, and Justin knew this must be the guy Tee. He was the biggest guy in the room, and he was dressed all in black. Justin rounded the table and then turned back to look at him. The kid was on a cellphone. There was nothing on the table in front of him. He had no knapsack. There were gold rings on several of his fingers.

For a second, Justin stood still. The day was over and he didn't have to deal with this right this second. He could do it by e-mail. But Janice had said the kid seemed stressed. And then the guy looked up and stared right at him, and he knew he would have to say something.

So Justin walked over to the table and said, "Excuse me? Are you, ah, Tee?"

The kid looked up and said something rapid and incomprehensible into his phone. He was wearing dark glasses. Then he folded up the phone and leaned back in his chair. He did not look again at Justin. He looked slowly around the food court. And then he said, as if to someone next to him, "Who wants to know?"

Justin smiled. "I'm Justin Harrison. From Communications Studies. The secretary said you wanted to talk to me."

"You Justin!" The kid gave a laugh. "You the big Justin."

Justin kept the smile on his face. Sometimes he found it hard to tell when the students were joking. "What can I do for you?"

The kid spun his cellphone on the table. "No, I don't want to talk to you. I got no time for you." He had a heavy Jamaican accent.

"Excuse me?"

"I got no time for you. I need to talk to her."

"To her? To who?" But even on saying this Justin knew who they were talking about. And he knew now, a little too late, that Tee wasn't a student. Even the toughest of them didn't talk this way to the teachers, and they didn't speak patois on their phones and wear black glasses in the food court.

"Yeah, who? Who?" Tee waved a finger in the air like a query. "You don't know." He laughed, showing gold in his teeth. "Yeah, you're a smart guy. You a teacher. You know, you such a smart guy you shouldn't be making mistakes like getting messed up with her. There are things you don't understand."

Justin smiled brightly. "I think there's been a misunderstanding. I teach Communications and Media at Constitution. I thought you wanted to get into one of my classes. I don't know who you're talking about." He was conscious, on saying this, of lying, something he didn't do very well, so he made a show of looking at his watch. And he was faintly excited, too, perhaps at the fact that he was lying, which was exciting in itself, but also at the thought of the girl, the curly streaked hair, the taut pale belly. He had not heard from her. And now he had.

"Listen, mon." Tee hauled his bulk upright. He was housed in great swaths of black fabric, clothing like a parachute. There was still the plastic table separating him and Justin. "I really don't care. I don't want to know what's going on between you, right?" He picked up his cellphone. "But if she tink she can avoid me she's wrong. You just tell her I'm a find her. You tell her to call me."

"You're talking about Jenna," said Justin.

"Ahh," said Tee. "Smart guy remembers."

"Listen, I really don't know her. I met her on the weekend,

she was in trouble, I helped her out. I haven't seen her since. I don't know her at all. I have no idea where she is."

"Right. Whatever. Listen—"

"What made you—how did you find me?" But Justin already knew: the business card he had given her. The address of the college. He wondered how far Tee had come on a highway or in a subway to find him. Then for a brief second he wondered if Jenna was dead.

"You tell her to call me. And you watch yourself, mon." And Tee was loping away, shrugging his shoulders as if to an internal beat. Justin watched him all the way through the food court, until he disappeared at the exit that would have led him to a bus stop, not the parking lot.

Justin's heart was beating quite fast.

He walked to the other end of the food court and through the tunnels till he emerged in the parking lot at the front gate. He squinted in the glare on the field of windshields.

He was walking towards the front gate when he saw his boss, Mike, beside his red Thunderbird. It was one of those new Thunderbirds that looked retro. It was a convertible, but the top wasn't down. Mike was standing next to it talking to someone else, a girl. They were both leaning against the side of the car.

Justin changed his path between the cars so he could come closer to them. He walked behind them.

Mike was talking very intensely and closely to the girl. It was the girl he had seen with Mike two days before, the girl in the stretchy pants in the corridor, Justin's student. Now she was talking a lot too. Mike opened the car door, and she looked about to get in. Then Mike said something else and the girl turned and walked away, quite fast, between the cars.

43

Mike didn't follow her. He got in his car and slammed the door. Justin heard the engine roar up. He kept his head down. For some reason he didn't want Mike to see him.

As Justin got close to the front gate, Mike's red Thunderbird buzzed by him. The tires squealed as Mike turned into the road. Justin didn't see where the girl had gone.

He was boiling water for pasta that evening when Genevieve called. She had to cancel their drink the next day. Justin was sweating, shirtless, in his little kitchen. He had the door to the fire escape open, but the air that came in was hot and damp. There was no other window in his kitchen. It was on the third floor. He felt embarrassed talking to Genevieve looking so sweaty and pasty, even though she couldn't see him.

She said, "So. Sorry. I've just been so busy I can't even think. We've just got a whole pile of new clients. We got the Child's Last Wish foundation, finally."

"Oh." He pulled down a plastic bag of pasta. It was nearly empty.

"Which is really great, a pretty big deal, actually."

"That's good." There was another bag of another kind of pasta, twisted into a little cone in the cupboard. It might not be good to mix them, because they would take different times to cook.

"So we're really excited about that. But it's a ton of work, because we already had the Yummy Mummy Awards and the peddie bar, and I was already pretty much flat out on those already."

Justin poured the remains of the rotini and the remains of the farfalle into the boiling water. "That's too bad." He wiped his dripping forehead. "What's the peddie bar?"

"The manicure bar. I told you. It's like the best manicures, pedicures. It's the new one. I told you about it."

"Yes." He unscrewed the jar of pasta sauce. He would have to wash a pot to put it in.

"It's all organic stuff, and it's all woman-run, it's really good for you. It's all fair trade labour, too, like no illegal Vietnamese workers like most of them use. They're doing a lot of men, too, straight men too. You should go. I can get you a coupon."

"What do they need publicity for?"

He could hear her sighing. "Because. It's a whole new concept. It's like the future of peddies."

"Of peddies."

"They don't use toxic chemicals. It's the way all these things are going now. I'm so glad we're on this before anyone else. It's a project I can really get behind, because I really believe in it."

"You believe in organic peddies."

"Shut up. It's not a joke." She waited while Justin banged around with pots. Then she said, "They certainly make a lot more money than you do."

"I'm sure they do. I'm sure they do. And that's wonderful. How are you otherwise?"

"Well, I'm really excited about the Child's Last Wish thing."

"Now what is that again?"

"I told you about this too."

"I know you did." He slopped the sauce into the pot and turned up the gas. Now the kitchen would get really hot. "It's going to be nice and toasty in here," he said.

"What?"

"Hot hot hot."

"I don't know why you don't get an air conditioner in there. I couldn't stand it."

"I told you. The wiring's too old. It would overload it."

"So why do you stay there?"

"The Child's Last Wish. It's for dying kids, I guess?"

"Yeah, terminally ill kids. And they fundraise for, you know, anything they want to do. Like going in an airplane, or a balloon, or meeting Tie Domi, or whatever they want."

"So the kids get to live out a fantasy." He stepped out the kitchen door and stood on the iron fire escape. The haze was so thick he couldn't see the skyline. A dog was penned in the yard below, barking. If he could simply select "RPG" from the bottom of this screen, he could shoulder it and blow that thing away even if he couldn't see it exactly. The whole yard next door would have to go, boom. He could always duck from the flash.

"Right," said Genevieve.

"Before they buy it." There was a bamboo stick on the fire escape. He picked it up and sighted down it towards the barking dog. Laser night vision.

She said, "Buy what?"

"The farm."

"Before they pass away, yes."

"Before they kick."

"It's a really sweet thing, Justin."

"Before they go to the great McDonald's Playland in the sky." He could hear his pasta sauce start to plop. The plopping meant he would have to stir it, but that would mean re-entering the furnace of his kitchen. It would be okay if it were a little burned at the bottom.

"I never understand how you can be so superior about everything," said Genevieve.

"Here we go," said Justin. "I'm not being superior. It's your work, I think it's great that you're working, everyone has to work. I know it helps you if you believe in all the projects you're working for. It helps you to sell them. I just don't know why you have to feel you ... I don't know, *really* believe in them. You know? I mean do you really, really, deep down believe in this one?"

"What's wrong with it? What could you possibly find wrong with helping terminally ill children?"

"Well. Let's see. I find it sentimental. And fundamentally useless. It's basically, I don't know, some kind of religio-mystical thing, it sounds like. I don't see how it's helping the world at all."

"How it's helping you, you mean. It's not helping you at all."

"No, that's not what I—shit—hang on." The pasta sauce was smoking. He dove into the kitchen and pulled it off the flame. The boiling water had foamed up, too, and was splashing onto the stovetop and hissing in the flames. There was nowhere to put the hot pot on the little counter, because it was covered with dirty dishes, and it would burn the Formica anyway. There was a cutting board on the kitchen table but it had a loaf of bread on it. With the phone under his chin, he tried to pull the cutting board out from under the loaf of bread and leave the bread on the table, but of course the bread fell on the floor. Then he placed the hot pot on the cutting board.

She said, "Are you okay?"

"I am fine. I'm burning my dinner." He reached for the boiling water and stepped on the bread, which was on the floor. "Shit. Fuck. Fuck."

"Justin."

"Sorry. Sorry. Everything okay now. I'm a dorkwad."

She sighed. "Is that funny?"

"What, dorkwad? You don't think that's funny?"

"I don't know. I would have thought it funny when I was about sixteen. Or maybe fourteen."

"Huh. I guess that's where I get it from. My students. They all talk that way."

"Yeah," she said. "And they're all eighteen."

"And I think they're quite funny and clever."

"What are you making?"

"What do you think? I'm making dinner."

"It's pasta and bottled sauce."

"What else does one eat for dinner? If there is anything else, I'd be glad to hear of it."

"It's amazing to me."

"What is?"

"That you can sit there in your little unairconditioned apartment where you've been for five years and you can hardly feed yourself and you can still make fun of people who are trying to do something with their lives."

"Okay," said Justin. At higher levels of this game there would be available to him, for sure, the shoulder-mounted Stinger missile which, although quite useless in such confined quarters as these, would easily purée not just the barking dog but the entire yard and the fire escape and the garage behind it. Swoosh, blam. "Let's leave that one alone for tonight. Shall we? Let's leave the improving lectures for now."

Genevieve was silent for a while. "How is work, anyway?"

Justin exhaled. "Work is. Work is the same. Not great."

"Have you spoken to Mike yet?"

"Mike. No. I haven't spoken to Mike. Mike is too busy. Expanding my class size, threatening me, that sort of thing."

"Justin. Listen to me. You have to learn to stand up for yourself. If you don't learn to stand up to him, you're going to be stuck in that awful—"

"Listen," said Justin. "Something else happened to me. Something kind of strange."

He sat at the kitchen table. While the water boiled and steamed, he told Genevieve about the encounter with the girl, the trip to the hospital. He didn't tell her about the visit from Tee.

Genevieve was alarmed enough already. "So this was a total stranger?" she said. "She's just standing there and she asks you for help and you just get into a car with her?"

"She didn't ask me for help, no. I offered to help her. She was in trouble."

"Well, first of all, you have no way of knowing if she was telling the truth, and she could be—"

"And it wasn't a car, it was an ambulance, with two paramedics in it. It wasn't as if I was in any danger."

"Not now, no, but you have no way of knowing what she wants from you. You have a way of kind of lying down for people. Especially women who come on to you."

"She didn't come on to me. She was standing there, crying."

"Oh, no, they never do, do they, Justin?"

"What the hell—"

"A hot girl, or even a not hot girl, anyone with some cleavage or something comes up to you and you do whatever she wants. You can, no honestly, I know you, you can be naive about

49

women. I bet you gave her your number. I hope you didn't give her your number."

Justin stood up. He stirred the boiling pasta. "No. No, I didn't." Again he felt that little tingle, the thrill of telling a lie. It was like pretending your name was Fernando or something; it made you into someone else.

"Well, that's good. It sounds like a bad scene. She sounds like really bad news. I would sincerely advise you not to get involved."

"I'm quite certain I'll never hear from her again."

"If she calls you, Justin, don't just do whatever she wants, okay? Honestly. You have to be a little more tough with people."

Justin laughed a little. "Yes. I suppose I do. Anyway. You don't need to worry about me. Any more."

"What's that supposed to mean?"

"My pasta's ready. The sauce is getting cold."

"Does it irritate you that I call you?"

"No. No. I need to hear how you are. You still haven't told me."

"Told you what?"

"How you are." He cleared his throat. He hoped the question was clear. He didn't want to have to ask her point blank.

"I'm fine. I told you."

"Okay." He supposed this was as clear as she was going to be. If she were seeing someone, she would probably have answered differently. There would have been some other kind of hint.

After he hung up the phone, he drained the pasta and poured the sauce on it. He sat and looked at it and he thought for some reason of Tee travelling out to the college on the subway, in his hot clothes.

The steam rose from the pasta and the sweat squeezed

through his pores. He looked out the open door onto the fire escape. The sky was grey. The dog was still barking downstairs.

He looked at the phone and it rang.

The display said, "Unknown caller."

He let it ring twice before he answered it.

Her voice was high and sweet. "Justin?"

"Yes."

"It's Jenna."

Justin stood up. He went to the kitchen door and looked at the skyline. There were tall buildings farther away. His dinner was too hot to eat anyway. "Oh yes. Hello."

"You remember me?"

"Oh yes. How are you?"

"How are you?"

"I'm fine. I'm very well, thanks. How are you?"

"I'm fine. I'm fine."

Justin put his hand on his belly as if to hide its slackness. Actually, it wasn't too bad. He was more skinny than flabby, really. "So everything worked out, at the hospital? With Andrew, and—"

"Yes. I'm fine now. He treated me really well."

"Were you in there for a long time?"

"Kind of, yeah."

"Did they keep you overnight?"

"Listen, I'm fine. It was just something normal."

Justin drew in his breath. "Still. It must have been unpleasant."

She laughed a little. "It wasn't a whole lot of fun, no. Not something I want to do every weekend."

"No. Well, that's awful. I'm sorry you had to go through that."

"Well, listen, I hope you don't mind my calling you."

"No. No. Not at all. I was wondering how you were."

"Did I catch you at a bad time?"

Justin closed the door to his kitchen and his cooling pasta. He stood on the tiny fire escape. "No no."

"Well, I was really just calling to say thanks. Thanks so much for helping me out, and getting your friend to see me."

"You're welcome. It was no trouble."

She sighed. There was a pause then, and the sound of a door slamming and a man's voice, then another woman laughing. "And I wanted to kind of apologize, too, if my friend bothered you."

"Oh."

"Hang on one second, okay?" Her receiver was covered, and there was some murmuring for a minute.

Her voice came back. "Okay. Okay. Sorry."

He said, "Which friend are you talking about?"

"Oh, I guess my friend Tee came to talk to you. I'm really sorry about that."

"He's your friend? He didn't seem very friendly."

"Yeah, I know. I'm really sorry about that. But he's really nothing to worry about."

"So," said Justin, sitting on the fire escape, "I take it he found you. I was a little worried about that."

"Oh, it's nothing to worry about. Everything's fine."

Justin took a deep breath. "Is he threatening you?"

"No!" She sounded surprised. "No, no, he's . . . he's nothing to worry about. Everything's fine."

"What was it that he thought—"

"Listen," said Jenna, "I'm really sorry he did that to you. He won't do it again."

Justin's stomach rumbled. He stood up. "Is he your—"

"Actually," said Jenna, "there was another reason for my call." She gave another giggle. "I wanted to tell you that I think you're a really nice guy. A real gentleman. And I kind of wanted to, I was wondering if you wanted to get together. Have coffee or something some time."

Justin exhaled at length. He was almost laughing. "Sure," he said, smiling broadly. "I would love to."

When he hung up he had no hunger left. His fingertips were buzzing and, he realized with a mild alarm, he had an erection.

4.

He arrived early to get the table by the window, looking onto the patio on College, the street of cafés near the university. It was still the only part of town he thought of going out in, even though he hadn't been a student for six years. He read the paper for half an hour, and looked at the girls in the patio in their low-rise jeans. He was hoping that Jenna, when she arrived, would be wearing jeans like this, because he had never been out with one of these girls before. She was only fifteen minutes late. She stood in the doorway with her belly pushed out and looked around. She looked strangely confident for someone so tiny. The only tremble in her poise was the second she took to bunch her hair with her hand and pull it backwards. Her hair was a bushel, and its colour had changed: now it was peroxide white, in ropy curls.

She did wear the jeans, low on her hips, tight as under-garments, and a green silky top with smocking over the breasts and tiny straps on her shoulders. The fabric was loose under the bust, and hung not quite to her hips, so that of course a stripe of her belly was visible, with the metal rod in her navel and the tail of a tattoo in her groin. She had a tiny black leather purse on a strap like a thread, hanging over one shoulder.

She saw him and smiled and shrugged her shoulders like an excited little girl. She came towards him swaying and he saw that she was on fierce heels: pointy red shoes with a strap.

Every man in the café turned to watch her walk.

Justin stood to greet her and then jammed his hands into his pockets, as he didn't know if he should kiss her, and shaking her hand seemed formal and nerdy.

"Hi!" she said, still smiling, and she lifted both arms up to smooth her ropy hair back. Her eyes were blazing bright blue.

Justin did his best not to glance at her shaved underarms and said, "Hi. Nice to see you." He knew he was smiling like a maniac.

"Nice to see you too."

"Have a seat. This place okay?"

She looked around and sat and said, "It's okay." She was looking out the window at the patio and its girls.

"How've you been?"

She turned to look at him and he saw that her eyes were slightly puffy, and pink-rimmed. She was extraordinarily pale.

"Your hair," said Justin. "It's different."

"It's kind of crazy," she said. "You like it?"

"It's super cool. It's like dreadlocks."

"But it's not."

"How did you do it?"

"It's some stuff you put in it. It's just product."

"Cool."

"You've never seen it before?"

"No. No."

"It's what Christina Aguilera used. Then everyone used it. You've seen it before."

"Ah."

Then the waitress was on them. Jenna asked for a Tom Collins, which they didn't have because it was an Italian café and they didn't do mixed drinks like that. So she ordered one of those sweet vodka drinks in a bottle. He ordered a beer.

"So," he said, "how are you feeling?"

"I'm fine. I'm all fine."

"Did Andrew, my friend Andrew, the doctor, was he, did he help you out?"

"He was great."

"Good. Good. I knew he would be." Justin tried to drink his beer slowly. He let his eyes rest for a second on the deep cleavage of a girl sitting just outside the window. He looked back at Jenna and she raised her eyebrows at him. He said, "I guess that whole thing must have been extremely stressful. Not just because of the pain, I mean the physical side of it."

Jenna closed her eyes for a second. She sighed and shook her head. Her lips were so full they looked swollen. She opened her eyes and said, "Did you grow up here?"

Justin laughed a little. "Okay. Yes, I did. Not here exactly. In a suburb."

"Which one?"

"Don Mills, as a matter of fact."

"Oh."

"And you?"

"No."

"What no? You mean you're not from Don Mills? I could have guessed that."

She laughed freely and swung her hair back. Her face flushed in blotches. Her skin, so pale it was translucent, seemed vulnerable to this, to swirls and mists of blood. "No, I mean I'm not from here. I grew up in Belleville, near Kingston?"

"Ah yes. Belleville. I've been through there. Or I've seen the signs. On my way to Montreal." His beer was almost finished. He put it down. "So what brought you here?"

She shrugged. "Not much to do in Belleville."

"Right. So how long have you been here?"

"Two years now. A year and a half."

"Not long."

"No. I came for college, at first."

"Really? Which one? I teach at a college."

"I know," she said, and she raised her eyebrows again. It was something she did. It wasn't clear if it was a query or disapproval.

He said, "Right. Right. I gave you my card. What are you studying?"

"Oh, I'm not there any more. I was at Sheridan, for a while."

"Sheridan, right."

"I did hospitality."

"But not any more."

"No," she said, and giggled. "It wasn't for me."

"But you work in hospitality now?"

"Yeah. I guess. I waitressed for a while."

"Uh-huh." The café was filling up. Occasionally Justin would recognize someone he knew here, someone he had gone to school with at the university nearby and who was now in advertising or wrote for magazines, and he had rather hoped that would happen now, not just because he wanted to be seen with Jenna but also because he could have used some help with this conversation. And because it would have made him look popular. But there was no one.

"You come here a lot?" she said.

"Yeah, I guess. Not really. I don't go out a lot. But this place is nice because you can come here in the day and work. Mark papers, stuff like that. And sometimes I know people here."

"The waitresses?" She said this with a little smile.

"The waitresses? No. No, I don't know them. I mean guys, usually. The kind of guy I went to school with. I went to university, to school, here in the city."

"You seem awfully interested in the waitresses."

"Do I?" Justin felt an unpleasantness in his stomach, for this was—had been—a subject dear to Genevieve, when they had gone out together. "Really."

"I don't blame you, star," said Jenna. "She's cute."

"Which one?" said Justin, peering at the bar. "Our one?"

"No, not our one. I mean, she's cute too, but I mean the one in the white top. Don't tell me you didn't notice her."

"Yes, sure I did. I was trying not to look. There's not much to that top."

"It looks good. If you have a chest like that, you should go for it, I say."

"Yup." Justin's beer was empty. He would need another one to continue negotiating this particular topic.

"You like our one, though? The little one?"

"I didn't say that. I thought that's who you—"

"She's cute. I like her hair. But girls who are a little bigger shouldn't wear, I mean they don't look good in those short pants."

Justin stared again at their waitress. She wasn't exactly big. She was short and curvy. She was quite lush, actually. He would have slept with her, had she ever made herself available to him. Perhaps this was what Jenna was trying to ascertain.

"Tell me which girls in this bar you like."

"Yikes," said Justin. "I'm not sure I want to do that."

"Why not?"

He blew out his cheeks. "You tell me which ones you like."

"I'm not into girls," she said.

"Well, if you were a guy, which ones would you like."

"I don't know. I'm not a guy."

"Okay. Let's drop that one, then."

"You scared I'm going to get weird on you, star?"

"Well, yes, actually. Most girls do."

She laughed at this, too.

"It's funny," he said, "I used to have a lot of arguments with people about looking at girls."

"Well, if you look too much, especially if you're on a date, it's rude."

"Yeah, there's that, but it was really deeper than that too. At university . . ." He hesitated, really wanting to talk about this but knowing that it was risky. There was the nauseating feeling of saying too much, too early in the evening, to someone he didn't know, or perhaps finding out something too early about who you were talking to, destroying some kind of spell, before you needed to. But he spoke quickly before he could stop himself. "At university a lot of my friends, taking the same kind of courses I did, like literature or film studies or politics, they used to say that if you looked at girls, at women, because you were turned on by them or were judging their bodies or anything that guys normally do, you were controlling them in some way, exerting power over them. Just by looking at them. It had a lot to do with the history of art and how men were always painting naked women and how naked women filled up all our advertising and stuff like that. I never really understood it, though, I never really got the argument, because in my experience there is nothing more powerless than a guy staring at women." She smiled, so he took a breath and went on. "I mean I know because I do it all the time. I sit in a café and I just love staring at the girls and women of all ages and what they're wearing and, you know, if they catch my eye we both look away, because we're both embarrassed that they caught me."

"They're probably not embarrassed," said Jenna. "Everybody likes being looked at. You're just not supposed to show it."

"Well, maybe," said Justin. "Some people would say they don't like it, because, I guess because when I'm looking I'm judging. I'm judging who I find attractive and who I don't, although to tell you the truth I find most women attractive, but still I can see how that would make people feel nervous or uncomfortable, to be judged. But what I mean is I still feel powerless. You feel totally helpless sitting there looking and lusting. You're the loser, I mean I'm the loser. It feels as if the people you're looking at have all the power. There is nothing more pathetic than a guy just staring at women."

She laughed. "Of course. I know that."

"You do?"

"Who doesn't? It's the guy who doesn't look at you who seems the most powerful. That's the guy, you want his attention."

He smiled, breathed out with great relief, and said, "Have you eaten?"

"I'm starving."

He met her eyes and she smiled and leaned forward towards him. He could smell the candy smell, a fruit flavour like green apple or grapefruit, perhaps her lip gloss. He let his eyes caress her bare shoulders and then fall, quickly, over the tight round-ness of her bust and then he raised his hand for the waitress.

She ordered calamari but seemed surprised when it arrived. It was grilled and plain and looked good. She picked at it, tried it, put it aside. She tasted his odd beef wrap thing. She had a glass of white wine with the food. They talked about the city; she thought it was okay, better than Belleville, at any rate. She hadn't really lived right in Belleville, but just outside it. That was where her mother lived, anyway.

She liked movies, so they talked about movies for a while. She liked going to movies by herself. She spent a lot of time by herself. She liked action movies, crime movies, science-fiction adventures, big Hollywood blockbusters. Justin was actually, himself, pleased with this, not because he liked these movies, but because her taste for violence was rather sexy, and it was sexy perhaps because it was masculine, or perhaps because in such sharp contrast to Genevieve's taste, which had been sensitive to violence or indeed to seeing too many male characters at all.

Jenna very much liked Samuel L. Jackson, and admitted she kind of had the hots for Vin Diesel. This made Justin feel some-what small, but he didn't say so; he said he thought Vin Diesel was quite good-looking, but he had never seen him act.

She had some friends in town, sure, some good friends. She had an easier time with guy friends than girl friends. She didn't know why; guys just seemed easier to get along with. She liked the same things guys did. She had one friend, a girl though, who was having a hard time, she was helping her out. This girl was too stressed out. She was having trouble sleeping. She had been meaning to ask him, Justin, because he was friends with doctors, if he knew anyone who could get this girl the medication she needed.

"Doesn't she have a doctor?" said Justin.

"No, she just moved here. It's really hard to find a doctor these days, you know?"

"I know. You have to know someone. I can find her one. I can ask Andrew, the guy who took care of you."

"Oh. That would be nice." She toyed with the lettuce under the calamari, and said, "Could Andrew get her the medication?"

"Well, he would have to see her. He's very proper about that sort of thing. He can't even write prescriptions outside the hospital, yet. I think. I'm not sure where he is with that. I'll have to check."

"Oh, that's okay. Ask him, when you see him, though."

"What's the medication?" said Justin.

"It's just a regular sleeping pill. She gets really stressed without it. It's like Valium."

"Like Ativan, Xanax?"

"Yeah. Xanax. Or any one of those."

Justin nodded. "I love those. I've taken them all myself. I used to have trouble sleeping."

"Really? Can you—"

He shook his head. "I don't have a doctor right now either. Mine died." For some reason this made him laugh, and she laughed too. "No, it's true. That's the second doctor I've had who's died. Anyway, no, I don't want to take them any more anyway. You can get, you know. You want to take them all the time."

Jenna pushed her plate away and arched her back as if stretching. "So tell me about being a teacher."

"Ha." This came out as a sort of bark. Justin pretended to cough. "Well, its a bit odd. I don't teach what I studied, what I was trained to teach. I teach really boring things."

"What did you study?"

"I studied literature. English literature."

Jenna leaned forward, her eyes wide. "I loved English. In school."

"Really."

"It was my best subject."

"Really."

"I write poems, too."

"Really? What about?"

"And stories. About anything. I used to read a lot. I had a lot of time on my own, in the country. What are your favourite writers?"

"Wow," said Justin.

"Wow what?"

"Nothing. Let me tell you about my favourite writers. Do you want another glass of wine?"

Then they talked for some time about books and reading, actually he talked most of the time, and she listened with what seemed like genuine interest. She wanted him to write down all the names of writers he was saying because she hadn't heard of most of them.

She really liked Shakespeare, when they did it in school. And Italo Calvino. And Steve Martin, his novel *Shopgirl*. It wasn't bad. She was working in a store when she read it. The back of her hand brushed against his, lying on the table.

He said, "You want to go somewhere else? For another drink?"

She shook her ropy curls all over her shoulders and looked him in the eye and smiled and said, "Sure."

They walked down the crowded street. Jenna had not made a move to pay for any of their meal and drinks. He guessed that was the way it was going to be. She produced a cigarette and a lighter from her tiny leather bag and smoked it.

When they passed the groups of girls in their skinny jeans and their clingy tops, those girls didn't look at Justin, they looked at Jenna, up and down, and then they turned with a kind of curiosity to Justin, and then looked away. This was better than not being looked at at all.

There was a crowd outside Superfat. A bouncer was checking IDs.

"Sure," she said.

It was red and hot inside. He got her another vodka cooler and himself a beer and they watched the pretty people dance. The music was bassy hip-hop. The girls were dancing slowly, just swivelling their hips round and round. "This is fun," she said. "I never go out." Then she said, "Oh my God, I love this song," and she just walked onto the dance floor.

He followed her.

She danced like a black dancer on a video. She turned her back to him and planted her feet wide apart and started rotating her hips. Then she started sinking low to the ground and jiggling her buttocks. Then she turned to face him, her face all lit up and smiling, and her hair a big halo, and pushed close to him and put her hands on his hips while she rocked, side to side. "I love dancing," she said.

"I can see that," he said. He was sweating a little.

She pulled away from him and danced some more and he knew that she wanted him to watch her. At this point he began to be aware of a certain nervousness: he wasn't sure, at this point, if he wanted to have sex with her or if he was afraid of it.

She came back to him every few minutes, dancing so close to him she was almost rubbing against him, but she wasn't. On her hair was the cigarette and the candy juicy-fruit smell, and something else, the smell of her skin as she grew warm. At one point she brushed her cheek against his. He tried to put his hands on her hips and pull her closer to him, but she pulled away again.

They went back to the bar and had another drink. Justin tried not to calculate the cost of the evening. She still was not offering to pay for anything. He suggested that they dance again but she said she had to go, she had a long shift the next day.

So they walked out onto the hot street, which was starting to feel a little aggressive, with cars roaring past and guys shouting between them. He said, "Which way are you going?"

She said, "Oh, I'm going back towards Ossington. Dover-court. Around there."

"That's not far. I'll walk with you."

They walked past all the patios and through the groups of young people and Justin wondered if he could take her hand. He chattered all the way about the different restaurants and which ones he'd been in and which ones he'd like to try, even though he wasn't very interested in restaurants.

They passed Ossington and the bars started to thin out. There were guys sitting on doorsteps and shouting to other guys in parked cars. The guys went quiet as Justin and Jenna passed. One of them snickered. Justin wondered what it would have been like for her walking alone. He said, "So, you live right here?"

"No, no. I'm not living here. I have to go to my friend's place."

"Oh."

She took his arm and held it close to her as they walked. He said, "Where is it?"

"At Dufferin. That's like—"

"Ten blocks. Fifteen. This side of Dufferin, or past Dufferin?"

She said, "You don't have to go all the way there. It's no problem."

He said, "No no. It's no problem. No problem at all. I was just asking."

"Really," she said, "I'll be fine."

"No no," he said. "I'd love to."

The street began to curve northwards. There were mostly dark houses on either side now, and not many people. They passed Dufferin. They passed a park and a church he had never seen before. It was remarkable that he had never gone this far west on College before. She didn't seem to have any problem walking so far in her heels.

She stopped in front of a brick apartment block, one of those four-story blocks with wooden balconies and a recessed door in the centre. The entrance hall was lit with a fluorescent light. He said, "This is where your friend lives?"

She turned to him and said, "Do you have a pen?"

"A pen? Why?"

"I might have one." She opened her little leather bag. Justin caught a glance inside it: scraps of paper and chewing gum and lipstick. She pulled out a ballpoint pen and a fold of paper.

"Ah," said Justin.

She wrote her number on it and JENNA in a curly script. She said, "I would love to see you again, if you'd like to."

"I'd love to," said Justin, holding the paper away from his body as if it were fragile.

She moved close to him and put her hands on his shoulders. She was only a half inch shorter than he was, in her heels. Very slowly, she pushed her face in to his. She kissed him very softly, but kept her lips on his. He put his hands on her waist and pulled her closer. Her lips were astoundingly soft and gentle. She kissed him very gently for what felt like a long time. She didn't put her tongue in his mouth. It was very tender and caressing. Her lips were sweet with fruit flavour.

He opened his eyes to see that hers were shut. Her eyelashes were very long. He closed his eyes again. He could smell her neck, a soapy scent and warmth. He had his hands on the taut flesh of her waist. He was aroused.

She pulled her lips away and rubbed her cheek against his, and pushed her belly and hips against his. He knew that she could feel him, and that she knew what she was doing.

"Bye," she said, and she turned and walked into the building.

He saw her buzzing a code on the intercom. She turned and waved to him, so he walked away. He had to go to a bank machine to get a cab home.

5.

In his Online Writing class, he checked the name of the girl he had seen with Mike, his boss. The class was writing a test. It was not a test he had devised himself; it was a multiple-choice test that Mike had suggested. It had come from a textbook. The test asked them to decide, among other things, whether meeting deadlines when given a writing assignment was (a) very important (b) not as important as the quality of the writing (c) as important as the content or (d) subject to change depending on the obstacles encountered when doing the research. Justin was not sure what the right answer was; he would read the textbook before he marked them. This one would give them trouble. Mike was big on the multiple-choice, because that's what the provincial test would be, and they would have to get used to it.

The girl was sitting towards the back. Justin had given them a sheet on the first day with squares where the chairs were and had them write their names where they were sitting. He should have known them all by now. This girl didn't talk much. She looked a little different from the others: something about the cut of her hair and her fingernails looked a little more expensive, something about her clothes, he wasn't sure what. Perhaps she was a year or two older than the rest of them.

Through the wall came the drone of Mike's voice. He was teaching in the classroom next door, and he was loud. Some of the students looked up at Justin and he smiled back; they were all used to Mike's presence leaking through at them from wherever he was. Justin had given many a lecture punctuated by Mike's vague yet insistent points from next door. These buildings had been built rather quickly, in the sixties. They had been built largely of concrete, except the interior walls, which were really just partitions. They were probably just drywall. And Mike's office was on the other side, so you could hear him when he was on the phone in there, too, laughing with people mostly, it seemed.

Justin looked over at Mike's girl—he was already thinking of her as that, although he had no evidence of anything—at the top of her head, bent over her desk, the neat blonde ponytail, and he checked his sheet and saw where she had written her name, Cathy Heilbrunner. He remembered this now, of course he should have remembered this name. There were not many German names at this college. She always did well on these tests.

She was wearing a cotton sundress and bare legs, but had a little cardigan to cover her shoulders.

He got up to stride up and down between the rows of students, as teachers had done when he had been in school, and the class looked up at him. They put their pens down. "It's all right," he said. "Keep going. Just walking around."

But they weren't used to this. He tried to walk slowly to the back of the classroom, but they just stared at him as if he were going to ask them something. One girl put her hands over her test as if he were going to copy from her.

"Just walking around," he said. He tried to put his hands behind his back as invigilators in his own exams had done. He tried to pretend he had an academic gown on, a pipe in his pocket.

"You're making me nervous," said a girl in a high voice.

"You'd better get used to this," said Justin. "In the provincial tests they'll have people walking around, just checking on you. When I was in school they used to do this on every test."

There was some sighing.

He passed Cathy Heilbrunner and she did not look up. She was working quickly though the test. He glanced at her brown smooth legs and feet, neatly crossed to one side of her chair. She wore real shoes, pointy leather shoes with a heel, which was unusual in this room full of running shoes.

After the test, he went to the departmental office and asked Janice if he could use the phone. She waved him to a desk behind her, the elderly Erna's desk, where he stood to use the phone with a sense of transgression. Erna was gone. He kept his eye on the back of Janice's head as he dialled. He was hoping she would be kept occupied by students and by her own phone.

Just as he had the number out of his pocket and was about to dial, Mike came in. He leafed through some folders that Janice gave him, and then he looked at Justin standing there and frowned.

Justin waved and smiled and held up one finger as if to say one minute.

Mike ploughed into the office. He gave the impression of scattering papers as he arrived in any room. "Hey Justin," he called, although he was two metres away, "you don't have a cellphone?"

Justin shook his head, still smiling. "Don't have much of a need for one, Mike."

"Well, obviously you do." And Mike passed into his own office and shut the door.

Justin waited till Janice was occupied with another would-be gang member at the front desk, and he dialled the number Jenna had given him.

It rang a few times before a woman answered.

"Jenna?"

"Jenna? No. Who's calling?"

"Justin. Tell her it's Justin."

"One minute."

He breathed out as he waited. He was relieved it wasn't Tee who had answered.

"Hello?"

"Hi," he said.

"Hi. How are you?"

"Great. Great. How are you?"

"I'm fine. I'm glad you called."

Justin felt his chest expanding with some kind of hot sweet gas. It was an almost pleasurable sensation. "Good. I had a great time last night." He said this extremely softly, as he was not far from Janice.

"Me too. A really great time."

"Would you like to—" At this moment Janice stood up and turned around and walked towards him.

Justin cleared his throat. Janice went to a filing cabinet across the room.

He whispered, "There's a party this weekend. It's some old—"

"Why are you whispering?"

"I'm in a very public place."

"I can't hear you."

Justin cleared his throat again. Janice went back to her seat. "Sorry. I'm in my office, it's very public. I'm using someone else's phone."

"So what? Are you embarrassed?"

Justin laughed. "No. No, I guess I'm not. I don't know. It's a bit of a weird place here."

Janice turned around and stared directly at him. She gave him a little smile and turned back.

Justin decided to go for it and make it fast. "I was wondering if you wanted to go to this party on Friday. It's some friends, old friends, acquaintances, really, they're people I went to school with. It's not in a house, they've rented a bar, it's somewhere downtown."

"Sure."

"You might find it a little boring, I don't know. They're a little older than you. You might find it interesting. I don't know."

"Sure."

"If it's boring, we can go somewhere else."

"Sure."

"Okay." His chest was expanding again.

Janice came back to the filing cabinet.

Jenna said, "What do I wear?"

"Wear? Oh, nothing. It's not a big deal."

"So I wear nothing? That would be a pretty big deal."

"No, I mean nothing, like it doesn't matter." Janice was taking her time at the filing cabinet. Mike came out of his office.

"I wouldn't mind wearing nothing, though."

Justin laughed. He held up the one finger to Mike again. Mike grimaced and began talking loudly to Janice.

"I wouldn't mind that either, actually. But really, it doesn't matter. It's casual."

"Okay."

"Okay then."

He offered to pick her up but she said she didn't know where she would be and it would be easier if they met somewhere. He told her he'd meet her at the Rivoli and they'd walk from there. He had to tell her where the Rivoli was. She asked him a lot of questions about it, and it took him a while to recognize that her most pressing concern was what people in these places would be wearing. He could have given her a very detailed rundown on what people in the Rivoli would be wearing, and indeed what the people at his college reunion party would be wearing, too, which he would have enjoyed, but Janice and Mike kept glancing over at him. He told her she'd look fine, which he knew to be true, and hung up.

Mike said, "Cellphones are very cheap these days, Justin. They're almost free. In fact they often are free. We teach our students to be aware of these things."

"These phones are cheaper, I find," said Justin. "Unlimited free local calls, all the time."

"Justin has a very busy social life," said Janice.

"Yup," said Justin, walking past her. He rifled through the mail in his pigeonhole. He could feel her staring at him. He knew his face was red.

He glanced at her before he left, and she winked at him.

He walked through the food court, as usual. He walked through it rapidly and attentively these days, looking for Tee. He had not seen him again.

He did, however, see the girl, Cathy Heilbrunner. She was sitting at a table with a coffee, talking on a cellphone.

Justin changed his path to walk past her. He slowed as he approached her table. She saw him but her expression didn't change. He smiled as naturally as he could and stopped beside her.

She said, "I'll call you back, okay?" and closed her phone. She looked up at Justin with a blankness that could have been described as a mild alarm.

He tried to smile wider. "Hi," he said. "Cathy."

"Hi."

"Didn't mean to interrupt your call. Just wanted to say hi."

"Oh. That's okay."

"How did you find the test?"

She shrugged, turned down the corners of her mouth. "Fine. No problem. I hope, anyway."

"Good," he said. "Good. That one was a tricky one, I think. I'm not a big fan of the multiple-choice, myself, it's not very interesting. But it's helpful to get to know them, you know, get to know the style, because that's what the provincial tests are like."

"Yes." She pulled her cellphone towards her, as if to protect it.

"Okay. Well, see you. Have a nice week."

"Okay, you too." She gave him a wincing smile. She was opening the phone and dialling as he walked away.

He went and got a coffee and a newspaper and took it outside. It was not so insufferably hot that one couldn't sit outside, in the shade at least, under one of the trees in the strip of grass between lots H and I. He sat and drank his hot coffee and sweated. This was supposed to be good for you.

He pretended to read the paper and studied the students who were streaming out of the building and through the parking lots. He was almost invisible there under his tree. He still felt some resentment at those who climbed into cars. Most of them had cars, it seemed. How did they afford cars? He did not have a car. He did not have a space to park a car near his apartment. Where did they park their cars?

There was a blonde ponytail passing between cars a few metres away. It was Cathy Heilbrunner. She walked confidently on her high heels, in her little sundress.

Justin half rose to see what car she would get into. He hoped she would not walk to a distant lot.

She stopped by a shiny new Mini, metallic blue, and got in.

Justin folded up his newspaper, for now he had to face the subway.

6.

"Brian."

"Justin. Nice to see you."

"This is Jenna. Jenna, Brian. Jennifer. How are you. Jenna. Jennifer."

"I *love* your dress," said Jennifer.

Jenna said *thank you* almost too quietly to be heard.

"So," said Brian, staring at her. "Surviving?"

"I guess so," said Justin. "Still teaching. You a doctor yet?"

"Is it cotton?" said Jennifer, touching Jenna's waist.

"I think so." Jenna smoothed her flat belly. The dress was white and tied behind her neck. Her hair was up.

"Soon," said Brian. "You? Still writing?"

"No no," said Justin. "Gave all that up. I'm teaching. I teach English at a college. I think I told you last time."

They had come a little too early. Or perhaps not many people were going to come. There was Dorothy Liu and Guntar Haus over by the bar, and a group he knew from the student paper by the window, and he hoped for some reason

77

that Dorothy wouldn't in fact come over and talk to them, as she was looking awfully slim and had narrow jeans and a silk top on, an outfit which he feared might make some uncomfortable. At least he was sure Genevieve wasn't going to show, having ascertained from Jennifer long before that she was with her parents in Barrie.

"I can't wear white," said Jennifer. "Makes me look like a ghost, or a tomato, probably a tomato right now, since I've had two glasses of wine already. But you're so pale and it still looks fantastic. It just suits you. I love the eyelets. I should try wearing a dress some time. I haven't worn a dress in I don't know, years. If I don't have to I don't, and that's just fine with me."

"Jennifer is a big runner," said Justin. "You still do that? Marathons and all that?"

"I did a half last month. I'm doing a full one in the fall. I'm not doing triathlons any more, it was getting expensive. How do you stay in such fantastic shape?" This was not directed at Justin.

"I don't know," said Jenna, looking at the floor. "Nothing." Her face was red in blotches. Justin glanced around and had the feeling that everyone else was trying not to look at them.

"That pay okay?" said Brian. "Teaching?"

"Has anyone been to Blacktable yet?" said Jennifer.

"That the place just opened down on Queen way west?" said Brian.

"It's in the new area," said Jennifer. "Around Lansdowne. Crackville. Everything is opening there, you just have to step over a few junkie hookers to get there. It's Damian Buhr's new place. He was at—"

"Trade, I know. I should check it out. Have you?"

"Fabulous," said Jennifer. "Amazing. All international fusion."

"I went to that new bar," said Brian, "Hex Key, which was stupid fun. There's a DJ in the washroom. There were girls dancing on the bar. It was like a movie."

"How's your drink?" said Justin, to Jenna.

"Okay," she murmured. "I might go out for a cigarette, though."

"You want me to come with you?"

"No no."

"*Justin.*" This was Dorothy Liu, squealing. She put her arms around his neck and put her nose against his cheek and kicked her leg up behind her as if she was in a movie about women. "How *are* you?"

"Dorothy. This is Jenna."

Dorothy did not release him. "I had to come over to see who this gorgeous creature was." She put her palm on Jenna's bare arm, uniting Justin and Jenna with her own hot flesh, and Jenna flinched. "This is the most beautiful woman I have ever seen, Justin, and I don't just mean with you, I mean like anywhere in the world. *So* nice to meet you. I *love* your dress."

"Everyone seems to like it," said Justin.

"How *are* you? You're looking not so bad yourself. You're looking great. How's the writing?"

"Not writing. Teaching. It's fine."

"I would so love to get together with you, you know? There's a project I'm working on that I think you would be perfect for. Top secret right now. I should get your number."

"How do you stay in shape?" said Jennifer.

"Oh," said Dorothy Liu, "this is ridiculous. This is stupid but it's really fun."

"What?"

"I've been doing this strippercizing thing. It's like a pole dancing workout. It's fantastic."

"Is that with Hotgirls?" said Jennifer.

"Yeah. They have a studio right by my office."

"You are paying to learn how to strip?" said Justin.

"It's more of a workout," said Dorothy. "It's totally acrobatic. It's like gymnastics but with better music."

"Well," said Jennifer, "it's certainly working."

"I'm going to go get a cigarette," said Jenna in his ear.

"Sure," said Justin, "you want me to—"

She was walking away.

"Anyway," said Dorothy, "Justin, it's a writing thing, at least you could advise me on who would be best for it, it's commercial, you know, like maybe not your kind of thing, but I'd really like to pick your brain about it."

Jenna had disappeared down the stairs, or perhaps into the washrooms. Justin listened to Dorothy Liu, or did not listen, for a few more minutes and then she had had enough of him and she and Jennifer stalked back over to the bar and Justin was left with Brian the almost doctor, who said, "So. *You're* doing all right. Obviously. Where'd you meet her?"

"Ah," said Justin. "We were both. A restaurant. She works there."

"Way to go. Way to go. She's a knockout."

"What were you guys talking about back there, a restaurant?"

"Oh. Yeah. Blacktable. It's in the area that was all sketchy and it's all bars and stuff now. Meme is down there. It's like a movie theatre with art videos and a bar."

"Is it expensive? Blacktable?"

"I would think, yeah. That's what's happening to that area, that's why all the artists and punks and rummies are all upset over it. They spray-paint the front of it with stupid stuff every week."

"I don't keep up with this stuff. I suppose I should."

"You're going to be dating girls like that, you should," said Brian. "Guntar."

"Hey, Guntar."

"Brian. Justin." Guntar wasn't looking terrific. He hadn't shaved and his hair was turning grey. His face had always been grey.

"How's married life?"

"Terrific. Fantastic." Guntar started to cough. "Working a little too hard."

"Really. In journalism?"

"No no." Guntar was coughing so hard now that he could hardly speak. "Journalism. No." He coughed for a minute more. "Impossible to make a living in journalism. Advertising."

"Wow," said Justin. "Even though you were the editor-in-chief of the student paper. I thought that was a pretty big deal."

"Yeah," said Guntar. "No." He began to cough again.

"Excuse me. Good to see you." Justin put his beer on the bar and went down the stairs and outside. The street was crowded. Jenna was standing on the curb looking into traffic. It looked as if she was going to step into it. He almost ran over to her.

"Hey," he said.

"Hey."

"You okay?"

"Awesome." She sucked on her cigarette, then threw it away. "Are we going to stay long?"

"No," said Justin, "no, no, not at all. I just have to say hello to a couple of people, then I'm ready to go. I thought it would be more interesting than it was. Than it is."

"You want to go back in and do that? I'll meet you in a second."

"You sure you're okay?"

"Yeah, totally. I'm fine. Just going to get some air for a second and I'll be right back in."

"Okay. I'll just wrap it up. Then maybe we can go somewhere more fun."

"Whatever you like. We can stay too, if you're enjoying it. Or you can stay and I can go."

"No no no. Come on back in with me and we'll just stay a few more minutes. The more interesting people will come soon. I just spoke to Guntar, who's really intelligent. He was the editor of the paper, the student paper, he was quite a star. We all thought he was going to—"

"Okay, I will. You go on back in and I'll be there in one second."

"Okay." Justin patted her shoulder as he walked away, a gesture that made him feel like a dad, as if Guntar had rubbed off on him.

Upstairs, he found Brian again. They leaned against the bar. "So," said Justin. "Medicine. Like everybody. Why is everybody a doctor? My old buddy Andrew did this too."

"Really? I thought everybody wanted to be a great writer."

"One or the other, I guess. So, right now, hospitals for you. All day long and all night. How you holding up?"

"Oh," said Brian, "it's okay. You sleep once in a while. It's kind of fun actually. The nurses are fun." He put his bottle of beer to his lips and lifted the bottom to the ceiling.

Justin tried to laugh. Then they toasted each other. Then he said, "You get to have access to all these great drugs and you get addicted like doctors on TV. It's kind of cool."

Brian laughed. "Yeah, I guess. I guess you could if you wanted. Some guys do. I don't know how they find the time."

"Yeah, sure. But seriously, you must be tempted. You get all screwed up in your sleep because of the shifts and hey, you could just grab an Ativan and you're fine. I would find it hard to resist."

"Oh, God, I have no problem sleeping. That's the least of my worries."

"Yeah. Of course. But how does it work, though? If you really wanted to get something harmless just to help you sleep? Isn't it all over the place?"

"Sure. Some of the heavier stuff is under lock and key, but there are samples of all kinds of stuff we have."

"But you can write prescriptions anyway. Can you write them for yourself?"

"No, of course not," said Brian. "Where did Dorothy go?"

"I don't know. I think she's with Jennifer."

"She's looking all right, isn't she?"

"You want another beer?"

And there she was, Dorothy, striding towards them. She pushed herself between Brian and Justin and put her hand on Justin's arm and said, "So. Tell me everything. Where'd you meet her and everything."

"I'll see you, man." Brian winked as he moved off.

Dorothy said, "So I guess things are really over with Genevieve."

Jenna was standing in the doorway, looking for him. Justin waved. She saw him standing with Dorothy and stopped. "I totally knew that would happen," said Justin.

"What was that?"

"Excuse me one second." He walked over to her. "I'm about ready to go."

Jenna said, "Who's Genevieve?"

"Genevieve? Who mentioned Genevieve?"

"A girl outside asked me if I knew her. Then she got all weird when I said no and she wouldn't say who she was."

"Oh good. Wasn't that nice of her. Which girl?"

"The tall one in mom jeans."

"Jennifer. Wasn't that sweet of her. Listen, let's get out of here."

"I guess she's your ex."

"Yes, my ex, Genevieve. I'm sorry about that. Everyone here knew her and ... I guess they like gossip." He was almost pushing her out the door.

"Don't you need to say goodbye to people?"

"Nah. No. Not at all."

They stopped on the street and he breathed in. The side-walk was crowded. People were sitting on the patio with bare shoulders and laughing. There were beats booming from the cars lined up. "Okay," he said. "Lovely night."

"Where do you want to go?"

"Yes. Let's go ... let's go a little further on. There are some patios away from all these stores."

They walked and she didn't take his arm. They sat outside a Spanish restaurant and she said, "Did you go out with her too?"

"Her? With who?"

"With that Chinese girl."

"Dorothy? Oh no. Good lord no. She would never have been interested in me. I mean, I wouldn't, I mean, whatever, no."

"Never interested in you? Why was she coming on to you then."

"Yes, I guess she was coming on to me. Even I noticed that. That's interesting. That's kind of cool."

"Oh, it's cool, is it? Why don't you go back there if you—"

"No, no, it's cool because she honestly has never come on to me before. It was because you were there."

Jenna was silent and he could see she was thinking about this and was not upset by it. Her face was like a stage: it showed great shifts of emotion without her knowledge, and it occurred to him that he had been reacting to its drama, fearful of its torments, ever since meeting her.

He said, "You should see it as rather flattering too."

"I guess. I guess it's flattering when girls are bitches."

Justin laughed, relieved that they were now back to joking.

"Especially girls in cheesy-ass polyester tops."

"Whoa now," said Justin. But he was laughing. "I used to spend all my time with those people. That was my life. But I can't really keep up with them now. They like going out to restaurants and talking about them, and I don't earn quite as much money as they do, and you know I'm honestly not all that interested in restaurants."

"Me neither," she said.

"Really? I mean I like nice places, and I like nice food, I just hate talking about it. It's like talking about renovations or furniture, which they also talk about a lot. It seems kind of, I don't know, boastful, like competitive."

"Sure," she said, nodding and frowning. Perhaps she didn't know people like this.

"So," he said. "It's early."

They still hadn't been served their drinks. She said, "You really don't have to take me anywhere. It's expensive to keep paying for drinks if we don't really feel like them."

"Oh, that's—"

"Where do you live?"

"Where do I live?" Justin looked around for the waitress. He could have used at least one more. "I live near where we met. Uptown and west."

"Is it nice?"

"Nice? Not really, no. It's small. It's kind of hot. But I live alone, at least, which is nice. I had roommates for years."

"Tell me about it," she said. "You're lucky." She threw her hair back over her bare shoulders and leaned forward. "You want to just go back to your place? Just chill there?"

"My place?" The waitress was coming towards them. "Sure. I mean, sure. We'd have to grab some beer or something."

"Do you smoke at all?"

"Smoke, no, but, you mean cigarettes?"

"No." Jenna smiled and reached across the table for his hand.

"Hello guys," said the waitress. "How you guys doing tonight?"

"We're great," said Justin. "I think we're going."

"Wicked," said Jenna.

They sat on the old loveseat he had covered with a tablecloth. He put on some folky stuff Genevieve had liked. It was the only girl music he had. Jenna produced a bag of weed, rolling papers, asked for a magazine to work on, scissors. She was very focused and very careful in how she constructed it. She cut the weed up with scissors, rolled the paper, then cut a square of cardboard from the paper package and rolled it into a filter. Her joint was perfectly cylindrical.

Justin took a long drag and tried not to cough. They were drinking Grand Marnier because his uncle had given him some at Christmas and he had never opened it and it was the only thing there. It was soothing after the smoke.

When they had finished the joint they kissed stiffly for a while and he put his hand on her breast. When he started kissing her neck they were both breathing a little harder. She was writhing around a little, arching her body up to his.

He stroked her bare thigh for a while, which was exciting, for it was smooth and firm and hot. He pushed his hand up her thigh as far as he could, to find the edge of underwear, and still he could not find it. His palm slid up to her hip. It was high on her hip that he found the fine string that signalled some kind of minute thong. He traced it towards the small of her back, where he found a tiny triangle of lace, then around to the front, where the string began a descent into her groin. He imagined the shape of tattoos under his fingertips. She made no move to stop his hand. He withdrew it.

He didn't know if he could untie the halter top of the dress there on the sofa or if it would be more polite to suggest that they move into the bedroom. He thought perhaps it would be more polite to remove his shirt first before he had her naked, more gentlemanly or something. He said, "Would you like to move into the bedroom?"

She shook her head. She was unbuttoning his shirt. Her face was flushed and her eyes were focused on his buttons.

He reached behind her neck and pulled on the ribbon of fabric that held her dress up. His heart was beating quite fast. The ribbon came undone and he pulled the front of her dress down, something you get to do in dreams. She smiled and looked down at her little breasts, as if she were just as delighted to see them.

By the time they were mostly undressed, Justin kept suggesting they go to the bedroom, and she kept refusing. She kneeled on the floor and tugged his jeans off. Then she straddled him and ground against him. She pinched his nipples. He held on to her hips. Her whole body was a muscle, an elastic band, it was both soft and firm at the same time. The tattoo in her groin was a green dragonfly. It was one long filigreed wing that usually rose slightly above her waistband. He had to kiss it.

He took each nipple in his mouth and sucked till it was hard. He said, "Let me get a condom."

She said, "If you like."

He went to the bedroom and got the condom and still she didn't follow him. They ended up on the living room floor, on the dusty rug.

She wasn't completely shaved, as he had expected; she had a fine thatch which he licked and sucked and probed till he was dizzy and his face felt shiny. At first she giggled through his licking, and then became silent and taut and then panting.

She rode him for a while and touched herself and she seemed to come close, whimpering.

He turned her onto her back and lay on her and pushed into her. Her eyes were intensely blue and green and grey. Then she closed them. She drew her knees up and locked her ankles around his back. She ground against him slowly and began to moan. He let her control it until she began to really pant and he knew it was going to work like this, without his even touching her. She came almost silently, gritting her teeth, squeaking a little, but so strong he could feel the contractions, all her muscles flexed like a terrible fit. He pinned her down and thrust until she was finished.

He shifted off her and without speaking she turned over, shiny with sweat, face down, and arched her back and spread her legs and raised her white buttocks off the ground.

It was all so slow and easy. He had never felt so free. He had never felt so invited; he had never felt that he didn't have to ask permission for anything.

He pushed in between the wet lips and thrust as slowly as he could, to control himself, and to stare for as long as he could at her back, the taut little buttocks, the bumps of her spine, her shoulder blades; he wanted to appreciate it and remember the image, and the feeling of muscle under skin under his fingertips. She was grunting a little with each thrust, as if he was hurting her, which he knew he wasn't, but he was grateful for the feeling that he might be, that he might be so big he was uncomfortable for her.

He leaned forward and reached around and caressed her underneath, where she was slippery and engorged. He found the rubbery button. She sighed and whimpered and he felt her tightening again. He worked at it as slowly as he could, having difficulty keeping his balance, slowly thrusting and rubbing her in tiny circles until she began to cry out and shudder again. He felt her contractions begin again and he almost laughed with pride.

This time she came loud, wailing and swearing and shuddering. She sounded as if she was crying.

89

By the time she was finished he was thrusting savagely and she was murmuring something between her gasps.

He leaned forward to hear her, and was astounded to hear that she was giving him encouragement in unbelievably crude terms. No one had ever spoken to him like this before. He came quickly and collapsed.

She didn't want to lie there long. She bounced up and grabbed her drink. They sat together naked on the loveseat. She began to roll another joint. Justin let his head roll back and for the first time was aware that he had smoked a joint, staring at the ceiling and letting amazement wash over him. He was dizzy and floaty and shaky, as if he had been running, or as if he were old. Perhaps he was. He had his hand on the back of her neck, under her hair and her skin was damp and hot. She crossed her legs. She seemed unaware that she was naked. He wondered if something terrible would happen now; it had to, for he would surely pay for what had just happened. He lifted up the mass of her hair to look at the black sun tattoo on the back of her neck. There were tiny letters traced around the spiky black rays. He leaned in to read them. They spelled RYAN.

He let the hair fall. He sat back. "So," he said, "who's Ryan?"

"Oh," she said. "A family member who died."

"Ah. Sorry about that."

She said, "You want to get something to eat?" and he almost laughed with relief. He leaned forward and kissed her all over her face, until she giggled and pushed him away. "You're nice," she said.

90

They ordered pizza which she ate naked, then they watched celebrity gossip on TV. The weed felt like sand in his veins, and he was yawning. He said, "Let's go to bed," and she looked frightened for a minute.

She said, "You want me to stay here?"

He said, "Yes, I do."

"Really?" She looked at him and then looked away and down and she blinked several times.

"Very much. I would love it if you did. We'll wake up together."

She put his arms around her neck and kissed his cheek, and he felt her nipples brush his chest and he was aroused again.

In the stuffy bedroom in the darkness they coupled again, simply and quickly and hard. He pounded into her as hard as he could, trying to get her to say the naughty things again, and she did.

He could not get her to orgasm again, but he couldn't wait either, and came inside her too quickly.

Afterwards, she said, "You can come inside me without a condom if you want. It's okay."

There was grey light in the morning and when he looked at her she had her eyes open and was staring at the ceiling. Her mouth was tight. She looked at him with wide eyes and did not smile. He kissed her for a while and got hard against her but she pushed him off.

He made her coffee. He had frozen waffles in the freezer, which she was very pleased about. She ate them in a flood of syrup and exclaimed several times about how much she loved them. She had to go to walk her dog. He asked her what kind of dog it was and she said some kind of terrier he hadn't heard of. The dog's name was Amanda. It wasn't her dog, really, it was her friend's but she was taking care of it.

She was wearing his white T-shirt and her white thong. There was a blue bruise on her thigh that perhaps he had given her.

He said, "Do you have to work today?"

She was quiet and staring at the table.

He said, "I have to mark a bunch of tests in the afternoon, but that's it. If it's going to be stinking hot again, I might try to find a public pool."

She put her knife and fork down.

He said, "I still haven't asked you where you work."

She was perfectly still and her eyelids were lowered. Then the corner of her mouth twitched, because she was crying.

"Oh," said Justin. "Hey. Sorry." He took her hand. "What is it?"

She shook her head. Her hand was limp, but her shoulders were tense and shaking.

"Hey," said Justin. "Where did this come from? You okay?"

She just sat there and shook. He got up and went to the washroom and brought her back a roll of toilet paper. She took it and bunched some up and wiped her eyes. Then she laughed. "I'm sorry. I'm sorry."

"That's okay. That's okay. Are you going to tell me what's wrong?"

"It's really nothing." Her voice was strong again. "It's just that." She blew her nose. "I'm sorry. That's gross."

He laughed and stroked her bare knee. With his other hand he pushed her hair behind her ear. He wanted to touch her everywhere at once.

"I've just been having a rough time lately, nothing serious. My family . . ."

Justin waited. "Your family?"

"I've never . . . they're all screwed up. And I've never been very happy. I'm always like this."

"Oh."

She was silent for a while longer and Justin decided this was all he was going to get. He said, "Okay."

She blew her nose again and said in a shaky voice, "But you've been so nice to me. You're a real gentleman." She leaned and kissed him on the cheek. Her face was wet.

"Ah," he said. He rubbed her shoulder for a bit more and then got up to clear their plates. He wasn't sure if she had really stopped crying or not. He wanted to find out about the fucked-up family but he wasn't sure if she was inviting inquiry. He poured them some more coffee.

He sat down again, in his grey bathrobe, wrapped it around his skinny legs and said, "How's your health these days. Since you had that thing. When we met."

She sniffed. "I told you. I'm fine."

"Do you want to tell me what it really was?"

She looked at him quickly. Her eyes were red but she had stopped crying. "It was exactly what you thought it was. Do you really want me to go into details about how that happened?"

"No. I mean not if you don't want to."

"Well I don't."

He took her hand, which was limp and hot. "How old are you, anyway?"

She answered so quietly he had to ask her again.

"Twenty," she whispered.

Justin had never actually seen anyone choke on a drink at surprising news, except in children's cartoons, but he did it now. "Holy," he said. He had spilled coffee on his bathrobe. He got up to wipe it.

"That freaks you out."

"No no," he said from the sink. "No. Not at all. Yes. Sure it does. I had no idea."

"How old did you think I was?"

"I don't know. Older. Like twenty-five, twenty-six, easy. You seem so confident."

"So what difference does it make? Twenty or twenty-five?"

"Not much, I guess. I don't know. People seem to think it does. Twenty sounds really young. But I guess you're not. Jesus. Twenty." His ears were buzzing, as if he had been listening to loud music. "Jesus."

She said, "So how old are you?"

"Thirty-two."

"Huh. That's about what I thought."

"Right. Ho boy."

She drew her knees up to her chin. "Is that really a problem for you?"

"Of course not."

"You want me to go?"

"No, no. I mean, you have to walk your dog, right?"

She nodded, and pushed her coffee cup away. Then she got up and went to look for her dress.

7.

Justin went out for a drink with Andrew on Sunday evening. Andrew said he could stay out till nine at the latest. He had to catch up on sleep whenever he could. And he hardly drank at all. You just couldn't, when you were working shifts like this. Whenever he had a few hours he just had to sleep and then do laundry.

They went to a patio on College. Andrew ordered a beer and sipped at it. He said, "So, you're having fun, at least?"

"Oh yeah. I'll say. Definitely." Justin tried not to giggle. He wanted very much to describe the fun, but he knew that would be immature.

"That's good. That's what you need."

"It's good for now. It's terrific. It's just a fun thing, you know. I know it's not going to last. You know. It's just what I need right now." Justin stared at all the passing bare shoulders and all the bouncing, teasing breasts in their stretchy fabrics and felt very hot. He felt a little buzzy, unsettled, not really there, as if he hadn't slept for a couple of days, even though he had been doing nothing but sleeping since Jenna had left on Saturday morning. He had not called her, and she had not called him.

"Let's hope she feels the same way," said Andrew.

"Yeah. I hope she doesn't get all hung up on me. That would be the last thing I need." Justin drank his beer. His was already mostly gone.

"How old is she?"

"How old is she? Ah." Justin took his time swallowing. "Ah, twenty-one, I think." He started to sweat. He could feel it prickling on his forehead.

"Twenty-one?" Andrew pushed away his beer. "Holy shit. Really?"

"Yeah, I know."

"Holy shit."

"I didn't find out," said Justin, "till we'd already, you know. I should have asked earlier, I guess. She seemed older."

"Holy shit."

"Stop saying that."

"That's like the same age as your students."

Justin shook his head. "I know. But she seems so much older than my students. It's hard to imagine . . . I can't imagine dating one of my students."

"Oh."

"My students live with their parents in suburbs. The girls wear headscarves."

"Headscarves."

"They're Muslim."

"Ah," said Andrew. He rubbed his face as if exhausted by this topic.

"It would be like dating one of your patients, I guess."

"Okay."

"Although," said Justin, "I think my boss does."

"He dates my patients?"

"Yes. No, he dates mine. I have a feeling he's doing a girl in my class."

"Uh huh. Cool." Andrew was also staring at the passing stream of breasts. It was like some kind of very uneventful contest—it could have been one of the long days of qualifying rounds for the gruelling final pageant, the great city-wide beauty pageant. But he was listening, a little. "Isn't he not supposed to?"

"Oh, he's very much not supposed to."

"Is she hot?"

"Kind of, yeah. She seems to have a little more money than the other kids. She's also, coincidentally, doing extremely well on these stupid multiple-choice tests. I just marked a bunch today. It's incredibly easy to mark them, which is nice. And I saw this girl's name, she's got a funny name, German or something, and I noticed someone got eighty-nine per cent on this, which was unusual to say the least, most of them failed it, or half of them anyway, and so I checked the name and it was hers."

Andrew was yawning. "Holy shit," he said. He took off his sunglasses. "Check it."

"What?" Justin scanned the five girls walking in front of them. "Which one?"

"Twenty-four zee. That's the new one."

"Oh."

"Six cylinder supercharged. It's got some new computerized traction control which is retarded intelligent, it thinks for you, basically, like it tells you when it's going to rain and you should call your mom, sort of thing. It's basically magic."

"Huh," said Justin. The car was small and silver, parking laboriously across the street. "Looks like a shark in a cartoon."

"It's supposed to be four-thirty or four-forty horse, something stupid like that. It's stupid fast."

"I forgot you were really up on this stuff."

"Oh, I'm not, really. I would just love to own one."

"Really?" Justin stared at the car. He would not have noticed it. "I suppose it's because you might, some day."

Andrew laughed. "Maybe."

"Who's driving it? I can't see."

"Some fuckstick with a shaved head, of course."

"You have to be a titwad to get one." Justin watched the big guy walk away from his car and slap some other shaved head jerkwad's hand. They were all wearing linen drawstring pants like pyjamas. "Asshat," said Justin. Then, "My boss is a total prick to me, so maybe I should call him on it."

"Huh," said Andrew. "I wouldn't. What are you going to do, threaten him?"

"I guess not."

"What does he do?"

"Uch. What does he not do." Justin drained his beer. "He is just generally a dork-knob."

"A dork-knob. Is that anything like a titwad?"

"It is. No, a fucknuts. Or no, it's more like a dildobucket."

Andrew laughed and was thus emboldened to take another tiny sip of beer.

Justin wanted another one, but he didn't want to call attention to it. "Genevieve says that's very immature humour."

Andrew didn't reply to this. It was as if someone had mentioned his dead mother or God and it had got embarrassing.

Justin looked around for the lithe waitress who although almost illegally young was still probably older than Jenna.

"With me," said Andrew, "it's nurses."

"Really? No way."

"Oh way. There's a lot of time spent together in the hospitals. And the doctors kind of have all the power. At least, almost doctors. They know we're going to be doctors."

"Really. That must be fun. So you date them, or you just—"

"Sometimes. A lot of shit just happens in the hospital."

"No way. I am consumed by jealousy. Where in the hospital?"

Andrew smiled, shrugged. He let his dark glasses slide down his nose and peered at Justin. "You haven't really fucked till you've fucked on the birthing bed."

"No shit. You mean with the stirrups and legs up in the air and all that?"

Andrew nodded. He pushed his glasses back up his nose, a little too smugly.

"Are you supposed to do that?"

"Well, not on the birthing bed, no. But there's no specific regulation against relations with the nurses. It's discouraged, of course."

"Huh." Justin watched the girls for a while, the gleaming car he would never drive. "I guess there must be all kinds of temptations at the hospital. Like you must have access to all kinds of fun drugs."

"Yeah. It's there. I'm not tempted though."

"What about if I wanted something?"

"You?" Andrew turned to stare at him. "What would you want?"

"I'm having trouble sleeping. I don't know. Just something mild to help me sleep."

RUSSELL SMITH

"So why don't you go to your family doctor?"

"Oh, shit, family doctor, that's a good one. That's a funny one. I haven't had a family doctor in years. They're impossible to get now. There aren't enough of them. They're not taking on new patients. You should know this. This is why you're in med school."

Andrew frowned. "So you go to a walk-in clinic."

"They won't give out anything good there. They figure you're just a junkie and you're prescription shopping, or you're going to sell them or something. You want another beer?"

"No," said Andrew, "no thanks."

The waitress took Justin's order and they both turned to watch her undulate her way back inside. They had to all wear tight black trousers at this café.

"Well," said Andrew, "if you're really in trouble I can always prescribe you something. But it has to be totally legit. Like I have to see you in a formal appointment, examine you, and so on."

"Examine me?"

"I just mean I have to interview you, get your history."

"Oh. That would be great. No problem. Thank you."

"But you know," said Andrew, "there's always the internet. You just buy whatever you want from Mexico or India or whatever. They make you fill in a form and they give you a prescription. It's expensive. You need a credit card."

"Oh. I hadn't thought of that."

Andrew yawned again. "I should get going."

"Sure." Justin looked around at all the girls he could be seducing and buying drugs for and couldn't stop himself from smiling. He felt rich and powerful. He had a credit card. He could call Jenna that evening, he had a reason to now.

Although he shouldn't, for it would look weak. She could easily call him. He was a little surprised that she hadn't.

The next morning he took the long bus ride out to Constitution. When he got to the concrete corridor to his office he saw a queue of four students outside Mike's office door. The door was closed. Mike probably wasn't even in yet. This troubled him vaguely—perhaps because students were rarely lined up to see him, Justin, and he didn't see why they would, if the tests were all multiple-choice and all had right or wrong answers; it wasn't as if there was any philosophy to be discussed—but he forgot this immediately on seeing Annette the PR idiot striding down the hall towards him like the angry host of a home decorating show. She was wearing a tight skirt with a little ruffle below the knee and high heels and a little jacket that was open to reveal a clingy white tank top and the lines of some kind of rigid bra. Her legs were attractive and the heels high, but she wore flesh-coloured pantyhose: it was exactly the kind of suburban sexy outfit that Justin resented finding attractive.

He braced himself for her brisk greeting, and forced his eyes up from her chest to her face, and he even arranged his features into a kind of concrete smile, but she passed him in a rush of air. He even nodded as she approached. Her face did not flicker. He could have sworn she looked him in the eye, too.

It occurred to him after she had passed that it was not a snub: she simply did not recognize him from the meeting of other sad-faced teachers she had had to address. He was invisible to her.

In the departmental office, Janice greeted him with the news that someone had called for him, a girl, a lady she should say, and she said to call her urgently. Janice handed him the pink message with JENNA written in Janice's curly capitals, and a number. Her face looked as if she was trying not to smile or even laugh. "I didn't ask," she said, "what it was about."

Justin turned and left the office again. He walked all the way to the food court with a strange sense of trouble. It was good that Jenna had called him, but he didn't like any messages that people said were urgent. He found a pay phone and a quarter.

She answered right away. She said it was nothing serious. Just that her living situation had got all screwed up. No, she wasn't in any danger or anything, nothing like that. She just needed to get away from her roommates for now. She couldn't stay there right now.

"Of course," said Justin. "A couple of days is fine. Or longer. No problem."

And when he hung up he was smiling, he was so happy and excited at the thought of sleeping with her every night for the rest of the week, and trying hard to calm his happiness, to temper it with the knowledge that he knew he should have, that he was trying to conjure from somewhere, that this would bring complications, but he could not see them, he could not see them anywhere for happiness.

8.

"I would get my boobs done," she said.

They were in bed, looking at her body.

"What? You're kidding." Justin stroked them. He tried to let his fingers be lighter than they were, as if by barely touching her skin he could feel more of it. "You're insane. Your boobs are perfect. What do you want?"

"Bigger, of course. A lot bigger." She cupped them with her hands and pushed them together to make cleavage. "See."

He pushed her hands off. He kissed each one on the side and then between them and then teased each nipple with his tongue. "That would be a travesty. That would be a crime against God and man. These are the most perfect breasts ever created or witnessed in the history of humanity."

She sat up. "Do you believe in God?"

"Ah. No. I do not." He tried to reattach his head to her chest. "But you see, these breasts may change my mind. They may be evidence of a divine plan."

She looked down, sternly, objectively. "You don't think they should be bigger?"

"You've never seriously considered that, though, really, have you?"

"Sure I have. If I had the money."

"No, really. Seriously." He heaved his head up, stared into her eyes, now a slatey grey. "Don't ever think about that. That would be a terrible, terrible mistake."

"Really?" She was smiling, as if genuinely surprised that her breasts were perfect. She kissed him on the forehead. "That's sweet of you."

"It's not sweet of me at all. I am a very objective judge."

"Of women's bodies."

"Uh. I guess. Let me analyze the rest of you." Her belly rose to meet his lips: the skin of a drum. "This part cannot be altered. This shape here is . . . well, it can't be altered. And down here . . ."

She let him lick and stroked his hair as he did so. She said, "What's your favourite part, on you."

"My favourite body part, of myself?"

"Yeah."

"Yeah. I don't think I have one."

"Come on. You have nice shoulders."

"I do?" He tried to look at his own shoulders.

She pushed him onto his back and studied him. He felt like a fish in the bottom of a boat.

She stroked his shoulders. "You have nice broad shoulders."

"I'm all bony."

"Bony is sexy. Better than pudgy, star."

"Ah."

She traced the middle of his belly with his fingertip. "You're in great shape. I can see muscles."

"It's called undernourished."

"Six-pack."

"Ha."

"And this thing is fantastic."

"Ha."

"It is. It's beautiful. I think of it and I get a little rush, a little shiver. I think of it and I want to suck it."

He sat up and kissed her face, under her eyes, on her nose, on her chin. "I'm sure that is not true but it is a lovely thing to say."

"I'm serious."

"Is it . . . I'm always curious, I don't really care that much, but I—"

She laughed high and fast and threw her hair back. "Every guy," she said. "Every guy."

"Every guy what?"

"Every guy wants to know the same thing. Every guy is worried."

"Ah." He lay back, folded his hands on his chest. "Well?"

"You have nothing to worry about."

"Average," he said. He affected great interest in his fingernails.

"No, not quite. Slightly larger."

"Really? Honestly?"

"Quite large, yes. Honestly. It's a beautiful cock."

Justin laughed. He felt his ears turning red. He could not help smiling.

"And you know how to use it. You're a stud, star."

"I should do porno movies."

"You could, you know. Seriously."

"Shut up," he said. "Do you think we should think about getting up?"

"You want to?" She said this with such sadness he had to kiss her shoulders.

He said, "What would your porn star name be?"

She shook her head. "Whatever."

"What's that game, where you take your pet's name and your street, or your mother's maiden name or—"

"What kind of porn do you watch?" she said.

Justin looked around for his watch. "We should maybe think about dinner."

"Don't be embarrassed. Every guy does."

"Well, yeah." He tried to laugh but it came out as a whinny. "But it's embarrassing."

"No. It doesn't bother me."

"Well then," he said, "you're unusual in that regard."

"Everybody does it," said Jenna.

"Do you?"

She sat up and folded herself so she was cross-legged, an operation that was intriguing and beautiful. She started combing her hair with her fingers, which made her breasts jiggle. "Sure."

"You do. You look at porn."

"Sometimes."

"And." He sat up now, too.

"And what?"

"Well, lots of things. I have a lot of questions. This is the most interesting conversation I have had in some months and I am suddenly quite excited about it."

"Don't have a fit, star."

"Okay. What I want to know is this. Several things. First of all. Where do you find it? Online?"

"Sure. My roommate's computer. Or whoever's. If I had my own I'd be on it all the time."

"Okay. What about movies, videos? You ever rent them?"

She sighed. "Not personally. But I have watched them."

"Okay. Next question. Do they turn you on?"

"Why else would I watch them?"

"Okay. Excellent."

She laughed and lay back. "That makes me okay, does it?"

"Well, yes, yes it does. Most women deny it. Or they won't even look at it to see. They're terrified of it."

"What about you?" she said. "What turns you on?"

"I have way more questions. I've only just begun my interrogation. I need to know what you look for, what turns you on. Then I need to know, in detail, what you do about it."

"Hey, that's what I asked you. And I asked first."

He thought about this. "Okay. I don't look at it a lot. Okay? And this is really hard to talk about. Because we've all . . . I have come to believe that you should never ever mention ever even accidentally coming across a picture of a naked woman, if you're talking to a woman. It's supposed to be like admitting to puppy torture or something."

She flipped over so that he could admire her back, which he did. She said, "My God. You must have been going out with some fun girls."

He laughed. "I'm not alone in that, I assure you."

"Okay, so what?"

"What what?" He was stroking her buttocks now, trying to get her to part her thighs a little.

"What do you jerk off to. Describe it to me."

He pried the legs open a little more. "All right. I like, ah . . . this isn't every day, you know."

"Okay."

"Okay. When I do look at it, if I'm really bored or something, it's really pretty embarrassingly normal. I mean I just like naked girls. Women. Pretty basic. I like naked ladies."

"What kind?"

Justin blew out his cheeks. "All kinds, I guess."

"Big boobs or small?"

"Hmm. Both, really."

"I don't believe it."

"No, really."

"And what kind of sex. Rough, gang bangs, money shots, what."

"No. No. Honestly. Wow. This makes me uncomfortable for some reason."

"Sorry," she said. "I'm just—"

"No, no. It's also . . . I don't know. It's thrilling. I will tell you, if you really want to know. I'm just scared."

She pushed him back and hauled herself on top of him. She put her sharp chin into his chest and whispered, "Tell me. What gets you off."

"Everything does, actually. Any picture of—"

"Close-ups?"

"Yes. Close-ups of penetration. That'll do it."

"Big swollen cocks pushing into tight little pussies."

"Yes." He giggled.

"Or assholes."

"Yes."

"What else."

"I like videos of girls when they're coming. Really coming, though. I want it to seem real. Lots of moaning and writhing."

"That's sweet."

"And I kind of like amateur stuff too. Fat housewives in their rec rooms, with their faces blurred out."

"Gross."

"Hey, you asked. See, it's never a good—"

"No no." She put her hands over his cheeks, as if calming a child. "It's okay. It turns me on. I want to know."

"That's incredible," he said. "That's fantastic. You're amazing. What do you like? Like what do you watch, that gets you—"

She laid her head flat on his chest. "I like all kinds of kind of gross stuff."

"Like."

"Like when it's a little bit rough."

"Rough on the girl?"

"Yeah. Or where there's more than one guy."

"Like a gang bang."

"Yeah. Not that I would want that in real life. But I get turned on when I see them sort of passing the girl around, and talking about her like she's not there."

"Really. Wow."

"Does that freak you out?"

"Nope," he said. "No, it doesn't." He played with the ropes of her hair as if he was counting money. She writhed against him and her skin was hot.

She didn't leave the house much. Once she went to the grocery store and came back with the ingredients for a chili which she spent an hour and a half making. She didn't seem happy with his music collection: she had a little case in her bag with pop music with big dance beats. She sang along to it and danced as she cooked, so he didn't mind.

She had a big bag of weed with her and they smoked it every night. He liked this as it made him sleepy and tactile; he liked the feel of her nipples under his fingertips, the feel of the room expanding around him as he smoked it. But he disliked the coughing and the sore throat in the morning, and he hated the tarry smell of his stuffy rooms. He hated too that she frequently woke up with red eyes and lit a joint for breakfast. They sat in silence as she smoked in the mornings. He asked her why she needed it and she said she didn't need it, it was just nice. Then she said that sometimes she woke up all freaked out in the mornings.

"Tell me about it," he said. "So it takes the edge off."

"Yeah."

"But doesn't it make you sleepy all day? I could never get anything done."

She laughed. "I couldn't get anything done without it. I get too freaked out."

Justin didn't ask her what exactly she wanted to get done, for it was the kind of question that seemed to make her angry or tearful.

"I'm going to run out soon though," she said. She puffed out her cheeks. He had never seen her do that. "Which is a big drag that I'm just going to have to deal with."

"Ah. Is this due to a cash flow problem, as my friends in business school would say?"

She kept blowing air. "I guess you could call it that. I have a serious cash flow problem."

"Right. Well, might not be a bad idea to take a break for a while anyway. It's probably bad for our lungs. I heard that smoking one joint was like smoking a whole—"

"Yeah," she said, "no. It's a little more, it's a little more than that. The weed is just one thing. I owe money everywhere. I owe my roommate for rent."

"Well, I guess you're not working right now, right."

She turned to the sink and began clattering with dishes. It was sweaty hot in the kitchen. He watched her hips shift as she put her weight on one leg and rubbed the back of her calf with her foot. He wished she were naked and not in her track pants.

"Yeah," she said, "I'm going to go back to work soon."

"Do you have something lined up?"

"Oh yeah. It's no problem."

"Waitressing."

"Yeah."

He said, "Don't do those. I'll do those. It's my turn."

She kept splashing and washing and clinking. "I'm not going to quit smoking," she said.

"Okay," he said. "Fair enough. I was just—"

"Smoking's about the only thing I like." She put a glass onto the drying rack with such force that it cracked. Then she dropped her hands to her sides and stared at the soapy water.

He came up behind her and put his hands on her hips but she was stiff. "Okay," he said. "That's kind of harsh, but okay."

She pulled away from him and grabbed another glass.

"Hey, take a break," he said. "You're going to smash everything I own."

She flicked the water from her hands and pushed away from him. She went out onto the fire escape. He heard her dialling her cellphone.

He finished the dishes while she talked. He tried to listen but it would have been too obvious if he stopped washing and stood in silence so he couldn't hear anything but a few words. He definitely heard the word Tee.

When he was finished she was silent. He smelled the earthy smoke coming from the open door. He went out and sat with her. The night smelled of garbage and dogs. It was noisier on the fire escape, from the traffic and the dogs.

"I'm sorry," she said. "I just really need a little cash. I'll get some soon and it will be all no problem."

"Exactly," he said.

"It's stupid though. I need to get some more weed before I get psyched up to get work. And I need the work to buy the weed."

"Huh." He didn't know what to say to this. He was trying hard not to offer to lend her money. He didn't know why it was a bad idea.

"Usually he spots me," she said.

"Is this . . . is this Tee, the guy you buy from?"

"Sometimes. I have someone else too. But they've already spotted me."

"You mean they've . . . I don't get it. They give you stuff up front?"

"Sure. Then I pay when I can. But I'm behind now."

"Shit." Justin thought about this. "Holy. You mean you owe these guys money?"

"I guess."

"You owe drug dealers money."

She laughed. "You say it like it's some kind of crime movie. It's no big deal."

He stood up. There was sweat on his neck and he prickled. "You owe drug dealers money. I don't know. That sounds really not good to me. I don't know these guys—"

"I've done it before. I do it all the time. It's cool. It's fine."

"I've met Tee, don't forget. I don't think he's cool or fine at all." He wanted to pace around but there was no room on the fire escape. He went into the kitchen and back out again. "And I don't think you should be owing drug dealers money. I don't think it's a good idea at all."

She was laughing at him. "Relax. Calm down. You're getting yourself all worked up. You act like you know all about everything."

He sat with her again. He took the joint from her and took a long drag. He said, "You're right. I don't. I just have this idea of—"

"They're not going to come after me with guns, if that's what you think."

"Okay. Okay." He took another drag and looked out at the rooftops. There was a glow over the horizon that was the city's light reflected in the haze, still there after dark. "I can't lend you any money," he said. "Not to buy drugs."

She was silent. The joint was finished. She flicked it down into the dog's yard. She said, "I never asked you."

"Okay. I'm just—"

"I wouldn't."

"Okay," he said.

"Is that what you think I want?"

"No. No. Listen—"

"I would never ask you for money."

"Okay," he said. "I know you wouldn't." He coughed a little on the night air and the weed smoke. It was almost midnight and he would have to be on the train by seven-thirty in the morning. He already had a headache. "Okay. I should go to bed." He got up and went inside.

In the kitchen he began to put the drying dishes away. He heard her come in and close the back door that didn't close properly. She did it gently.

Then she was behind him and her hands were around his waist and she was standing on her toes so her lips were at his ear. "I'm sorry," she whispered. "I know you're just concerned about me."

Her skin was hot on his neck and he could smell the shampoo on her hair. "Yes," he said, "I am. I'm just trying to help."

"I know you are." She squeezed him, her cheek on his shoulder. "You are so sweet, you really are. You want to take care of me."

He wiped his hands and turned and embraced her. He cupped her buttocks as he had begun to do every time he touched her, he couldn't help it. And he was aroused again, as soon as he touched her. He kissed her eyes and her lips. He said, "Listen, I know I seem really silly and naive about this, but I really don't like this drug dealer thing. I would rather you paid them off. Let me give you some money, just for now, just to deal with this thing. I'd rather."

"No," she said. "I'd rather not. It will be—"

"I know it will be fine, but just indulge me on this one. Let me lend you a little money. Just for my peace of mind. How much is it? A couple hundred bucks?"

"Not even. Like one fifty."

"To each guy?"

"Yeah. No. Not quite. Like a hundred to one and—no, listen, forget it, this is silly, I don't want it. You shouldn't have to—"

"I know I shouldn't. But just let me. For me. Okay? A hundred and fifty, two hundred, it's no problem. Just to get this behind you."

She looked at him with her eyes of blown glass and said, "You are so sweet."

"Okay then?"

"Okay. Sure. If you really want."

"Yes I do."

"And if you're really *sure* you want."

"Yes I am."

"Wicked." She smiled. "You are so . . ."

"So what?"

"I don't know. Grown up. You're so serious and responsible. It's cool. It's sexy. I admire you. I admire everything you do."

He lifted up her T-shirt, cupped her little breasts, sucked her tongue.

They didn't turn on the light in the dank bedroom. In bed he impaled her and she was already wet.

When she was bucking and panting and had come once already and he was still thrusting mercilessly she whispered in his ear, her arm tight around the back of his head, "What do you want to do that you've never done before?"

He was silent in the darkness, aroused and fearful. He reached under her buttocks and parted them, stroked her there. Their eyes were close together, staring.

So softly he could barely hear, she whispered to his ear, "You want to fuck me there? Do you?"

He thrust harder in response. She put both hands to his chest and squeezed his nipples. He was going to burst. "Don't come," she said. "Don't come yet." Then she pushed him back, wriggled out from under him, and turned over on her front. "Come on," she said. "Yes. I want you."

9.

The next day at work he saw Annette the PR idiot coming down the white concrete hall at him from afar. He smiled at her and she smiled briefly and vaguely at him and did not slow down. He put himself in front of her. "Annette," he said. "Hi. Justin Harrison. I'm one of the instructors here. We met in a meeting, a few meetings actually, about the fundraising. The capital initiative."

"Oh of course," said Annette. "Justin!" Her smile was blazing. "I didn't—"

"No, of course," said Justin. He held out his hand and she took it. "You must meet a lot of instructors."

"Yes, I do. You're in—"

"Communications and media. I teach Business English, and other things."

"Of course. Well," she said. She was already edging past him.

"Been here a few years now. Good to see you again."

"You too." She turned and then stopped. She said, "You know, we're always looking for feedback from instructors. You

117

know. About how we can improve our best practices. We like to hear about things from your end."

Justin almost laughed. "Well, I'm glad to hear that. That's great."

"My door is always open."

"Ah. And where, ah, where exactly is your door?"

She laughed. "Touché, touché. I don't actually have an office in this building, but, here." She pulled up her briefcase and stuck her hand into it. She withdrew a manly black wallet and then struggled to extract a card from it.

"Let me hold that," said Justin.

"No no, I have it, here you go. Here's me. Feel free, any time you want to chat."

"Thank you," said Justin, "I will."

He was whistling when he made it into the departmental office. He felt that he could maybe just lean over Janice's desk barrier thing and take her hand and she would meltingly follow him anywhere, into the janitor's closet perhaps, if there were still such things as janitors' closets. "Good morning," he fairly shouted.

"Good morning," said Janice. "Are you okay?"

"I am wonderful, Janice, which is, I suppose, surprising, I concede. How are you?" He was pulling out the bundled papers in his cubbyhole and dropping them onto the floor to make clear that he had no intention of reading them.

"Fine," she said evenly. She handed him a yellow envelope whose flap was tied with a red string.

"Wow," said Justin, "that is cool. That is so archaic. I haven't seen one of those before."

"You haven't seen an envelope full of transcripts?"

"I think this is what they mean when they say *manila*. Did you ever wonder about that? When you read books they always say 'she handed him a manila envelope' as if everyone always knew what the hell a manila envelope was. Do you think they came from Manila?"

"Not this one. This one came from Mike."

"Ah, Mike. How is Mike?"

"He wants you all to go over the midterm marks."

"I guess it just means yellow. Why manila means yellow is something to Google. I totally love the red string thing. It's almost a wax seal."

"Yeah," said Janice. She was wearing her reading glasses which were unbearably adorable and they had ridden down her nose and she was peering at him over them which was even sweeter. "He just said to take a look at all the other instructors' marks and see where you fit in."

"I like your glasses," said Justin. "Very studious."

"That's me." She swivelled in her chair, back to her computer screen.

"Hey," said Justin, "what do you mean, where I fit in?"

She shrugged. "That's what he told me to tell you guys."

"Like how our marks match the other teachers' marks?"

"I guess so. I don't know."

"So we can see if our marks are higher or lower, and whose class is doing the best. I get it. Clever. Clever." He bent to pick up the papers he had scattered on the floor.

"He didn't say if you were supposed to get back to him or what."

"On the principle that the better the marks, the better the school. Brilliant."

"Justin."

"Yes."

"Talk to Mike, not to me."

"Recycle this crap for me, will you?" He handed his garbage to Janice.

He taught his morning class on E-Mail Etiquette, which was always a popular one, ending in mass chattering about bitches and douchehos. The class left in anticipation, for once, of writing their next assignment. The assignment was to write a cordial response to a rude e-mail. They would complete it by writing the nastiest imaginary e-mail to an imaginary shitwad boss of their ever entire lives. Justin had an hour before the next section, in which he would teach exactly the same thing again, and so repaired to the cafeteria, where he could scan the grades given out by the other instructors.

He sat at a plastic table that had slightly less red sauce and coffee on its surface than the others. There was always a barely perceptible buzz of fluorescent lights in there, which niggled like an expectation of nausea, but it was at least cooler than the hell outside, and there were no windows to remind one of freedom. And there were legs, of course, legs and breasts half-covered, restrained by elastomers and filmy cottons, and hair, everywhere, swinging and scented, with hairbands and ribbons and other fetishistic items. It was quite a pornographic place, actually, the cafeteria.

He had a cup of the liquid that came from a machine marked COFE and he had put enough sugar in it to mask the taste, so he was ready to open the envelope.

He actually had no interest, no interest whatever, in what the other instructors' marks were like, and he was absolutely not going to play Mike's game of competing to give out the highest marks, and he knew that none of the other instructors were going to play along either, so it was pointless even to look. He would do it merely out of curiosity and he would not let it affect him. It would be instructive to see how they had dealt with the standardized tests, at any rate.

He unwound the red string with pleasure. He would enjoy doing it up again, too. It was like writing with a fountain pen, or finding a bus with wooden seats.

Inside the envelope was a red folder, and stuck to the outside of the folder was a yellow sticky note with Janice's girl's writing: "Enjoy these, sweetie! J." Then there was a happy face. Janice wrote notes like this for everybody.

Inside the folder were the computer printouts, not the handwritten lists each instructor had submitted. They were photocopied, marks from the midterm tests from every single class taught in the department, arranged by instructor. Mike had marked the median mark at the bottom of each class list, without any other comment.

He delayed looking at his own.

Meredyth Solberg-Spencer's median was 72, unsurprisingly high. Top mark 85, lowest 24. She was remarkably good with stupid stuff, despite her seeming impatience. Justin felt momentarily sorry for her; she wasn't really silly at all. Although she was going to make the rest of them look bad.

Joe Montalino had a depressing 58. Mike B. and Michael M. had pulled off mid-60s medians. Highest marks in the low 80s.

With great dread, Justin uncovered his own. If his median was lower than 60, he'd be in for a threatening lecture.

Median mark 79.

"Holy crap," he said aloud. Then he looked around at the startled students and smiled.

Reddening, he looked back down at his page. How the hell had he pulled that off? His lowest mark was a 17, poor old Dushan who still couldn't quite read.

Top mark 92. Cathy Heilbrunner, of course.

"Holy crap," he hissed. "Well, thank you. Thank you, Cathy Heilbrunner." Then he pretended to cough because he was talking to himself.

He gathered up his papers and stuffed them back into the envelope. He carefully wound up the red string.

Then he sat for a while. He sipped his gritty liquid. He tried to be happy, but there was something unpleasant about his success. He didn't know what it was. Perhaps he just didn't know how he had done it. Good old Cathy Heilbrunner, thank God for Cathy Heilbrunner. She was the one he had seen hanging around Mike all the time. He wouldn't ask any questions about that, as it was not his concern.

Ninety-two per cent. Perhaps she was genuinely intelligent, although intelligence wasn't exactly what that test measured.

He didn't really know why he opened his backpack and went through the crumpled file folders that lived in there. Since he did not deserve an office, he carried his entire course record in there all the time; he had grown used to it.

He found the file with his handwritten records of the test

results. He had typed them up to give them to Mike. He went down the list. Poor old Dushan, 17. Cathy Heilbrunner, 89.

He put the sheet down and looked around again. He had an uneasy feeling, as if he looked noticeable there on the crowded cafeteria floor. But he knew he looked almost like the students. No one was watching him or, of course, cared about him.

Of course he knew that he had not typed it incorrectly when he had submitted it. He distinctly remembered this girl's mark. It was an 89, and he had been so surprised by that that he had even mentioned it to Andrew. Maybe Andrew would even remember that. In fact, he had a photocopy of the sheet somewhere, maybe at home. He hoped he hadn't lost it.

He unwound the red string, opened the yellow envelope. He checked Mike's printouts again.

Cathy Heilbrunner, 92.

He puffed out his cheeks. He was trying not to say something loud.

He put all his papers away and carried them gingerly to his next class, as if they were a bomb.

He called Jenna from a pay phone after his class. He knew that he was going to have to get a cellphone now, this pay phone business was nonsense. He had known it would happen some time. It would probably cost a month's rent or something, or perhaps it was free now, he had no idea.

Her voice always sounded frail or afraid when she picked up. He said, "You okay?"

She said, "Yup," but her voice was faint.

"What's wrong?"

"Nothing. I'm good."

"Good?"

"Really good, actually. It looks like I have a place."

"A place? To move into?"

"Yeah, with a girlfriend. My friend Deenie. It's a place I've stayed before. Or the same building anyway. She's cool. She needs a roommate."

"Oh. That's good."

"I'm going to go move some stuff this afternoon."

"Cool. That's good." Justin looked around at the sad ugly students and felt sorry for himself in the fluorescence. "I'll be off early this afternoon as well." He twisted the phone cord as tightly around his fingers as he could and still it did not hurt him.

"You want to come over later, maybe in the evening?"

"Oh," he said, dropping the phone cord. "Sure. Really?"

"Sure. If you want. You could meet Deenie."

"I'd love to."

She said, "Do you like dogs?"

"Dogs. Sure. Love dogs."

"Deenie's the one with the dog."

"Ah yes. Dog called a girl's name."

"Amanda."

"And Deenie," he said, "is the one who has trouble sleeping at night."

"That's right."

"I've done something," he said, "that might help her out."

"Sick," she said. "That's nice of you."

"All right," he said. "Where is it?"

"It's the place you dropped me off before. Where I was staying before. On College."

They made a plan to meet there and Justin hung up the phone not feeling quite as happy for Jenna as he should.

10.

He waited outside the building for her for a while. It was evening. There was a great deal of garbage in bins and out of them around the front door and it smelled bad. He saw an elderly woman come out with a little cart and slippers and socks, and he saw a tall black man who looked Somali or Ethiopian go in. There was Indian music coming from one of the windows. Justin was damp from the trip, from the subways and the streetcar and from carrying his pack like a house on his back. He had had a Jamaican beef patty for dinner. He was not in the best of moods.

He heard his voice being called and looked up. Her white head was poking out of a window on the third floor. She was giggling. He waved. She said she would buzz him in and go to 304.

He went through the glass door into the fluorescent white vestibule where there was an intercom and junk mail was piled up, and then the next glass door shrieked like the security doors in documentaries about prisons.

The stairwell smelled of cat urine but the corridor smelled of curry. The floor was linoleum and the doors and the mouldings were painted a shiny brown, but they had not been painted for some time.

When he found 304 his stomach was upset although he had no reason to be actually nervous. He knocked and there was hysterical barking and scrabbling at the door. When it opened he stepped back. It was Jenna, holding a dog by a studded collar.

The dog was short and stout and striped in grey and black. It had an enormous head and jaws and wide-set eyes that looked unfocused. It was barking and snarling and trying to get at Justin. Jenna was holding the collar with both hands and screaming, "Amanda, Amanda, sit, sit," and then another girl came up behind her and they both wrestled the dog away.

The apartment was two rooms, it seemed, the main one being a kitchen and living room in which someone had been sleeping, as there were a duvet and pillows piled up on the sofa. There was a sleeping bag on the floor, too, although this may have been the dog's bed, in fact it probably was, as it was strewn with chewed rubber and plastic and leather things. There was a large metal cage in one corner. The room was a little cramped.

Deenie held the dog at one side of the room while Jenna kissed Justin quickly on the cheek. Justin tried to greet everyone as cheerily as he could, although the dog was still straining to get at him, and the barking was deafening. "Don't worry," Deenie shouted, "she just wants to get to know you."

"You want something to drink?" shouted Jenna. "Water?"

"No, thank you," shouted Justin.

"Have a seat," shouted Deenie. "I'll put her in the cage."

While this was effected, Justin cleared a space on the sofa and sat, and Jenna brought him a glass of cloudy water. It was a little close in the room, not just because of dog smell but because of piled up dishes and the sweet smell of beauty products, of powders and shampoos and creams. It was steamy.

Deenie, he noticed surreptitiously, was as tiny as Jenna but with larger breasts, possibly not real ones. She had shiny straight black hair, a little gothy actually, with coloured tattoos all over her arms and possibly elsewhere. She had rings in her nose and eyebrows, and one of those Cleopatra bangs cuts that he always associated with sadomasochism, probably because of whatsername, famous fetish model. He tried to remember her name as he watched, alternately, Jenna trying to pull dirty dishes out of the sink to fill it with water, and Deenie struggling to cage a monster almost her size. Both the women wore the yoga sweatpants that showed their thongs and their lower back tattoos, although Deenie's yoga costume was entirely black. It was clever that there was goth yoga wear. This was clever.

"Do you do yoga?" said Justin, to Deenie, and she said "Yoga?" with such bafflement that both girls laughed, and Justin laughed too.

"Oh, hey," he said. "I forgot. I've got something for you." He picked up his knapsack and fished out the envelope that had arrived that morning. It was a long brown envelope covered in strange stamps. The stamps were also brown. It looked like an artifact from a museum. "These arrived this morning. From India. It was super fast. They said it would take ten days." He pulled out the two silver foil racks. The pills in their bubbles were yellow and tiny. "They pack it really flat," he said, "so it looks like paper. And there's nothing on the envelope that says what it is. I guess it's not entirely legal."

"Cool stamps," said Jenna.

Deenie sat on the coffee table. Her eyes were focused as she took the blister packs. "Sick. You tried them?"

"Me? No. But they say lorazepam one milligram, I looked it up, and it's the same thing."

"How much do I owe you?"

"I printed out the receipt," said Justin. He lifted his bum off the sofa to try to find it in his back pocket.

"Don't worry about it," said Deenie. "How much do I owe you?"

"Oh." He found the paper and unfolded it. "It was sixty-nine U.S., for fifty, so let's just call it seventy. Here."

"That's okay," said Deenie. She got up and went to the kitchen counter, where she opened a small tin and took out a wad of bills. She counted off four twenties for Justin.

"Oh," he said. "I might not have change. Hang on." He was trying all his pockets.

"Don't worry about it," said Deenie. "It's for the exchange rate."

"Okay. Thanks."

Deenie went back to the counter, and she was already popping open a blister pack. Justin saw her swallow a pill at the sink, with her back to them.

Jenna showed him the other room, the bedroom, which was Deenie's room—so Jenna would be the one sleeping on the couch, presumably with the dog at her side, on the floor—and it was painted dark purple, with clothes piled on the floor and bed and the closet door open and bras and stockings hanging over it. There was a bamboo blind over the window and a red scarf over the lamp, so it was rather dim.

Justin had to use the washroom, which also had panties

drying on a rack in the bathtub. There were more hair products than could fit on any of the porcelain surfaces. The tiles of the walls were interesting, black and white, maybe the original deco of the building, which made sense, it would have dated from the forties maybe. "Bettie Page," he said aloud, remembering.

Back on the sofa, Jenna offered him a beer, which he took, and then she sat down to her focused work of cutting weed and cardboard for the filter. The dog had settled to whimpering and screeching and scratching at the metal floor of her cage with her claws, which was a little quieter. The dog's stripes made her look like a tiger, but not as cute and friendly as a tiger.

Deenie interrogated him a bit, wanted to know how old he was and did he have a job and how much he liked to party, which was sweet really, a bit older-sistery. She did look a bit older than Jenna, late twenties or maybe even thirty. She was really very pretty too, incredibly so, actually; if Justin allowed himself to think about how unbelievably sexy and almost unclothed these two women were on either side of him he would get nervous, so he tried not to. But a part of him warmed to the idea that he was already used to it, that he was not going to really care if Deenie liked him or not. This was improvement in his life.

Jenna was a little excited, it seemed, to tell him that she was going to start work at a new place that weekend, a job Deenie had got her, a really nice place, a fancy place. It was a hostess job at a lounge called Mirror, which was right downtown and business guys went there. They blew tons of money in that place. Deenie said that Jenna would be perfect for it because they wanted a really pretty girl at the front but someone with a little bit of an edge, because the suits liked that, and she knew Donnie, the owner, had known him for years, actually, and he was all right.

Justin said he had passed the place a few times and it looked really exclusive, all red and glowing, but he had never been inside. He was pleased about this news, too, and he was thinking that he would enjoy coming to pick up Jenna there at the end of her shift, greeting the doormen like an old buddy, maybe being invited by Donnie for a drink after last call, as Jenna did her cash, having the drunken bankers eyeing him and wondering how he got to take her home. But he didn't say any of this.

He was enjoying the smoke and the beer. He sank back into the sagging sofa. "Why," he said, "did you name her Amanda?"

Deenie took a long toke and pointed her nose at the ceiling as if thinking hard about this question. She let out the smoke in a stream, and then lowered her face to Justin and said, "What?"

"Amanda. Sweet name for a dog, kind of scary dog."

"Oh, but she is sweet. She's super sweet. She wouldn't hurt a fly. She wouldn't hurt a bee."

"She wouldn't hurt a rabbit," said Jenna, coughing. "She wouldn't hurt a bunny."

"Okay," said Justin.

"She already had that name when I got her," said Deenie. "The guy had named them all already."

"Which guy?" said Justin.

"A guy selling them. My sister knew him. He had a bunch of puppies. I just met him and he had a bunch in his truck." She began to giggle. "In a KFC parking lot."

Jenna laughed too and Justin laughed a little. "Okay," he said. "I see. Is it, is she a pit bull?"

Deenie put her finger to her lips. "Shhh," she said. "We don't say the P word. Pit bulls are illegal. And they're super hard to define anyway. They're all mixed up. We say she's a Staffordshire terrier."

"Which just means pit bull," said Jenna, "but it confuses people." Jenna's eyes were already red and puffy. The apartment was hazy with smoke.

"What time is it?" said Deenie. She had already asked this a few minutes before. She was waiting for Armando, it appeared, who was going to drop by.

Justin glanced at Jenna, who said, "He's cool. You'll like him. He dresses well."

"Maybe you guys could take Amanda for a walk, when he comes?"

"Yikes," said Justin.

"She'll get to know you," said Jenna.

The intercom buzzed feebly and the dog yelped as if electrocuted and started barking hysterically. "Come on up," yelled Deenie to the machine.

"Are you staying here tonight?" Justin whispered to Jenna.

"Sure," she said. "I'd better. I mean, it would be a good idea. To start."

"Okay. Sure. But you're welcome, you know you're welcome to come over. If you feel like it."

"Okay."

"Okay, piggie," said Deenie, "you big fattie, you big stinkie, who's going for a walk now? Who's going for a big walkies?"

The dog was trying to tear open the door of the cage with its teeth. Deenie struggled with the latch. Justin stood up.

"It's okay," said Jenna, "she's a nice dog."

Amanda was released just as the apartment door opened and a stocky guy walked in. "Hey stinkie," yelled the guy, "come here piggo." The dog bounded past Justin and leapt up to the guy, who boxed her away and then boxed her away again as she leapt. She was apparently trying to tear the guy's throat out. "Hey baby," said the guy. He was wrestling with the dog now, holding it by the snout and shaking it. The dog was growling and snarling.

"Hey," said Deenie. "This is Justin."

"Hey," said Justin.

"Armando," said the guy. He somehow managed to stick his hand out and Justin leaned over the snarling dog to shake it. "How's it going."

"All right," said Justin, suspecting that there was some cooler answer he could give.

"They're going to take her for a walk."

"Cool. Hey baby."

Jenna had got up and put her arms around Armando's neck and kissed him on the cheek, which was a little startling.

"The leash is behind the bathroom door."

"All right, get down," said Armando, "that's enough. Down."

"Sit, Amanda, sit," said Deenie.

With one hand, Armando grabbed the dog's collar and twisted it, and with the other he somehow pulled her legs from under her, so that she was flipped over onto her back. "Down," he said in a harsh voice. Amanda flipped herself back onto her stomach but did not stand up again. She lay at his feet and whimpered. "There," he said, "good girl."

He was about Justin's height, this guy, but quite a bit broader. He was wearing a filmy white shirt that might have been rayon or even silk. He was clean-shaven, and his black hair was shiny. His shirt was unbuttoned to show a silver cross on his chest. He was wearing cologne. "You kids partying tonight?" he said.

"I don't think so," said Justin.

"We're just hanging," said Jenna. She was attaching the leash to Amanda's collar. The collar's studs were actually quite pointed, like spikes. "You ready, star?"

"We'll see you later, I guess," said Justin, and shook the guy's hand again, just in case he hadn't been polite enough.

Amanda dragged them down the stairs. When they were on the street the two of them both had to hold the leash to stop her from running. It was getting dark.

"Where are we taking her?" said Justin.

"There's a park. Just that way."

"Let me hold her." Justin wrapped the leash around his knuckles and leaned back to rein her in. Amanda turned on him and leaped up.

He pushed her away but he distinctly felt a spike of tooth on his knuckles. "She bit me," he said.

"Don't let her," said Jenna. "That's bad."

"Yes, that's bad."

"Bad girl. No nipping. Push her down, on her neck. Put your fingertips against her neck and push."

"Christ. She's nipping at me."

"It's a dominance thing. She's seeing how much she can get away with, and then she'll take more."

Yanking the dog's head towards him with the leash, Justin bent and thrust his stiff fingers into her neck. "No," he said firmly. "I'm the boss now. Not you."

The dog sat, looked away, and tried to run again.

"There," said Jenna. "That's good."

"Jesus," said Justin. "I'm exhausted."

"Just keep doing that. Teach her who's boss."

He yanked hard on the leash again and Amanda slowed and walked at his heel. "Good girl," he said, "good girl."

He could see, ahead of them, one of those cafés that only had guys in it, and the guys were all standing on the sidewalk and watching them approach.

"Oh good," said Justin. "You know these guys?"

"They know me," said Jenna. "They're okay."

The group went silent and staring as Justin and Jenna passed. But they weren't staring at Jenna, not all of them anyway, they were staring at the dog.

"Hey," said one of the guys, nodding at Justin, and Justin realized he had been greeted.

"Hey," said Justin.

"Nice dog," said the guy.

Jenna was silent, so Justin said, "Thanks. Yeah."

Amanda was pulling towards the guy, yelping a little, so they stopped while the guy extended his hand and then withdrew it quickly as Amanda nipped at it.

"Shit," said the guy, laughing a little.

"Sweet," said a fat guy.

A smaller guy, a teenager maybe, holding a beer and a cigarette, with his underpants showing, said in a high voice, "That an American red tipped pit?"

Justin look at Jenna. She shook her head.

"No," said Justin. "Uh, terrier."

"Staffordshire terrier," said the first guy. "Red tips are orange."

"Tail," said the fat guy. "You mean red tail."

"Pit's a pit," said the first guy, and everybody laughed.

Jenna was moving forward, so Justin pulled the dog and they walked away. "See ya," he called, and the guy said, "All right."

They found the park which was completely dark and Jenna bent to unhook the leash from Amanda's collar.

"Jesus," said Justin, "you're going to set her loose?"

"She's *fine,*" said Jenna with some annoyance.

Amanda rocketed off into the darkness.

"What if there's someone walking a smaller dog?"

"Then it's up to that person to protect her dog. Besides, she won't hurt anything if it just rolls over. She just has to be the boss."

"Great. What if there's a cat?"

"You think a cat would stick around to say hello if she saw that coming at her?"

Justin grunted. "I guess not."

They were walking across the grass in darkness. They could see the rapid shadow of Amanda flitting through pools of light between trees. The light was coming from the streetlamps around the perimeter. It was cooler in the darkness. There was a smell of weed in the air. Justin could feel damp on the grass, through his running shoes. He could hardly see Jenna at his side. He took her hand, and she let him.

"What about a baby?" said Justin. "What if there's a toddler walking around."

Jenna sighed loudly. "Justin, think about it. Would you bring a kid to this park after dark?"

"Okay. Okay."

Then she giggled. "It's funny, though, sometimes it's the smallest dogs that are the stupidest."

"What do you mean?" He was squinting into the darkness to try to make out the shapes of other dog walkers. There were some thugs sitting on a picnic table at one end, in their hoodies. He could see the glow of their joint. The rest of the darkness seemed empty.

"Oh, it's always the little yappy ones that want to start a fight. It's true. Little poodles and shit. They stand up to her, and then that's . . ."

"That's dangerous."

"Yeah, a little. But nothing bad has happened so far."

Justin sighed.

She stopped, put an arm around his waist. "Those guys thought you were pretty cool."

"Ha. Yes. They thought it was my dog. I felt like a dork."

"Well, you looked pretty cool. They probably thought you were running me or something."

"Running you?"

She was silent for a second. Then there was a thundering of paws and Amanda was on them at full speed, panting and drooling. Jenna wrestled with her for a minute, throwing her down and letting her leap up again. The dog seemed to love being treated as roughly as possible. She was yelping with joy.

"Ah," said Justin. "Running you. I get it. Like I'm a pimp?"

"You stinky," Jenna was saying, panting too. "You big stinko. Let go. Let go."

"Hey," said Justin, "about how old is Armando?"

"Armando? I don't know. Maybe twenty-six."

"Wow," said Justin. "Younger than me."

She threw a twig and Amanda leaped off into the darkness to find it. She turned to him and pushed her belly against his.

She put her arms around his neck. Her face was a pale moon in the darkness.

"Hey," he said.

She kissed him and he put his hands on the taut fabric around her hips. Her skin was warm through it. He let his fingertips run over the ridge of her thong, then up over the seam and into the warmth of bare skin around her middle. He was swelling fast.

"You want me to stay over at your place tonight?" she said.

"Yes," he said. "I always do. I want you to stay over every night." His heart was beating fast, as if he had said something important. He was moved by it, at any rate.

They kissed a long time in the park and then Amanda raced up to him and jumped up, but she was trying to lick his face.

"Amanda," said Jenna, "no kissing. No kissing."

"It's all right," said Justin. "Good girl."

11.

She said she was going shopping for a dress for the new job, on Saturday afternoon, and he asked if he could come with her. She said she never bought new things and he said he didn't either and he was excited about it. Indeed, he had to admit to himself that he was as excited about this as about any event of his professional or academic life, or indeed as any event of the preceding five years, and she seemed just as excited. This was strange, as he did not recall any excitement preceding missions to buy specific items of clothing with Genevieve. Even when Genevieve had asked his advice about her clothing, his advice had seemed to provoke disapproval, and so he had done his best to avoid these missions. He had also found it almost impossible not to stare at the salesgirls and the other shoppers and this had provoked tension.

He was quite prepared for this tension to recur today, so he had steeled himself like a Buddhist, no, a Jain, or whoever was the absolute purest of the ascetics; he would have no conscious-ness of womankind other than Jenna; man and woman would look the same to him, like bodiless brains, like God's creatures, not like *sexual objects.*

He said this to himself, "*Sexual objects,*" hissing a little, as he waited for Jenna to emerge from a mirrored cubicle in one of the big chain stores. They had tried some of the boutiques on the artsy strip downtown but she had been dismayed by the prices. So now they were in a giant glittering cube three stories high with escalators and glassed galleries around the upper floors. There was shrieking music, so loud you could fire a revolver and no one would notice, in fact this was probably why so many people did fire revolvers in these places. Or not revolvers, semi-automatics was what they used now, Glock nine-mills, Tec-9s, whatever—a shooting might indeed break out, since it was the one day of the year he had chosen to step into one of these places. Doubtless he would be one of those crossfire people you read about after each of these mall gang things. There was only one exit, at the front, but the sales counter looked pretty solid, and one could throw oneself behind it pretty quickly from where he stood and roll into a ball. They wouldn't come in here anyway; there were no running shoes for sale, as far as he could make out.

All this was to distract himself, of course, these practical thoughts, to prevent for as long as was humanly possible his eyes from following every set of breasts or thighs that emerged from the neighbouring cubicles, every set of tiny sock feet visible under the door, the dropping of jeans and skirts to the floor and the stepping out of them by bare feet, all of that was not for him. He would stand and wait as long as it took and he would consider the architecture and the music and the fire escapes. If they did come at him with Tec-9s he would just scroll down to his little armoury at the bottom of his screen and select the equivalent Uzi 9 mm, nothing larger, and standard Kevlar body armour.

The music was interesting, actually; it was the kind of music one only heard in these places and sometimes in the back of taxis on Friday nights, dance music, but not the popular kind with a female singer that Jenna had brought to his house, just the hard pounding kind with a lot of clicks and pops and buzzes and the occasional siren. It was designed to make your heart speed up, he had read this, and this was working on him; it was irritating and exhilarating at the same time. On balance he had to admit that it was enjoyable, sort of troublingly enjoyable like pornography. It was not helping him control his desire to stare at every woman's body. He would ask Jenna to tell him where he could buy some of this music.

She had taken one clingy black thing and one clingy red top into the change room. He was excited to see the black thing. She was wearing strappy shoes with spiky heels, shoes that were impossibly arched, and he had never seen anyone so young walk so confidently in them. They turned her legs into dancer's legs, into permanent flexion. She had put them on because she knew she would be trying on dresses, she said. He thought this was a good idea.

Before she emerged, the girl in the next box did, wearing a blue dress with a low back. She turned from side to side, pulling at it. Her back was bare almost to her bum, which showed that she was not wearing a bra. She clutched at the front of it to make it cover her breasts, which were visible from the side. The bumps of her spine rippled. She had curly black hair.

"Hey," said Jenna, making him jump.

"Hey. Wow. Wow."

"You like it?" She was frowning at herself in the mirror, spinning just as the girl next to her was.

"Holy crap."

She puffed out her cheeks, put her hands on her hips. It was a little black cocktail dress made out of something like rubber, something worn by aliens on television. It was high on her chest, almost to her neck, but it clung to her breasts and their nipples. You could see the outline of her thong on her hips.

"Well, it certainly fits you," he said.

She sighed. "It looks cheap."

"Well, I don't know. It looks sexy."

"You couldn't wear any underwear with it."

Justin coughed. "I have no problem with that."

Jenna looked at the girl next to her in the blue dress and this woman looked at her.

"I like it on you," said the blue dress. "I'd wear it if I could."

She also had shoes with heels, although not quite as pain-fully high as Jenna's.

"I like yours," said Jenna. "It's a little more sophisticated."

"It's a little loose in the front, right here. I'm scared I'm going to flop right out."

Justin looked away.

"Justin, look at this one. That's what I'm looking for, more."

The two women were staring at themselves and each other in the mirrors. Justin nodded as seriously as he could. "It's very nice too." He looked at their calves flexing as they spun on their pointy shoes. The heels clicked on the concrete.

"You want to switch?"

The blue dress giggled and said okay and they both went back into their change rooms and handed Justin the flimsy garments over the tops of the doors. Justin could just make out the tops of their heads and their bare feet under the door as he passed them over.

Then they came out and he had to look at Jenna's bare back and then the other girl's breasts in the tight black fabric. The other one had bigger breasts, but wider hips, too. She looked squeezed into the black dress.

"I look like a sausage."

"Oh my God," said Jenna, "I'm skanky." The blue dress was loose on her too; she was holding the front over her breasts to cover them. But she twirled and admired her back in the mirror.

"I like them both," said Justin.

Jenna was smiling. "You like this, don't you, star?"

"Yup."

The women went back into their cubicles and Justin handed the two dresses back and forth again. He looked around with a little more confidence as he waited. Some of the shoppers were teenage girls, too young for him, but still they were wearing miniskirts and long socks or stay-up stockings that went over their knees. They probably sold those things in here; in fact there was a whole underwear section with fantastic stockings and stay-ups. Although it would be a bad idea to suggest going over there to look at them, as it was summer and too hot anyway and nobody needed stockings. Why were these girls wearing them then?

"Hey," she called. "Take this too." She pushed a piece of fabric over the top of the door. He took it and she giggled. It was her thong, made of some fiery orange cotton.

"Thanks." He put it in his pocket. Then he pulled a string out so it was just visible over the top of his pocket.

She opened the cubicle door but she didn't step out. She was wearing the black dress. "Hey," she said. "You like it better like this?" She lifted the skirt up to her waist. She had shaved herself completely, and the bare lips were startling in the fluorescent light. She dropped the skirt.

Justin stood in the doorway to block the view. "Show me more," he said.

She pulled the top of the dress down and her breasts were bare, the nipples erect. "Come in here."

Justin glanced around. The girl in the blue dress was gone; the attendants in their tights and heels were elsewhere. He stepped into the cubicle, closed the door, and put his lips to her nipple. The music screeched and banged.

"You want to do it right here?" she whispered. She had her hand on his crotch.

"Jesus. It would be pretty obvious. People can see our feet."

She turned her back to him, hiked up the dress and rubbed her buttocks against him. "Just put it in. Do me."

"Christ. No. I can't."

"Chicken."

"Yup."

"Let's do it somewhere else, then," she murmured. "We'll find a place that has a real room with a door that closes."

"Okay. Like where."

"Big department stores have them. And that sex store in Yorkville."

"Wow. How do you know that? No, don't answer that. Okay. Let's go."

"I have one more thing. The top." She pulled away from him.

"Okay," he said, relieved. "You're getting the dress."

"You think?"

"I'm getting it for you. You have to. You'll make two hundred bucks a night at this place, wearing this dress. More. I don't know."

"I was hoping for a lot more, actually."

"Okay. I don't know. That's great. But you're getting it. Take it off and I'll go pay for it."

She wriggled out of it and stood there naked in front of him, laughing. She put one foot on the little bench and a finger in her mouth to wet it.

"Stop it. I'm going to pay for it."

"Go." She stooped to pick up her jeans.

"I'm keeping your panties though."

He opened the door a crack and tried to slip out so that no one could see inside. No one was looking anyway. He went and got in the line at the cash. His face was hot.

The line was too long and there was only one clerk and she was chatting at length with everybody. He went to find the stockings.

He selected a pair of opaque black thigh highs and then a pair of white ones. He knew the white ones were cheesy but what the hell. They were for him, really, after all, so what the hell. They were only about twenty bucks each.

Jenna was standing in the line. She was holding the red top.

"Shit," he said, "I missed it. On you."

"You'll see it at home."

"Here. You'll have to model these for me too." He handed her the stockings, and then smiled sheepishly, prepared for a reprimand.

"I see," she said, fingering the packages. "You have a kind of a fetish for these things, eh?"

"I guess." His face was really red now.

"Cool," she said. "They'll look great with the black dress."

"That's what I thought. The white ones . . . they're really for me."

"I can't wait. Thank you. I love wearing these."

"Whoo." He exhaled at length.

"This lame-ass girl is taking her sweet fucking time."

"So," he said. "Are we going to do that thing? Now?"

"If we ever get out of here."

"Yes," he said. "We're doing it next. We'll take a cab uptown."

"That girl was hot," she said.

"Which one? The blue dress? Yes, she was. Ha." He laughed aloud in the lineup of the big store in the hard music, a laugh that felt like a great relief. "This is the most fun I've ever had."

"We're not even moving forward," she said. She was staring hard at the overworked girl behind the cash and the girl was not looking up. "She prefers chatting. I just want to get this cheesy-ass dress and go."

"Hey, where do you get music like this?"

"You mean like hard house?"

"I guess. It's not techno?"

She screwed up her face. "Not at all. This is more like hard house, hard trance. It's more teenage."

"Oh. What's the difference?"

"I'll get you some mixes. Deenie knows DJs."

"Wow. Cool. I have to learn about all this stuff."

"No," she said, "you don't. Come on, bitch. Stop chatting with your hoochie friends. Let's go."

"We should go dancing again soon," he said. "I totally love this."

"We should go shopping for you soon," she said. "Get you some new clothes."

"Me? Yeah. I guess so. I can't really afford it."

"Then what are you buying me clothes for."

"Oh," he said, "that's different. Believe me. It's really different." They moved forward a little.

"It's like waiting for the fucking bus," she said.

"No," he said, "it's okay. It's all cool. Everything's great." He rubbed the back of her neck, under her hair, and it was damp. She said she was too hot and pushed his hand away. "Everyone hates shopping," he said. "But I think I love it."

"Hey," said Jenna, to some girl beside her, "we're *next*." Her voice was high and sharp and the girl looked alarmed and stepped back. "Finally," said Jenna. She slammed her purchases down on the counter.

"Easy," said Justin, "it's all good."

"What was that?" said Jenna loudly, whirling around. She was staring at the girl, a pale redhead, who had dared to try to get in front of her.

"Do you have a problem?" said the girl.

"Do you have a problem with me?" said Jenna.

"Whoa," said Justin, "cool it. Easy now."

The redhead's girlfriend giggled and murmured something.

"What was that?" said Jenna, stepping towards them. Her face was white with bright red patches on it.

"Would you fucking calm down, you psycho," said the redhead.

Everybody in the line and all the clerks were all staring now. Justin grabbed Jenna's arm and pulled her back. "Leave it," he said. "Come here."

She shook off his arm and hissed, *Fuck off,* and it seemed to be directed at him.

Justin moved himself between her and the girls and said "Come on," and he noticed when he looked at her that there were tears on her cheeks and she was breathing violently. She turned and ran towards the front doors.

"I guess you don't want these," said the girl at the cash.

"Just hold on to them for one second," said Justin, and went after Jenna.

He found her half a block away, walking rapidly. She was staring up at the sky and sobbing. People were giving her a wide berth as they walked past her.

He walked with her in silence for a moment and then put his arm around her shoulder to try to slow her down. She let him.

He asked her several times what was wrong, what had happened, but she kept crying in almost complete silence. Her face was twisted, her mouth stretched downwards, her eyes red, a picture of agony. He kept saying soothing things until she slowed a bit.

"It wasn't a big deal," he said. "Why'd you get so mad?"

"I just can't handle shopping," she said. "I can't fucking take that shit, that stupid shit."

"Okay. Okay." He was trying to breathe deeply, but he was a little shaky himself. "Okay. Whoo. I thought you were going to kill her."

"I would have fucking killed her," she said, but then she laughed a little and wiped her eyes, so he knew she was coming down from her rage and he'd be able to talk to her like a human in a second. It was amazing how quickly one learned to understand new people.

They were almost past the shopping zone by then, into the bank towers. "Listen," he said, "I just left that stuff at the cash. I still have to pay for it. Let's turn around and I'll just dash in and pay for it. You don't have to come in the store."

"I don't want it."

"You don't want it? That's . . ."

Her face crumpled and she was crying again.

"Whoo. Okay. Okay. But that's silly. You looked so beautiful in it. It will just take me two seconds to go in and get it. It would be a waste."

"You don't fucking get me at all," she said in a cracked voice.

"Okay." He tried rubbing the back of her neck. "Okay. I guess I don't."

"I could never touch that fucking stuff now, okay? It's poisoned for me now."

"Okay. Okay. You want to sit on this bench for a minute?"

"No. I just want to get off this fucking street, away from these fucking people. You don't get me."

"All right. I want you to slow down, to sit for a second. You need to calm down."

"I need to get *away*." Her voice was raspy.

"Okay. Let's turn off the street. We'll go down this street. Okay? There's a park, I think, a couple blocks."

He got her onto the side street and she was still walking as fast as she could, so fast he couldn't keep his arm around her.

When they got to a very quiet bit of city, an area of parking lots, she slowed and said, "I'm sorry. I ruined everything for you."

"No no. I mean yes." He laughed. "But I just want you to be okay. I need to understand what happened, too."

"I never could do shopping. I fucking hate shopping because I fucking hate people. I can't take people at all. I can't be around them."

"Ah," he said. "That's . . ." He stopped and rubbed his forehead. He was damp. He didn't finish what he was saying because he didn't know what that was. He didn't know what it would be like to hate people, or to feel that you did. "I don't know what that is."

She stopped completely and looked at him and said very softly, "Where are we going now?" It was as if she was just waking up.

"Home," he said. "Let's go home."

"I need to be alone," she said just as softly.

"Okay. Okay. You want me to take you to your place?"

"No. I'll see you later." She put his arms around his neck and kissed him gently on the lips. "I'm sorry," she whispered.

He stood there and watched her walk away. She was walking south, away from her house. He could have walked after her but he knew it would not do his dignity any good. He just stood there feeling bereft. He felt as if something had torn in his gut.

He walked back to the clothing store and paid for the stuff. He thought it would make him feel better, give him some sense of having done something nice, but it just made him sadder to carry around her silky things. He resisted calling her phone. He went home.

There was a voice message there for him from Dorothy Liu reminding him about the networking dinner thing that night, which he knew he was not going to now and had never wanted to go to. He wanted to talk to Andrew then, as he hadn't for a while and felt a bit guilty about that. Now he would be the kind of guy who only called to recount some disaster or angst. He called, but Andrew's cell was off, so he was probably on another marathon shift and he wouldn't see him for a week.

12.

"Andrew told me about it," he said. "The doctor who, you know. Or no, it was Brian, the guy you met at that, anyway, he keeps up with restaurants and stuff because he has a little more money, I guess."

"Huh." She hadn't picked up her menu, but was looking around. They were perched on high stools, at a high table. The tablecloth was black. There was a candle in a square glass thing. "It's cool."

"Apparently there are all these new places around here. You been to any?"

"Oh. Yeah. I've been to a thing, a dance club, I think. Around here."

"Persimmon? It's right next door."

"Yeah. I guess so."

"Really. That's cool." Some guy had taken her, of course. Briefly, he hated this guy and resented her for going to Persimmon with him. "How was it?"

"Oh, it was . . . fun. It was okay. I had a good time."

"Huh. It sounds cool. But you never know what that means. If it's too fashiony it could be a bunch of, you know, guys with large Chanel sunglasses."

"It was a bit like that. But not totally. Younger guys, not older," she said. "Young douchebags." She sipped her sparkling wine.

"Kind of like not exactly hipsters but not full-on douches either."

"Douchesters," she said.

"Exactly. That's a bit what this place is like. Slightly more douche than hip, but still."

At the bar were a couple of guys in narrow jeans and fitted suit jackets and T-shirts, and they hadn't shaved in exactly two days. And the waitresses were Asians and Russians in heels, not the paint-stained short-haired girls that had been running all the other bars in this neighbourhood since it had started to clean itself up. The room was lovely, though: its ceiling was twenty feet up, there was a mirror the size of a swimming pool over the bar and a chandelier that looked like a spaceship. A DJ with a beard and a ball cap was setting up a mixer and a speaker at the end of the bar.

"Wasabi eel dumplings," he read. "Kimchi pie. That sounds ridiculous. They're all small dishes, I think. You order a bunch and then you share." They were all also over twenty bucks. He did not say this. "The turnip tartare looks kind of okay."

Jenna frowned at her menu. Her eyes were red-rimmed and she was kind of dopey, which means she had been burning fatties like a kid before coming, but still, she had her hair up in a nineteenth-century bun, like a Russian countess in a movie, and her neck and shoulders glowed pale against the darkness. She had a black dress that tied up behind her neck and left her back bare, and a choker made of silver threads. The dress was cheap, he knew that; all her clothes were cheap, they were the kind of slippy thing you could buy in a rock store for forty bucks and you could only ever wash it once, and anyone who weighed ten pounds more than her would look like a ham in it, and she looked like a fashion magazine, albeit the kind of fashion magazine that also had photo spreads of drug addicts in condemned hotels.

He wanted to reach and stroke her knees under the table but wasn't sure if they had both recovered from that afternoon enough. He hadn't brought the dress they had bought, hadn't asked her to talk about it. When he had weakened and apprehensively phoned and promised a fancy dinner she had pretended nothing was wrong and nothing had happened, or perhaps she hadn't pretended at all.

He wanted, very badly at that point, to know if she was wearing any underwear. He would be patient and this question would be answered.

"Why don't you order for us?" she said. "I'm not going to eat any eel."

"Sure. Let's go for basic stuff. The marinated ostrich strips and the almond salad. And the vanilla quiche, I guess—oh, no, there's eel in it. What's with the eel? Huge specials on eels at the food terminals today. Great vats of writhing eels they had to sell off. How about quail? It's a tiny little bird. Okay. How about another salad, then? There's this cracked peppercorn salad, it can't be just cracked peppercorns, it has to have something else in it. We'll try it. Hey, we could go out after, if you like. To Meme, which is right down the street. It's kind of small though. Or to, we could go to, to Persimmon."

"Sure."

"Unless you think it's like a guest-list kind of place."

"Like full-on douche," she said. "Do you like those shoes?"

The waitress was tottering around on black pumps with silver spikes.

"I do," said Justin. "But she can hardly walk in them."

"Takes practice," said Jenna.

"You think you could do it?"

She narrowed her eyes at the shoes, considered, then nodded. "No problem."

"Cool." He looked down at the wine list to hide his silly smile. "What do you think I am? I'm kind of too old to be a hipster."

"No you're not. If you want to be a hipster anyway. There's a fine line between hip and douche."

"That's what I mean. Would you say I'm more hip or more douche?"

"You have zero douche."

"Maybe I'm more hipbag than douchester."

"You guys ready to order?" said the Asian girl who looked like a wax sculpture.

Jenna was giggling and sniffing too hard to speak. Justin ordered a bunch of ridiculous stuff, trying not to count twenties in his head, and a bottle of Portuguese wine for sixty-four dollars, which was towards the bottom of the list. They just should have ordered the wine; he knew neither of them was going to eat the food anyway.

"How am I dressed tonight?" he said "How douchey am I?"

"You look nice," she said. Then, "You could wear less tan and beige stuff. And that navy jacket you wear."

"It's gay-ass."

"Don't take offence."

He laughed. "So what's not gay-ass?"

"Some colours. I could see you in red or orange or something."

"That's completely insane."

"Well, you asked."

Their wine came and he tasted it and he noticed she was smiling at him, and all around her. When the waitress had left she said, "Thank you. For bringing me here."

"That's okay. I mean you're welcome. I just wanted you to feel a little better. After today."

She played with her necklace and said, "Did you notice the sky, coming here?"

"The sky?"

"It was so gorgeous. It was like a blue slate. It was like rock."

"Yes. No, I didn't. That's beautiful. You should write that down."

"I do. I write stuff down all the time."

"Cool. I should do that too." She put her hand on his on the black cloth.

"This wine is okay," he said. He was reminding her to drink it.

"Yes," she said, "it's nice." She sipped some more. One of the guys at the bar had just elbowed his buddy and gestured with his chin to look over at her. Now they were both staring at her back. She couldn't see them. He was happy for them to enjoy it.

"Do you ever wonder," she said, licking some wine off her lips, "maybe you can answer this, you're smart. I always wonder this."

"Yes."

"How do you know if something is true or not?"

"What? What kind of thing? Like something someone says?"

"No, like what you're seeing."

"Ah. I see. That is a famous question."

"Like even if you see it, you don't know if it's real. You could be dreaming, or hallucinating or—"

"Or," he said, "you could know what you see but you can't be at all sure that I see the same thing."

"Exactly. Like I see this cloth as black, and you call it black too, but you may be seeing a completely different colour."

"Yes. A lot of philosophers have wondered about this. You don't even know where your perceptions are coming from. I mean, your hand touches the tablecloth and your fingertips, I mean the nerves in your fingertips, register a sensation, and they send a message up to your brain, but it's only in your brain that you register what the texture is. If the nerve was cut you wouldn't feel anything, even though you touched it. So you could be just a brain in a tank, somebody could be—"

"Exactly!" Her voice was high. "I have so thought about this. Like you're just a brain in a tank and somebody is feeding you pictures and tastes and stuff."

"Yeah. It's in a lot of science fiction movies. But it's a serious question." He was happy now, because he could lecture a bit about this—he wouldn't go too far, he would stop as soon as he felt her attention wander—but he could because she had actually asked him to talk about something interesting, to teach her, in fact, which was something he was good at and usually, it seemed, told not to do.

The food, when it came, was sweet and prickly; there were flavours of fire and tar and vanilla. They had a few mouthfuls of each thing. He was drinking most of the wine.

She wasn't quite as pleased as he had expected to hear of the philosophers who had worried about reality. Perhaps she was genuinely disappointed that it wasn't her idea. But she seemed to like hearing him talk. She looked at him with a smile that was almost protective; it wasn't condescending, it was perhaps maternal. He didn't mind it. Women always smiled at him this way, when they got to know him.

She started talking about things she was going to do with her life. "There's one great idea I've had," she said, "which you are not allowed to steal."

"Okay. Deal."

"A modelling agency."

"Okay."

"But it's special. It's for alternative models. Like specialities."

"Like you'd have dwarfs?"

"No, gooftroop. Like goth girls, punk girls, rock girls, anyone who has lots of tattoos and piercings. They need them all the time for advertising, for videos, for night clubs, promotions, whatever."

"Huh. That's not a bad idea, actually."

"And they would have to be ready to take their clothes off," she said, looking thoughtful. "Like it wouldn't be for porn, it would be for art photography, but it would be kind of sexy. Like if you need a girl to wear rubber or be painted blue or get in a bathtub in a party dress, that kind of thing. There are so many of these beautiful girls out there and the modelling agencies don't want them. But the photographers love them."

"That sounds okay. Have you—have you posed for stuff like that?"

"Like it wouldn't be for porn. But it would be kind of sexy."

"That sounds okay."

"I'm serious."

"I know you are. This sounds like a good idea. You're a businesswoman. I never come up with anything like that."

"I have another really good one," she said. "But you totally are not allowed to steal these, or even repeat these ideas to anyone else. Do you promise me that?"

"Sure."

"You're smiling, like you're not taking me seriously."

"No, no, of course I'm serious. You don't need to worry about it though. You can be a little paranoid sometimes. Anyway, go on. What's your next idea?"

"A travel book, a travel guide. But it would be for sex tourism."

"Ah. That's good," he said, "but I think there are already a few of those."

"Yeah, I know, but this would be more high end. This would be for couples, or both sexes anyway, it wouldn't just be for disgusting—"

"Douches. It wouldn't be a douchefest."

"Seriously. It would have like sex clubs, fetish clubs, places to pick up, dating services, sex shops."

"For where is this?"

"Every major city. You'd do a series. But it would be mainstream, like not porny. Respectable. It would start with Europe, mostly. For classy people who go to Europe."

"Huh," he said. "You're all about marketing sex. That's quite smart, actually, right now."

"I know it is, star. I just need to get a little money and I can do these things."

"Yes, you can. That's cool." Then, "Hey, I really like going out with you. It's fun."

"Can I get you another bottle?" said the waitress.

There was a small crowd outside a nameless bar which must have been Hex Key, or possibly Meme, and as they got close Justin saw that they were guys in undershirts and ball caps and basketball shorts, not the guys with the narrow moustaches who were listening to seventies disco inside; these were the guys who used to live here before this all started. They leaned against a car and stared as Justin and Jenna approached. She put his arm around his waist and he put his arm around her shoulder, which was maybe insecure but what the hell.

One of them, the biggest, a white guy, raised his eyes at his friends and they all laughed. Justin knew the guy was going to say something to Jenna as they passed and he wondered what he would be supposed to do about it.

They walked straight at the thugs, who didn't move. The thugs stared hard at Jenna. At the last minute the biggest stepped aside, and he glanced at Justin and said, "You got lucky, guy." He was smiling.

Then they were through and past them.

Jenna giggled and squeezed his waist tighter. "That was nice."

"Was it? I can never tell. It wasn't aggressive?"

"No, that's not aggressive," she said. "That's respectful."

"Huh. I can't tell. I guess it's on the line. It's admiring, but it's hostile too. That's a combination I've never really understood before."

"Well, you do now."

"I guess I do."

There was a line outside the black door and velvet ropes that must have been Persimmon. There were guys checking names on a clipboard with little penlights. The women in the line had heels on and shiny dresses.

"Fucknugget," said Justin.

"Don't worry," said Jenna. "We'll see what happens."

She led him by the hand along the line. She just stepped in front of the front person and smiled up at the black guy. "Hi," she said.

He looked her up and down and then glanced at his partner, who had the clipboard. He took her in too, and then he nodded.

"Come on in, folks," said the black guy, unclipping the rope.

As they moved through the first door and into the bass boom Justin could feel the eyes of the people in the line on the back of his neck.

There was a fifteen-dollar cover to pay, two of them actually, which he paid in cash; he could use a credit card at the bar. She could hardly wait for him to get his change and get their hands stamped; she was dancing already, swinging her hips and her head. She took him by the hand and led him right past the bar, and she let go of his hand as she stepped into the thick of the bodies around the dance floor; he could barely keep up as she disappeared into the purple darkness.

13.

Instead of the usual queue of supplicants outside Mike's office there was just one girl, another pretty one, but she wasn't from one of Justin's classes. She was like Cathy Heilbrunner: white, with straight hair in a ponytail and grown-up clothes and no funny colours in her hair, a little makeup. She could have been a shop clerk or a secretary or someone in PR, but she had that brightness of a student waiting to see someone she had to impress. And she had a green knapsack, so she had to be a student.

Justin smiled at her and she smiled back. As he passed, Mike's door opened and Mike loomed. He had that peculiar leering smile he took on with female students, or perhaps with everyone; it was only with these girls that it particularly irritated Justin. He nodded at Justin, perhaps even winked, and then stepped aside to let the girl in. Justin stopped to say hello as cheerily as he could, and also to get another look at the girl. She was frowning as she went in. She looked scared, in fact.

The door closed with a click.

Justin padded into the departmental office. He had his usual hour to kill before the torture of Media Studies 125 (Introduction to Media), in which he planned to try to get them to read news stories on their computers and then talk about what news might consist of, which was not as easy as it sounded, as they usually refused to read the news stories because those stories were gay-ass. So he was going to look at Janice at her desk and see if there was anything in his mail hole. Janice had been extra friendly to him since she had overheard him making a date. In return, Justin had been even more reserved with her.

She almost leaped up from her chair when he came in. "Hello sweetie! How was your weekend?"

He coughed a bit and fumbled in his pigeonhole as if extremely distracted. "Fine, thanks."

"That's it? Nothing exciting?"

"Not really." He frowned as he opened an envelope and pretended to read a flyer from a car insurance company. "Huh," he said. Then he turned his distant eyes onto Janice, as if noticing her there. "Ah, how was yours?"

"Oh, nothing special. Mine was kind of lame, actually. That's what happens when you're an old married couple like us."

One of his flyers was a folded letter from Mike to all staff. The key to the answers of the final test of the term—which was coming up in about three weeks—would be posted on the departmental website and just before the test instructors would be given a secret passcode to access them. Justin glanced back at Janice, who was still beaming a smile and her huge eyes up at him like a dream. He said, "You're not married, are you?"

"No, no, not at all, but you know what I mean. When you're

with someone." Then she stretched, arching her back and pushing out her cleavage.

"Not getting bored, are you?"

"Oh no, I love it." She pulled at her ponytail and shook her black hair out over her shoulders. She put the elastic in her mouth and then lifted her arms to begin gathering her hair back into its previous shape, brazenly showing her shaved underarms. Justin recognized this operation from Jenna; it was meant to invite attention, so Justin stared. "I'm very domeshtic," she said through the elastic in her mouth.

"I can see that," he said. "Listen." He put his elbows on her partition and leaned over, looking right down into her cleavage. "Mike. He's only teaching the one class right now, right? One section of Marketing, right?"

"I shink sho." She removed the elastic from her teeth and began the process of working the ponytail into it.

Justin stayed focused. "So why are there always so many kids lined up to see him?"

"I don't know. He's the head of the department."

"Yeah, I know that, but . . . yeah. Never mind. None of my business. I'm just curious what they all want to see him about. Can you appeal your marks, for example, to him, if you're a student?"

"Well, I would guess so. Why don't you ask him that?"

"Oh I will, I guess, but it doesn't really matter. I'm just curious. If he has the final say, if he's kind of the final arbiter as far as marks go."

"Well, I would imagine he is."

"But you'd think he'd consult with the instructors who gave them. Anyway, forget it. Just wanted to know if he is actually teaching any other classes."

"Not as far as I know."

"Thanks, then. You look lovely in that top."

"Go away," she sang.

"Bye."

On leaving the office he turned, for some reason, not right towards the cafeteria, where he would spend the next hour, but left, down the hall that passed Mike's office. He didn't know exactly where he was going. But he did know that the classroom right next to Mike's office was empty, because that's where he had taught his last class and where he would teach his next. He would perhaps sit in there for just a minute.

He slowed as he passed Mike's door and he heard the big guy's voice droning from within. He was very quiet as he went into the empty classroom and gently closed the door. He sat on a chair close to the wall and was still.

He couldn't quite make out any specific words, but he knew the tone: Mike was lecturing. He didn't seem pleased. It was his intimidating tone.

There was clatter from the hallway that came and went, obscuring the signal. Justin try to slow his breathing, stop any ambient noise.

If he closed his eyes he could hear a couple of words. He heard "level playing field," one of Mike's favourites. He was never sure what it meant; indeed it usually seemed to mean the opposite.

"Certain advantages," he heard. "Certain advantages which aren't available to."

A laugh and a shriek from a gang of girls in the hallway obscured the rest.

He waited. There was a silence, possibly indicating a response from the student whose voice was not so authoritative as Mike's.

Then Mike agreeing. "Oh absolutely, absolutely. That's not the issue here, not."

Justin's knapsack fell off his lap with a rush and a thump, and Justin swore. For a second he thought that Mike's voice had stopped, perhaps because Mike had heard the thump, but it recommenced.

He heard, "Life's not fair," and "the best advantage you can possibly have."

The student murmured something. One of the words may have been "parents."

"If you have to," came Mike's voice, then more droning. Phrases came and went, with pauses as the unhearable student spoke.

"On your side . . . life is unfair . . . work out some kind of . . ."

Then the air conditioning or the heating or some other rushing noise filled the ducts and the voice was gone.

Justin gathered his bag and went to the door. He peered into the hallway as if he had been doing something illicit, all alone in there.

And in fact, exactly at that moment Mike's door opened and the pale student emerged. Mike came behind her, no smile on his face this time. She did not say thank you or goodbye as she paced quickly away. Her head was down. Mike glanced at Justin and grunted. He frowned slightly.

"Mike," said Justin. "Hey."

Mike looked at his watch. He closed his office door behind him and locked it with a key. "Just going to get a tea," he said.

"Hey," said Justin, "I'll come with you. I was just going down there. Before my next."

"Huh." Mike began striding down the hall and Justin kept pace.

"Not that the coffee in that place is any good," said Justin. "I can barely stand it, but I take it like a pill."

"Don't drink coffee," said Mike.

"You don't?"

"Nope. I don't. Not at all. Bad for my training."

"Ah. Training. What kind of training is that?" They were passing into the open concourse now, moving so swiftly that people were having to stop and move aside for them with startled expressions; Mike didn't seem to mind this. Justin could smell the curry and coffee air of the cafeteria approaching.

"Triathlons," said Mike. "Some bodybuilding. I do the fitness competitions though, not the bodybuilding. Fitness is a whole lot healthier. Coffee just increases your glycemic levels. It works on the pancreas to screw with your insulin. It's really the enemy of good nutrition."

"Ah."

"You should avoid it too, my friend."

They were at the coffee urns now. Mike grabbed a styrofoam cup and filled it with hot water. He perused the rack of brightly coloured herbal tea bags. He picked a strawberry thing, which struck Justin as strangely girly.

Mike had paid for his tea by the time Justin made it to the cash. Mike waited impatiently.

"Shall we have a seat?" said Justin.

"Oh, no, I'm heading back to the office." Mike stood still for a moment and stared at Justin. "Why? Something you wanted?"

"No no. Purely social, Mike. Just killing time."

Mike glared at him for a moment longer, as if evaluating the possible truth value of this statement. "Hey," he said finally, "I've been meaning to say. Good job with the last test. I don't know if you noticed. Highest grades."

"Oh yeah, I noticed." Justin took a sip of his coffee, looked around as if he was still hoping to have this conversation seated. Mike didn't move. "Thanks to that one high mark, though, in my class. It was way off. Raised the median. Not really a reflection of how the whole class did."

"Well, hey, a median's a median. That's what the province is going to look at. That's what counts."

"Yeah. Yes. Well, thank God for that one high mark, then. It was way up there." Justin closed his eyes as if thinking. "Cathy Heilbrunner, I think it was. Amazing student."

"Oh, yeah, that one," said Mike. "She's definitely a bright one." Mike was fishing the teabag out of his cup, looking for a napkin to wrap it in. Justin grabbed one for him. Students were pushing past them with their yoghurts and bananas and herbal teas.

"You know her?" said Justin.

"Oh, no, not really." Mike moved to the table with cream and sugar and Justin followed him.

"Ah," said Justin. "Rich girl, it seems like."

"Not that I know of." Mike snapped the lid on his tea. He was ready to go. "You have a class this afternoon?"

"Yeah, of course. Right now."

"See you." Mike nodded and stepped into the flow of knapsacks down the concourse, and was carried off as if by a current.

Introduction to Media was not terribly bad, although his mind wasn't really on it. He was able to get them talking about a video they had all seen of a cop beating the crap out of an environmental protestor. Allegiances were divided because cops were obviously douchebuckets but then so were environmental protestors, for they were rich kids who had never had anything serious to worry about. Several opinions were ventured on how to fight back against cops when there's only one of them, and how the protestor was obviously a pussybag for not knowing any of these techniques. This was clear confirmation of the protestor's dickhat social status. It was an almost enjoyable hour, in that it went quickly.

Cathy Heilbrunner was not in this class.

Justin took his time going through the parking lot. It was glaring hot and ugly, and he could have hurried to the bus stop, but he wanted to find Mike's car.

He wandered for a few minutes, scanning for red. The sun was like the screen-filling image of the yellow orb they used in Westerns when the guy had been beaten up by Mexicans and was tied to a stake in the desert and losing consciousness. There would be vultures circling, too, and a dully booming drum. The air shimmered over the adjacent highway.

There was the Thunderbird.

There was no licence plate on the front end, so he went around to the back. He kept jerking around, in case Mike were to stride out of a stairwell and find him circling.

The rear licence plate read WNDRKD.

Justin walked to the grass lozenge in one of the dividers between lots, so that he was well away from the car, before he withdrew his notebook from his bag and wrote that down. Then he walked along the highway in the sun to find the bus stop.

14.

Justin's computer was in his bedroom, on the plywood desk he had had since undergrad. It was an old computer, and he didn't have the highest of high-speed connections, he had the basic service thing, so he didn't use it much, except for e-mail and for Sandstorm III (Sheikh Assassin). The machines at school had high speed if he needed to look something up. So it took its time, grunting and clicking, in hunting down the Constitution College Instructor's Web Page for test keys. Justin's room smelled of dirty sheets and Jenna's lip gloss, and stale weed smoke. She had left a silver bangle on the bedside table.

First there were ten e-mails. Three penis enlargements, two pleas from Africans with a great deal of money for him, one warning from a bank he had never used that he must update his password with them. One from his mother asking if he wanted the chest that was in the garage as it might make a nice coffee table and his father was about to throw it out. One from Dorothy Liu, a group e-mail reminding everyone that the annual Victoria College reunion pub crawl was next week and to sign up with her to get the required T-shirt. Then there was another one from her for him alone, wondering how he was doing and why he hadn't shown up at the eighties night thing she had arranged at Lee's Palace. Then there was one from Guntar Haus, announcing that there were still spaces in the regular Ultimate Frisbee game he was setting up in Riverdale.

Justin answered his mother (negatively) and just ticked the ones from Dorothy and Guntar. For some reason he didn't want to answer them even to say no at that moment. It seemed like a tiring thing to do.

The Constitution College test answers page was up and running. First you got the logo of the college and then a sign-in square. It said please enter password.

This was interesting because the answers would not be available for another three weeks, after the test was to be given, so there was no reason for the key to be available to anyone yet.

Justin tried his college e-mail address and password, which were incorrect. He took out his notebook and copied from it WNDRKD.

This was incorrect.

He tried it in lower case, then tried WONDERKID in upper and lower case, and with one majuscule. Then he tried wunderkind, Wunderkind and WUNDERKIND. Then Wonderboy, both ways, then Wonderkid00, Wonderkid01, and Wonderkid69, which he thought would appeal to Mike's sense of self.

He got up and picked up Jenna's bracelet. He looked around for other items that might bear some of her scent. There was a hair elastic with a few white strands stuck to it. He picked it up and smelled it. Jenna had not called for a couple of days. He had tried her and left a message on Deenie's voice mail.

The phone rang. He jumped into the kitchen to peer at the display. It was only Genevieve.

"Hey," he said.

"Hey you."

The preliminary how are yous were a bit stiff.

"So," he said, "what can I do for you?"

She was quiet for a second. "What can you do for me? Nothing. I was just calling to chat. See how you're doing."

"Ah. You haven't done that in a while."

"Well, neither have you."

"No," he said. "I had the feeling you weren't too keen on me calling too much."

"What? That's ridiculous. You can call me any time you like. In fact I wish you would."

Now he was silent. He had wandered back into the bedroom. He sat at his keyboard and tried JERK as a password.

"Well," said Genevieve, "what's going on?"

"What's going on? Same. Same old. Work, you know." He entered JERKOFF, ASSWAD, TITSTICK and FUCKPAD.

"How is that poor woman who has cancer?"

"Who? Oh, Linda. You know, I forgot to ask. She hasn't come back yet. I'm still teaching her students."

"That's awful, Justin. Don't you want to know?"

He typed DOUCHEHAT, and the page told him he wasn't allowed to attempt any more passwords. "Yeah, I guess I should. Maybe go visit her or something. I don't think she'd want that though."

"Well, still. What if she dies?"

"Well, then there won't be much point in visiting her, will there?"

"No, I mean your classes. Will they replace her?"

Justin sighed. He closed down his web browser and reopened it. He loaded the instructors' page again. He watched it painstakingly build itself. It was like listening to a skipping CD. "What was that?"

"What are you doing? You're so distracted."

"Nothing. Nothing. My classes. I don't know. I'm sick of trying to get anything out of Mike."

"Listen, Justin, you really have to—"

"Hey, listen, I think Mike may be actually up to something. Something quite bad."

"Bad?" she said. "What?"

The page was loaded. He tried ASSKNOB. It would have been great if that one worked. "I think," said Justin, "that he's selling test results to students. I know it sounds ridiculous."

Genevieve laughed. "Yes it does. Why would he bother to do that?"

"I don't know. I don't think he needs the money. Although he seems to live pretty high on the hog, for a young guy. I think he just likes the power. He likes having control over people."

"Well, what makes you think he's doing that?"

Justin typed DICKASS, and the page shut down again. He went to a search engine and typed *amateur girls tattoos*. "Well, there's one girl in one of my classes who sees him a lot, in his office. She does really well. And he boosted her mark on the final transcript. He altered the mark I had submitted."

Genevieve thought about this. "Maybe he's sleeping with her."

"Maybe that too. Maybe both. But he's put up a page of answers to the test that—on the web, I mean, he's posted a page of answers to a test that's not going to happen for three weeks."

"What? So anyone can go and look at the answers?"

"No, you need a password. And he's going to give us, the instructors, the password after the test, so we can mark them."

"Shouldn't you know all the answers anyway?"

"Yeah, well, no, they're really stupid tests. Sometimes you don't know the answers, because sometimes the answers are stupid. It's this stupid province-wide test designed by the kind of idiot who thinks Business English is a real subject. Anyway, the point is if you have the password now you can get the answers before the test. And I think he's playing favourites and giving out the answers to girls."

"What makes you think he's getting money for it? Maybe he's just getting laid."

"Yeah, I don't know. Something I overheard. I can hear what he's saying in his office sometimes." Justin clicked on a line that said *pierced and tattooed sluts in your neighbourhood*. If it really had pictures, the page would take an hour to load. There was really no point to porn on this computer.

"You mean you're spying on him? Justin, you can let that get out of hand. What are you doing, going through his files, or what?"

"I would," said Justin with energy. "In fact I've been thinking about that. I have to find some way to get into his office when he's not there. Or maybe get his BlackBerry for an hour or so, something like that. I wouldn't mind really knowing if the test keys are already up or not. I've tried a bunch of passwords, but I think—"

"Justin," said Genevieve firmly. "*What* are you *talking* about. *Listen* to you. You're talking about breaking into someone's office, or computer? What is happening to you?"

"Aha," he said. He had a half a girl on his screen. So far, she was promising: she had a bushel of dreadlocks, like Jenna, except they were dyed black, and cat-eyed makeup and some kind of corset. Her lower half was not yet visible. "What?"

"I'm kind of worried about you, Justin. You sound different."

"Ah. Different. Maybe a little."

"Well, you want to tell me what's going on?"

"Going on? Nothing. I told you. Same old."

She sighed. There was a silence. The girl on his screen still had no crotch. It was probably just a welcome screen anyway; there would be pages of clicking and passwords to prove you're not a minor.

Genevieve said, "Are you seeing anybody?"

"Ah," said Justin. The girl's black thong and garters had materialized. It was as good as he could have expected from a welcome screen. He searched for the age verification box. "Ah, yes. I am. I guess. I'm not sure."

"Oh. Well, that sounds promising."

Justin's age was eighty-seven and he lived in Aruba. "Hah," he said.

"Well, as long as you're happy."

"What about you?" he said, to keep it going. "You seeing anyone."

"Um."

"I see. A similar situation."

"No, not really, to be honest. I've been with . . . I've been on a few dates, I guess. But nothing, you know."

"*Been* with?"

"What?"

"Never mind." Members area. Free tour. He clicked.

"Well, are you happy?"

He puffed out his cheeks. "Yes, as a matter of fact. I am."

"Okay. Good."

"Good then."

"Do you want to tell me about her?"

"Not really."

"Why not?"

"Well, I just don't think that . . . I don't think that's necessary. I don't think that's something we should get into telling each other."

"Are you embarrassed by her?"

"No. Quite the opposite, I would say."

She said, "It's Dorothy Liu, isn't it?"

"Dorothy Liu?" He laughed. "No. Christ no."

She said, "All right."

"This is a silly game," he said. "I'm not grilling you on who you've . . . *been* with."

"Okay. I know. I'm just . . . I'm worried that . . ."

"You're worried about what?" His screen stuck on an image of a fantastically cute goth girl in her bedroom. She was lying on her front and smiling at the camera. Her ankles, kicked up behind her, were wrapped in some kind of leg warmer, and even that was sexy. There was a bruise on her shoulder.

"I don't know. I just have a funny feeling. I don't know why. That whoever you're seeing . . ."

There was a electric guitar leaning against the wall of the girl's bedroom. He tried to make out the CD titles in her CD rack. It was such a familiar-looking bedroom, and that was what was so exciting about these shots; one had been in so many bedrooms like this, although probably not with such a deadly raven-haired girl with pierced labia. It was unlikely, of course, that the girl was actually from his neighbourhood or even from his town, but one could always hope to recognize an apartment one had been in, maybe a glimpse through a window of a familiar streetscape. It was fantastic to imagine that there were girls like these, gleefully taking their clothes off for cameras, all around one, in one's own town, that maybe even the pierced skinny girl at the Starbucks might appear on your screen one night. Even if it never happened, the thought alone that it was possible was reassuring. He said, "If you don't finish your sentence there's no way I can know what it is you're trying to say."

"Well, nothing then."

"No, go on. Whoever I'm seeing?"

"That whoever you're seeing is, is not good for you."

"Not good for me? What would be good for me?"

"No, I mean that . . . I just worry about you. That's all."

"Thank you for your concern for my welfare."

"Okay. Well, it was well meant."

"Your feedback is appreciated. I will pass it along to a customer service representative."

"Okay," she said. "Forget I said anything."

"Okay."

"I'd better go."

"Me too. It was nice—"

"Listen," she said, "just don't do anything that's . . . that isn't you."

"That isn't me? What, for example, would not be me?"

"Well, breaking and entering into someone's office, for example. Stealing someone's property. You're not exactly a cat burglar."

"Cat burglar. That sounds so cool. I would wear a sort of

tight black bodysuit and a black skullcap. Like a mime. That is me, though! That is so me!"

"Oh yeah. You're such a tight black bodysuit kind of guy."

"Okay," he said. They had laughed for a second. "Okay. I promise I won't do anything that isn't me. It is nice of you to worry about me, actually. I mean that." There was a crunch and a tone on the line. "Hey, listen, I have to go. I've got a call."

"Okay," she said, and her voice was small. "I'll talk to—"

"Hello? Hello?" There was a hissing but he wasn't sure if he'd heard a voice. "Hello?"

Then it was definitely her, but faint. "Hey, star."

"Where are you? You're very faint."

"I'm okay. How are you?"

"I'm good. Good."

More hissing.

He said, "You on your cellphone?"

"What's that?"

"You okay?"

"Yeah yeah. I'm fine. How are you?"

"Listen," he said, "I can hardly hear you. You want to come over?"

"No," she said, a little too quickly. "I can't."

"Oh."

"I'm exhausted," she said.

"How is work?"

"It's good. Really good. It's great."

"That is so good. That is excellent. That is—that's a relief. So tell me about it. You making a ton of money?"

"Well, not yet. I'm only getting tip-out right now."

"And the people are okay? Not too scary?"

"No, they're cool. There's one bitch. But I don't want to talk about her."

"Okay. And the big guy, the owner, is he sleazy with you?"

"Sleazy? No, he's nice. He's cool."

"I wish I could see you there. In your sexy dress."

"Well," she said, "you could come and check it out. I'll put your name on the list."

"Really? When?"

"Friday?"

Today was Tuesday. "Friday, yeah sure. I'd love to. Am I going to see you before then?"

"Hey," she said, "Deenie wants some more of those nice things you got her."

"Deenie. Oh yes." He considered this. "She wants more? Jenna, there were fifty of them. That was like less than a week ago. That was five days ago."

Jenna was silent.

"Jenna, is she taking all those?"

"I really don't ask her what she does with them."

"That would be ten pills a day."

"Shh," she said. "Don't say that on the phone."

"Say what? Pills? You think we're being monitored by the, by the what, by the feds, by whoever taps the phones of college English professors?"

"Shut up. I'm serious."

"Okay. Okay. Maybe we should have code names. You could be Dolphin and I could be Mister Orangutan. No, I would be Viper or Demon or Top-Ass or something. Or you want to be Top-Ass?"

"Listen, I'm going to have to go pretty soon."

"Okay, Jenna, listen. Let's say she's doing . . . she's listening to ten *albums* a day. That would make you pretty much a zombie."

He could hear her sighing through the wires. "I don't *ask* her what she *does* with them."

He clicked on *view full photo set*. That would take a decade to load. He said, "Jenna, is she selling them?"

"What are you so worried about?"

"Well, I don't know if I . . . I mean I don't know if I like that idea."

She said, "Aren't *you* selling them?"

The first photo was already clear. It was tantalizingly non-graphic, all black mesh underthings and artful shadows. "Huh," he said. "I guess I am."

"Well then. Do you think you can get her some more?"

He sighed. "No. No I don't think I can. I just wanted to do her a favour. I didn't want to get into—"

"But this would be doing me a favour. If you do her a favour you're doing me a favour."

"Hey. I just got them off the internet. Anyone can. I'll just give her the address and she can go nuts."

"Do you pay for it with a credit card?"

"Yes."

"She doesn't have a credit card."

"Ah."

"It's just a small favour to ask someone."

"Okay. I'll think about it. Listen, speaking of which, do you think you could get me some weed? I find I quite enjoy it."

"Justin," she said deliberately. "Don't talk like that on the phone. Okay? I mean it."

"Jenna, really, this is silly. It's a bit paranoid. I really don't think, I mean we're not exactly on the radar of the secret police, if there are any secret police. You can't just go around bugging people's phones in this country. That's only in movies. You think they have their eye on me because I'm looking at goth girls in their stockings on my computer? So is everybody else. I really don't think they care so much about that."

"I have to go," she said.

"Okay. Okay. Sorry. Don't get upset. Listen, I miss you. I'm looking forward to seeing you."

There was static on the line.

"Jenna?"

"Yeah."

"I'll see you Friday."

She said, "Are you really looking at goth girls in stockings?"

"Yes, I am, as a matter of fact. Because I miss you so much. Not one of them is nearly as sexy as you are."

"Describe them to me."

He snorted. "Okay. I'm looking at one . . . let's see. Okay, this one's better. She has her top off now. She's got the shiny black hair, you know, with the Cleopatra thing, and a few studs in her face, and—"

"You're not looking at her face."

"Well, sure I am. That's part of it, sure. She's very pretty."

"Okay."

"And she's got kind of boy-cut black panties, kind of tight shorts panties, and they're black mesh, so like see-through, which I like."

"Uh-huh. Is she shaved?"

"It's hard to tell, the way she has her legs. It's kind of covered.

184

I like it when you can see a little bush through the mesh. That's a total turn-on."

"Huh," she said. "That's interesting."

"I can't believe I'm telling you this."

"Go on. I like it."

"That's cool. Okay. So she's on a tabletop, in a dungeony kind of place, with straps and buckles everywhere, although she's not tied up yet, but she's spread out on the table, lying back, with her arms outstretched and her back arched and her hair sort of spreading all over the tabletop."

"That's sexy," said Jenna.

"Yes, it is sexy. Her skin is very pale, only a few tattoos, there's a greeny dragon on her shoulder but that's about it. Pierced belly."

"Does she have big tits?"

"No, actually, she has perfect little pale taut breasts, like yours. Pale pink nipples, like yours. In fact yours are a little bigger. Yours are the most beautiful breasts I have ever seen," he said sincerely.

"Shut up. So what turns you on about it?"

"Well," he said, "I guess the fact that she's all arched with her arms out and sort of take-me-now. She's looking . . ."

"Submissive."

"Yeah, hah, submissive, I guess." He giggled.

"I like that about you."

"Huh. And she's all small and pale and dangerous looking. She's kind of snarling. And I guess I like all the cheesy dungeon stuff. I would love to tie someone up like that."

"We should do that."

"Whoo. Yes. We sure should. Wow."

"Are you turned on right now?" she said, her voice soft.

"I sure am. I am bursting. It's incredible. Just talking to you."

"That's really hot, to think of you getting all turned on there alone."

"I have stuff of yours here, like a hairband, and that turns me on too."

"That's sweet. You are such a sex machine."

There was a bit of silence and then she said that she had to go and he said okay, he would see her Friday.

He hung up the phone and clicked on the next photo. While it was loading he looked at the browser's search history and saw that there were about ten porn sites listed there. He would have to find a way to clear those, or set it so that they didn't stay in memory at all. He began to go through the options on the browser, which was so absorbing he forgot to click on the next picture.

He found "clear history" and then, after a few minutes, "clear history on exit," which would mean, he assumed, that every time he shut down the program it would erase his tracks. He tried closing it and opening it again a few times just to make sure.

He wasn't interested in looking at porn any more. He opened Sandstorm III (Sheik Assassin) but he quickly got back to the same damn bunker he had been having trouble with for a week. Every time he ran out of 40 mm grenades the same cocksucking T-72 loomed up over the berm. He was bored with running away from it so he shut it down.

He opened and closed his browser again to check on his tracks. When it was good and closed, he looked around him.

Just behind him was the bedroom window, which looked out at the wall of the next house. It was just a blank wall, so no one could see in, and he had no blind on that window. He went to the window and peered out.

There was, in fact, a dark window on the opposite wall just a few feet away, so it was possible that if you looked from it at a certain angle you might be able to see into a corner of Justin's room. He turned and looked back at the computer to see if it would be in the line of sight. It might be. If you could see into the room you would see exactly whatever was on Justin's computer screen, which was facing his window, which was completely uncovered.

He walked back to the computer, the screen blazing blue in the darkness. It would have been incredibly bright if you were able to look in from outside.

He shut it down and sat there in the darkness, blinking away the white burn on his retinas, feeling silly. He knew this was silly. But he would have to find some sort of curtain.

15.

"This one's four, though. It's awesome."

"Four what," said Justin. The music was some kind of coun-try rap. It was too loud.

"Nicole?" said the girl beside him. She was shouting into a phone. "This is a new phone. I'm just testing it."

"Four megapixels," said the guy. "It's a deal."

"Megapixels. What do I need megapixels for?"

"I said it's *really loud in here*," shouted the girl into her phone.

"You mean the camera? I don't need a camera. I just want a phone."

"They all have cameras," said the guy. He was about twenty-one and he had the burgundy golf shirt of the phone company. There was only one other guy working and there were three people waiting to see each guy. The other guy was helping the girl who was shouting. "You might as well get a good one. For the price—"

"No, I don't need the text thingies, I don't need the internet, I just need a phone, a really basic phone. To make calls on."

The guitars twanged. The music was probably programmed by the mall.

"Is it clear though?" shouted the girl. "I think it's clear. It's better than the last one. Hey, did you get a birthday present for Shayla?"

"Okay," said the guy. "This is about the most basic one. And you can get the different coloured face plates. It's popular with ladies." He turned to watch his colleague handing a selection of coloured flat machines to the shouting girl. She was Indian or Arabic or something and wearing a clingy white top which was quite hot. This kind of thing would make up for working in a stall in a mall concourse, Justin supposed.

"So how much is this one?"

"Ah. That's two thirteen."

"Two thirteen? And that's the most basic one? Hell. I thought they were all free these days."

"Well," said the guy, still staring at the Indian girl. "You can get them free if you sign up for a plan. Or you can get a discount. You can get a hundred bucks off this one if you sign up for a twenty-four-month plan."

"No *way*," she said to her phone. "I was totally going to get her the blue one too. The pink is kind of cheesy-ass."

"Okay," said Justin. He was sweating already. "Tell me about the plan."

Sighing, the guy handed Justin a leaflet. Justin tried to read it for a minute and a half. It was covered in phrases like *The Nomad, The Family Man, The Weekender*. Each one had a series of abbreviations after it. He folded it up.

"Okay," he said. "I'll pay full price."

It took another half hour to pick a phone number and pro-gram the phone and fill in forms. The mall must have been air-conditioned but under the lights of the phone stall it was enough to make you lose weight through dehydration. Justin's head was buzzing as he stepped into the hotter and more humid air of the street. He walked for a block with the big bag full of packaging and his new phone until he found a little square of concrete with some benches. The benches were all occupied by sleeping people, so he sat on the concrete shelf around the non-functioning fountain and began to unwrap. He worked his way through boxes and moulded plastic shapes until he found the tiny phone, which was unfortunately red (this being the only faceplate available for that particular unsophisticated model), and the battery, which was separate. The guy had been nice and given him a battery which he had already charged.

He put all the packaging and the heavy instruction manual into the plastic bag and threw it in the garbage bin which was conveniently next to him.

He dialled Jenna.

Of course she didn't answer. He had resisted calling her for a day and a half, maybe twenty-four hours, because he had a feel-ing she wouldn't answer. But the phone was a sort of a special occasion. He had something to tell her at least.

He got her faint-voiced message. "Hey," he said "Mister Oran-gutan here, come in Pink Dolphin. The cat is in the cage, repeat, the cat is in the cage. Do not respond to this message. Mouse bites are imminent. The cat has consumed the red flag and responded to the treatment. We are go for system repositioning. The matter of the Chinese watch . . ." He sighed. The garbage bin stank and one of the sleeping bodies on the bench had opened its eyes and was staring at him dully. "No, hey, it's me, I just wanted to try out my new cellphone. It's amazing. Apparently I can dial numbers and they ring and you can communicate with me anywhere I want. It's an amazing technology. Next they'll be transmitting moving pictures from afar. Anyway. Everyone should have one. You know this because you have one. Okay. Just calling to see how you are. Call me on my new machine. The number is six four seven five six six two, which is cute because it spells *knob,* five six six two. I tried jerk and goof but they were taken. Anyway. Easy to remember. Six four seven knob. Call me. Bye."

He gathered up his technology. He jammed the bulky charger and its wire into his shorts pocket. He held onto the phone, in case it rang, and walked towards the subway. He wished there were a streetcar instead that would get him home, as the phone would not ring underground.

As he walked, this little heavy thing in his hand grew hot, a freshly poured ingot. It really was stupid to walk around with it like this, waiting for it to ring. He put it in his pocket and left it there for a block but then took it out again in case he didn't hear it there. There would be some way of making it vibrate that he would figure out later.

He held it slightly away from his body like something radioactive.

When he got home he saw that the light on his home phone was not flashing. "My land line," he said aloud. He would get used to saying that now. *Call me on my land line. Wait till I get on a land line.*

It was possible, of course, that Jenna had simply not answered her phone when he had called her with his cell—his *mobile*—because she had not recognized the number on her phone display. She wouldn't answer any stranger's call, of course.

He poured his mail on the kitchen table, all bills and offers for credit cards, and dumped his electronic equipment in a pile. He picked up his home phone and dialled her. She answered right away. "What now?" she said.

"Whoa," he said. "You mad at me?"

"Oh," she said. "It's you."

"Who did you think it was?"

"Oh, nothing. Sorry. Nobody. I was expecting a call."

"Oh. Did you get my message?"

"Oh," she said, "yeah."

"Oh. Okay. I got a new cellphone."

"Yeah," she said. "Nice."

"So, how are things?"

"Not so good," she said with a twist in her voice.

"Oh oh." Justin sat down. He was tired then, from the long walk and the heat. For a second he wished he hadn't called, which was odd. "What's up? Is it work?"

"I quit."

"Oh, shit." He put a hand on his belly, which was queasy. He had not noticed it before. "Why? I thought it was great?"

"It was all fucked up." Her voice had gone quiet now, and wavery. "It was just totally douchey."

"Why? What happened?"

"It's just a shitty place, what can I tell you? I wasn't going to take shit any more, that's why."

"Shit from whom? From the manager, the big guy?"

She sighed. There was a TV playing in the background. On Justin's end, the dog next door started up. "From him, yeah, and from this one girl. It doesn't matter now, it's over. I just have to find something else I guess."

"That's terrible. That's terrible." Justin opened the back door to let some air in, and more barking. He had to speak louder over the dog. "Can you tell me what happened? Is it a secret?"

"I just don't get along well with girls, I guess. Listen, I don't want to go into it, I'll just get really upset. Who cares? You want to cross-examine me, decide if I was right or not?"

"No," he said. "I'm just curious. It's terrible."

"Don't worry, I won't be a burden on you."

"Jenna, that's not what I was thinking at all. Listen, don't be mad at me, I'm on your side."

"Then let me not talk about it, okay?"

"Okay, sure. No problem. I just . . . I feel for you. What are you up to right now?"

"I don't feel great right now."

Justin stood on the fire escape and looked at the city. Since yesterday, it seemed, they had destroyed a block of houses just past the next alleyway. They were digging now and would build foundations soon and another tower would go up and he would see less of the city, which was all towers anyway so what did it matter. He wouldn't mind living in a tower, actually, as long as he had air conditioning. "I haven't seen you for a while," he said.

"I really don't feel well."

"I would really like to see you. I miss you." His stomach twisted as he said that. That was always an idiotic thing to say. His voice had gone slightly higher too.

But she was silent, so perhaps it had had an effect.

He said, "Come over this evening. I'll make you something nice to eat. Relax, take your mind off stuff. We'll watch a movie if you want."

She exhaled. "Sure," she said. "Why not."

"Cool. Exactly. Why not. What time?"

"I have to do some stuff."

"Sure. Whenever. When do you think?"

"What time is it now?"

"It's four. I'll go shopping for food. Come over at six."

"Six."

"Yeah. That okay?"

"Yeah, okay. Six or six-thirty."

"Perfect. I can't wait to see you."

After he hung up he saw the apartment differently. It was covered in crap. There were envelopes and newspapers all over the kitchen table and a pile of more newspapers by the front door. There were dishes in the sink and a shopping bag of tins and bottles for recycling. He would have to shop and clean up and shower and cook before six. He started piling things up. He turned on the radio very loud.

He took a cab to the market, which was like a travel documentary about Phnom Penh or Mombasa. He stood in the sewer-smelling fish shop until he was shouted at by a red-faced Portuguese alcoholic wielding a long curved machete with visible rust stains. Justin selected two translucent marlin steaks, as gruffly as he could.

He went to another shop for vegetables and stood in line to pay for them. Then he stood in line again for bread and again for cheese and again for a bunch of orange lilies. Then he stood in line for a single lemon. His bags were then heavy and he walked with them to the liquor store, where he stood in line to buy some white wine. Then he walked with the bags and the wine to the streetcar and the subsequent subway, which were quite crowded.

It was five to six when he got home and he was damp and thirsty. He dumped the food and got in the shower. He had a feeling she would be a bit late anyway.

By six-thirty he was shaved and dressed in a white cotton shirt and linen trousers, which had been a gift from Genevieve three years earlier. He began to slice his vegetables, which he was planning to grill on the little hibachi which should still be hidden somewhere under the fire escape, if it wasn't too rusted. The radio was playing something cheerily baroque and he was humming along. If she was a little late she'd be just in time. He opened the wine.

By seven-twenty he had found and cleaned the rusted hibachi and located a half a bag of charcoal and some toxic starter fluid. He set it up on the fire escape and lit it and watched the flames scorch the siding. He wanted to go inside and get a tub of water in case of disaster but he didn't want to leave it alone either. The flames died down soon anyway. The smell of the lighter fluid and the coals was satisfyingly summery; he hadn't smelled summer like that since the year before.

He went inside to start the rice.

The rice was done by quarter to eight and she wasn't there. The coals were ready so he put the vegetables on. He called her phone but of course she didn't answer.

From his front window he scanned the street. He squinted at the few stragglers on their way to the subway. Just a couple of bursts of five-five-six rounds would clear them. You wouldn't even need two magazines.

He called her again at eight. The vegetables were done and cooling and so was the rice. The coals were almost consumed. He could fry the fish if he had to but it would be a waste. He had consumed three-quarters of the bottle of wine and he suspected she wouldn't be bringing any more.

He sat out on the fire escape and watched the evening grow yellow.

His feeble buzzer sounded at quarter past. He let her in without saying anything. She was wearing baggy camouflage military trousers and a loose plaid shirt that looked like a boy's shirt. She had a baseball cap over her hair which was flat and dull. She looked tired. She didn't mention her lateness.

She sat at the kitchen table and said, "So how you doing."

He said, "You said you'd be here at six. It's almost eight-thirty."

"I'm sorry." She put her head on her hands on the table and closed her eyes. "I told you I wasn't feeling good."

"I would say 'dinner is ruined' if it didn't sound so gay."

"Well don't then."

He stood there with his arms folded. He wasn't even hungry any more.

She said, "I ate anyway."

"You ate? I told you I was going to cook for you."

"I'm sorry. I'm not hungry."

Justin tried to breathe deeply. "Jenna. I spent an hour in the hot market carrying bags of food around. I bought us two beautiful marlin steaks. I lit the barbecue. It's almost all gone now, so I don't know how I'm going to . . . Now you tell me you don't want any? What did I spend all that—"

"You want me to go?" she said from the table. Her voice was very quiet.

"No. No I don't want you to go. I'm going to . . . I'm going to cook my steak now and eat it. You sure you don't want one?"

She was silent. Her eyes were open but she was just staring sideways along the table top. Her eyes were red.

He said, "You been smoking?"

"Who cares?"

"Just curious. I could use a puff if you have any more."

She hauled her head up and felt in her pockets. The process seemed difficult. She extracted two baggies of weed. She pushed one over the table at him. "I got some for you."

"Cool," he said. "Thank you." He picked up the bag. It was quite large and puffy, as if packed quite tightly. "Jesus," he said. "How much is that?"

"That's eighty bucks worth right there."

"Holy shit. I'll never smoke all that."

"I got a deal on it. I only paid sixty for it. So it was worth it to get more."

"Won't it dry out, if it just sits there?"

"Keep it in the freezer," she said. She pulled out her rolling papers. "It should be all right."

He rummaged around for the kitchen scissors.

"So you only owe me sixty," she said.

"Sure. You want it right now?"

"No, whenever."

But he went to get his wallet.

When he handed her the money she was in the middle of her careful construction, cutting and rolling, concentrating like a child with crayons.

He stepped onto the fire escape and smacked his fish on the barbecue. The coals were grey and it made no sizzle. But it would cook. It would be something like a smoking process.

He went back in and she still wasn't finished rolling her joint. He really wanted some now. She said in her soft voice, "I don't really eat fish anyway."

"Ah. I should maybe have asked you that. Okay. You want some rice and vegetables?"

"Sure. Maybe a little." She finished her joint and licked it up and down in a way that always seemed obscene. She lit it and took a drag that lasted thirty seconds. She must have consumed half the thing in one toke. She handed it to him.

He tried the same thing and coughed. Then he tried another. The apartment expanded slightly around him. He thought of having her naked beside him in bed, all sleepy like this. "All right," he said. "No harm done."

His fish cooked. He served her some cold rice and vegetables but she didn't touch them. He poured her the last glass of wine and she sipped at it but didn't finish it. He ate in silence next to her.

He asked her if she was ready to tell him about what happened at Mirror and she said not really. He looked at her slack face, her red eyes and said, "You're totally gazooed."

"Yup," she said, and put her head back on the table. "Did you get a movie?"

"Oh. Shit, no, I forgot."

"Great."

"Hey," he said, "sorry. I went shopping for supper for two hours and I forgot the movie."

"Forget it. I should just go to sleep."

"Okay. Whatever."

She stood up and shuffled into the bedroom. He cleared the dishes and scraped the oily fish bits into a plastic bag, which he put under the sink. He was supposed to have some sort of recycling tub for the green box but he had never got one. He hoped he remembered the fish bag the next day. The apartment was smoky with fish oil and smoke. It was not unpleasant. It was a bit sexy. There was no sound at all from the bedroom. He imagined her sprawled on his bed and went to wash his hands.

There was no light in the bedroom. He stood in the door for a minute to let his eyes adjust. She was on her side, curled up, almost fetal. She hadn't even taken her cap off. He sat beside her and rubbed her shoulder. She didn't respond. "Hey," he said. She muttered a little. He pushed her onto her back and she moaned. Her eyes were screwed shut and she swatted vaguely at her face as if it was itchy. "Hey," he said. "You're fast asleep."

"Yeah," she sighed, without opening her eyes.

He switched on the lamp beside the bed and she said, "Huh."

He took off her ball cap and stroked her hair. He looked at her twisted body. Her baggy pants were low on her hips and her hip-bones jutted. The green and blue dragonfly was curved inwards, in the convexity of her groin, in the shadow of the bone. An edge of white thong. He caressed her belly and bum a bit but she didn't stir. In fact, her eyes twitched as if she was irritated.

"All right," he said, standing up. He pulled off her running shoes. Her little white socks were dirty. He peeled them off too, and kissed her painted toes. He got her to sit up which she did docilely and he unbuttoned her shirt and pulled it off. She had a plain white cotton bra underneath, some kind of sports bra. It was beautiful. He pulled it off her and could look at her breasts with their sleepy soft pink points for only a minute before she sank back. He unbuttoned her trousers and pulled them off. She pulled her knees up and grabbed at the cover, stuffing herself into the bed. "Okay," he said. He turned off the lamp and left the room. He closed the door behind him.

He put his puffy bag of weed in the freezer. He picked up the remains of the last joint she had smoked, and the wine she hadn't finished, and carried this loot out to the fire escape.

16.

He didn't sleep much, aware of her body next to his, inert and untouchable. It wasn't until the room was filling with light that he felt its warmth. He rolled against her and put his nose into the mass of her hair. The room was hot. She smelled a little sweaty. He was hard against her and he rubbed himself against her bum. She sighed and stirred a little. He reached a hand around and found her breast. He caressed her nipple and she pushed his hand away. He slid it down over her belly, brushing the metal button there, and down into the stubbly groin. His cock was so distended he knew he would burst at her first touch. He was even breathing hard already.

She let him stroke her there for a second and then rolled onto her back. She put her hand on his to still it. She looked up at him with eyes that were grey in the dawn.

She didn't say anything, so he said, "Hey."

Her eyes flickered away. They panned the room as if she was trying to recognize it.

He said, "You okay?"

She yawned. "What time is it?"

"No idea. Early." He tried stroking her belly again, rubbing in wide circles. He tried to keep his touch as light as he could. "How are you feeling?"

"Okay." Her voice was faint and her eyes closed again. She turned away from him and sighed.

"You were pretty wrecked last night."

She didn't answer. He didn't know if she was sleeping or staring wide-eyed at the wall.

"You sure you're okay? You were all sad."

More silence, but a quiver passed over her body and he knew she was crying.

He tried stroking her and turning her over and kissing her wet face and asking her what was wrong but she wouldn't answer. She kept saying it was nothing, really nothing, and that she had to go.

He let her get up and get dressed. His cock had subsided but it swelled again watching her heave the waistband of the camouflage trousers over the curve of her hips and close the snap against the swell of her belly. Then she wrestled with her bra. "What are you looking at?" she said.

"I'm looking at how beautiful you are. If that's all I get, then I'm allowed."

She kissed him quickly and said, "What did we do last night?"

"Nothing. You were too stoned and you fell asleep."

She thought about this for a minute and said, "Sorry. I'll make it up to you."

At this he swelled again. He hugged her and breathed in her hair. He could almost circle her waist with his hands. Her skin was always hot.

She said, "Next time we'll fuck like mad dogs. I'll let you do anything you want to me. You can punish me for being so bad."

He bit her ear and her lip and rubbed her nose with his. He resisted lifting up her shirt and ripping off her bra with his teeth. "I've got to shave and rush. You want breakfast? I've got to be fast, I have to get on the subway and get up to the college."

"You're so sweet, but no."

When he came out of the bathroom she was folding up a piece of paper at the kitchen table. There was a pen out on the cloth too. She put the paper in her pocket and said, "Ready, star?"

"We could grab a coffee together on the way."

She stood up and put her arms around his neck. Her eyes were blue-green again. "I'm sorry I'm such a drag."

"Listen," he said quickly, afraid she was going to start crying again. "Is there any way I can help you? Is there anything I can do to help you?"

"Help me with what."

"Well, you seem to be having a hard time with something, and you won't tell me what it is."

She was looking around for something. "That's just normal. No, there's nothing you can help me with. Did I have a hat?"

At the subway she kissed him and said, "Hey, did you remember to get that stuff for Deenie?"

"I'll order it. It takes ten days."

"Whenever you get around to it."

"Hey," he said, "when am I going to see you again?"

"I might have to go home for a couple of days. See my mom."

"Okay."

"So I'll call you when I get back?"

"Sure. Can I reach you up there?"

"Sure. You can try. The reception's not always good."

She embraced him again and reached quickly down his pants and squeezed his balls, right there in the crowd of people rushing the swinging grimy doors. He jumped and giggled, and then she was walking away and he was waving at her flashing hair.

It was around lunchtime that he found the note in his pocket. He sat at a sticky table unit in the ferocious white light of the cafeteria with his tray with its spilled orange soup and a bun and an apple that was now splashed with orange soup and felt something crackle under his bum. He extracted the folded-up paper and saw a loopy handwriting in ballpoint and he knew it was hers. He looked over his shoulder before unfolding it. No one was watching him or paying attention to him.

Dear Justin, I am so greatful for everything that you do for me, your beautifull smile and amazing body and your huge cock that fills me up so I feel like I am bursting, and your great sense of humor and the fantastic places you take me too and great food and experinces you give me. Thank you for your generosity and how sweet you are to me. I remember every moment and great orgizms! I ❤ Justin Harrison, your slave and lover Jenna Whibley.

Then there was a little happy face with circular breasts under it.

She must have stuffed it in his pocket when she was goosing him at the subway.

He read it again and then looked around the room, which seemed to be buzzing somehow; perhaps the fluorescence was flickering. The students in their stained running shoes were pale. The whole room with its hissing food machines and stained plastic and rubber surfaces whined in the light. He felt a heat in his chest and throat and knew it to be an onrush of tears, a childhood feeling he hadn't felt for years. He blinked back his tears and felt around for a handkerchief. He had none, so he grabbed a soup-wet napkin and pretended to sneeze and blow his nose. His whole chest wanted to empty itself out through his eyes. He coughed for a minute and it passed. It was of course because he was exhausted, because he had hardly slept. He felt very exposed there, crying alone at his table, so he folded up the note, put it back in his pocket and tried to eat his soup in the angry light.

He tried calling her cell from his cell the next day, and then again from his land line the following evening, but she didn't pick up. It was quite possible that there was no reception where she was, but then he had an idea that Belleville was a pretty big place, not far from Kingston which had a university in it, but then she had said she was in the country somewhere anyway. He decided not to try her again until she called him.

He ordered a hundred tablets of generic lorazepam from India.

He left another voice message for Andrew. It wasn't so much that he missed hanging around with him, it was just that he wasn't talking to anyone about this shit, and some voice of conscience, perhaps of guilt, told him that he should. But he didn't really want to.

He was leaving the department after Online Writing, cutting through the cafeteria again to avoid the hot asphalt of the parking lot for as long as he could, when he saw the hulking black jacket and the black do-rag of a guy sitting at a table with his back to him, and he knew it was the same guy, Tee.

Justin stopped and moved sideways, towards the central coffee stall. Once he was behind it he could turn and walk down another corridor. He would go underground through C building and then up and out at the other end of the parking lot. He could even walk almost to the next bus stop, at the end of the campus, underground. He doubted that Tee knew the corridors very well.

Tee turned around at this moment and saw him, even through his dark glasses. Justin turned his back and lined up at the coffee stall.

Then Tee was behind him in the line. "Mack daddy," said Tee, fairly loudly.

Justin turned around and looked at him.

Tee looked down at him. He wasn't smiling. "Mack daddy mack daddy."

"You want to talk to me?" said Justin.

"I think you got something for me."

Justin looked around. There were the usual students but no one he recognized from one of his classes, and none of his colleagues. "You think so."

"Ahee."

"I'm sorry, I can't help you." Justin walked between Tee and the coffee stall, towards the tunnel to C building. He walked as quickly as he could, through the plastic tables, but Tee followed him, his jacket flapping and rustling with his big gait.

"Mack daddy mack daddy," he was chanting.

Ahead of them were the double doors to the tunnel. There would be a short stretch of hallway and then a set of stairs they would have to go up to get to the next level. That stairwell was usually deserted. So that wasn't a good idea. And even of he did get all the way out to the parking lot, it was an empty wasteland and nobody would notice or care if something bad happened there.

Justin stopped and Tee almost fell over him. Justin turned around. "Look," he said, "you want to talk, let's talk. Let's have a seat." He walked back to the food court and Tee followed.

Justin sat at one of the four-chair units. "What can I do for you?"

Tee looked around for a minute before folding himself and sliding into the chair opposite. He must have been wearing ten pounds of clothing. Again, Justin marvelled at their heat on such a day, at the effort of the long subway ride from downtown, or from wherever Tee was coming from, which was quite possibly not downtown.

There were students and staff at every table around them. Nothing could happen here. For a second, Justin hoped that Mike would walk past and see him sitting with this apparition. Justin smiled at him pleasantly. "So. What can I do for you?"

"You know what you can do for me. Money money money."

"You're asking me for money?"

"My money. That you owe me."

Justin tried to laugh. "Listen, I don't know why you're trying to scare me. I don't even know you. I met you once before. There's no possible way I could have anything of yours. Now try to explain to me what makes you think—"

"Don't play me," said Tee, loudly again. "I know you're the bank, you're the bankroll, you want to play the mack daddy, fine—"

"Keep your voice down." Justin's heart was pounding and he knew he was red. He tried to keep his voice even. "I assure you I am not the bank or the bankroll for whatever you think—"

"You buyin me weed, right? You buyin me weed from girlie-girl and you sellin it, right?"

"I am—no, neither, I am neither buying nor selling your weed, I have absolutely no idea what you're—"

"So you buyin from me, means if punanni don't pay me you do."

Justin closed his eyes for a second. "Christ."

"Me na foolin aroun na more." Tee's accent seemed to come and go. "Jenna's a nice girl, I used to like her, I'd help her out. Now it's gone too far."

"How much does she owe you?" Justin was calculating how much cash he had in his wallet. If he could pay it off, if it wasn't a lot, he could just make this whole thing go away.

"Tree unred," said Tee.

"Jesus Christ." Justin breathed deeply. "Jenna. Jenna."

"And I want it now."

"Listen, I'm not even in touch with her. I don't even know where she is." Justin stood up. If he walked with the crowd right now, through the busiest corridor, he would be surrounded by people all the way to the bus stop.

Tee didn't move. "I know she been stayin with you. Wheer you live?"

"No, she hasn't. She was there three, maybe four nights ago. But she's gone now. I think she's left town. Listen, man. Tee. I'll tell her you're looking for her. But I'm really not your guy." Justin wheeled and walked away, as quickly as he could. His heart was racing so fast he felt a little dizzy as he moved. He didn't look behind him. He pushed through the next set of swinging doors and blazed through the next corridor. He had put a few clusters of girls behind him by the time he came to the next doors. He went up a crowded set of stairs and then was on the main level.

Even in the parking lot, he didn't look behind him. He walked in the middle of the roadway till he came to the bus stop, where at least ten people waited. When he was in their midst, he looked back. No one had followed him.

She didn't call until the next evening. He was at home. "Hey," she said sharply. She sounded close by.

"Hey."

"How are you?"

"I'm fine," he said. "I've been missing you. I tried to get hold of you."

There was a silence.

Justin said, "There's stuff I have to talk to you about. How are you, anyway?"

"I'm good," she said. "I got another job."

"Wow," he said, "cool. That's terrific. Where, out in the country?"

"No," she said, "here, downtown. I didn't end up going out to my mother's after all."

"You've been here all this time?"

"So what are you doing this evening?" she said.

"You've been here all this time. Why didn't you return my calls? Did you get my calls?"

"My phone hasn't been working well. So you want to get together or what? I need to get those things from you."

"Things? Those things for Deenie you mean? That's why you're calling me?" Justin was breathing fast again. He felt a burning in his belly as if his dinner was rebelling. There was a fine pain spreading through his chest, as if the tears he had had in the cafeteria were gathering again. "I can't believe this."

"It just didn't work out," she said, "going to my mother's. She wasn't ready for me there. So I stayed here and got a job. Aren't you happy for me?"

Justin tried to breathe deeply. "What kind of job is it?"

"Cocktail waitress. In a good spot. It pays good money. Or it will, anyway, once I get into it."

He looked at the dirty plate on the table in front of him. It was smeared with hardened tomato sauce. He felt a little dizzy. "Where is it?"

"It's in a good place. Just trust me."

"You don't want me to know? Why on earth not? What, are you torturing kittens for a living or what?"

"Listen," she said, and her voice was high, "I am not comfortable with you wanting to keep tabs on me. It's like I have to report to you on where I am all the time."

"Holy shit, Jenna. Relax. What are you talking about?" He got up and away from his dirty plate.

"So you don't have that stuff I asked you for?"

"No I don't. And I don't think I will. I don't feel comfortable with that."

"So you're changing your mind now?"

Wherever he moved in the apartment there were dirty things. He stood out on the fire escape where the signal from the phone was buzzy. "Listen. This is getting out of hand. There's really no need to be upset. It is a little strange, that's all, that you told me you were going away to visit your mother and you stayed here instead and pretended you weren't here. That, to me, is a little, it's a little not—"

"Listen," she said, and her voice was shaky. "I just asked you for one favour, one small thing. It doesn't cost you anything—"

"Yes it does. It costs me one hundred and forty dollars, as a matter of fact."

"Which I will repay you as soon as—"

"This is all you want?" Now his voice was shaky too. "You call me because you want these stupid pills, and you won't even tell me where you've been or why you lied to me or where you're working? How do you think that makes me feel?"

"You're saying I'm a liar now."

"Well aren't you?" And now his voice was loud. He couldn't control it. There was a red fury heaving in his chest. It was sparking out through his fingertips, his hair with little pricks of pain. "What the fuck else are you then? You never planned to go to your mother's at all, did you? You just wanted to get rid of me for a few days, is that right? Isn't that lying?"

"Oh, get upset, that's right. Have your little temper tantrum like a little boy. How old are you anyway?"

"Oh, that's good too. That's very good. You get me really furious and then you make fun of me for it. I've got some fucking goon following me to work and threatening me, because he did, again, I was going to tell you that, by the way, your good friend mister Tee again, if you want to hear it, but I'm not allowed to get angry because then you can say how old are you? That's clever. Every woman knows how to do this, right? They love to ask how old you are." He was aware, as if from a distance, of how stupid and destructive this all was, but it was completely beyond his control now. "Well I'll tell you. A whole lot older than you, let me tell you that. And a whole lot more responsible."

"You know what, little angry man? Why don't you just keep your fucking grimy little apartment all to yourself and stop—"

"And why don't you find some other sucker to—"

"And just fuck right the fuck off." She disconnected.

Justin ducked back into the kitchen and threw the phone onto the table, but not hard enough to break it. Then he went back out to the air to breathe. His chest was constricted. The air he was breathing felt like the gust from an oven when you open the door to check on a piece of pizza.

He waited till this had passed, then went back in to call her again. He called her twice and she did not pick up each time. The second time he left a message saying listen, let's both calm down, I'm sure we're both sorry for the things we said, let's get together and work things out.

Then he drew the new curtains and went to the computer. He had discovered a site where pierced and tattooed girls gave little confessional monologues about their incredibly banal lives and giggled while they removed their clothes and stroked themselves or applied lotion to various parts of their bodies. This was distracting but unarousing. That and the weed soothed him enough to curl up in bed and fade in and out of dreams about roof repair and very high ladders.

17.

He did have enough time, on leaving the house, to make his Business Communications class, as long as he caught a train right away and then a bus before eight-thirty. It was tight, and everything had to run smoothly; there could be no construction on the 400, for example, as there had been. And he had to find all the folders and binders, all the stuff he should have a regular place for so he didn't have to go sifting through piles like this every morning, with a shirt with a collar that was far too hot already and would be drenched even before he wedged himself onto the crowded bus. He cursed and dripped as he sorted his papers. And his head was buzzing from an uneven and largely drugged sleep.

It was at this inopportune moment that his quavery doorbell rang, or rather hummed, whined and failed. There were perhaps batteries in it that needed replacing. This was not his responsibility, it was his landlord's.

It could not be, at this hour of the morning, anyone he actually knew. It would be a Portuguese Jehovah's Witness or a neighbour with an inquiry about a pile of garbage. He snapped up his nylon briefcase thing. The doorbell rang again, and then again. Someone was leaning on it.

"Fucknugget cockgobbler," Justin called. He left his bag on the table and ran down the narrow stairs in his socks. "Douche-prick." He opened the door.

There was the stocky guy, the gangster guy, Deenie's boyfriend. Justin couldn't remember his name.

"Hey," said the guy. He wore a white soccer jersey in some shiny synthetic material. It had gold trim and the word Umbro on it in blue letters. It was kind of flashy in a way that Justin couldn't decide was cool or not. And he wore those long shorts that stop just above the ankle, and tiny little socks above his running shoes.

"Hey," said Justin, and the guy was already moving towards him.

He put one hand on Justin's shoulder and pushed him out of the way. He walked into the narrow stairwell and up.

"Hey," said Justin. "What the fuck."

"Relax, tough guy," he called down. "Just need to talk to you."

Justin followed him up the stairs and into his own kitchen. The guy was already sitting on his kitchen table, flipping the pages of the newspaper.

Justin stood against the fridge and was silent.

"Remember me?" said the guy.

"Deenie," said Justin. "Deenie's guy."

"Armando."

"Armando. We met. You were friendly then."

Armando laughed. "I'm not here to make trouble for anyone. We just need to sort this shit out. Right?"

Justin sighed. "Here we go again. What shit?"

Armando seemed interested in an article. "You're a professor, right?"

Justin was silent.

"My uncle was a schoolteacher. He made good money by the end."

"Sort what shit out," said Justin loudly.

"Don't play me, all right?" said Armando quietly. "I know the game. I've been around long enough to know the game."

"All right," said Justin. "I've had enough of this. I have no idea what you're talking about and I think you know it. So I'm going to call the cops if you don't get the fuck out of my apartment." He turned to where the phone was on the wall but it wasn't there; it was on the kitchen table beside Armando.

"Yeah, all right, tough guy, cool down. Calm down." Armando picked up the phone on the table and put it down again by his beefy thigh. "You really don't know who you're dealing with here, do you?"

"No," said Justin, almost smiling. "I honestly don't." He felt like laughing; it was rather amusing after all. "What is Umbro, anyway?"

"What?"

"Umbro. It's on your shirt. You see it on a lot of soccer shirts. I've always wondered what it means."

Armando looked down at his chest for a second. "Some kind of company, I guess."

"Well, I guessed that. I wondered what kind of company."

"Listen," said Armando. "We don't need to drag this thing out. Jenna has something of mine. I think you know this. Whatever. She needs to know that I wasn't born yesterday. I've been around. I know the game. And she can't play me. She needs to understand this."

"Whatever," said Justin. "Listen, what you need to know is that I have no idea where Jenna is, let alone what she has of yours. She isn't even speaking to me right now."

"Is that right?" Armando grimaced, then reached around and began massaging one part of his back with his hand. "Is that right."

"Yes it is. Now I would like you to leave. I have to get to work."

Armando didn't move. "Listen, if Jenna has a problem, I understand that. She should talk to me. If she has a problem she should talk to me. But she can't play me. Tell her she should know that. We just need to get this thing sorted out."

"Are you threatening her?" said Justin. "What did she do to you?"

Armando eased off the table and stretched his back and arms for a second.

"Because if you are threatening her then I'm going to just call the cops about it."

Armando swivelled his head around on his neck as if warming up. Then he lurched towards Justin and Justin's arms flew up to protect his face. But Armando just put his face right into Justin's. He was smiling. "You're a fucking douchewad, you know that?"

Then he raised his knee and stamped down hard on Justin's toe.

Pain knifed up through Justin's leg and struck cold into his belly. His knees buckled and he was on the floor. His leg was clenched and useless. He was panting.

Armando was at the top of the stairs. "That was dumb, wasn't it?"

Justin felt bubbles of sweat bursting through the skin of his forehead. The pain was receding from his guts but still burning in his ankle and foot; his toe was on fire and throbbing. He got to his knees.

Armando was thumping down the stairs. "Sorry I had to do that," he called. "That doesn't have to happen. You just let her know."

Justin heard the door at the bottom of the stairs open and slam shut.

He stood slowly and shuffled to a chair, where he sat and breathed hard for a while. The pain was not diminishing in his foot. If anything it was growing stronger. It was all-absorbing; he could not think about what to do next until it subsided. He was afraid to try to wiggle his toe or take his shoe off. If it was broken he would have to spend the day in emergency, miss his classes. Mike would love that.

He picked up the phone and called Jenna's cell but of course she didn't answer.

Then he sat and thought some more.

He had to find a phone book because he could never remember the number of his own department at the college and he didn't have it written down anywhere. He tried moaning but it didn't help the pain. He found the number of the college and dialled and then had to push buttons for two more minutes before he could enter the extension for Communications. He got Janice in the end and told her that he was sick and that he had to cancel his classes. She agreed to put a note on the classroom door.

"Wow," she said, "you sound terrible. Get lots of rest."

He tried walking around the kitchen a bit and the burning began to diminish. He went and lay down and felt it throb for a while. But it was subsiding. His body was cooling too, as he had sweated so much. He felt sleepy.

When he had the courage, he slowly took off his shoe and sock. The toe was red and swollen, but it wasn't broken. With pain, he could wiggle it a little, but he knew by the end of the day he wouldn't be able to.

He changed into shorts and a T-shirt and put his shoes back on again. He found that he could walk, if with a limp.

He put on some sunglasses and went into the street. He made sure the front door was locked, and he looked around in every direction before he started off for Deenie's apartment.

He didn't want to buzz up in case anyone inside looked out to see him there. He waited there by the front door in his dark glasses for someone to come in or out. He wished he smoked, as it would look more natural to be out there for a smoke.

Finally an old lady came shuffling out with a shopping buggy. She didn't look at him as he grabbed the door behind her and slipped into the lobby.

Then he couldn't remember which floor was Deenie's. It was apartment 4 on some floor. It wasn't the ground floor.

He tried knocking on 204 and there was no answer.

He went up the stairwell to 304 and knocked there. He heard the insane barking of the dog and a scrabbling of claws.

"Who is it?" came Deenie's voice.

"It's Justin," he called as cheerily as he could. "Jenna's friend."

The door swung open and the dog lunged at him. He put his arms up around his head and neck, but the dog was only licking. He tried to push the dog away but his hands got wet with tongue. "Christ," he said.

"Wow," said Deenie, in the doorway. "She likes you. Come on, stinkie, inside."

He followed the girl and the dog into the apartment. There was no one else there. Deenie wore loose jeans and a spandex tank top with spaghetti straps. She wore no bra and her nipples were huge.

"So I guess you have something for me," said Deenie. She released the dog again and Justin had to fight off the frantic tongue again.

"Oh those things," he said. "I ordered them. For you. They won't be here for a week or so."

"Oh, those," she said. "No. I mean, that's cool. But that's not what I meant. I thought you had something else for me."

Justin laughed. "Everybody seems to think that. It's like being in some kind of mystery movie. It's sheer Kafka."

"Amanda, leave him alone. No kisses."

"I just had a visit from your boyfriend."

"Oh." She stared at him for a second then, her face confused. "When was that?"

"Just now. He was very angry about something."

"Oh." Frowning, Deenie sat, folded her legs and her bare feet under her, and reached for a pack of cigarettes on the coffee table. "And you have no idea about what."

"No I don't. I was hoping you or Jenna would tell me."

She lit a cigarette and Justin felt his stomach curl a little at the airplane hangar smell. There was no air in the room to start with. "Well," she said, exhaling, "you won't find her here, as I'm sure you already know."

"Good Christ," said Justin, "why is everybody always telling me that I know things? Where is she?" He pushed the dog off roughly.

"I have no idea," said Deenie evenly, reaching out and grabbing Amanda's collar. "You *sit*. She hasn't been here for a week now. And something disappeared from this apartment at exactly the same time she left. Something of Armando's, that I was keeping for him. And now we can't find her. Isn't that strange?"

"Okay." Justin breathed deeply. "I get it. Well, you tell Armando that I have no idea where she is either and I have nothing of his. Okay?"

Deenie shrugged. Her nipples protruded like rivets—what had she been doing, breast-feeding?—and it was impossible not to stare. They were there for no reason but to suck on, and to see them was to think of sucking on them, and surely she must know that?

Justin said, "And if you see her, Jenna, you tell her I would love to talk to her too." He backed towards the door.

"Yeah, well, you do the same for us." She released Amanda's collar and the dog bounded up to him again.

He tried grabbing her giant head to stroke it but she was too frenzied; she kept trying to lick and bite him. He pushed his outstretched fingertips into her neck the way Jenna had shown him to do and she lay down and rolled over. "Good *girl*," he said. He rubbed her belly and she writhed. "She really does like me."

Back out on the street, he put his sunglasses on again. The sun had gone yellow and brutal. He didn't know where to go next. He had the whole day ahead of him. He hobbled along the sidewalk trying not to put weight on the one foot.

He got on an eastbound streetcar for a few minutes of air conditioning. He got off where the cafés started to thicken on the street. He thought he would have a coffee in the sun somewhere, pretend he was living a normal life.

He was scanning a terrace full of blondes with laptops when he saw her crossing the street. She had huge sunglasses on, and a baseball cap, but he recognized the bushel of blazing white ropes. She had a loose top on and her camouflage pants, as if she had not changed since he saw her last. He watched her walk across the street in the way she could not disguise, her little hips gliding as if on springs. She walked as she danced; she walked to make people want to fuck her.

He was on the other side of the street from her. He kept up with her as she strode past a few cafés. She didn't seem to be looking for anyone.

He crossed and came up behind her. He called her name and she didn't respond. He walked as quickly as he could and came up alongside her. "Hi," he said. "Hey. Jenna."

She looked over at him and didn't stop walking. "Hey," she said. "What's up?"

"Oh, not much," he said. "I've been looking for you. Would you slow down a second?"

"I don't have a lot of time."

"Oh, come on, Jenna." He stopped and she stopped too. She looked up and down the street. "So what's up?"

"Someone just tried to hurt me. Did hurt me in fact."

Now she looked at him, over the rims of her black glasses. Her eyes were pale. "Who?"

"Your friend Armando. Deenie's good buddy. Came to my apartment to threaten me, and then stomped on my foot and damn near broke it. That makes two guys trying to hurt me to get to you. And I have no idea why."

"Are you okay?"

"I don't know. It's all swollen. And I'm limping."

"Oh, shit." Her face twisted and he knew she was going to cry again.

"Listen," he said, "let's sit down. Have a coffee. Relax a little bit. I need to know what's going on, and what we can do about it."

She nodded, and he took her hand—this was the moment that would tell him if she was going to fight him or go soft again, and she went soft and limp like a child—and led her onto the terrace of a place called something like Concubine. They sat in the sun and it was not unpleasant. Around them were couples having breakfast as if it were a weekend. They were probably waiters who didn't have to be at work till five. There was a pretty student with her books and her laptop. There was a business couple in their hot jackets and their communications devices laid out on the table like chess pieces. They had file folders with their business plans and they were nodding and smiling and reassuring each other that the opportunities were there.

Justin hated them all, hated them and envied them with something more than envy, it was a longing to be not impatient with them, not bored by them, to have nothing to worry about but breakfast and the newspaper, to not feel superior about their wimpy little dogs—there was some kind of white poodle sheepdog thing flopped under the breakfast couple's table—because he would always prefer a bigger, stronger, scarier dog—what was he thinking, exactly? He wished he were somebody else.

"I'm sorry about Armando," she said in her small voice.

"Huh," said Justin. The gay waiter was on them and Justin ordered them cappuccinos. "It's on me," he said after the waiter had spun away. "So fill me in. What's Armando looking for?"

"Nothing that I have, that's one thing," she said.

"Jenna, I'm not fucking around any—"

"All right, okay, chill, I'm telling you."

"Okay. Okay."

She sighed. "Okay. Armando is missing something that he left in Deenie's apartment."

"That she was taking care of for him. I know that part already. It was drugs, I suppose."

"It was some coke. Justin, I don't do coke, okay? I wouldn't touch it. I hate that stuff."

"Okay. Okay. So why would Deenie have it in her apartment?"

"Because he doesn't want it on him."

"All right." Justin scanned the street. It was so pretty, so flowery and domestic. The delivery trucks were roaring up and the men slamming their doors and greeting the shop owners and people were sweeping the street and laughing and rolling out café awnings. It was like a set; it was like a children's movie about a town; perhaps they would all break into a song. "All right. Treat me like a complete idiot, okay, because this stuff must be obvious to you but it takes me a while to figure it out. Armando and Deenie are both dealers, is that right?"

"Deenie? No, God no. No no no." Her voice was slightly louder and she seemed genuinely startled by this idea. "Deenie doesn't want anything to do with it. But he can't have a large quantity—listen, Justin, you know you can't mention this to anyone in any way, don't you?"

"Of course not."

"I mean seriously, not your closest friends, not anyone you talk to. Not even as a joke, or to show off, you know—"

"Show off? What kind of guy—"

"Shh." She put his hand over his and her skin was cool. "I know guys. And they want to show off. I'm not saying you. You just need to know that I'm really serious, it would be a really bad idea to spread the word about this to anyone, in all kinds of ways. God."

"Okay, okay. Don't worry, I won't." And Justin was sad for her again, seeing her so shaky and worried in this make-believe world of threats and traitors. It couldn't be really that bad.

The gay waiter arrived with their coffees and was cheery about it; the café owner was out standing on the street with his hairy forearms folded and calling jokes to a guy getting off a motorcycle, who yelled back. Everyone was laughing. There were long-haired girls gliding by on bicycles, wearing bikini tops and shorts. Even they seemed to be smiling. "Okay," said Justin, "I promise not to say anything to anyone. Now listen. Did Armando threaten you too?"

"Oh yeah." She threw her hair back and laughed a little. "He sure did."

"Really? What did he do? Did he hurt you?"

"No no. He wouldn't hurt me." She sounded scornful. "He just plays the big man. He thinks he's a lot tougher than he is."

"He seemed pretty tough to me," said Justin.

"He's good at scaring people if they don't seem like they're going to . . . whatever, anyway. I have nothing to do with what's missing, and he's going to find his stuff, or who has it, and he'll calm down and everything will be back to normal."

"So what did he say to you?"

"Oh, he was just all cool, like I know what's going on, just happened to let me see the gun in his coat, like—"

"Gun? Gun. The gun in his coat. Jesus Christ. The gun in his coat. You sure it was a gun?"

"He has a gun like all drug dealers, Justin." She spoke slowly. "They all have guns."

"Oh good. Good. Now I know. Silly me. Of course. All drug dealers have guns."

"They just think they have to."

"Okay," he said. "So how much coke is he missing?"

She looked down. She had hardly touched her coffee. She put a teaspoon in it and took it out again. "I don't know. I'm not sure. A lot."

"How much."

"I think—I'm not sure—but I think it was around three Gs."

"Three grams? Is that a lot? I have no idea."

"No no. Not grams. Three grams is only an eight, that's only two hundred and fifty bucks. I mean three large. Three thousand."

"Three thousand dollars? Three thousand dollars' worth of coke?"

"That's why he's kind of upset."

"So there was three thousand dollars' worth of cocaine in that apartment when I was there?"

"I don't know, Justin, honestly I don't. I didn't want to know anything about it. I swear to you."

Justin sat back. He took off his sunglasses and wiped his face. The day went from yellow to white. It was bleached. His toe throbbed. "How much is that, in terms of weight?"

"Don't know. A small brick. It would be wrapped in plastic. I don't even know where they were hiding it. Listen, a lot of people come into that apartment. It could have been anyone. He thinks it's me because I had a kind of a fight with Deenie and I left. Then it went missing."

"Huh. So he thinks you—and by extension I—owe him three thousand dollars. And by the way he has a gun."

"You know, it's not really that—"

"Do you ever think of just going to the police?"

"Don't you ever think of that," she said sharply. "Deenie is my friend, the closest friend I've ever had. And she doesn't want to be involved in this either."

"Well then, explain to me why she keeps ... no, don't. Forget it. Forget it. Okay. There's still one more thing you haven't told me. About this fight with Deenie. Where did you go?"

She pushed her coffee away and stared at the street. She stared without moving for some time. Justin thought she wasn't going to answer him or even move any part of her body ever again when she said, "So Armando came right into your apartment, right?"

"Yes. He did."

"You might want to think about changing your locks."

Justin thought about this. "Why?"

"Armando has ... kind of a way with things like that. If he's been inside, he'll figure a way out. I mean a way in."

"Okay," said Justin evenly. "I'll change my locks. You were telling me. Where you'd been."

She said, "Do you ever wonder if all the people around you are really people?"

Justin coughed. "You mean if they're illusions?"

230

"No, if they're just, I don't know, masks. If they really have brains like yours. Or if they're . . . if they see everything differently and have different reasons for doing things. Like they're some other kind of animal. Like how do you know what a cat thinks?"

"Huh. This is kind of like your am-I-the-only-brain-in-the-universe thought." Justin glanced at his watch. It was only nine-thirty.

"Sort of. But I mean . . . I can never know that if you and I see a colour, like the green thing over there, that we both see the same colour? We just call it the same colour."

"Yeah." Justin yawned. "Let's talk about that. Anything but about where you went for the past five days."

She sighed and frowned. "It's not a big deal. I wasn't anywhere. Deenie and I just weren't getting along so well. I don't get along with people. Maybe I just can't live with people. With girls, anyway."

"So where did you stay."

"I had a friend's apartment. They were away. It was nice, actually."

"They," said Justin, smiling.

"What?"

"Nothing. *They* were away. My students always say that. Nothing. So you just didn't want to see me for a while."

"Sometimes," she said, still staring at the street, "I don't want to see anyone. I didn't want to see you, Deenie, anyone. I'm sorry if it was mean. It wasn't about you." She looked at him and took her sunglasses off and her eyes were violently blue and red-rimmed. "I like you very much, Justin. And you've been really good to me. I didn't mean to hurt you."

Justin folded his fingers into hers.

She said, "I'm just a fuckup. Sometimes I don't want to talk to anyone because I just don't want to answer any questions. I don't want to have to explain what I'm doing or not doing, like why I don't have a job and why I might spend a half a day smoking weed on the couch. I feel guilty about it, I guess."

"Jenna," said Justin. "Are you seeing somebody else?"

"What?"

He withdrew his hand from hers. "You heard me."

"I can't believe you would ask me that."

"It's not such a ridiculous question."

She said, "You really don't get me, do you."

"Obviously not."

"Justin, I'm not like that. I can't sleep with more than one person. Unlike you, obviously."

"What?"

"Well, I wouldn't even think of that. The fact that you asked me means that's what you're thinking about."

"Jesus Christ," said Justin. "That doesn't even make the remotest—"

"What about you?" she said. "What did you get up to while I was away?"

"While you were—you weren't even away, as it turns out."

"Well, whatever."

"Listen," he said, "I'm not even going to answer that or I'll get angry, and there's no point to that. Let's talk about your new job. Can you talk about that?"

She screwed up her forehead. "Oh. You're not going to like it."

"Uh-huh."

"But it's good. I'm making good money for once."

"So you're a mercenary. You're going to Iraq to protect the oil executives. What."

"It's just cocktail waitress. I told you."

"But."

"But it's in a strip club."

Justin laughed. "Well, that doesn't sound so bad. You don't have to do it topless or anything, do you?"

"No. I have to wear a kind of a stupid outfit, it's a white shirt with a black bowtie which is lame-ass unsexy, but they don't want you to compete with the girls. They want to make it clear who's a waitress. I can wear a short skirt though."

"Cool. I have no problem with that. I've been to a strip club before. Although I can only remember it vaguely. Which one is it?"

"You wouldn't know it. It's on the east side. But it's a pretty good one, it's not sketchy. There's lots of businessmen and stuff. But I don't want you to come by. I'd be embarrassed."

"All right. Sure."

"The problem is I'm only getting two shifts a week right now and that hardly pays for the Metropass. They say next month I'll get a few more."

"Uh huh." Justin felt, like a person walking behind him, a request coming up.

"So I'm still totally fucked with this Tee situation. He's becoming a pain."

"Yes," said Justin, "he paid me a visit too. At my work. I almost paid him off just to get rid of him, but then I didn't know where you were and . . ."

"There is one favour you could do for me," said Jenna. "I could do it, but it would be better if you did. It would help me out a lot."

Justin put his sunglasses back on to soften the glare of her hair and the pain in her eyes. He looked at the happy street and all the people with their boring little lives. He had no urge, really, to be in on that business meeting with all the cellphones on the table. He wanted to sleep with Jenna again, every night. He wanted her naked with him that afternoon. He wanted her white belly and thighs. "What can I do for you," he said.

18.

And this is how he came to be standing, that Friday afternoon, on an industrial strip of street far from downtown, a street
of auto mechanics and warehouses, waiting for some guy called
Devonne or possibly Devawn who would see him there and
come out to him. He had taken two buses to get here and then,
from the unbelievably depressing intersection of Lansdowne and
Dupont, where there were a gas station and a coffee shop and a
lot of trucks coming out of blackened factories, he had walked
north. At least there was a big hardware store near there, where
he could go afterwards to inquire about getting new locks and
how to install them. That idea was almost as stressful as this current mission.

He had found the railway lines and walked along them until
he found the street and the house. The tracks ran along one side
of the street and were guarded by a metal fence. There was no
sidewalk along that side but a strip of grass with a path worn in it,
and he had walked along that until he had found Mundial Auto
Repair and the house was right beside that, a sole residential

house in a street of concrete boxes. It was brick painted brown and the windows on the ground floor were blocked with cardboard boxes. There were open windows on the second floor and Justin stood across the street as he had been told to do and looked up at those windows, because someone would be looking out of them at him.

There was no bench, no tree, nothing to lean against except the chain link fence along the tracks. This made him look so obviously like a guy waiting for a drug deal that he had to smile. The whole idea of sending him was to keep this surreptitious, as people in this neighbourhood might recognize Jenna if she were to show up (particularly Tee, who used to live in this house and was known to pass by from time to time), and he began to reconsider this logic, standing there, as he was possibly the least congruous element in this whole heterogeneous scene. He was quite obviously not a mechanic on his lunch break.

For future ventures like these, were there to be any, he would have to buy some of those long shorts that Armando and guys like him wore, and maybe a European soccer team jersey. He wouldn't look so bad in the bright yellow and green of Brazil, but he knew he couldn't carry it off.

There was really nothing more idiotic than what he was doing, and yet he felt like smiling and wasn't sure exactly why; perhaps it was at the idea that he was even considering wearing a soccer jersey in colours not found in nature.

Every time a car rumbled along the potholed road he studied it to see if it was an unmarked police car. Most of the cars that passed were small and had tinted windows and booming from within.

He wished he had brought a bottle of water.

There was really no danger to this, though, no exchange of cash: the guy Devonne was fronting Jenna a small quantity of weed because he liked her. Jenna could easily sell this in the new place where she worked, God help her—Justin wasn't going to think about this part—and thus easily earn back the three hundred bucks she owed Tee. Tee was really the only problem, Armando wasn't, Armando would find out who took his brick and leave her alone. It was probably Deenie anyway, and he'd figure that out and leave everybody alone.

The girls at work were apparently always looking for weed. There wasn't nearly enough around to satisfy the demand. This would bear some thinking about later, too. There wasn't enough weed circulating in a strip club in the east end. This was strange, but he would think about it later. Now he just had to say hello to Devonne, get the bag and leave.

He had to do this because he wasn't a heatscore like Jenna. "I'm not a heatscore," he said aloud.

There had been no twitch of curtain or anything in the windows. But it had only been ten minutes or so. He didn't suppose drug dealers were terribly precise about times. He sat on the dusty ground.

After a half hour of near-insane boredom, the door of the house opened and a burly black man gestured to him. Justin got up and walked over. The guy in the door was older than he had expected: his dreadlocks were mostly grey and he had a sparse grey beard. He was wearing a kitchen apron and wiping his hands on a towel and smiling. "Justin, ya," he said, shaking hands wetly. "Come in, come on in. I'm cookin." He turned and walked down the dark hall which rang with reggae music and Justin had no choice but to follow him. It was a slight deviation from plan but nothing to get uptight about. He seemed friendly enough.

And he was friendly, very friendly. The house was thick with curry smell; in the cramped kitchen he was stirring a stock pot full of a yellow stew. "Oxtail," he called, "for my family." He stirred and splashed yellow on the yellow surfaces. Justin was sweating; it was a humid oven in there and the curry was overpowering. The reggae was so loud he had to shout. "You're Jenna's friend, ya. Good friend of mine. Sweet girl ya. You tell Jenna I miss her and am thinkin of her. I'm happy to help her out." He laughed and jiggled. He was quite fat, really.

The jovial cook. It was really quite a cliché. Justin was smiling as hard as he could.

Devonne offered him a taste of stew or even a whole bowl and assured him many times of its quality. It took some effort to refuse the many entreaties. Justin accepted a bottle of Ting and an offer to sit at the kitchen table. There were stacks of poker chips and neat packs of cards on the table.

Devonne wiped his hands and sat with him. He pushed stacks of chips to one side, careful not to upset them. Justin helped him.

"You play?" said Devonne.

"Poker?" said Justin. "No. Have played."

"You want to play, any time, you let me know. Friend of Jenna."

"You run a game from here?" Justin tried to keep a straight face, saying this. He didn't even know if this was the right phrase.

"Shit, no, mon. We got a place. You want in, I let you know."

Justin coughed. "I don't know. High stakes?"

"No, not really. Whatever stakes you want. Small, big, different tables. Good for a beginner, if you are."

"I'm not much of a gambler."

Devonne laughed. He was fumbling under the table for something. "Oh, I think you are. You here, you are." From under the table he pulled a clear plastic bag and put it on the table. "Everybody's a gambler, you know."

Justin was not good at judging these things, but the bag contained what must have been a pound of marijuana. It could have been two pounds. It was the size of a medium Kitchen Catcher but it was clear and tightly packed. Devonne also produced some stained and ancient scales.

Justin sweated with abandon. The whole idea of this deal was that the guy would have measured the stuff already and Justin wouldn't have to be inside here with all this stuff. If a SWAT team had burst in at that moment, he would not have been surprised. But still it was kind of cool to see that much weed. It was a story he could tell later. But then of course it wasn't.

Devonne chattered and laughed as he measured out the stuff, but Justin could hardly hear him over the music. He was talking about his kids and the joy of having kids, mostly. Justin didn't seem required to say anything much.

Justin's segment was about half of what was in the bag. Devonne wrapped it tightly in several layers of cling film, and then wrapped that in an opaque black film, but it was still larger than Justin had imagined. It would barely fit in a pocket. He would have to carry it in his hand.

"You want a grocery bag or somethin?" said Devonne, frowning for a second. He gave Justin a yellow plastic No Frills bag and Justin was able to leave.

"You tell Jenna," said Devonne, "she ever want to play again, we got the game running."

"Jenna plays poker?"

"She'll kill your ass."

"I bet she will."

"Or you want to get in, you let me know."

"How do I reach you?"

"Jenna knows."

On the front steps, Justin breathed in the carbon monoxide air, as it was much fresher than the curry air.

He tucked his yellow bag up under his arm and began to walk briskly.

At the end of the street, about a half a block away, was a police car with two policemen in it.

Justin kept walking. He would have to pass the car to reach the intersection. He could turn around and walk the other way but he suspected this street was a dead end because of the railway tracks.

As he walked towards the car, one of the policemen looked up at him and then they both got out.

Justin stopped then. He could possibly vault the fence and run down the railway tracks, flinging his package into the bushes. But then it would be ignominious if he got caught or stuck or simply didn't make it over. He wasn't in the best of shape. And the cops were bigger than he was and could probably get over it too. He could turn and run down one of the alleys between the buildings. Or he could just stand there, which is what he did.

The cops approached him and one of them said, "Hey there."

"Hey," said Justin, looking at their guns as they bobbed on their belts. The handles of the pistols were matte black and thick.

The two men stood in front of Justin and put their hands on their hips. They were both young white guys. "That your car?"

"Sorry?"

"That one. It's blocking the drive."

"Oh. No. No. No, it's not."

"You know whose it is? It's been there two days and we got a call about it. They can't get cars in and out of the garage."

His mouth was dry and his tongue was thick. "No," was all he could say. "Nope."

"You live around here?"

For a second he thought he was going to cry. He shook his head. He shrugged, as if to show he was a simpleton who was baffled by everything.

"All righty," said one of the cops. "Have a good one." And they turned to knock on Devonne's door.

Justin walked away at a moderate pace, and then when he rounded the corner accelerated. He couldn't quite run, as he might still be in sight of the car, but he walked like one of the racers in those funny walk competitions. The rules were you had to have one foot on the ground at all times. If you lifted both feet off the ground in a springy step then you were running.

He made it to Dupont, which was busy with traffic, and then almost ran, sort of cantered to Lansdowne. He ran this way almost ten blocks and then calmed a bit. He was almost at the subway station, which he could disappear into like a gopher down a hole.

His sweat was evaporating now and cooling him. His yellow package was slick. He wrapped the bag as tightly as he could and stuffed it into his shorts pocket. He could swallow again.

He looked up at the sky, which was astoundingly blue. He felt a bit high.

A pretty Portuguese girl passed him in her short denim skirt and he smiled boldly at her and she looked away, but she was smiling a little too. He laughed out loud. He felt like sex right then, like fucking someone then and there, and then a long nap.

There, a half a block away, was New World Lumber, fortified with barbed wire and metal fences like an outpost in the desert. He had to do the stupid lock thing in there.

With his hand on the package distorting his shorts, he walked in, trying to look like a contractor. It was at least air-conditioned. It was a sprawling hangar that smelled of paint and wood, and there were groups of men around the counters, shouting. Nobody looked at him.

He waited near the counter for a while before he saw the dispenser for paper numbers. He took one that said 105. The electric sign above the counter said 87, so he wandered a bit through the store.

There was a room of plumbing fixtures, and lots of electrical outlets, but no locks. There was an entrance to a warehouse full of lumber. There were some pretty walls of paint chips. There was a wall of fishing tackle which distracted him for a moment. The rods were gorgeous, all metallic greens and blues and reels that looked like robotic surgical equipment. Justin had no interest in fishing, but he wanted one of these.

Next to them, behind glass, was a row of rifles and shotguns which were equally absorbing. And in a display counter with a glass top were handguns. He peered at these for a while, his scalp prickling a little, as they made him think of all the silly things he was doing, but they were so solid and menacing you just had to stare at them. It seemed strange you could just buy a handgun so easily.

Some were all black and some a mixture of silver and black. They were all automatics. He looked for the smallest one. There was a squat silver one with a short barrel and a heavy magazine. The tag on it said "Lifelike! Walther PPK!" The price was only $120, which seemed ridiculous, and then he realized that these were not guns at all. There were boxes of BBs and pellets in the same case. They were BB guns, designed as replicas. Of course it was illegal to just walk into a hardware store and buy a handgun. Although it wasn't clear why one would want a BB gun that looked exactly like a Walther PPK. Just for fun, possibly. It was kind of fun. He stared at the Walther for a while and wondered how heavy it would feel in the hand.

He heard a number being called and walked back over to the counter. They were at 91. His sweat had cooled on him and he began to shiver. He threw his paper tag on the floor and pushed through the doors out to the glare.

In the heat, he walked slowly, but he kept looking behind him. It was not relaxing. He was aware of his package again. And there was the entrance to the subway, cool and dim.

19.

"Finally."

"What?" he said.

"Oh hi. Sorry."

"You thought I was someone else. Again. Who is it you are having these conversations with? Whoever he is pisses you off a lot. Does he hang up a lot on you in mid-sentence or what?" Justin had taken his shirt off and was catching the late afternoon sun from between the houses on his fire escape. He felt healthy. He felt he would join a gym someday, or go running or perhaps a triathlon.

"What's up your ass?" she said.

"No, seriously. Who is it you're waiting for all the time?"

"Did something go wrong?"

"No it did not. It went very smoothly. With one amusing hitch that I'll tell you about when I see you. You want to come over now?"

"I'm getting ready for work."

"You want to come over before you go to work? I wouldn't mind you taking—taking over from here."

"Yeah," she said. "Okay. But I can't stay at all, like at all at all."

"No problem." He disconnected without saying goodbye. That was only going to make her crankier when she arrived.

He closed his eyes in the sun. He would have to try to calm down a little. He felt like yelling at someone but it probably didn't have to be Jenna. He breathed deeply until the sun had passed behind the house.

Then he went back into his stuffy bedroom and fucked his bed hard until he sprayed wet into his sheets.

He dozed for a half hour and got up and took a shower. In the shower he thought about how he was going to pass his evening if Jenna wasn't going to be around. He thought too, he couldn't help it, about how Jenna was going to pass her evening and why she wouldn't answer him about who the hell she was expecting on the phone all the time. And about why the fuck she wouldn't tell him where she was working. He asked himself if he trusted Jenna and the answer was yes he did.

When he was dressed she still wasn't there and so he walked to the beer store. He didn't leave a note for her because she could fuck herself if she showed up when he wasn't there. It might show her what it was like to spend your life waiting for someone.

He knew this was no mood to meet her in.

When he was waiting in line at the beer store there was a harsh electronic bleeping which annoyed him until he noticed that people were turning their heads to look at him, which indicated that it was coming from his pocket. This was the first time his cellphone had ever rung. He had no idea it would sound like an alarm on a factory floor. It took him a minute to extricate it from his pocket, during which time it seemed to grow louder.

"Customer service," he said to his phone.

"Hey star," said Jenna. "You're not home."

"No, I'm not," he said. "Where are you?"

"Standing at your frigging front door looking like a douche."

"Ah," he said. "I got tired of waiting for you and I went to get some beer. I'll be there in ten minutes." Before she could reply he folded his phone. If she wasn't there in ten minutes it would be her problem. He was aware again, as if of a buzzing noise that was just low enough not to be noticeable for a while, of a sourness at the bottom of his belly, a slowly turning nausea that was the inevitable result, these days, of any telephonic contact with Jenna.

The line inched forward. He really wanted a beer.

She was sitting on his doorstep, right on the street. She wasn't dressed for work: she was wearing her white yoga pants and a tank top. She looked like one of those ads for American underwear. She had an old blue knapsack which pierced him with a quick sadness, perhaps because it must have been something she had taken to high school with her, not all that long ago.

She had her head down on her knees. He said hi as nonchalantly as he could and stepped past her to unlock the door. She followed him quietly up the staircase.

"You want a beer?" he said.

"I'm late for work now."

"Sorry," he said. "I thought you were coming right over."

She sat at his kitchen table. "So how did it go."

He cracked his beer. It wasn't quite cold enough, but it tasted like blue ocean in an ad for a resort. He drained a quarter of it before he answered. "Kind of funny," he said.

He told her the story of the jovial cook and then his encounter with the cops. She didn't laugh. "Anyway," he said, "here's your stuff. Go nuts." He pulled the yellow No Frills bag out of a kitchen drawer and pushed it across the table at her.

He watched her open it and examine its contents. She was frowning as she did it but she was probably just concentrating. She unwrapped the layers of cling film and pulled out a tuft of herb. It was a dusty greeny grey. She pulled it apart in her palm and Justin could smell the muddy hay smell from across the room. "That Devonne," he said, "he's okay. Funny."

"I bet," she said, "he's your new best bud."

"He tried to be, yeah. He wanted me to come to a poker game."

She was sniffing the weed.

"I've always kind of wanted to try that," he said. "Poker for money."

She put a strand of green on her tongue.

"I used to be okay at it, in school," he said. "Never played for money though."

"You want to play in a poker game for money with strangers. With D."

"Yeah. He said it wasn't all that high stakes."

"Justin, I don't think that's really you."

"I watch it a lot on TV. And I've done it online. Anyway, he said I could find out where it was through you."

"Okay, star."

"He said you were pretty good at it."

She sighed, put the piece of crushed grass back in the plastic. "I don't think you're ready for that, star."

"Oh. Thanks very much. For your vote of confidence."

She was rewrapping the package. She put it back in the yellow bag and said very quietly, "Thank you very much, Justin."

He sat down at the table and took her hand, which was cool. She closed her eyes and put her forehead down on their hands. It was damp, a little clammy. "I owe you so much," she said to the tabletop.

"No, you don't," he murmured. He stroked her head and her neck and her arm. Her skin was calming to touch. He felt every invisible hair under his fingertips.

He felt the familiar warm liquid on his hand as she cried silently. It didn't alarm him as much as it once did. He tried to squeeze the muscles of her shoulders but it was awkward. He said, "I just hope it helps you out now. And I hope you don't get in this fucked-up situation again. Now that you're working."

She shuddered and hauled herself upright. "You have a tissue," she said soberly. "I have to do my makeup again."

He got up and looked for something she might use. He said, "I thought you had to wear a uniform."

"I do. It's at work. They have lockers."

"Huh. All I have is paper towel."

"I'll have to use your washroom for a minute."

"Sure. So how late do you have to work? You want to come over here after?"

"No, star, it'll be super late."

He didn't say anything. He waited for her to finish in the washroom.

When she came out she hugged him tight for a few minutes, then took his face in her hands and kissed him long and wetly. She ground against him until he was hard and then shivered against him and sighed.

"Come by afterwards," he said.

She said, "I can be a little late for work." She began to undo his belt.

He pushed the strands of fabric off her shoulders and kissed them. He pulled the top slowly off her breasts, and they sprang free. He kissed her nipples. Then he pulled back. "Jenna," he said, "will you tell me where you've been staying?"

She put her head on his shoulder and pulled him against her. "I've been staying at a friend's apartment," she said very softly. "He's away and he's lent me his apartment. He's not a boyfriend. He's just a friend. There is nothing for you to worry about."

Justin stood there, stroking her bare shoulders with his fingertips. There was a numbness spreading through him, as if his muscles were stiffening.

"I wouldn't cheat on you," she murmured to his neck.

"So where did you meet him?" said Justin.

"I've known him for a long time."

"What does he do? Why is he such a mystery man?"

She pulled away from him and pulled up her top. She snapped the straps into place. She wiped her face and turned from him. She leaned against the fridge. "I don't like it that you don't trust me."

"I don't like it either, believe me."

"So you don't. You don't trust me."

"I'm just curious. I just don't know why everything has to be a big secret. I tell you everything."

"Oh do you."

"Yes I do."

Jenna was stiff and staring at him. Here eyes were blue again, a bluer blue, in the dim apartment.

"What?" he said.

"You tell me everything."

"What?"

She picked her blue knapsack up off the floor and fumbled in it. She pulled out a curled strip of yellow paper. She handed it to him. "What's this then?"

He took it and unrolled it. It was a square sticky note. On it was loopy ballpoint that said, "Enjoy these, sweetie! J."

Justin laughed. "Where did you find this? You going through my papers?"

"It was on the floor. I was trying to clean up for you."

"No, it wasn't on the floor, it was stuck to a red folder that had a pile of transcripts inside it. And the folder was in my briefcase."

"It must have fallen off."

"It must have. It must have. That's funny, though, because I haven't taken it out of my briefcase yet. Not in here I haven't. Anyway, it's from the departmental secretary, Janice. She's nice that way."

"I bet she is."

Justin laughed again, this time a little higher. "Jenna, I hardly know her. I work with her. She's the secretary."

"And she calls you sweetie?"

"Sometimes sweetheart, too. Sometimes babe. She calls everybody that. Even the women. Listen, this is getting silly."

They both stood there breathing hard and staring at each other.

"It's kind of a joke," said Justin. "She knew I didn't want to go through everyone else's test scores. She's being sarcastic."

"I want to trust you," said Jenna. "I really do."

"Hey," said Justin, "you're the one hiding out in some guy's apartment."

She dropped her bag and put her face into her hands.

"Whoa," said Justin.

When her voice came, it was high and whiny. "What do you think this means to me, Justin? You think I'm like this with everybody?" Now she was really crying again. "You think I just jump into bed with people? You think I would let anyone do what I let you do to me?"

"Do to you?"

"You think this doesn't mean a lot to me? You could really really . . ." Then she just sobbed for a moment, really wailing, her face red and twisted and her shoulders shuddering.

"Whoa," he said. He wrapped his arms around her and cradled her. "I could what?" He wondered if the downstairs people could hear her wailing. He waited for the convulsions to subside. "Jenna. I could what?"

"You could really hurt me," she wailed, "if you wanted to."

"Okay," he said, rubbing her bumpy back. "I won't. I won't. I wouldn't hurt you."

"I wouldn't," she hiccuped. "I wouldn't cheat on you."

He kissed her violently and ripped her top down. He cupped her ass and kissed her shoulders. He cupped her between the legs and rubbed her there. She had her hands down his pants and was clutching at him. Her face was salty with tears. He got his hands inside her underwear and found her wet there. He pushed her towards the bedroom.

When he had her down on the bed and kissing her bare breasts he had an unfortunate sensation. She was limp; compliant but unenthusiastic. Of course she was tense about their fight and getting to work, of course, but she might also have been thinking about someone else. It was really unpleasant to think about, as he nuzzled her trimmed cleft with his nose, but it was not impossible that she had done this already somewhere else today. He couldn't fight the idea of someone else kissing her there. He imagined for a second that someone else's saliva had been on her.

He fucked her briskly and she moaned and wailed a lot although he didn't think she came. He pulled out and shot an arc of semen across her belly and breasts, which was something he had fantasized about, he didn't know why. And as he lay there panting and sweaty beside her, the image was on him of someone else's stickiness on her. He couldn't relax; he was buzzing.

She said nothing. After a few minutes she got up and went into the bathroom. He heard the shower running.

He got dressed, fighting the image of someone else's vile mucus on her white skin. "Fuck *nugget*," he yelled, to clear it.

He watched her dress.

Picking up her knapsack, she said, "I don't want you to wait up all night for me. I'll call you tomorrow."

He smacked her bum as she left and watched her flit down the stairs. Then he went to the bathroom window, which looked out onto the street, and watched her walk away.

She didn't walk towards the subway; she walked in the opposite direction.

He hit the soap dish with the back of his hand and it snapped across the room and shattered, leaving ceramic shards and soap scum all over the walls and floor.

After cleaning up the broken soap dish, he went to his computer and looked up all the strip clubs in the city. This was silly; he couldn't go to them all.

He looked at porn for a while. It was idiotic. And he didn't even open Sandstorm III (Sheikh Assassin). He had no urge to play.

Then he typed in "Walther PPK" and learned that it was a blowback-operated semiautomatic manufactured by Carl Walther GmbH Sportwaffen in Germany and under licence from Walther in France and the United States. PPK stood for Polizeipistole Kriminalmodell, which apparently meant Police Detective Pistol Model, not criminal model. These pistols featured an exposed hammer, a double-action trigger mechanism, a single-column magazine, and a fixed barrel which also acted as the guide rod for the recoil spring. The pictures looked exactly like the BB gun in the hardware store.

It was James Bond's favourite weapon.

All this was more interesting than porn.

He typed in "Walther PPK buy" and found The Gun Warehouse which offered him one for $505.99 used, and new from the manufacturer for $579. Of course they would not ship firearms directly to any consumer. Nor would they ship outside the United States or its possessions, including Guam and Puerto Rico.

20.

There were, according to touristic websites, only three strip clubs worth checking in the east end, and two of them were so seedy he doubted the waitresses wore uniforms. The one pretentious one was the Manor, and it was one tedious streetcar ride from the subway. The streetcar took him past prostitutes on the street whose gender he couldn't ascertain. Most were rather tall.

He remembered something and pulled out his cellphone. He dialled Deenie's number. There was no answer and he hung up before the message came on.

Then there were dark parks and wide open streets with queues outside shelters. Then there were just dark buildings. It was just before eleven.

His phone buzzed.

"Hey," said a girl. "You just call me?"

"Oh, hi Deenie. Yes I did."

"You got something for me?"

"No, sorry, sadly I don't."

There was a silence.

"Pretty brave to call here," she said.

"I was going to hang up if whatsisname answered."

"Uh huh."

"Actually," he said, "I wanted to ask you a favour."

"Huh." Amanda started to bark behind her.

"I'm looking for a poker game. Guy called Devonne told me I could go."

She laughed. "You're a big player now, eh?"

"I guess."

"How'd you meet Devonne?"

"I get around."

"I bet you do."

"Look," he said, "I just want to play poker. Stress relief, you know."

"Oh right," she said. "You're not going to find her there, you know."

He said, "You going to help me out or not? I helped you out, remember."

"Okay. You help me out with my problem first."

"Deenie, I have no idea what . . . I can't help you there."

"Help me out, I'll tell you where to go. I have to go."

He got off at the intersection he had written down and saw a building half a block away glowing purple. It was a stone building that had possibly once been a hotel. There were no huge billboards of half-naked women; just a ten-foot purple neon sign, a black double door under purple lights, and a couple of black bouncers in black suits and ties, with earpieces.

His guts burbled as he walked towards them. He knew he had the stupid half-smile on his face that meant he was trying to look relaxed. He stopped before the door and nodded at one of the men. The guy just looked away. Justin didn't know if this meant he was being rejected or allowed to go in. Then the other man said, "Good evening, sir," and so Justin stepped forward and heaved the door open.

There was a vestibule with a coat check, which was closed because it was summer, and then a corridor with another bouncer in it and a woman behind a window who took money. He stopped there but the woman just smiled at him; there was a sign that said "No Cover." It was all very confusing.

It was dark of course and loud with dance beats. The main room was huge and sprawling; there seemed to be subsidiary lounges on every side, like grottoes, chapels off the nave, with their own saints and candles. A gallery ran round the top. There was a woman on the stage under purple light, writhing around in a not unusual manner, and the usual scattered guys close to the stage. It was so dark it took him a minute, standing there and staring around, to make out the other women circulating. There were indeed waitresses with black skirts and white shirts and black bow ties, which was encouraging. Justin just stood there at the back, staring, until he had counted three cocktail waitresses moving to and from the bar. They all had dark hair.

A bouncer in a similar white and black getup, with a headset, approached him and said, "Can I help you, sir? VIP lounge upstairs, ten-dollar cover."

Justin nodded and grinned like an idiot and shook his head and gestured to the main room. He walked down a couple of steps and took a table as far from the stage and in as much darkness as he could find. He sat there and waited for a waitress.

It was perfumed in there, a smell of hair product and skin cream, and it was overlaid with alcohol. Boozy perfume.

After a while he could see the strippers all around him, sitting with men or on them. A couple were sitting at the bar playing a video slot machine. They were almost naked; they had the sheer bodysuits and the bikinis and the clear plastic platform shoes you always saw. Their skins were uniformly caramelly, and they turned dark brown under the black lights. Most of them had chosen outfits that were entirely or partly fluorescent that picked up the black light like beacons. The glowing triangles and thongs moved around alone in the darkness in the private lounges. He couldn't see anything over the railing of the upper gallery, the VIP lounge.

A cute and perky waitress with black hair in a ponytail and bangs leaned over him, smiling, and called him sweetheart. He ordered a beer.

He could see into one of the side chapels; it had a glass partition. Inside were black leather couches and a coffee table. There was a guy in a business suit with a naked girl rubbing herself against him like a kitten.

Just a few tables away from him a guy was getting a regular dance. The girl was standing, at first, her back to him, bending over and pushing her buttocks into his face until his nose was almost between them. Then she reached back and spread them apart. He must have had his nose almost touching her anus. If you really liked anuses, there could be no better view.

Then she sat on him, leaned back and pushed her breasts up into his face. Justin saw him take a nipple into his mouth. The guy's hand was stroking the inside of her thigh. When it got too high up into her crotch, she gently pushed it away. She threw her hair back over his shoulder, closed her eyes and writhed as if in ecstasy. She was grinding her buttocks into the guy's groin as if she was trying to get him off right there. Justin looked away.

He wanted to walk around and peer into the dark booths, but he knew that wouldn't be tolerated. If this is what you got in the open room, then the special treatment would be interesting.

A girl in a white bikini and a mesh wrap was prowling. She was tall and caramel like all of them. Justin shrank in his seat and stared into his beer; he didn't want to be chosen. But there she was, standing next to him, leaning down, her palms on his table. "Hi," she said.

Justin smirked and nodded.

"You mind if I sit down?" she said, sitting and pulling her chair close to him. She put a hand on the back of his neck. "How are you?"

Justin muttered the formulas. He wasn't sure if he was supposed to buy her a drink. She put out her hand and asked him his name; hers was Monique, although her accent sounded more Slavic than French. She was completely hairless and glowing. He felt warmer from the proximity of her skin.

She asked him if he had been there before and if he had had a stressful day and everything you could ask someone who doesn't want to talk to you. Then she asked him if he wanted a dance, and he said no thanks, and she said she thought he was the kind of guy who would prefer the privacy of the Champagne Room, and he should check it out with her.

She smelled of candy, like Jenna. The music had changed to some whiny romantic diva. It was curious how feminine the whole environment was, for a place so masculine in intent, a place full of big bouncers and erections; the girls got to choose their music and it was the softest purest mush and that was what set the tone for the whole place, that and the sweet smell. It felt as if you were trespassing in a suburban bedroom, but then it really didn't. He felt the eyes of the bouncers on his back.

"Well," said Monique, "I'll come back and see if you're ready for a visit to the Champagne Room. I think you're really going to enjoy it." She stroked his cheek with the back of her hand as she got up.

It was just behind her as she turned that he glimpsed her, her hair in its bushel, and his belly went cold.

She was right at the other side of the room, and she was half-naked too. It was her. She was sitting next to a guy, a middle-aged white guy in a suit, and she was in a clingy green spandex minidress. Justin stood up to stare, then ducked back down again. He picked up his beer and moved to a section a few steps up, his back against a low wall.

He watched as she stood in front of the guy and peeled off her dress, and there were her perfect breasts, his, glowing pale in the black light, and she was throwing her ringlets back and laughing. She kept a tiny green thong on. She climbed on the guy's lap and began grinding against him. Justin watched the guy's hands circle her waist. He saw his nose against her ear, and she was still smiling and laughing.

Seeing this contact, the hands on her especially, caused a pain right through his body that was almost nausea and almost terror. He felt like shouting and crying at the same time. He picked up his beer and his hand was shaking.

He got up and went to the washroom, avoiding her side of the room. He felt he might throw up but he didn't. It was almost like a dream.

In the mirror he looked the same, perhaps a little clammy and wide-eyed.

He took as long as he could in the hope that she would be finished her dance when he came out.

But she wasn't, she was still writhing against the old guy and his hands were all over her. And now her thong was off and she was spreading her legs for him, touching herself right under his face.

Justin sat and watched the girl on the stage. He ordered another beer and drank it slowly, trying not to glance over at where Jenna was almost having sex with a guy, but did every few minutes anyway. The guy was buying dance after dance. He would probably take her upstairs soon. There was a possibility that Justin might not be able to stomach this; he wondered what he would do.

He could buy a dance himself, from someone like her, and she would probably see it and it would be interesting to see how she reacted. But that would be idiotic and he didn't want a dance anyway; his body was dead.

He glanced over and she was finally getting off the guy. He watched the guy count out a wad of twenties and she took them and leaned over and kissed him on the forehead. She was still naked. She sat naked next to him and they chatted for a while as if she was clothed.

Then she got up and pulled her dress on. She was beautiful as she straightened it and pulled at it to cup her breasts.

She walked directly towards him.

Justin stared frozen at the stage. He hadn't prepared anything to say to her.

She veered towards the bar and sat there with one of the girls at the video machine.

Justin watched her shoulder blades glide; they were a kind of perfect beauty, and this hurt him like ice in the face. He knew he should just get up and go now; he had seen what he needed and there was no reason to talk to her now. But he sat there and sipped his beer.

He was about to go, in fact, when she got up again and looked around. Her eyes passed over him and she did not recognize him. But then she walked to his corner and he knew she would.

She was about to pass him so he stood up. She couldn't miss him; she was ten feet away. She stared right at him and stopped. They looked at each other for a second and she approached him. He could tell from her clenched jaw that it was not going to be good.

"Hey," he said.

"What the *fuck*," she hissed.

"Jenna," he said, and his voice was shaky, "I don't want you to do this. You don't have to do this."

She put her hands on her hips, looked around. "You shouldn't be here. I don't want to see you."

"Jenna, you really don't have to do this. I will help you out if you need money. Let's go, right now. Let's get out of here. Go and get changed." His voice was cracking because if he wasn't careful he was going to cry. He could feel tears behind his eyes already.

"Justin, get out of here. You need to leave, right now."

"Come with me. Please. Go and get your stuff." He took her forearm and tried to lead her towards the exit. She shook off his hand.

"Do not do that."

"Please, Jenna. Please." He touched her arm again and she slapped his hand away. At this point he was aware of the big men just behind her and behind him. They must have been watching the whole thing.

"Sir," they said, and they had hands on his shoulders. They were between him and Jenna and moving him towards the door.

"Okay," he said. "Okay. I'm going. I'm going."

"Justin," she called, "I don't want to see you any more."

The street-level door to his apartment was ajar, which was strange because no one else used it.

On the narrow staircase up to his own door lay a single sock, his. It was a clean sock and must have come from his sock drawer. He looked up the stairs and saw the upper door wide open, and that's when he knew what had happened.

The kitchen floor was strewn with smashed crockery and food. The fridge door was open. A jar of mustard had been thrown at the wall. Every drawer was open.

In the bedroom, the mattress had been dragged off the bed. His clothes were everywhere. His computer, strangely, had not been taken, but had been pushed onto its side. It might even still be operable. He thought this in a calm way, as if he were seeing all this on a screen.

There was a damp patch on the bedroom floor that smelled of urine.

He went through every room slowly. Everything in his medicine cabinet had been poured onto the floor of the bathroom, even a bottle of Aspirins.

Yet nothing seemed to have been taken, except for a little basket of change on his dresser. There had been nothing of value anyway.

The freezer door was open, a bag of frozen corn thrown onto the floor. But nothing was gone from there, because he had taken his bag of weed and put it in his pocket before he had left. He did not know why he had done that. Perhaps because he had hoped to placate Jenna with it if he ran into her.

Mechanically, he got a bucket from under the kitchen sink and began to fill it with hot water. He squirted some dish soap into it, and put on rubber gloves. He began to cry, but not because of this; this he hardly saw. It was as if he had noticed a mosquito bite next to a stab wound. He had no affection for any of his things, any of his life.

21.

He spent the next few days mostly crying. He missed another day of work and lay on his bed and cried. He felt poisoned. Genevieve called him twice, for some reason, and he didn't answer.

It didn't take him long to clean the place up. There were only some dishes broken and food ruined. Someone had pissed on his bedroom floor, which was nasty, but most of it had hit a hooked rug that he had been able to throw out.

This was of such little interest to him that he didn't even tell anyone about it. He took breaks from the cleaning to call Jenna's cell, and she didn't answer.

He knew that he had to talk to the landlord about changing the locks, and that he should feel frightened, but he didn't, because he was worthless anyway. He called a locksmith out of duty.

His computer worked mostly. The mouse had been smashed so you had to get around the screen with buttons, which was a distraction. There was an e-mail from Dorothy Liu, inviting him and "the whole gang" to a barbecue in Uxbridge. He stared at it for a while like something in code before understanding that it was a friendly party among people he knew and who still thought they knew him. He could not imagine such a thing. He did not really know where Uxbridge was.

On the third day he called Jenna's cell again and she answered. She said that she didn't want to talk to him, that she didn't appreciate what he did and she didn't like being spied on. He told her he was terribly sorry and terribly sad and needed to see her to work things out, that he knew they could work things out, and she said that he had to understand that things weren't going to work out between them, and she had to go.

When he did go to school, seeing the girls everywhere— on the bus, in the cafeteria, lined up outside Mike's office, with their miniskirts and chubby legs or skinny legs, their jeans not as tight as Jenna's, their baggy T-shirts that Jenna never would have worn—was painful. They were all beautiful but not as beautiful as Jenna. And he was alone, he did not have one of them, he did not have any woman in his life; he had been abandoned. He thought of the word "bereft" and it made him cry on walking from the washroom to his classroom. He pretended to be sneezing.

He could not believe this had happened. He thought it likely that Jenna would get over her temper, as she always did, and that he might possibly get over his horror at what she was doing for money—he kept seeing the hands on her waist, the hairy chin on her breast, imagined the hard penises pushed up against her back, all night long, and did she masturbate them through their trousers, did she give them blowjobs in the Champagne Room? It was impossible not to imagine, and horrible—no, he couldn't accept that, he would never get over it, and perhaps he wouldn't have to. When she calmed down and talked to him he would convince her that she didn't need to do that, he could lend her money, he would help her find a job, a really well-paying job in a restaurant or night club, as a hostess, or he would help her apply to community colleges to learn some skill, he would help her find a bursary. He imagined them living together in the country in five years, as he taught in a rural high school and wrote a book and she painted and baked bread and wore white cotton dresses.

He thought of nothing but Jenna all day, on the bus, in his classes, and especially at home. He couldn't look at porn on his computer. He carried his cellphone with him at all times and could hardly bear to charge it as it would mean switching it off. He looked at it in the middle of lectures he was giving, over-come with anxiety about its not ringing. How could she not want to call him, to work things out?

He found the note she had written him that ended with "I ❤ Justin Harrison" and was stricken with pain and then reassured and happy and then worried and then stricken with pain again.

He was not eating very much, either.

Even Janice the secretary, nice sweet dull Janice with the lovely breasts, made him think of Jenna and her breasts, and when he saw Annette the PR idiot he stared as usual at her tight thin trousers over her always surprisingly firm and round bum and saw the line of her thong and it didn't excite him in the least; it just made him think of Jenna's hips and her legs and her sparse bush and he wrinkled his face and said "Hahh" aloud, as if he was suffering from gas or about to sneeze.

When Genevieve called him a third time that week he finally picked up, in case she wanted to tell him she had cancer or some-thing. But she just wanted to know how he was doing, and he asked her why and she said because it was weird that he hadn't returned her calls, and she was concerned about him. He told her that he had just been really busy and he'd been a little bit down, and he cut her off when she tried to ask him why. He actually wanted to get off the phone as soon as he could in case another call came through.

He reflected afterwards that it was odd that he wasn't feeling any interest, not even any curiosity about Genevieve now, in fact he hoped that she was seeing someone else, and he wondered when that had happened. She just seemed like a rather annoying and uptight middle-class girl and he supposed she had always been and he wondered why he had been such a cretin as to not have seen that.

He called Andrew and told him that he was really down so they went out for a drink. They sat on a terrace on College and sweated. It was humid and hard to breathe even at night. Justin felt he was always shining, like someone with a fever.

Justin said, "I have a feeling it's going to work out, actually. I have a feeling this is just one of her hysterics. She goes into these black moods when she can't talk to anyone and when she comes out again it's like she's just woken up, she's a different person."

"She does that a lot?"

"Yeah, she does. She has problems. But she's an incredible girl, A. She's a lot of fun to talk to sometimes. I feel a whole lot more . . . I think we have more fun together than Genevieve and I ever did."

"Huh."

They watched the sweaty girls pass. It was no longer as fun as it had been at the beginning of the summer; everyone just looked too hot.

"So you think," said Andrew, "if she does come back, I mean change her mind, that this is like a long-term thing?"

"What, you mean are we going to get married?"

"Well, not married exactly, but like a serious thing."

"It already is a serious thing. It was pretty serious, dude."

Andrew looked at him and there was a tension to his smile. "Right."

"What are you trying to say? She's not right for me, right?"

"I don't know. I'm asking."

"All I know is it's really exciting. To be around her."

"Yeah." Andrew was shaking his head. "I don't know if exciting is always good. Exciting is maybe not long-term relationship material."

"Christ I hate it when people talk like that." Justin realized after he said it that it had been a little too loud and intense. Andrew was smiling uncomfortably. "No, seriously, do we really believe this, that relationships should be calm and stable and passion doesn't really enter into it? Do you really believe the women's magazines that say that passion cools off in every relationship, that's totally *normal*, it turns into something else, it turns into a *partnership*, and that's something we should all be *happy* about and look forward to. Fuck that. No, really, fuck that. If a happy relationship means what everyone else seems to want, I don't know, shopping for curtains on Saturday and then hockey on Sunday, whatever, talking about real estate and floor finishings for the next ten years, then I don't want a happy relationship. Trust me. I'm going to want garter belts and fishnets when I'm sixty-five. And if my wife doesn't want that then I'll find another wife."

"Whoa. A touch defensive."

Justin drained his beer.

"I think . . ." said Andrew.

"Yeah."

"I think you're inventing attacks, dude. Nobody is pressuring you into any of that. I don't even know where you get that from."

"Hah. I think . . . I don't know. Maybe my ex. Maybe I thought that's what she wanted."

"Maybe it was."

They were quiet for a moment. Justin wiped his face with his T-shirt. It was impossible for it to be so hot after dark; it was possibly even hotter than in the day; there was no breeze, no relief, it was like a small dark hotel room where you couldn't open the window, and they were on the street.

"No," said Andrew, "it's more the cultural gap I think what I'd be, I'd be concerned about."

"Cultural gap?"

Andrew smiled again. It was surprising that he had thought about Justin's relationship, but not unpleasant. It was a little flattering.

"You mean," said Justin, "she's from the wrong class."

"Hmm." Andrew finished his beer. "Well, you do have a lot more education than she has."

"Yes."

"So how are you going to talk about things, about the things that, that interest you, that are important to you? How are you going to talk to her about all the books you read, and your views on publishing and racism and everything you get all excited about. You just cut that off when you're around her?"

Justin laughed. "This doesn't sound like you too much. Sounds like you've been talking to Dorothy or Jennifer or something. You guys have been talking about this, right? You going to do some kind of intervention?"

Andrew smiled and shook his head. But he wasn't denying it.

"Listen," said Justin, "Dorothy Liu can think what she likes, and she can have what she wants, she can have her theme parties and her engagements and her . . ." He was going to say *you can all have your little marriages and your little lives.*

"Okay, okay. Easy."

"Next you'll be telling me the difference between love and lust."

Andrew sighed. "Well, yeah, actually. I think you could actually use a lesson in that."

"I knew it."

"You love her?" said Andrew. "You really love her? In a way that isn't just—"

"Desire. No, I don't. Because I don't understand the difference. No one has ever been able to explain the difference to me, and I don't, I just don't buy it." Justin was really unbearably hot now. They would have to get up and run to the lake and jump in or put their heads inside freezers, or their blood would boil, their hair would catch fire. "And nobody can tell me he's ever felt a difference."

"Between love and desire? Oh, I think I could tell—"

"Nope. Nope you can't. It's something you explain to yourself after you feel desire. Nobody has ever felt or experienced a difference. They're both highs."

"Highs," said Andrew. "What do you know about highs? I got to go to the can." He went inside.

So Justin had offended him. He didn't know if he had meant to or not. It was clear that he would have trouble explaining things to people like Andrew, people so much like him, from now on, as nobody seemed to get it.

When Andrew came back Justin was thinking about something else. He said, "Listen, I know you're really not supposed to talk about your patients, but this thing, she didn't really become your patient, and there's something I've been wondering about, and it would really help me a lot if I knew the answer to this thing."

"You mean when I treated her."

"Yes."

"You're right, I'm not supposed to talk about it."

"I know that," said Justin, and then tried hard not to say anything else. He said, "I don't want details. I just want to know if what she had was what she said she had."

"Didn't she tell you all about it?"

"Not really, no."

Andrew had a funny look on his face, either surprised or disgusted. "That's a little odd."

"Well, she said it was a miscarriage. But she didn't want to talk about it. I just wondered."

"You mean you don't really trust her," said Andrew. "You don't believe her."

"Of course I do. I just never . . ."

"Okay," said Andrew. "It was what she said it was. It wasn't serious. It was really early. Early in the . . . early in the process. Technically it wasn't a miscarriage at all. Technically it's called chemical pregnancy. It was just heavy bleeding. We kept her overnight. I left before she did. Usually it's uncomfortable for a while and then it's over. She didn't need blood or anything. Okay?"

"Okay." Justin exhaled. He had been clutching the arm of his chair quite tightly and now he released it. "Thank you."

They sat in silence until Justin said, "See, that's what she said it was. I do trust her."

"I know you do," said Andrew gently.

"Yes, I do."

"Okay."

Justin motioned for another round.

"No," said Andrew.

"Just one more."

Andrew sighed. The waitress smiled at them and nodded.

"The burglary," said Andrew. "Did you call the police?"

Justin shrugged. "That had nothing to do with her."

"So why didn't you call the police?"

"What could they do?"

"Well," said Andrew, "most people would think that was a pretty big deal."

Justin wanted the next beer now. It would probably be ten minutes on a night like this. "What makes you think it was her?"

"I didn't say that," said Andrew.

"It's what you're thinking."

Andrew said nothing.

"I know who it was," said Justin. "It was a guy she knows. He's looking for something he thinks she has. It's ridiculous."

"Jesus Christ," said Andrew.

"It couldn't have been her. She never had a key anyway."

"Jesus Christ. So how did this guy—I can't even believe she knows someone who would—"

"Oh, he's just a—it's no big deal," said Justin. "I doubt it will happen again." There was really no point in talking to Andrew.

"Hey," he said, "we should get together and play poker again, hey? That was fun."

Andrew was yawning. "Yeah. That was fun."

"Get the guys together again."

"Yeah. I would love to. But just, for a while anyway, I'm not going to be able to stay out late, you know. Until the end of this term anyway."

"Right. Right. Okay." Justin's next beer arrived and he sucked on it. "Well, when you're ready. Next time, next time I'd like to play for real money."

Andrew raised his eyebrows like a cartoon character. "You?"

"Why not?"

"Well, you lose a lot of money fast that way. But if you're suddenly rich or something—"

"No, no, that's not it. Just makes it more fun. More serious. Just small stakes, you know. A few bucks. Try it out."

"Okay." Andrew was nodding but his eyelids were closing every now and then.

"Yeah. Well, forget it for now. When you're back in the loop. Let's get the bill."

When he got home he called her phone and incredibly she answered right away. "I'm sorry to bother you," he said, and he already felt like crying. It was too soon for crying.

"What's up?" she said, and her voice was at least soft if distant. At least she wasn't mad.

"Can we get together, just for a coffee or something? Just to talk."

"What for?"

He spoke quickly. "Jenna, I have no idea what this is about. We had one fight, one misunderstanding. I apologize for my behaviour sincerely. I was really upset at the time, because I was surprised. But we can work things out, I mean I really think we can. I need to at least talk to you about it, about why you're so upset and being so firm. I don't even understand."

"Justin, I really don't think there'd be any point." There was chattering behind her voice, as if she was in a public place.

"No point? Jenna, what about the last month? Did that mean nothing to you?" And on that his voice did crack. "I have no idea what this is all about. We can get over this, we can."

"Justin, I'm really sorry you got that surprise. And I'm really sorry you're so upset. But I just think that it shows that we're not going to get along. There are things that . . . there are things I can't hide from you, things that you obviously can't handle."

"But I can. I can. Of course I can. I can handle anything, anything at all that you want to do, anything you want to tell me. I want to be with you and that means accepting you and know-ing—" He stopped and she was silent too. "Can't we just meet for coffee? This is killing me. I want to understand what you feel. Even if, okay, even if you decide it's over between us, we need to have this talk. Please. I need to understand."

"Justin, I'm sorry. I'm sorry but I don't think there would be any point."

He was pacing in his hot apartment. His insides were burn-ing and he couldn't stop moving or they would spill out and corrode the floor. He couldn't believe it was getting worse. The thought came to him as if from a rational planet far away that he was going to be a mess all evening now, and possibly for the next few days, and that he had better create some plan to deal with it now, some kind of sop to panic. "Jenna," he said, and now he was crying, "you have no idea what a mess I am. I'm sorry, this is embarrassing. I know I am humiliating myself in telling you this, I know I am losing my dignity, but I know that we had something, have something that's real and serious and that you really care for me. I know that. I can't believe you don't miss me. I can't believe you don't want to work this out. Don't you miss me at all?"

"Justin, this is hard for me too. So I don't want to talk to you any more. I am sorry you're upset."

"Upset? You have no idea. You have no idea. I am thinking of nothing but you all day and all night. I can't sleep or eat. I am, I don't know why. I'm devastated."

"I know. I know you are." Her voice was very quiet; he wondered how she chose to be calm or hysterical. "I want you to really try to get over it. It's the only way. Maybe we can talk in a while, like in a few months, but—"

"Months? A few months?"

"I've got to go now."

"Are you going to work?"

"I'm not going to answer the phone for a while, okay?"

"Jenna don't, please don't."

"I don't want to hang up on you."

"Okay," he said. "Goodbye. Goodbye."

Then he was alone in his apartment. His limbs were alternately hot or cold. He felt quite high. He smoked a joint and cried loudly, choking, and then stopped. He couldn't sit still. He thought of calling Andrew but knew he would cry and that would embarrass everyone. He went out on the street and walked to the park, past the parking lot and the pay phone where he had met her, and he started to cry again so he had to turn and go home again. He tried looking at pictures on the computer and couldn't even see them. The thought occurred to him to go to a strip club, to look at writhing hairless naked bodies and touch and stroke them until he had replaced hers with them.

He called Deenie. She said, "What?"

He said, "My apartment got trashed."

"Huh."

"Whatever, whoever it was didn't find what he was, what they were looking for."

"Oh yeah."

"So maybe you could spread it around that I'm not your guy?"

She said, "You found Jenna?"

"Yes, I sure did. She won't talk to me now. So I'm really not your guy. With her. Okay?"

"Okay."

"So listen, we're finished about that, right?"

"It has nothing to do with me anyway, tough guy. It's Armando you have to talk to."

"Right," he said, "well I'm not going to do that. Just give him a friendly word for me, will you?"

"I'll try."

He said, "Trashed like wrecked, destroyed. Someone pissed on my bedroom floor. They threw food all over the walls. You think I deserve that?"

"I don't know if you do or not."

"All right."

"Justin, I'm sorry that happened. I am. I had nothing to do with it. I don't know anything about it."

"All right," he said. "So make it up to me. Help me out with this little thing. That poker game."

She giggled. "That? All right. If you're sure."

"I think you owe me right now."

"What day is it?"

"Friday."

"You're in luck," said Deenie. "It's on tonight, I think. It doesn't really get going till the bars close. Get a pen. Write this down."

He didn't shower or change. He just wiped his face off and left the apartment. He went by a bank and took out two hundred bucks. This left four hundred until his next pay, which was in a week and a half. He was telling himself this was about a distraction and fun but he knew it was more than that. He knew he might see someone there who knew her. He knew that there would be something more vaguely advantageous, too, in doing things like this, and it wasn't just in impressing her, for she wouldn't be impressed, she was more impressed by the fact that he read books and liked poetry, but there was a simple advantage in knowing the kind of people she knew, perhaps in being one. It would get him closer to her.

He hailed a cab. He was going to Chinatown, of course. "Of course it's Chinatown," he said to the cab driver, and giggled.

"Okay boss," said the cabbie.

"Forget it, Jake," said Justin.

It was only just past one when he got to the main intersection Deenie had described. He had to walk and find an alley from there, but it wouldn't be going yet.

He went into a red bar full of white students on the main street and sat at the bar and drank a big beer and listened to the bland rock music and watched the girls with their strange ugly outfits—their skirts with knee socks and high-tops, their skirts over jeans—and the skinny boys with their silly facial hair and mops in their eyes and tried to see himself in them, for this was exactly the kind of bar he had come to when he was at school just a few blocks away. They had dressed in similarly silly clothes that they had bought in second-hand stores in the nearby market and it had been romantic. And yet he felt different from them now. The music was all angst and irony and pretension. The boys singing it sounded whiny. It seemed sheltered. And he didn't want to sleep with any of the girls any more, with their spectacles and their police boots.

He had to drink three pints and really take his time to get him to two o'clock, and still he didn't leave till the place was emptying out at two-thirty. Then he read over his scrawl on a slip of paper and stepped out into the loud street. He took a side street into the heart of the open-air market that was all closed up and piled with garbage, and then found the alleyway beside the store called Hostile. It was narrow and completely dark. "Saigon," he said to the street, in his rumbliest voice, "shit."

He walked very slowly down the street. He could see a dim yard at one end, but there was no light in it. He stepped carefully. The walls were textured with graffiti.

He got to the open yard. It was full of junk and a picnic table. The wall to his right was covered in graffiti. There was supposed to be a door, but there was no door. He moved towards the wall to see if there was a bell. A crack of light appeared in the wall, a door with no outline opening. Then there was light from the door and a figure in it. The figure was silhouetted from a lamp behind. It was a big guy, standing a foot or so higher than Justin. There must have been a step up.

"You were going to knock," said the big guy. "Weren't you? Never knock. Never knock." The guy stepped aside. Justin stepped up a step and past the guy—a white guy in a motorcycle jacket and a ponytail—and then looked down a set of stairs into a basement. There were two more white guys waiting at the bottom of the stairs.

Justin went down, and the door closed behind him.

"Hey," said one of the guys at the bottom.

"Hey," said Justin. "Friend of Devonne's."

"Tembucks, bro."

"Right." Justin got out his wallet and they gave him change for a twenty, all very politely. There was a TV monitor on a stool next to them with a grainy image of the courtyard on it. They had watched him on that as he stood next to the wall, and then they had opened the door for him.

"Never knock, eh?"

"Got it," said Justin. Then he was inside a basement with a low ceiling, next to a bar. The bar had a fluorescent white tube overhead and was stark. A short black man was behind the bar. The rest of the place was a little dimmer, but it still had some pools of white light from naked bulbs in crooked standard lamps. It was messy: there were some sofas and some chairs, and newspapers and empty paper cups on them. There were a couple of little guys in hockey jackets and ball caps on the sofas. There was a TV hung up with a wire snaking down the wall. The TV was showing the weather channel. There was some music from somewhere but it wasn't loud. There were a couple of tables with green felt tops but nobody sitting at them.

Justin went to the bar. The guy nodded at him. "Beer please," said Justin. He pointed at one. Then he leaned against the bar and tried to breathe deeply. A little Asian guy in a pair of basketball shorts and flip-flops was walking around and picking up papers. Every now and then he'd murmur an order to one of the guys at the door and the guy would go off somewhere. The little Asian guy didn't seem happy. "The fuck is this?" he said, picking up a big McDonald's paper cup. "Who the fuck let this in?"

Nobody said anything back to him.

Then the little Asian guy sat at one of the poker tables under a low-hanging light and read a newspaper. The T-shirt he was wearing seemed to be from a lacrosse team. It was now a quarter to three. Justin was surprised he didn't feel in the least drunk. Although he must have been.

There were a couple more guys in the bar, though. There was perhaps another entrance. There was not one woman.

Beside the poker table there was a dead potted plant on a stool. Its dried spindles hung down to the floor. It was hard to imagine who had wanted to decorate the place with plants. Especially since there didn't seem to be any windows. Perhaps a plant could survive on fluorescent light. Justin didn't really know these things.

A cluster of guys clattered down the stairs, all bulky jackets and hats, and one of them was Devonne the weed dealer, you could tell from the shock of half-grey dreadlocks. Devonne laughed loudly with the guys at the door and smacked their hands. He went over to the little Asian boss who half stood up to smack his hand. They did a handshake that seemed to have three parts. Devonne sat at the table, and a tall white guy sat with them.

Justin waited for a minute before he went over. He nodded and smiled at Devonne, who looked at him blankly. All the guys at the table were staring at him silently now.

Justin stuck out his hand. "Hey Devonne. Justin. Jenna's friend. I came by your place one time."

Devonne smiled and laughed. "Justin my brother," he said. He grabbed his thumb to shake his hand. Justin was smiling as widely as he could.

Someone had brought a couple of packs of cards to the table. The little guy was shuffling them.

"You here to play?"

"Maybe I'll just watch for a bit."

There were glances round the table.

"We don't really do that here," said Devonne, still smiling.

"He's with you," said the little guy, "he's cool."

"Cool," said Devonne. "You just sit back from the table a bit."

"Cool."

"Ricky," said Devonne, "this is my boy Justin. Ricky owns the joint."

Ricky had a limp handshake. The other guy was called Shank.

"Five and ten?" said Devonne.

"Five and ten. Hundred dollars in," said Ricky. He was still peering at his newspaper.

"Sounds good." Devonne and Shank got up and went to the bar. Justin followed without knowing why. He stood behind them as they handed over a hundred bucks each to the barman. He counted out chips of three different colours to them.

It was dimmer now. Someone had turned off the naked bulbs. And there were more people sitting on the sofas now, a couple of women in the tight scoop tops of club waitresses. It was subdued. Everyone looked tired. There was one young guy, maybe a teenager really, darting around the room and shaking hands with everyone. He had a ponytail and a baseball hat and a bulky team jacket, even though it was muggy in there. Most of the time he just stood against one wall, and people came up to him. He was a little jumpy.

Justin sat and watched the game. It went very quickly, with phrases he didn't recognize. It was hold'em, which he knew, and he got that the blinds were five and ten dollars. But he was taking a few seconds to figure out who the winner was in each hand, and someone was scooping up the chips before he could. There were rapid hand signals and taps he wasn't catching either. He made sure he was far enough from Devonne that he couldn't see his cards.

"Shank," said Ricky, "what I tell you about beer bottles on the table."

"Sorry man." Shank pulled his bottle off the felt.

Justin had his own beer bottle on the table. Nobody said anything to him. He pulled it off and cradled it on his lap.

After a few hands Devonne was out of chips. He said to Ricky, "You spot me for some more?"

Ricky shrugged. "Sure. Tell Rav."

Devonne heaved himself up and off to the bar.

"Justin," said the guy Shank. "You playing?"

"Just watching. If it's okay with you."

"Anything okay with Devonne okay with me. I'm just saying. You should get in the game. What are you afraid of?"

"You," said Justin.

"That's right, my friend," said Shank. "You should be."

A new guy showed up at the table, a little muscular guy with a shaved head and wraparound shades. The shades were a little silly in there. He was also missing a front tooth.

"I'm in?" he said. He put his hundred dollars' worth of chips on the table.

Ricky nodded.

"Bruno," said the guy, with a French accent. He sat. There were introductions all around.

Devonne came back with more chips. He had at least two hundred worth this time.

"You're welcome to play, Bruno, my friend," said Shank, "if you don't mind us taking all your money."

No one laughed at this, not even Bruno. "All right," he said, "all right."

Bruno lost quite heavily on the first few hands and Devonne and Shank started to needle him. "Don't stop, brother," said Devonne, "don't stop, bitch." He was not smiling, but Bruno was.

Justin was distracted by a woman coming down the stairs. She was dressed like a hooker, in thigh-high shiny boots and a shiny miniskirt and fishnets. Her hair was blonde and her face was a little rough. She berated the guys at the bottom of the stairs. "I was waiting for ten minutes out there," she said. "In the fucking dark. And there's a guy standing at the end of the alley watching me."

The guys seemed to know her and they apologized and she tottered to the bar and kissed the barman. Justin could see Ricky, sitting at his table, just glancing at that scene, as if he wasn't interested, but he was watching every second of it.

It made Justin sad to look at her and worried that he would start thinking about Jenna again, which of course he was now.

The little ponytailed guy in the team jacket who was just roving around the room and talking to everybody passed their table with a girl, a pretty girl, an off-duty waitress with makeup and her hair down, and they both went into the single washroom at the end of a short corridor.

When Justin looked back over at Devonne he saw that there was something new on the table, beside him: a black CD cover with white powder on it. Shank was leaning over and cutting it up with the edge of a credit card.

Justin looked away. His heart rate had just gone up and he was feeling heat in his face. It was something like exhilaration. He realized that this was what he was wanting, this was what he had waited all night to see. Stuff like this. It was now something he had seen, something he had done. Probably something he never would have done. Probably something Andrew and Guntar had never done. Although you never knew with Guntar. It was certainly something that would horrify Dorothy Liu. And Genevieve . . . he smiled about the impossibility of telling Genevieve about this.

Ricky, the owner, ignored the plastic plate of drugs on the table. Shank offered him some and he just shook his head. Justin loved this too.

The new guy in glasses, the toothless bald guy, Bruno, won a big hand and pulled in a bright pile of chips with a little smile. Devonne and Shank were wiping their noses and sniffing.

"Hey," said Bruno, "any chance of a little bump? Just to keep me going. Feeling a little sleepy. Just a small bump."

Shank was shuffling cards. "How about you start losing some fucking money," he said. "Then we'll see about a bump."

Bruno nodded. It was impossible to tell if Shank was being serious, but he sounded awfully serious.

The jumpy little guy came past them again, with the pretty girl walking behind him.

"Hey," said Justin, leaning over to Devonne. "Is that girl doing what I think she's doing?"

Devonne's eyes flicked at her as she passed. "What, like is she a professional?"

"Yeah."

Devonne laughed his big laugh. Then he said in a low voice, just to Justin, "I don't know what the official policy is on giving skull, you know? In the bathrooms. But I don't ask."

"Don't ask, don't tell," said Justin.

"A'ight." Devonne gave him a fist bump, which still made Justin feel silly. "I tell you, though, that's no hooker. That's not about sex. It's a little exchange. It's about what that guy has."

"Ah."

"I'm not saying the exchange doesn't involve a little head. I'm just saying."

"Don't ask."

"Don't tell."

"So," said Justin, "he's the guy to talk to. If I want anything."

"You mean any of this?" Devonne nudged the little tray beside him. "Here, have some now, if you want."

"Oh, no thanks. I just mean in future."

"Well, in future, you need anything you come to me. But not here. Not now."

"Okay."

"But yeah, that's the guy in here, if you're stuck. But only if you're stuck."

"Cool," said Justin.

"I guess. Hey," said Devonne, "here. Play a little." He pushed Justin a little pile of red chips. "All right if my man Justin plays a hand or two?"

"Oh, no, man, thanks."

"Come on man. Only way to learn."

"I'd only lose it. And you're losing enough already."

Devonne bellowed his laugh. "You watch me. Night is young."

Justin glanced at his watch, on his lap. It was four-thirty. The chips were in front of him.

"My man Justin's in this hand," said Devonne.

"All right," said Ricky. "No talking between you guys."

"Those are five each," said Devonne. "You're big blind."

Justin had a jack and a seven. He checked once and then folded on the flop. Little toothless Bruno won quite a big pot.

There was ten bucks gone out of Justin's fifty. "This is going to go fast," he said.

"It's for fun," said Devonne, leaning over the plate of powder.

An enormous white guy, a giant, was looming over the table. "How much is the buy-in?"

Nobody looked up at him. "Talk to this guy," said Shank.

"One hundred," said Ricky. "Five and ten."

"All right," said the giant. He was young, maybe even still a teenager. He had a massive team jacket. "I got sixty. How's sixty? That okay?"

"No," said Ricky. "One hundred at this table."

The giant took his bills out of his pocket. "Look, I got it right here. Cash. Sixty bucks right here."

"Not at this table," said Ricky. "Now get out of here."

"Hey now," said the giant. "Hey now. You can be nice."

No one was saying anything or looking at the guy, but there was a very slight stiffening around the table. Every guy was looking studiously at his cards.

The giant leaned forward, extending a meaty hand over the table. "Hey man, I'm being cool. You want to be cool."

"You're bothering me," said Ricky.

"What did I do? Don't be a dick, man. I'm being cool."

"I'm going to ask you to step away from this table."

"Am I being a dick? No."

The two guys at the bottom of the stairs were a little closer now; they had come up behind the giant without making any big procession.

"All right," said the giant, "all right. I'm cool. I'm not looking for trouble. But you don't have to be a dick."

He moved away, his hand unshaken.

"Ricky," said Shank. "What did that guy do to you?"

Ricky shrugged. "He was bothering me. He was drunk."

There was a pause, then everybody laughed. "No," said Devonne, "nobody drunk here."

Justin folded on the next hand, losing five bucks. Then he caught a jack ten and called the big blind. Then he folded on the flop. Another couple of hands and he was going to lose Devonne's money. He was a little scared to bet, he would have to get over that.

"You want some of this, you let me know," said Devonne.

"Okay," said Justin. "I do."

Devonne pushed the plastic square with the powder on it across the felt. There was a bank card on it for cutting up the lines. Justin had seen this in movies. He did it convincingly. He just cut himself a small one. There was a rolled-up twenty on the plate as well, but it seemed unhygienic to use that. He took a twenty out of his wallet and rolled it up. He looked around, but no one was watching him. The place was dark and full now, with almost as many women as men, and another poker table going across the room. He put the bill in his nose, closed the other nostril with a finger, bent and sniffed.

It smelled of bleach. Then it burned his nose. It was fierce. He thought he would sneeze, but he didn't. It was bitter and nasty.

He wiped his nose and pushed the plate back. It was undignified, this bending and plugging and public sniffing. He wouldn't do it again.

The bet came to him and he had an ace three suited, so he went all in with his remaining chips. Devonne raised an eye at him but clapped him on the back. "Now you're going," said Devonne.

Everyone else folded, and Justin had won fifteen bucks. There was a pleasure in raking the chips that made his ears feel hot. His teeth were also numb, and the back of his throat seemed to be closing up. He was having difficulty swallowing. There were no pleasant symptoms yet apparent.

By this stage Shank had already gone through his stack and had got up to buy more chips. The little toothless guy Bruno had quietly built a big pile.

"How about that bump?" said Bruno.

"Give it to him," said Devonne. "It'll make him start losing."

"Go nuts," said Shank, pushing the plate over to him. "We will take your money, you know that, don't you?"

"I guess," said Bruno, looking at his cards.

"I like your shirt," said Shank.

"My shirt?" said Bruno.

"Does it come in men's?"

"Hey now," said Devonne. "Friendly game."

"We're all friends and gentlemen," said Shank. "Just fucking with you, bro."

Bruno was bent over the CD case.

Over his head, Justin saw a hulking figure move from the stairs over to the bar. A black guy in a flowing jacket like a cape or a parachute, with a black hairnet.

"Hey, Jason," said Shank. He was rapping on the table.

"Justin."

"Justin, whatever. Check or bet, bro."

"Oh, sorry." Justin looked at his cards. Nine ten diamonds. "Raise twenty. Guess I'm all in." He pushed his chips forward and saw Bruno, to his left, immediately match them. And then so did Ricky and so did Shank. It occurred to him that he hadn't given his hand any thought at all, that he didn't know what he was doing, in fact. Devonne folded.

Shank had a pair of eights, and that was that.

"Sorry man," said Justin to Devonne. "I lost your money. I'll pay you back."

"Hey, it was worth a try. You enjoy it?"

"Yup," said Justin. He drained the rest of his beer. "I did." He stood up and looked over at the bar. The big black guy turned around and it was Tee, for sure.

Justin spun and walked to the bad-smelling toilet at the end of the hall. He stood at the urinal and thought for a minute. Of course Devonne would know Tee. It was not such a surprise. And he didn't have to run, either. The chance of a confrontation was unlikely in there, especially while he was sitting at Ricky's table. Still, he would avoid being seen by him for as long as he could.

And it was good, really, this scare, for behind Tee's black cape was a little glimmer of Jenna, somewhere in this darkness. Even if she too was running from Tee, he was a reminder that she was somewhere else, and wherever it was, they were all in the same city, and perhaps knew the same people.

There was only the one urinal, which lacked a flushing handle, and one stall. A murmur of voices, male and female, came from the stall. The plaster was collapsing from the ceiling. Justin zippered and left.

Tee was no longer at the bar, so Justin walked right to it and took out his wallet. He ordered another beer and then said, "And a hundred bucks in chips, please." He counted out the bills.

The barman said "You at Ricky's table?"

"Yup."

He got his chips and his beer and handed over his cash.

The barman said, "We take ten per cent when you cash out."

Justin nodded as if he knew this, for it felt as if he did, and left the guy a five-dollar tip on his beer. He turned around very slowly, his head down, scanning for Tee. He glimpsed him, now sitting on one of the collapsing sofas, sprawled expansively, his arm the length of the backrest, his stupid dark glasses still on, smiling at some girl, and the little ponytail guy rapidly making his way over to him. Justin kept his head down and went back to his table.

When he sat, he angled his chair a bit so his back was mostly to the room.

He noticed when he took his first hand that his hands were shaking slightly. Aside from that he still didn't feel anything special.

Devonne's stack was low again.

Justin asked him, "How much you in for?"

Devonne shrugged. "Few hundred now. Eight, I think."

"Eight? Man."

"I got time. I got time. I got patience."

"How late does this place stay open."

"I've been here till afternoon sometimes. Noon at least."

Justin nodded as if this sounded about reasonable. He folded on a couple of hands, bet modestly on one and was up twenty bucks.

"You getting it," said Devonne. "I don't like that. Have some more of this." He pushed the plate over—it was Shank who kept pouring more powder onto it from a little folded-up pocket of paper—and Justin tried it again. It burned still but didn't attack his throat in the same way as before. When he looked up again his vision was perhaps slightly clearer, but he didn't feel crazy or anything. It occurred to him from a distance that he hadn't thought about Jenna for the past few hands, since the urinal at least. And that he wasn't quite as worried about the presence of Tee as he should be. These were not bad things.

Little Ricky was on his cellphone. He just said "Hello" and then "All right" and he snapped it shut.

"What up," said Shank.

"Black Mike is coming down."

"Shit," said Devonne.

"He playing with us?"

"Yeah."

"Shit," said Devonne.

"What's the problem?" said Justin. "Who's Black Mike?"

Devonne sighed heavily. Everyone seemed despondent about this news. "He's a guy," said Devonne. "He's black. And his name is Mike."

"So?"

"So nothing."

"Is he, is he like dangerous or something?"

"No. He's just a good player. He's dangerous to your money."

"Oh," said Justin. "Is that all. I'll take him."

They played another hand and Justin found himself with an ace queen, which he played quite conservatively, just calling bets through the flop, and he found another queen on the turn and still stayed calm. He thought for a long time when the bet came to him. Then, with his heart racing, he pushed all his chips forward, and said crisply, "All in."

There were groans from around the table. And as Justin's face started to turn, he knew, very pink, everyone threw down their cards. He came away with another thirty bucks. "Here," he said to Devonne, and counted about fifty dollars' worth of chips for him. "These are yours."

He kept glancing over at the bar, and saw Tee moving around, but if Tee had seen him he wasn't going to do anything about it.

Shank's chip stack was low now and he was getting a little tetchy. "Devonne," he said, "my friend, I want to ask a favour of you, just a favour."

"What's that."

"When you bet ten dollars, you throw in ten dollars and you throw it a little fast. I know you are a gentleman and I trust you, but I would just like to see you put that ten dollars down, like here, one on top of each other, instead of throwing it in there."

"Shank, my man," said Devonne, "I understand what you are saying, I hear you, and I have no problem with that, and I will respect that. But if you are at all unsure about what I have put down, you just ask for a chip count. I have no problem with that."

"But I don't want to do that," said Shank, "I don't want to ask for a chip count, my brother, because I don't need to, because I trust and I respect you and I know that you are a gentleman. I'm just asking that you put your chips down this way, that's all."

"That's perfectly fine. I'm just saying you can ask for a chip count any time you want."

"Hey," said Ricky, "check or bet."

Shank held out his hand and Devonne shook it.

Justin wished he had a notebook. It was funny how all these handshakes were meant to reassure, but they did the opposite. Once the handshake came out you knew there was reason to feel nervous.

He folded two hands. Then he hit a pair of kings and raised everybody right through the river. He was fifty bucks up.

That giant guy came back to the table. "Hey, Ricky, right?"

"What can I do for you now," said Ricky.

"I'm sorry if I pissed you off earlier, man."

Ricky said nothing.

"I've got eighty bucks now." He put his bills down on the table. "I would like to buy in."

"Buddy," said Ricky, "I've told you this table is a hundred-dollar buy-in. And I don't want you at this table."

"What is wrong with you, man?"

"I don't want to talk to you any more. All right."

"I don't believe you, man. I don't believe this."

296

"All right then. I'm going to ask you to leave this club. Donny, this gentleman would like to leave now." Ricky said this in a normal speaking voice, and the older guy in the black leather jacket and the beard was right behind the big guy, as was the other guy from the bottom of the stairs. They had their hands gently on the giant's elbows, and he turned and went with them very quickly, saying, "All right, all right."

"Okay then," said Bruno the bald guy.

"Okay then," said Justin. He was smiling although this had been a little nerve-racking. He was smiling quite genuinely because it had also been quite impressive to watch, and instructive in its lack of politeness. He was thrilled, really, at such impoliteness. He shook his head a little, because he had in fact been a bit drunk and hazy earlier, but that had passed, and he wasn't the least bit drunk any more. He was just impatient for the next hand.

An older guy, a black guy with short hair and gold jewellery and office clothes, had arrived and sat and shaken everyone's hands. Justin shook his hand. He almost said, "Black Mike, right?" but he didn't.

Black Mike was very quiet. He folded a lot of his hands.

Now there were a couple of people standing respectfully back from the table and watching, mostly girls. Somebody brought him another beer, probably Devonne. He caught the eye of an okay girl, not one of the blonde club waitresses, who weren't much interested in the poker anyway, but a college sort of girl, in jeans and a tight top, with straight black hair and no makeup. He smiled at her and she looked away. Then she moved away.

But at least it was good he had tried.

Black Mike folded a hand, and Justin raised the big blind twenty bucks with a pair of sevens and to his surprise everyone folded. He just had to stay calm and playing this way and in ten more hands he would double his money. He wondered if he should try more drugs and thought he probably should, if someone offered it to him, anyway, because he really wasn't feeling anything from it and he would have liked to know what it was supposed to feel like at least. And still he was not thinking about Jenna, or feeling like crying, and it would be getting time to leave soon and then it would be time to be alone in the dark street again, or more likely in the daylight, as it was now almost six, which might be even worse, and so it might be best to prolong whatever it was for a bit.

The drug dealer guy passed the table, on his way to the washroom with another girl, and Justin half rose to scan the room. He couldn't see Tee anywhere, although he could have been slumped in one of the sofas with his back to them.

Surreptitiously, he counted his chips. He was now seventy dollars up, not counting the fifty he had given to Devonne, so he was well up. "Ricky," he said across the table, "what time is sunrise, do you know?"

"What time is what?"

"What time is love," said Shank.

"What?"

"Dawn," said Justin. "The dawn. What time is dawn today."

"The dawn," said Ricky quietly, his face in his cards. "Dawn is at six-thirty-eight today."

"Thanks," said Justin.

"No shit man," said Shank. "You really know that?"

"Ricky know everything," said Devonne.

"Of course I don't know that," said Ricky. "What do I look like, the fucking weather channel?"

Everyone laughed at this but Justin was scared once again. Devonne pushed the drugs over to him and he took another bitter hit. Then he leaned over to Devonne and asked him about the little drug dealer guy. He asked him if he could just go up and talk to him or if he needed an introduction. Devonne said he didn't need to, anyone in here could just walk up and talk to him, and Justin said no, he wanted to talk to him about something special and he wanted the guy to know he was cool. Devonne raised his eyebrows and said all right because he needed a piss anyway.

So Justin walked carefully behind big Devonne out into the room, right in the middle of all the sofas, looking around for Tee, and he didn't see him. They found the little ponytail guy at the bar and Devonne introduced them. He was Danny. Danny was very chirpy and very pleased to meet Justin. Devonne told Danny Justin was his boy and a good guy and then he left them alone.

Danny said, "You want to do a little business, we just have to go in the washroom for a second."

"No, that's okay," said Justin. "I was wondering if you could help me with something else. I just need you to tell me, maybe, who to talk to about something I'm looking for."

When Justin got back to the table they were waiting for him. Shank was tapping his fingernails on the table. They were quite long.

"Blind's to you, bro. We can't play without you."

"Oh. I'm sorry," said Justin. "I'm sorry, everyone. Didn't know. But listen." He looked at his stack of chips. Then he made a show of looking at his watch. "I'm sorry to say I think I'm going to cash out."

No one seemed to mind this, as he had feared. They were only irritated that he had made them wait. They were already on to the next hand. He got up and cradled his stack and walked to the bar. The barman took seventeen bucks off his hundred and seventy, and then he bought a round of beers for the table, which was only twenty-five. He brought them back in two trips. And on the second trip he did see Tee, first the back of his head and then his face. And they caught each other's eye, he thought, just for a second, and Tee frowned and looked away. So perhaps that would be that.

Justin shook everyone's hand at the table and thanked Ricky, who was distracted, and Devonne got up and gave him a somewhat odorous hug, and then he just walked up the stairs and the guy at the top opened the door for him and Justin fumbled in his pocket for a minute and handed the guy ten bucks, which he took with a nod. Justin didn't know if he was supposed to do that but it couldn't hurt. It was a pleasant transaction.

And then he was in hazy sunlight. The door closed behind him and he was in the courtyard, small and innocuous now, quite a friendly downtown backyard actually. There was even a picnic table. He walked down the alley towards the street with a bit of a floaty feeling. He had no sunglasses. The light was gentle and misty. It was already hot and humid. He was extraordinarily thirsty. He yawned although he didn't feel tired. He kept looking behind him but no one had followed him.

The shops on the street hadn't opened yet, but the piles of garbage had been taken away. There was traffic noise coming from the main street. And when he got onto it he saw the vendors already setting up stalls of vegetables and shouting at each other and there were streetcars rattling down the street. It was like walking out of a tunnel onto the other side of the world.

He knew it would hit him now, and it did, the remembering Jenna and the wondering where she was at that moment, if she had spent the night alone or with someone else. Because it was a beautiful morning and he would probably crash with exhaustion and hangover some time soon and at that point it would be better to have a girlfriend. She could have spent the entire night out somewhere doing something stupid, just like him, and he didn't know anything about it and probably never would.

He walked for a bit, smelling morning smells, and then felt a bit shaky so he hailed a cab. He had not spent any money at that place, and had even come away with extra for the cab, which gave him a rush of pride. He switched his cellphone on, because now he would be waiting for a call from that guy Danny.

22.

There were a couple of beautiful things you could glimpse
from the bus out there. There was the big highway flashing
like a river in the haze. There were the brown stretches of field
that had not yet been turned into townhouses; their emptiness
had a certain purity that was not without grandeur. There was
the great grey sky unobstructed by towers and perhaps slightly
bluer than it was downtown. There was the despair or resigna-
tion on the faces of the riders with their plaid plastic shopping
bags and their sleeping or wailing infants which made one feel
slightly better about oneself. There was the odd gorgeous black
girl with a long slender neck and tight jeans. Those girls were
very demure; they never returned his gaze, but stared at the grey
rubber matting on the floor.

He had taken two of the pills that had arrived from India that
Monday morning, one milligram each; he had started with one
with coffee and then had had to chew another before entering
the churning subway. He wasn't sleepy, not at all, but he was able
to concentrate on the blue in the sky and the plume of smoke

reaching straight up from the overpass. If anything he was more aware, more able to concentrate. He was aware of human smells, particularly of the black girl in the gauzy top crammed next to him, a creamy skin product tinged with sweat, and he wanted to breathe it in for as long as he could.

He had momentary panic on touching down on the side-walk in the hammering sun, seeing the glare of the thousand windshields that he would have to walk through on the black asphalt; he would be dripping by the time he reached his class-room, he would see Mike who would bark at him, he would see Mike with the pretty blonde with the expensive blue Mini and this would make him sad again.

But it didn't take too long to get to the swinging metal doors and burrow down the stairwell, where it was at least cooler, if rank with fried food and old coffee.

He was grinding his teeth when he went into the depart-mental office, for he did not know what crudity he would let loose on Mike if Mike said anything the least bit fuckwaddy to him, which Mike could of course not help but do.

Janice was looking frankly, honestly, beautiful, although he knew objectively she was not a beauty, she was just a pretty Por-tuguese or Egyptian girl with gorgeous skin, and she would grow to be dumpy in her thirties, but today she was wearing a loose linen blouse with lace at the collar and no sleeves and she looked like a Victorian photograph, a summer girl from a movie about a country house. Her hair was in two shiny pigtails and she wore her spectacles. Justin smiled dopily at her but could not speak.

She was not as cheery as usual. She said hi softly and then asked him if he was here to pick up his envelope.

"Envelope?"

"From Mike. Today's the day . . . didn't you read your e-mail?"

"Ah. I guess not."

"I thought that's what you were here for. Everybody has to come in today to pick up their envelope and sign for it."

Justin stared at her. She was opening a file folder full of white envelopes and sorting through them. "Are you okay?" he said. "How are you?"

"Oh." She sighed. "Could be better."

"What's wrong?"

"Nothing I want to talk about."

"I'm sorry to hear that."

"Harrison," she said. "Here." She handed him his envelope.

"What is it?"

"You should read your e-mail."

"Wow," he said, "you are in a bad mood. I'm very sorry I didn't read my e-mail. What is it?"

"You are giving your students the provincial test this afternoon, right?"

"I am indeed. That I have not forgotten."

"And to mark it you will need the correct answers, right? And to get the correct answers you have to log on to a website, and—"

"And this is the password to the website. Okay. Got it." Justin opened his envelope. There was a sheet of pink paper inside.

"So you need to sign for it here." She handed him a clipboard with a pen. There was a list of instructors' names. Everyone had signed for theirs already.

"Very top secret," said Justin.

"Well, it is, Justin. Obviously we have to be very careful about these. Only you guys have the key. I'm not even supposed to know it."

"I wonder why he chose bright pink then, for his password. It doesn't seem very Mike like. Not very macho."

"What?"

"The paper. Did everybody get bright pink paper?"

"Oh. I did that." She looked back at her computer screen. He was having a hard time getting a smile out of her this morning. "I had to photocopy it. That was the only paper around. It was for notices. We never used it, so."

"I thought you weren't allowed to see the password."

"Yeah, well, I had to do the photocopying."

"Okay. Thanks." Justin put the envelope in his knapsack. "I'm sorry that you're . . . You're usually so happy."

"I'm fine." She started to type on her keyboard.

There was no way Justin would have stayed there staring at her had he not been in that floaty state; he did not really know her and would not ask her a personal question. He knew this as he said, "You having problems with your boyfriend?"

She looked around with her eyes big. "Yeah, actually."

"I don't know how I could tell. I'm sorry to hear that." He was having a hard time remembering the fireman boyfriend's name. It was Todd or Rod or Brad or Dork. "I think I can tell because I'm having girl trouble myself."

Her face softened. "Really. That sucks."

"Yeah, it does suck. It totally sucks." He stayed there leaning over the partition, staring at her shining forehead.

She looked around; the rest of the office was empty. "Maybe you can explain to me then why guys can be total jerks."

"Ah. This is your guy, the fireman. Are you—"

"Brian."

"Are you splitting up? I thought you were together all the time, he was always spending big bucks on you."

She sighed again and shook her head and said, "Yeah, no, everything's fine. You're sweet though. Tell me you haven't had your heart broken. I thought there was something going on."

"Yeah, I have. I've been seeing—"

There was a rustling and a heaving as someone very large attempted to come into the room behind him; it was Meredyth Solberg-Spencer and her enormous bag. He shifted so that she could get to her mailbox, but she wanted to get to Janice's desk, so there was some awkward contact and Justin found himself excluded from Janice's aura. "My God," breathed Meredyth, "how anyone can work in this weather, get anywhere, do anything, I don't know."

"It's hot," said Janice sadly.

"How are you, Meredyth," said Justin.

"I am surviving, I suppose, but honestly not very well. I just feel faint all the time." She was damp and pale and her hair was limp, but then it usually was. She was breathing hard. "The poor things have to write their test today."

"Yes, mine too," said Justin. He might have been about to ask Janice out for a coffee to discuss their love lives. It didn't matter, as it wasn't possible now, but then it had never really been possible, as he had always thought that she belonged to a different class—to two different classes, actually; to a class of Portuguese secretaries and to a class of effortlessly sexy women who went out with huge brave dumb firemen called Brian. There was some overlap, of course, of these categories; they often went hand in hand; but membership in one alone was normally enough to disqualify him from imagining even a fantastic sexual encounter, let alone some kind of friendly intimacy. "Sorry?" he said to Meredyth.

"Your head's in the clouds," said Meredyth, peering at him from over her glasses. "Where were you?"

"Justin's distracted today," said Janice, looking at him with a not unsympathetic frown.

"I said how do you like this secret code business," said Meredyth. "I wonder if they need teachers at all."

"No," said Justin, "it could be much more easily done with computers."

"They could read the textbook and do the test online and a computer could mark it. We really don't even need buildings, a classroom."

"Do you have air conditioning in your car?" asked Janice.

"I don't drive," said Meredyth sternly.

"Oh, right."

"Janice," said Meredyth, her voice lowering, "have we heard any news of Linda?"

It took Justin a second to remember who Linda was, and then he remembered Linda Knelman who he used to sit beside and whose illness had caused his classes to double and he was stilled by a wave of guilt for not remembering her. "Oh yes," he said. "How is Linda?"

"We hear that she's doing okay," said Janice, also in a low voice. "She's come through her surgery. And she's back at home now."

"That's good," said Meredyth sorrowfully.

"Yes," said Justin, shaking his head, "that's good."

"But," said Janice, and she was almost whispering, "she's got a long road ahead of her."

"Yes," said Meredyth.

"Yes," said Justin.

"She's doing her chemo now. And then there's radiation too. I'm not sure what the difference is."

"Well," said Meredyth, "they're both quite awful." And as she began to explain the poisons and rays that were ravaging Linda Knelman's body, Justin tried to imagine someone whose tragedy was worse than his, unimaginably worse, and he couldn't really, but he felt it illuminate him somehow with a new sadness, as if he had looked into the sun and it had stung.

"Janice," he said, "if I wrote a note to her could you get it to her at home?"

"Of course, sweetie."

"That won't be the end of it, of course," said Meredyth. "She'll have scarring from that, and the exhaustion is, you can't imagine. And then she'll have to have scans every three months or so, and every time you never know what they're going to find."

Meredyth was showing no intention of leaving this topic or the room for a while, so Justin took his envelope with its secret code towards the empty classroom where he was going to prepare his Business class and of course spy on Mike.

And sure enough there was Cathy Heilbrunner, the pretty blonde, in another demure sundress, a squarish white one with short sleeves, like a nurse's tunic, and little white tennis shoes, waiting outside Mike's office.

"Ready for the test today?" he called to her heartily.

"I guess so," she said. She looked past him down the corridor.

"It's not so bad, I've seen it," he lied. "Listen, if you have a minute beforehand, I wouldn't mind talking to you."

Her eyes went wide. "To me?"

"Yeah, don't worry, nothing serious. I was wondering if you wanted to chat about what you're going to do after this year. You're finished soon, right, end of this term, middle of August?"

"Oh. Yes."

"So there are some things you should know about. With marks like yours. There are scholarships and so on."

"Oh. Sure." She kept looking past him, as if hoping Mike would show up and rescue her.

"It won't take long. I don't know if you've given any thought to going on in your schooling, maybe going to a university next year, but it's worth thinking about."

"Oh." She frowned.

"I kind of have to force you to look at these things," he said, smiling. "It's my job. So after you meet with Mike maybe? We can go and grab a quick coffee? I promise you it won't take long."

"Oh. Now, you mean? This morning?"

"It won't take two seconds. And if you haven't studied for the test yet, then it's too late, so you might as well relax."

"Okay, but I really don't know how long I—"

"There he is. Hey Mike."

"What's up?" said Mike, frowning. He was putting away his phone, which he had been thumb-typing on all the way down the corridor. He was a bit shiny and red, as if he had just come in from outside, and his cologne was strong.

"Nothing, nothing. I might need to steal your student from you, after your meeting—I guess you're having a meeting?"

Mike and Cathy Heilbrunner looked at each other.

"Just for five minutes, after you're done. I'll be working right here. Just come on in when you're done." Smiling and nodding, Justin pushed into his empty classroom and closed the door behind him.

He sat and loudly spread his books and papers out on the desk at the front. He heard Mike murmuring and then his door unlock and close as they both went into his office. Justin sat as silently as possible and waited.

He opened the white envelope and pulled out the pink sheet. The code written on it was neither Wonderboy nor Asshat, but TBIRD69, which was so brilliantly douchey, the ultimate douche password, that Justin could not have thought of it.

He could hear them talking then, but they were murmuring.

"My pleasure," was all that he heard Mike say, and then the door was opening again.

Justin jumped up and opened his door. "All done?" he said to Cathy Heilbrunner, who was already halfway down the corridor. "I'll just grab my bag, one second."

When he rejoined her in the hallway she looked miserable. Mike was glowering at them from his doorway. Justin ignored him and led the way towards the cafeteria. Cathy Heilbrunner followed. She clasped her pile of books to her chest.

"Too bad there isn't some more civilized place to talk," said Justin, "I hate the fluorescent lights in here, not to mention the smell. Would you like a coffee?"

She shook her head.

"All right, let's just sit then." He weaved among the knapsacks and the miniskirts and the track pants and the baseball hats and do-rags to a table at the back. He sat with his back against the notice boards—where he had always been sitting, since Tee had found him here, because you could survey all the entrances from there—and gestured for her to fit herself into the moulded plastic chair unit. "It's a bit like eating in a spaceship, isn't it," he said. "Your eating module. You can put your books here, no one will sit here." He tapped the tabletop. "There you go."

"So, listen," he said, and then he stopped to study the pile of books and folders she had just placed in front of him. There was a big web-design textbook, a guide to Business English, a three-ring binder and a slimmer notebook. Between the two textbooks was an edge of white envelope. "Hey," said Justin, "you're taking web design too?"

She shrugged. She had her eye on the textbook.

"That's an excellent idea," said Justin. "There's really a lot of opportunity right now for someone with a wide skill set. I didn't know you had artistic tendencies."

"I guess." She giggled, staring at him. It was as if she was trying to tell if he was being serious or not.

"You can make a whole lot more money as a designer than as a writer, of course, but it's useful to have both skills. Everything's online these days, and with budgets . . . You doing the hardcore coding part too, like HTML?"

"A little," she said, frowning. "Not really, mostly just Dreamweaver, stuff like that."

"Cool," he said. "I used to be really interested in that. Can I take a look at your textbook?" He put two fingers on top of the book and she flinched.

He let his fingers rest there for a minute and then withdrew them. She followed his hands. "Maybe later," he said. "Did you enjoy your courses here?"

"Sure. I guess."

"Did you find them useful? Do you think you learned a great deal?" He looked at the edge of white envelope again. He could grab it somehow, make her drop her books and pick it up or something. Or something goofy, like saying holy shit, look at that over there, what the hell is that, an elephant? Hey is that Snoop Dogg over there? And just grabbing it. Or he could just grab it right in front of her, just calmly lean over and take it from her. What was she going to do, tell Mike?

"Some parts, yeah," she said. "Are you saying I need to go back to school? I thought this was it, you go work now."

"Yes, it is designed as a practical diploma, sure, not really an educational thing, although I suppose that distinction is kind of old-fashioned. But with your marks, I mean, you're at the top of the class, of every class, did you know that?"

She put her hand on top of the pile of books. "Not in every class."

"So you should think of using that, maybe going into some-thing a little more challenging than web design."

"What's wrong with web design?"

"Hey," said Justin, jerking his eyes past her, "there's Mike."

She twisted her head around so fast her blonde ponytail whipped the air. Justin grasped the white envelope with two fingers and yanked it out. When she turned back around he was holding it up in front of him like a hand in cards. "That was silly," said Justin, "childish, I know, but it worked." The envelope had "CATHY" scrawled on it in a familiar handwriting, a small boy's handwriting.

She reached and tried to grab it from him but he pulled it away.

"What the hell are you doing?" she said.

"What are you worried about?" he said.

"That is mine. That is my private property."

"I don't think it is, actually." Justin opened the envelope and saw the edge of pink paper.

"Who the hell do you think you are? Give me that back right now." She stood up and leaned over the table, her hand outstretched. "If you don't give me back my property right now I'll call the police."

"No you won't. Sit down and calm down." Justin said this very quietly and slowly, and to his surprise it worked. She sat down and looked at him with her mouth slightly open. "You call the police any time you like. And we'll call Mike over here too, if you like, to talk about where you got this." He pulled out the pink paper and unfolded it. It was exactly the same as the one he had received that morning. TBIRD69. "I don't get it," he said. "Why would you do this? You don't even need to."

"It's none of your business," she hissed. "What do you know what I need?"

"Well, you don't need to cheat. You're smart enough. You come from . . . you seem to come from a comfortable background. I've seen the car you drive."

"What the fuck do you care?" Her voice was harsher than he had expected it to be. Her face was thin and pale and she wasn't as pretty now under the cafeteria light. She might have even been older than he thought; older than the other students at least. She was cold in the air conditioning too; her skin was bumpy. "You just said yourself the whole point of this is to get a job. Right? It's a qualification, it's just a hoop you have to jump through."

"Is that what Mike tells you?"

"Isn't your job to help us out? Isn't the whole point to get us a better start?"

Justin rubbed his face with his hands. "Jesus. Help you out by . . . no. I guess if helping you out means giving you an education—"

"An education? What, you mean like for fun?"

"I guess so, kind of, yes."

"You think I'd do this for fun."

"Well, not fun exactly, it's . . . phew. Listen, does helping you out mean giving better grades to the people with rich parents who can pay for them? How much is he charging you anyway?"

She made an incredulous noise, a kind of spitting and hacking noise. "Parents? Did you say parents?"

Justin shrugged. "Maybe you don't tell them directly what it's—"

"I haven't spoken to my parents for five years," said Cathy Heilbrunner. Her face was red now. "I don't even know my dad. If I had rich parents do you think I would go to this crap-ass school?"

Justin frowned. This surprised him. "How old are you?"

"I'm going to go now." She gathered her books up.

"How—so who's—where did you grow up anyway?"

"What the hell do you care?"

"I am curious now. Who's putting you through school?"

"I am."

"Entirely yourself."

"Well, me and the bank. I have loans I can't even think about. I'll be paying off my student loans until I'm sixty-five. That's the only way you can do it now. Or didn't you know."

"I know about student loans," said Justin, "I'm still paying back mine. That's the way it works. But you could do it the—"

"Mr. Harrison," she said, "You really don't get it, do you? I grew up in Scarborough, my mom couldn't take care of me, my dad was in jail left most of the time, I left home at sixteen. I never finished high school. I've been working for a while. I have to have the loans and the work. That's the only way to do it these days. Anything else you want to know?" She looked around and her mouth twitched; he had the feeling she needed a cigarette.

"So you're paying for everything? The car and everything? How do you do that?"

She squinted at him as if he was stupid. "I work, of course."

"Where do you . . ." But he didn't finish his question, because looking at her then, her brown tanned skin and her dyed hair and her tiny waist and arms, and the circles under her eyes that were apparent in the toxic light, he knew what she did and how she made so much money. She looked exactly, just then, like all the girls he had seen at the Manor.

"I do what I have to do," she said.

"Okay," he said. "It's none of my business." He stared at the pink sheet in his hands, then folded it up and put it in his back pocket.

She still hadn't stood up. "So what are you going to do?"

He sighed. He felt tired then, and sad. This hadn't worked out the way he had expected. He stood up. "I'm going to do nothing. Nothing to you anyway. But I'm going to keep this. You're on your own for this test."

She stood up and turned without saying anything. She walked quickly away through the tables.

And there, sure enough, was Mike, standing by the double doors to the tunnel to the parking lot, the real Mike, standing with his hands on his hips and staring at him.

Justin looked at him and then looked at the other routes out of the hall. There was the corridor back to the department, and then the main concourse leading to the bookstore and the other buildings. He could go back through the coffee machines and be surrounded by people for the next hundred metres; Mike couldn't confront him in public. But then it wouldn't really matter anyway. It wasn't as if he was really worried about his career here.

He walked straight at Mike. "Hey," he said. "We need to talk."

Mike said, "What the hell do you think you're doing. You're harassing students."

"Oh, you were watching me, were you?" They were both speaking quietly and had half-smiles on their faces because there were students passing close by.

Mike's right hand was clenched into a fist. He said, "You have no idea what you're doing."

"Listen," said Justin, "all we need is a quick chat and we can work things out. Somewhere in private. There are some things I've been meaning to ask you about. How about tomorrow, after all this stress about the test is over? Or the end of the week? Friday? Maybe we could have a coffee, maybe downtown if you're ever down there."

"Let's talk right now," said Mike.

"Sorry," said Justin, and he made a show of opening his knapsack and putting the envelope into it, with its pink contents peeking out. "I have work to do right now. Test this afternoon. And I have to think about what I want from you." He zippered up his knapsack. His heart was thumping.

Mike laughed. "You give it your best shot, tough guy."

"Friday then," said Justin. He was feeling that sparky feeling he had felt when he had walked away from the cops carrying a half pound of herb; it was a soaring floaty feeling of irresponsibility. It was as if he could punch Mike in the gut right there and deal with the consequences later; the point was he wasn't thinking about consequences. The Ativan had quite worn off; he was high on aggression. It was something he was coming to recognize now, and coming to recognize it was something he would have to be careful of, to resist.

He walked past Mike, brushing him carelessly with the bag on his shoulder, a bag which held Cathy Heilbrunner's cheat sheet and a tightly wound baggie of weed which he had detached from his home stock that morning. The bag also contained a hundred generic lorazepam from India, no, actually ninety-eight since this morning, and soon, as soon as he reached his classroom, to be ninety-seven.

23.

After the test he was sublimely calm, perhaps a little drunk.
On the bus, he actually got a seat. He felt the heat of the engine
under his bum roaring up through him. Sweat burst from his
temples. He tried to let it drip without wiping it, as it was supposed to cool you down.

He dialled Deenie's number. He got her voice mail so he
hung up and called again. She answered on the third call.

"Hey," he said, "It's Justin. Jenna's friend." He still had a pill
dissolving under his tongue. The sun was a heated iron ball, just
low enough in the sky to be visible under the top bar of the bus
window. It beat on him through the glass. He closed his eyes and
saw the red orb through his lids.

"Yeah," she said.

"I have something for you," he said.

"Is it Jenna?"

"Nope."

"Oh."

He still had his eyes closed. It was like what he imagined being in a tanning booth was like. A tanning pod. "I was going to drop in," he said, "but I don't want to run into your boyfriend."

"Oh," she said. "Okay. When."

"Now. An hour from now. I'm coming downtown right now. I can be there in, okay, an hour and a half."

She hesitated. "Yeah. Okay."

"You sure he won't be there?"

"He's out of town."

He snapped his phone shut and blinked at the other passengers, who were now bleached of colour. His mouth was dry and bitter.

"Hey stinkie," he said, wrestling with the dog. He let her take his whole palm in her jaw and she growled but didn't bite. Only when he withdrew it quickly did she try to nip at him. At the same time he was peering around the door to make sure the apartment was empty of armed Portuguese. He pushed her back with his fingertips in her neck as he had been taught to do and she sprawled backwards, and then leaped up and at him again, but now she was trying to lick his face. "She really likes me."

"You want something to drink?"

"Sure."

"I'll put her in her cage."

He sat on the collapsing sofa as she forced the wriggling animal into the cage. The cage seemed to have grown to fill more of the room. The bathroom and bedroom doors were open and there couldn't be anyone hiding in there whom he hadn't seen.

"You want a beer?"

"Sure," he said. "I've had kind of a weird day." He pulled out an envelope. He had counted out fifty pills to give her. They were in the original envelope from India, with curious Indian stamps and all. "The price went up, unfortunately."

"Uh huh," she said. When she looked up from the refrigerator with a beer in her hand she had an unpleasant smile. "I bet it did."

"What."

"So how much are they now, mister big dealer."

Justin shrugged. He thought for a second. He thought he had paid about $140 for the hundred. "I paid one twenty. For these. There are fifty here."

"Right."

"The exchange rate changed."

Deenie laughed. "Whatever. I'll give you eighty."

"A bill even."

"Fine." She went and found the tin with the rubber lid in the mess of the kitchen counter. She pulled out a wad of bills from it and counted off five twenties for him.

Justin took them with exhilaration, a little rush. "Hey," he said, "is it true Armando, your guy . . ."

"What?"

"I shouldn't know this, but don't get all stressed, I think it's kind of cool. Does he have a gun?"

She rolled her eyes. "They're not that hard to get."

"Really?" He laughed a little. "I would have thought they were quite hard to get."

"Don't ask me to get one for you, if that's what you're thinking."

"No," he said, "of course not."

"Jenna should not have told you that."

"I know she shouldn't. And I shouldn't have told you that she did. So just forget it, okay? Don't blame her. Just forget all about it."

"All right."

"I don't know about it," he said.

"Yup."

"Does he carry it with him?" said Justin.

"Would you shut up about that?"

"Okay," he said. "Listen, I have a little extra weed too."

"Huh," she said. "How much."

"It's only about . . . I'm not sure. I didn't have a scale. A little more than a forty, I'd guess. You can have it for fifty."

"Let me see it."

He rummaged in his bag and handed her the baggie. She removed the twist tie and sniffed its contents. Then she produced, from behind the fridge, a white electronic gadget. She set it up on the kitchen counter and plugged it in. A panel of red numbers flickered. She put the open baggie on its surface.

"Four grams, you're right. Good eye."

"So fifty then?"

"Let me give you some advice," she said, folding her legs under her as she turned towards him on the sofa. She was wearing a white tank top this time, but a disappointing bra. At least the bra straps, pale blue, were visible on her white shoulders. Her feet were bare, and the soles dusty. "If you come up with a price, just say it. Say it with confidence, like that's the price, take it or leave it. Don't ask if it's okay or people will always offer you less. Usually people will just pay whatever you ask."

"Got it." They smiled at each other. Then she got up to get him more money.

"So," she said. "You talked to her?"

He took a long pull from his beer. It burned in his nose. "I've tried. She won't . . . she's being very cold. I don't understand it. We were really close and now she's going through this thing. She's been really mad for a while. I keep thinking it's going to end. But it's gone on for a while. She talked to you about it?"

"You kidding me? She won't come near here."

"I'm kind of, I'm pretty broken up about it," said Justin. "I really like her, Deenie."

"She's always been like this," said Deenie. "She gets really mad, thinks people are against her."

"Does she usually change her mind?"

"Yeah, sometimes. Not always. She's always been kind of angry."

"Tell me about it." His high was drying up. A headache was building its foundations at the base of his skull. He knew he should do something about it, take some action; he didn't just want to take Ativans and drink beer all night. He'd be crying in a minute. "I wish I could just sit down and talk to her for a while, find out what's going on."

Deenie was rolling a joint.

"Why is she doing it? What she does. For money. She doesn't have to do that. Is there someone, or some problem that's, you know, pressuring her into doing that?"

Deenie looked at him sharply. "What's wrong with it?"

"What's wrong with it? Everything. It's just, it's ugly, I guess. It's ugly. It must be awful. Why do something you must hate every minute of, when you're so pretty you could—"

"What makes you so sure she hates it? No one's pressuring her."

He said, "Oh."

"It's easy money, it's fun."

"Fun?"

"Well, not always, but it's easy. You work whenever you want, you make a lot of money."

"Yeah, but she's so smart, she has so much potential. She doesn't even see it. What she could do."

"Potential," said Deenie. "Potential to be like you?"

"No. Not necessarily. But . . ." He stopped there, as she perhaps had a point.

"It's not against the law. Maybe this is her potential. Listen, a lot of girls do it. Even smart girls."

"Yeah," he said, "I guess they do." His insides were now well and truly cracked up, leaking warmth, deflating.

Deenie looked at him and shook her head. "Listen, I shouldn't tell you this." She licked her joint. "Because I don't want to tell Armando, but I have a feeling I know who she's staying with."

"You mean if you tell Armando he'll go over there and tear her head off?"

"Basically, yes."

"And you don't think she deserves that. Because you don't think she actually took your stuff."

"No, I don't. I don't think she would."

"Huh. Okay, so where?"

Deenie lit the joint. "She's working at the Manor, right? I know some girls who work there. They share a place near it. It's kind of gross. I bet she's there."

Amanda was whining and scratching at the bars of her cage. "Hey," said Justin. "You want me to take her for a walk?"

"Sure. I was just going to. I have to get ready for work."

"What time you work?"

"Not till ten."

He stood up. "Write down the address for me."

"It's right across town."

"I'll have her back by ten. It'll be good for her. She'll be tired and sleep all night."

"Jenna won't be there," said Deenie. "She'll be working. It's not worth the trip." But she got up and opened the cage. "Her leash is behind the door."

"Yes, stinkie," said Justin, "yes, we're going, yes, right now. Good girl. Yes."

Alighting from the streetcar at a corner about six blocks past the boundary of where he would ever know anybody to actually live, he was aware of what he was wearing. He was still dressed for school, in his khaki pants and his short-sleeved shirt. And his stupid knapsack. He should have thought of adding a pocket protector and some pens. With his slobbering striped pit bull straining at her leash, it was the oddest outfit in the neighbourhood: people might think he was in the vanguard of some impossibly downtown trend. They might think he was the scariest dude they had ever seen.

The streets were loud and bright. There was a ragged queue of people outside some kind of shelter or detox. Next to that windowless building was a windowless bar. People came out of one building and went into the other. Some people were sitting on the curb, a few feet from the traffic. The cars were cruising slowly up and down; sometimes people on the curb shouted noises at the people in the cars. It was not clear whether they were friendly exchanges or not.

Amanda had been subdued on the streetcar and sat at his feet. When they got off she didn't pull hard at him as usual; she looked up at him and hesitated. Justin didn't know where to go either. He had the address in a paper in his pocket but he didn't want to take it out like a tourist looking at a map. He set off down the main artery, past the detox queue, with Amanda trotting at his side.

The people standing around were of all races and ages and genders. It was surprising to see how many were women. They dressed like the men, in baggy jeans and hockey jerseys. They were missing hair and teeth and in one case an eye.

There was a big park across the street and he thought of going over there to look at his paper; it was still light out. But there were groups of guys sitting at the picnic tables.

He stopped at the next corner and looked at the address and the map Deenie had drawn. He had to go back the same way, through the crowd again, and go down a cross street for a while.

He did this as aggressively as he could. The guys he passed were all staring at the dog and its spiked collar. They said nothing.

He found the side street and walked down it. The building, when he came to it, was one of those squat brick five-story buildings, maybe from the forties. It had some effort at art deco detailing around the doorway. A cold fluorescent glow from the vestibule. In short it was very similar to Deenie's building on the other side of town.

Some of the windows had broken blinds in them, some had flags or blankets. He stared up for a while in case Jenna appeared at one of them.

He went into the vestibule and looked at the intercom panel. He was looking for a Rachel and she was on the fifth floor, but there was no list of names or apartment numbers. He pressed some numbers at random. After a few times a voice squawked from the intercom, "Yes?"

"It's me," said Justin.

"Who?"

There was someone on the other side of the door, an old lady with a shopping buggy, on her way out. She backed into the door and pushed it open. Justin held it for her politely. She didn't look at him as he and Amanda slipped inside. He heard the voice crackle behind him as the door closed. "*Who is it? Who is it?*"

"You're being a very good girl," he said to the dog as they walked up the staircase which smelled of bacon and cigarettes. Amanda padded her way up, glancing at him on the landings. She was less certain than he had ever seen her.

He didn't know what he was going to do if he saw her, Jenna, and he didn't want to think about it. The thought was present but distant that this was a silly thing to do, something that might end in humiliation of some kind, and he pushed it away; he was doing something, it was better. And discovering something, either about her or about himself, he didn't know which was more important yet.

He came to the apartment number. There was music or a television on inside. He said, "Sit," sternly and he knocked. He waited a minute and knocked again. A girl's voice came then, "Who is it."

"I'm here for Rachel." He smiled at the peephole.

"Who are you?"

"I'm Justin. I'm a friend of Jenna's. She's expecting me."

327

The door opened a crack. A pale girl showed her face. "You've got the wrong place."

Amanda leaped up and he yanked her back. "Sit," he said, "sit. Hi." He smiled as winsomely as he could. This word presented itself to him: *winsome*. "Hi." He put one hand in a pocket. "You must be Rachel."

"I don't know you." She was staring at the dog, who was whimpering, her tail wagging.

Justin knew she was just trying to lick the girl, but the girl didn't know that. "She just wants to play," he said. "Is Jenna in?"

"She's not here, and I don't know you, and I don't appreciate you coming to my door. I think you should leave." Then there was a male voice behind her, a guffaw.

Justin tightened his grip on Amanda's leash. "Could you tell her Justin's here, please, and it's urgent?"

The male voice called, "Who is it?"

The girl didn't turn around. "Get out of here," she said.

Justin was breathing hard. "Look. Please. I just want to talk to her. Tell her it's really urgent."

"Would you get the fuck away from my door please?"

Amanda started barking.

"I know she's in there," said Justin and his voice was loud, and he didn't know why. Amanda was jumping up now, trying to get through the door. "She can't just ignore me. Tell her she can't."

"What the fuck?" came the guy's voice.

"Tell her she owes it to me," said Justin, his voice embarrassingly high, and the girl slammed the door. He heard the locks being bolted. He was about to pound on the door, but he heard the man and the girl arguing and he stopped himself.

He jerked on the leash and Amanda followed him down

the hallway. What he was feeling was hard to describe; it was a prickly hurt that was turning into something else, a shortness of breath. It was rage.

He got outside and went around to the side of the building that he figured Rachel's apartment was on. He stood in the alleyway and looked up, trying to count windows. He didn't know what he was looking for. Perhaps he would throw pebbles against her window, or sing her a song.

Two men were coming down the alleyway. They were young guys, white guys, in the long shorts and tank tops and baseball caps. They were dark-skinned, with trimmed little goatees. One was short and sturdy.

"Hey," said the squat one. "Can I help you?"

Amanda barked. Justin said, "Okay, it's okay," to her. "No, thank you," he said to the guys. "Just looking for someone." He slipped his knapsack over both shoulders so he had his hands free. One held tight to Amanda.

"Who?"

"A girl," he said. "Friend of mine. Maybe you know her."

The two guys stopped in front of him and folded their arms. They were looking from him to the dog, who was barking without interruption. Justin held tight to her leash.

"You friends of Rachel?" Justin said.

They scowled at him. "She doesn't know you," said the taller one. "She doesn't want you bothering her."

"I'm not bothering anyone."

"Maybe you're bothering me," said the squat one. His forearms were hairy.

"Actually," said Justin without hesitation, "it looks like you're bothering me. Sit. Sit, girl. It's okay. It's all right." He had no idea what he was doing except that his muscles were jumpy and he wanted to smash these thugs in their brain-damaged faces.

The guys had their hands on their hips now, and had separated so one was on either side of him. Amanda was leaping up now and snarling.

"My dog doesn't like you," said Justin.

The guys were exchanging glances now, planning something. If he ran he could get away now. The alley was open at the other end, leading to another alley. But there was no way either one of them was going to get to him around Amanda.

He could just calmly walk by them and they would let him go, but for some reason he didn't want to. There was no point in walking away from everything. And there was the faintest possibility that Jenna was watching him from up there.

If one of them took a swing at him he would let the dog go. That would occupy the one guy, but then he'd be on his own to fight the other. But if he really let Amanda at him, the resulting trauma would be so dramatic it would distract everybody. He'd never get her off the guy.

"That dog so much as licks me," said the tall guy, "I'll cap it."

"Then back off." Amanda was focusing more on the tall guy now, growling and scrabbling to get at him. Justin was pulling so hard on her chain her front feet were well off the ground and she was whining for breath. "Douchewater." He did not know why he said this; he did not even say it loudly.

"What was that?"

"Yes, I'm afraid you are. You are a bag of douche. Water." He enunciated distinctly this time.

He almost didn't see the short guy raise his knee, he just felt it coming from his left side, saw the guy's eyes on his left foot and twitched his leg out of the way just as the thug stomped his foot down. He missed.

Justin yanked Amanda around and let out a foot of her leash. She leaped at the guy, her jaws snapping, and just missed his forearm. He had jumped back.

Justin reined her in again and said, "You don't want that, bro, you really don't. She can break that arm with her jaw. Once she bites—"

The other guy stepped up to him and Justin took a wild swing at him with his right arm. He was off balance because of Amanda. The guy pulled his head back swiftly and easily, like a fighter on TV, and then leaned in again fast and hard and Justin was blinded by pain. There was an explosion in the front of his brain and his vision was actually gone for a second. He went down onto his knees. The guy had butted him in the nose with his forehead.

Justin staggered up, blinking, and saw the guys turning their backs on him. They were walking away as if nothing had happened. He had somehow managed to keep a tight hold on Amanda, who was howling hysterically.

His eyes overflowed with tears, but he wasn't crying. It was just pain. There was blood running down his face, over his lips. He could taste the salt. He stumbled in the other direction, towards the back of the alley, where he would find a hole between buildings and sit for a second, then figure out if his nose was broken. He wouldn't be able to touch it for a while. He was laughing. "Whoo!" he screamed, and reached up and smacked a speed limit sign so hard it stung his hand and rang out like a bell.

24.

He and Mike were to have their meeting at the campus
in the late afternoon. They had had some e-mailed discussion
about when and where. Mike wanted to meet in his office, Justin
had said no, he wanted to go for a drink in the student pub or
in the depressing buffet-style "restaurant" that faculty patron-
ized in the administration building. He thought it was called the
Captain's Wheel or something like that. It had pictures of light-
houses on its walls and it looked out on the Physical Plant and
another parking lot. Mike countered with his car, in his parking
lot, somewhere they could talk in private. Justin said they could
talk beside the car but not in it.

It was unfortunate that it had to be after the end of classes on
a Friday when the whole place would be ghostly.

The shadows were already long when Justin floated from
the bus stop towards the campus. The road was dusty and the
cars seemed to be grinding along even more slowly, nose to
end, blindly following each other as if by smell. He yawned, an
unfortunate side effect of the Ativan which otherwise did not

make him sleepy. He enjoyed the walk. He enjoyed the coffee he had purchased in its efficient styro-cardboard. He enjoyed the golden light on the massed vehicles in the parking lot, although he still could not breathe through his nose or touch it. It was not broken, as far as he could tell, but he had slept with tissues balled up in his nostrils to stop the bleeding and now it was crusty.

He also had two incipient black eyes, still perhaps mistakable for signs of fatigue or illness, but growing steadily greyer as the day progressed. They would be respectable signs of idiocy by the next day.

He walked through the parking lot twice, looking for Mike's red Thunderbird, but it was not there yet, so he delved underground and strolled through to the department to see if Janice was there; perhaps she was wrapping up her work and would want to hang around to take his concerned advice about her love life. Perhaps she would even have time for a drink at the Bomb Shelter or the Pukehole or whatever the pub was called.

But Mike first. His scalp bristled and he coughed to mask an expletive he had been starting to say out loud, there in the musky corridor. There were still a couple of students filtering out, walking as quickly as they could towards the air. There wasn't the usual clamour in the air, though; in an hour it would be deserted.

He wasn't quite sure exactly what he was going to demand from Mike. A better course, more money, less teaching. General things. But he didn't really want those things, not any more. He wasn't quite sure what he wanted from Mike. Or why he wanted this job anyway. But he knew he did, an instinct he couldn't name told him he needed this victory, and not just as a victory, not just because it would be satisfying to beat Mike at something, and it would be, but there would be practical benefits from it. He would not continue in a job like this, he knew that. He would do something else, be someone else, he could feel that happening, but he didn't know what that would be yet, and he needed money, a bit more money, to help him do whatever it would be. He needed a base, a place from which he could begin being someone else. And while he became this person, he would take Mike's money.

He would see. He ground his teeth and considered then rejected taking another pill. He had a few in his pocket.

The door to the departmental office was open, which was strange; it was after five and Janice and Erna locked it when they left. So he was excited when he swung around the corner and into the room, for he would doubtless be the only one in there with Janice, if she was indeed working late.

Sitting in Janice's chair was Armando. He had his feet up on her desk and his hands behind his head. His hair was shiny black, as if combed with oil. He wore a white silky shirt with the buttons undone over a white tank top, and a couple of silver chains. One supported a clunky metal cross, which almost made Justin laugh.

Armando was just staring straight ahead.

He also wore shiny track suit pants—a track shell, it was possibly called—and puffy white running shoes that were absolutely new and clean.

Justin stopped in the doorway.

"Hey," said Armando.

Justin looked past him. Erna's office door was shut. Janice's desk was clear, her computer off, her desk drawers shut. "I am not going to ask you," said Justin, "how you got in here."

"Hey," said Armando, "it's a public place."

"Well, no actually, no, it's not. Technically. Jesus, did you tie them up and lock them in the safe or what?"

"What?" Armando scowled. "Who?"

"The girl who was working here and an older lady. Was this door—"

"Door was open," said Armando. He swung his legs off and heaved himself up. "Looks like you've been getting yourself in trouble."

"You should see the other guy," said Justin, backing into the corridor. He looked left and right. It was momentarily empty. He swung his bag onto his shoulder.

Armando was coming around the desk. "Where you going?"

"Come on," said Justin. "Let's walk and talk."

"Right here is fine," said Armando. "Close the door."

Justin began walking down the hall. Not too fast.

Armando was behind him. He left the office door wide open. "Hey," said Armando. "Where you going?"

"Come on," said Justin. He pushed through the swinging doors and they were in the dead strip of windowless, doorless hallway to the next set of doors, only ten metres or so but empty, and sound wouldn't travel. Through the doors and they were in the busy concourse that led to the cafeteria.

Armando had his meaty hand on his shoulder. "Hey."

Justin accelerated and pushed through the doors. The gust of fried food and the clatter of refrigeration machinery blew on him. Down the concourse, you could see the cafeteria opening up. There were a few ganglions of students in their plastic seating modules, all bright and unruly knapsacks in the glow.

"Hey," said Armando. "You have an office?"

"This is my office, right down there. Let's go sit down."

"No. We need to talk somewhere private."

Justin wheeled to face him. "What do you want? You going to break my toe again, or my nose, or what?"

"Looks like someone already tried." Armando smiled. "You should watch yourself." He folded his arms across his chest. Perhaps he was actually slightly impressed.

Justin smiled back. For a light-headed second he was looking forward to this conversation. He raised himself slightly on his toes. "Did you find what you wanted in my apartment?"

Armando smiled. "I don't know what you're talking about."

"Fine." Justin looked him up and down. The only place for Armando to be carrying a gun comfortably would be strapped to his ankle. The shell suit was so loose it was possible, but there were snaps at the ankle that were unbuttoned, which seemed a little careless if you wanted to hide something. This gun thing was really the only intriguing thing about Armando. One could probably buy an ankle holster online. "I know you didn't, anyway. You found dick all in there. So. What do you want?"

"You went to see her."

"Listen, I don't have a lot of time. Tell me what you want or I'm walking away."

"You try walking away from me," said Armando quietly.

"Are you threatening me?" said Justin not so quietly. "Are you threatening me with violence?"

A student was passing but she didn't hear.

"I am looking for something," said Armando, unperturbed. "That belongs to me. And if I don't get it, there's going to be trouble."

"That's what I thought. You are threatening me with violence. Which is a mistake. You want to scare me and you do.

337

You're right. You do scare me. But your problem is you think I give a shit about you. Or Deenie. See, you think I've been hanging around with Jenna and that I give a shit about what she says or wants too. You think I would hesitate to turn you in? A petty hoodlum drug dealer?"

Armando hesitated for a second, then said, "You watch your fucking mouth."

"You don't get it, do you? Think about it. I know something about you now. I know a lot about you. You think I give a shit about you and your girlfriend? I don't give a shit what you do, what you have in her apartment, the point is I know about it." Over Armando's shoulder, a shadow in the corridor they had just left, was the perfumed silhouette of Annette the PR idiot, walking behind them. Her heels clicked.

Justin waited until she had opened the door and was trying to get around them before he continued. He didn't try to keep his voice down. "You leave me alone I leave you alone. But you come threatening me, you lay a finger on me or on Jenna, I just go right to the cops. I have nothing to hide. Who they going to listen to? You, who they probably already know about, or an English teacher from a college?"

Annette had drawn up to them now and glanced at him, her eyes wide. Justin said, "Hi, Annette." She hesitated for a half a second, but he smiled and nodded at her, and she moved on. She was wearing a grey dress today; even in that moment he noticed how everything she wore was tight.

"All right," said Armando, "keep your voice down. Listen—"

"Yeah, I'd be nervous too if I were you. So I'll talk even louder."

"Listen, just shut the fuck up with all your big talk."

"No, you listen to me. I'm going to keep walking now and you're going to leave me alone. You know, Armando, you're after the wrong guy anyway. Number one, Jenna doesn't do blow."

Armando was rubbing his triceps now, frowning.

"Number two, she wouldn't steal anything from anyone, let alone Deenie. You're after the wrong person. I'm going to go now." He turned and walked after Annette.

"Hey, Annette," he said, catching up with her. "I'm going to walk with you for a minute. You remember me?"

"Hi, Jason."

"Justin."

"Justin, I'm sorry. How are things?"

"Fine. Fine."

She was looking behind them. "Everything all right with that guy? It didn't seem like much fun."

Justin looked over his shoulder. Armando was gone.

He stopped walking and so did Annette. He breathed deeply. "Okay. Wow." It would be cool to stop there, not run away as fast as he could. He tried to look at her. She had a string of pearls around her bare beck, which was a little sunburned, and her hair was that perfect metallic blonde colour that was perhaps meant to look partly grey, certainly not meant to duplicate a naturally occurring colour; it was more meant to duplicate a colour of paint for a bedroom wall, on a paint chip, something seen in a home decor magazine, something very recent and expensive and respectable. It would have a name like Malibu or Mousse. It was very probably the colour of her kitchen nook.

"You certainly told him off." Her face was a little red too, possibly not because of sunburn. She smiled in a way that he usually found aggressive. Perhaps it was her only smile.

"Listen," he said, "would you like to sit down for a second? You have time for a coffee?"

"Well, I'm in a bit of a—"

"No problem. No problem."

"Was there something in particular you wanted to—"

"No, no," he said. "Nothing at all. Purely social."

"Oh." She looked at her watch, which must have been a pose, for he knew she knew exactly what time it was, she must know the time to the second, all day. "Well, you know, why not. I'm always rushing around so much. I never get a moment to connect with the people on the front lines. I mean we have to keep reminding ourselves, you guys are the content."

"I'm content?"

"Well, yes you are, very much so. I mean that's why we have so much respect for you people. We couldn't do our jobs without you."

They joined the queue for coffee.

"You couldn't do your fundraising jobs without something to raise funds for, you mean," he said. "I'm not sure if that's exactly true. I could foresee a future in which we do away with the instructors entirely. We could do it all online, post the lectures, which would be written by some central government committee, post the tests and then post the answers to the tests. Or just sell them. We could do away with the whole instructional program. I mean we are just in the business of delivering a qualification, right?"

"I can't tell if you're joking or not," said Annette, "but I hope you are not. We really respect the educational—no, I want decaf. I'll get it. Thanks."

He watched her hands as she poured her coffee. She wore many rings, but he had never been very good at telling how exactly one distinguished a wedding ring from other kinds of rings. This was one of the things that were supposed to come to one naturally in adulthood, like knowing which day was garbage day. "I like to sit over there," he said "with my back against the wall."

"You seem to live an exciting life."

Justin actually laughed at this. When they had sat down he said, "What about you? Do you live an exciting life?"

"Well," she said, "I try to keep as busy as I can. And I am very busy. I'm very lucky I have this freedom, I guess, because I'm not married. I really don't know if I could ever give that up."

"Give up your freedom?"

"Sure. I think marriage can really slow a woman down, really." She crossed her legs; she wore white stockings and dark grey pumps. She pulled the grey skirt down over her knees. "There's something about it that can really age you. And when you're my age, believe me, you don't want to age any more."

"Your age? You're not exactly middle-aged."

"Oh, thank you, that's very kind of you, but I'm afraid I am. I don't feel it, I mean, I still feel like a teenager most of the time."

Justin smiled and nodded, but he didn't know what she was talking about. She couldn't have been older than forty.

She wasn't drinking her coffee.

"It's pretty vile," he said. "The decaf is the worst."

"Oh, it's fine. I've never been much of a coffee fan. They say middle-aged women prefer a cup of coffee to sex. Don't understand that myself, but then I've always been weird."

Justin laughed. "Good for you. Good for you." Now there was too much stuff in his head. He had almost forgotten about meeting Mike for a half a second. "I'll let you get back to your work."

"If you ever want to talk about how we can improve the optics, you know, the image of the college," she said, "you can make an appointment."

"That's right," he said. "I know."

He had to pass Mike's office on the way to the parking lot. And there was another kid waiting for Mike, a big black kid with cornrows, Justin's own student, Dushan.

Justin slowed. "Hey Dushan."

"Mr. H." Dushan always smiled. He was a nice kid.

"Listen, you're waiting for Mike, right?"

Dushan nodded.

"Yeah, listen, he's tied up. He asked me to come talk to you instead."

Dushan looked uncertain.

Justin looked up and down the corridor as if to make sure no one could hear him. "It's all right," he said to Dushan, "I'm in the loop. I'm working with Mike on this one. You can trust me."

"Oh." Dushan didn't make a move to follow him.

"Let's just step into my classroom, real quick. Won't take a second." He turned and Dushan followed him.

They went into an empty classroom and Justin shut the door. "So yeah," he said, "it's all cool, I'm in the loop. It's about the key to the next test results, right?"

Dushan wasn't smiling any more. He looked extremely nervous. But he nodded.

"All right. Here's the thing. The next test is the final, right? So it's worth a little more."

Dushan frowned. "You changin up the deal on me?"

"No no, I'm not. Mike isn't. This is Mike's deal anyway. I'm just helping him out."

"You takin a cut now too."

"Nope." Justin shook his head vigorously. "That's not it. Just a little system change. You're just going to deal with me instead of him. To keep him, you know, away from the action, you understand?"

Dushan nodded, still frowning.

"All it means it that when the time comes for the next test, and it's coming up soon, you come to me, and we do the deal, I get you the answers key, on a pink paper, like last time, right?"

Dushan nodded.

"And I get it to Mike. Price remains the same."

"A'ight."

"Okay. Except one thing has changed, and that's that Mike wants a little advance. Like a deposit. Some money up front."

Dushan smiled, but it wasn't a pleasant smile. "I knew it. You shakin me down now."

"Nope, not at all. It's just that Mike has had some problems with payment, you know, with some people who aren't too reliable. So it's half up front now. Or whatever. Some."

Dushan folded his arms.

"Listen," said Justin, "I quite understand if you need some confirmation from Mike on this." He took a deep breath, kept his features impassive. He was thinking of the poker game, the time he had won by keeping a straight face and saying, *I'm all in.* He was pushing his chips forwards. "You're quite right to want to talk to him, if you don't trust me. But there isn't a whole lot of time before the test. And he's going to be harder to get hold of from now on."

Dushan sighed, shaking his head.

Justin waited. He folded his arms, stared at Dushan.

Dushan fished out a wallet at the end of a chain. "A'ight," he said. "If that's the deal. How much you want up front? 'Cause I am stone fucking broke, man. This shit killing me."

"You got half?"

"Half? Three hundred fucking green? You think I carry that around, on the bus?"

"Three hundred, eh." Justin swallowed. "Well, what you got on you?"

"I got forty, and I need it for me little brother's lunch money, what I gotta pay when I go pick him up after. I owe the school."

"You pick up your brother from school?"

"No one else going to." Dushan pulled out a grimy twenty. "You take this, it's all I got. But it's like a deposit, a'ight?"

Justin looked at Dushan's extended hand, the thin wrist, the dirty fingernails. He had some faded plastic wristband that maybe meant he had participated in some charity event or that he believed in some new religion. He wore a T-shirt that said Raptors but it wasn't a real Raptors singlet. Justin felt a quick sadness, and a revulsion, as if his stomach had turned on him. "Okay," said Justin, "listen, forget it. I'll tell Mike you'll get it to us when you can. You keep that for your brother."

"Fair enough," said Dushan. "Thank you, Mr. H."

The shadows were long in the parking lot. There was a mild breeze; it was cooler than he had ever known it there, on the asphalt in the buttery sun. It was like a beach.

There were few cars left, so it was easy to spot the Thunder-bird and Mike leaning against it like a teenager. Mike was talking on his phone, of course. He had a white linen shirt on. You could see the glint of the silver chain he wore as a bracelet from three rows of cars away.

Mike folded his phone as Justin approached. "Let's sit down," he said, opening the door.

"Nope." Justin leaned against the next car.

"Okay." Mike put his hands on his hips and smiled at him. "So. What's this all about, anyway?"

"You tell me, Mike. What's it all about?"

"What are you talking about?"

"Oh, come on."

They stood in silence for a moment. They could hear the rushing of traffic from far across the lot. It was like the sound of wind when you're in an attic.

"So what are you after?" said Mike. "What's it to you?"

"You," said Justin, "have treated me like shit since I started working here. You run this thing like some kind of sales office. It's supposed to be a . . . anyway. I want you to do me some favours now."

"Like what."

"Three things. I want more money, number one. I want smaller class sizes. And I want . . ." He breathed in, stared over Mike's shoulder at the nearest tree, a solitary thing on a grass island ten cars away. It seemed to be wilting. He couldn't remem-ber for a second what the third thing was. It wasn't really that he wanted anything from Mike, now. He wanted a different life. But this was a start. "I want to teach what I want. Next term. I come up with two courses, English lit courses, I teach both of them. You can give my shit courses to someone else. Mike and Mike, Joe, whoever."

Mike rubbed his eyes as if tired. "English *lit*."

"Yes, English *lit*."

"What do you care," said Mike very slowly, "about how much English lit our students know about?"

Justin thought about this. It was not such an easy question. "I don't," he said finally. "I would just find it more interesting."

Mike laughed. "All right. And what are you going to do if I say no?"

Justin shrugged. "What do you think? I'll tell the administration about what you've been doing. And the police. I have evidence. The student admitted it. I'm sure she's not the only one."

Mike was shaking his head. "I still don't get it. Why do you . . . what's it to you? I'm making an efficient school here. I'm helping people get what they want. I'm helping them get professional qualifications that are going to improve their lives. Significantly. That's what they're here for. That's what—"

"No," said Justin. "No, no, it's not. It can't be."

"*And* it's preparing them for what the real world out there is like." Mike gestured towards the roaring road, his voice loud.

A black kid was trudging by, between the cars, his mammoth jeans frayed from dragging on the concrete. He glanced over, and Mike was quiet until he passed.

"It's a learning experience," he said more softly, "that is very useful to them, to know that there are various ways of getting ahead. The smart ones get it."

"The rich ones, you mean."

"Oh, listen to you, mister social activist with his English lit degree. What do you know about the kids I'm helping out?

You're on the side of the underprivileged now, with your university degree and your Converse running shoes? You're the snottiest guy I've ever met."

"Me? I'm snotty?"

"You think this is beneath you, don't you? Working in a suburb. You should be in an ivy-covered campus downtown, right, with all the other guys who don't like to shave, listening to indie bands, right?"

Justin laughed. "I've never really thought of it that way."

"It's always the rich ones who think everything should be tougher. If everything depends on what a good high school you went to, then the rich kids always win, don't they?"

"Yeah, maybe. But anyway, listen—"

"You'll never be able to prove it," said Mike. "All you have is an extra paper with the code on it. The girl won't back you up."

"Somebody will," said Justin. "I just talked to another one, too. I know there's more than one."

Mike pulled up the corners of his mouth. "Who? Who you talk to?"

"See. There is more than one, isn't there?"

"Who?"

"That poor fucking kid, Mike. You wanted to shake a kid from a fucking high-rise project down for six hundred bucks. See, I know exactly how much you're charging, too. It's disgusting."

"Dushan," said Mike. "That kid. He talked to you?"

Justin shrugged. "I tricked him. I almost got him to give me money too. But I couldn't do that. I'm not like you."

Mike snorted. "I gave him a special deal. I know he's got problems. So I cut him an extra-special rate. I know where these kids come from."

"How very generous of you. I know that six hundred bucks for a kid like that is huge. He's taking care of a family too."

"They all say that. They know it always works with people like you. They've seen it in movies."

"How much you charging the others? Whatever you think they can afford?"

Mike shrugged. "Listen—"

"Okay, so now I've got evidence from the girl, Cathy, and from Dushan. And he'll turn on you in a second if it comes out. So will she. You think they like you for this? And besides, you don't want an inquiry. You don't want the attention and the suspicion."

"I should pound the crap out of you," said Mike quietly.

"Yeah, okay, you do that, and I'll add assault charges too. Listen. Make me an offer, a salary offer, by tomorrow. Or Monday. Monday. I want a permanent position, and I want, I don't know, about five grand more per course per term. That will take me up to about fifty grand a year, fifty-five, it's not a lot. It won't look out of place, it won't attract attention. Then I'll decide if I accept it or not."

Mike screwed up his face. "You want to stay here? That's all you want? Why, if you hate it so much?"

Justin thought for a second. "No, I don't. I don't want to stay here. Long, anyway. I need a little stability for a while, and some income, and then I'm out. That's the final thing I want. I want to do the next term, no, the next two terms. And then you're going to give me a buyout. You are going to decide to end my next contract early, and you're going to pay me a large severance for it. That will be, say, March next year. So I'll have a full year's salary out of it. Okay? So I want this in writing. That my pay's going up, first, and my title, and later, say around Christmas, that you're offering me the severance. You can get me both letters by Monday. You can post-date the second one."

"You are trying to bully me?" Mike stood taller, stepped sideways slightly.

Justin looked around; Mike had waited for a moment when there was no one close, not even on the distant sidewalk or along the walls of the college buildings. Gently, Justin pushed himself off the car, watching Mike's right arm, waiting for it to twitch.

"Monday," said Justin, and then he saw the blow coming, a roundhouse that was just slightly too wide. He pulled his head back and felt the gust of air as the fist passed.

Mike staggered, almost falling as he missed, and Justin raised his knee and stomped down hard on Mike's toe. He had worn his leather-soled Australian boots for this eventuality. He hit a bull's eye. Mike screamed—quite a high-pitched sound, really, not the yell you would expect from watching fight movies—and he buckled and went down onto his knees. His eyes were tight shut and his head, was, unfortunately for Mike, bowed slightly, which allowed Justin to bring his knee up swiftly into his nose. Mike's head snapped back and then he was down on the gritty black ground, completely down, sprawled and writhing and clutching his face.

Justin looked around. There were two girls emerging from the building, another couple on the walkway from the other parking lot. Both groups were too distant to have seen, and none of them was looking his way. Mike was completely invisible between the cars now.

He looked down at him. Mike was trying to sit up, one hand over his face. There was blood streaming out from his nose now, dripping from between his fingers. His face was pale and he was clammy. But he was breathing and conscious.

"Monday," said Justin. He put his hands in his pockets, hoisted his knapsack and walked away through the cars, towards the road and the bus stop. He looked just like any student.

25.

The next afternoon he took the test papers to a café downtown on the street near the university to mark them. It was near where he had seen her last. He sat in the shade on the south side, in dark glasses, and watched the street with his pile of unmarked tests in front of him.

Part of him wanted to take the glasses off because he was a little proud of his black eyes; if Jenna were to pass by, she would see them. But he wanted to be able to see her before she recognized him, in case she was with someone.

There were plenty of other women to look at too, all the summer artist girls with their bare backs and bruised legs, all their hair unwashed or dreadlocked. And their guys were interesting to look at too, all their skinny boys with beards or sideburns and heavy spectacles and porkpie hats and their jeans as tight as stockings. Each time he saw one of these guys pass with his arm on the shoulder of a girl with a little tie-dyed dress on he wondered if he could take him.

Sometimes girls would glance at him but he didn't smile at any of them. His habitat was concrete, not the flowery city they inhabited; they could take that or leave it.

They were not thinking about him, of course, he knew that; this was the Ativan talking. Still, it was pleasant to sit there in the sun and drink sweet Italian lemon soda and feel it popping against the palate, to feel arousal at the sight of bare legs and shaved underarms, to feel everything, in fact, even the pain still silting up and ebbing away again in his nose.

His first task was to write to Linda Knelman, as she was dying, and he was not. He had a large card with some nineteenth-century still life on it; it was sombrely beautiful but innocuous. He did not know what would make dying people happy or sad. He started to write a short note in it about missing her at work and hoping she recovered soon, but it got longer. He had bought a nice pen, too, a fairly broad felt tip, and it felt good to write longhand. He wrote that he had always enjoyed working with her and respected her views, and then that he had always found that suffering, particularly suffering in the bright hot naked days of summer, made one more sensitive to lovely things as well, as if one were a violin string tuned particularly tight, and that these were times in which, contrary to popular belief, one could see the world more clearly and love it more. He knew that this would be small consolation to her in her discomfort, but he wanted her to know that he was feeling this sensitivity on her behalf.

He really didn't know Linda Knelman at all well enough to write this stuff, but he made himself seal the envelope before he could tear it up. It wouldn't matter to embarrass her anyway, if she was dying.

He wiped tears from his eyes as he wrote her address on the envelope. He didn't know if he was sad for her or for himself or just moved at his own nobility in thinking such noble thoughts. It was true what he had written, though, that he was as sensitive as the tip of a tongue. He would not have thought of Linda Knelman, probably, or thought of her so long and hard, had he not been so fucked up. It was true too that it made you feel better for a very short time to feel sorry for someone else and to feel that you had at least tried to do something nice.

He would deliver it himself that afternoon, to her house in the east end; that would make him feel even nobler.

He put the envelope in his bag and concentrated on perceiving things.

He could still feel the satisfying crunch under his sole of Mike's toe, the numbing thud of the nose against his knee. It was almost as if that spot on his knee was still warm from the contact.

He did not sight Jenna, but he had several heart-racing alarms as he caught a flash of blonde or a certain swinging walk across the street, between two cars, on a passing streetcar. It was always her, definitely her, and then it was not.

Halfway through his pile of papers, he called home to check his messages and there was another one from Genevieve. She had called twice before this week. He would have to give in and call her back at some point; she would be calling his mother next.

He ordered a coffee and called Genevieve on his cellphone. She seemed angry at first, that he had taken so long, and then solicitous. She asked him too many times if everything was okay and he got a little snappy. She asked him when they were going to get together, as if they had agreed to do such a thing, and he found himself saying sure, why not tonight? He would have to occupy himself some way in the evenings.

He told her to meet him down the street, in the same bar where he had first taken Jenna. It was convenient.

The next paper in his pile was Cathy Heilbrunner's. He burned through it; he knew the order of answers now (it was like a complicated rhyme scheme: a-b-a-c in the first stanza; b-a-c-a in the second; the third a symbolic b-a-a-d). She came out with a 65, which was a relief. If she hadn't passed it would have made things more difficult. He wondered for a half a second if Cathy Heilbrunner would be surprised by this result, perhaps even faintly pleased that she had done it on her own, perhaps even learning a lesson from it. But it was more likely to be furious, to take it as further evidence that the world of luckier people had conspired against her.

His phone was buzzing against his thigh and he was digging frantically for it in his pocket. "Hello?" he said several times before he had even pushed the green button.

"Hi," said Jenna.

"Hey," he said, and already he was dizzy, sick, fearful, joyous, the day had tilted. And beneath the thrill, the soaring relief that he still existed in her life, in her consciousness, there was the cloudy awareness of disappointment that it had happened; the day had been bearable up to that moment, and from now on it would no longer be.

"How are you, star?"

He sighed. "Why are you calling me? Now, I mean."

"Just wanted to see if you were okay."

"Ah."

"I'm sorry about what happened," she said.

"Okay." He tried to calmly sip his coffee and it was bitter and cold. A girl in a microscopic dress was passing, a thin blue cotton thing with a halter top, with a bare brown back and bare legs and breasts swimming like fish in a blue tank, the kind of sight that would normally make him feel the anguish of seeing something of great beauty, longing and excitement together, and he felt nothing at all, he just watched her pass. She was not Jenna. He said, "Do you want anything?"

"Want anything? No." She sounded convincingly offended, which made him smile.

"Would you like to . . . should we see each other?"

"I don't think that would be a good idea," she said, quickly, too quickly. "I'm really sorry you're . . ."

"I'm what."

"You're unhappy."

"Oh," he said. "Thanks."

"But I would only make you more unhappy."

"Yes, you probably would. And that's what I want, I guess. I mean I want it all, I want anything you have for me. I want you, so I want anything that comes along with you. You see what I mean?"

"No, you don't. You don't really want that."

"Are you seeing someone else?"

She exhaled. "Justin, I'm never really seeing anybody. I'm not good at it."

"Never *really*? As in maybe someone or some people but not really." Now his brain was all red. He felt the heat of pain like a burn spreading over his face, his neck, his scalp. "Just kind of seeing." *You belong to me.* He wanted to scream this at her but didn't.

"You see what I mean."

"See what?"

"Listen to yourself, Justin. I can't handle it when you're like this. I'd better go."

"When *I'm* like this?" And he was aware that he was speaking too loudly; he couldn't stop it. "That's funny. I learned it from you. You're the jealous one."

"Justin, I really have to go now. I just wanted to say I . . . I hope you don't think badly of me."

"Badly of you! No, I don't think that." Now he felt like crying again. He couldn't win this. "I only think the best of you. I'm in love with you."

"That's really sweet."

He pictured his quivering brain: incandescent red, like the sun through your eyelids. There must be a pill of some kind for this.

She went on, "But you've been mad at me too."

"Well, yes."

"And so I don't want you to be any more. That's all. I can't help who I am."

"Okay. That's okay. I'm not. I'm not angry any more." And he wasn't, as he said this, he knew he wasn't angry, only longing.

"Okay. Well, best of luck with everything."

"That's it then?"

"Yes. I had a great time with you."

"Hey, listen. I need to know, about your job. Where you work. Is there some reason you have to work there?"

She was quiet for a second. "I don't really work well other places."

"Well, yeah, okay, but this . . . I mean like does anyone force you? You owe anyone anything, or is there any—"

"Force me? No. Of course not."

356

"Okay. Okay." He closed his eyes and looked up and now he could see his brain clearly, as if on a surgery show on TV: it was a red mass throbbing like a lung; there were the pale blue sheets, parted, the hands in rubber skin, the fine silver poking and slicing instruments. He couldn't let her go; after that they would have to sew up the wound. "So it's like a last resort thing?"

"It's not that unusual. It's not a big deal. I'm good at it."

"Ow," he said. "I don't want to hear that."

"It's just a job."

"No it is not just a job."

"Yes it is. It's normal."

"No. You have such creative, you have such potential for lots of other things."

"Listen," she said, and her voice had that higher quality it always took when she was about to get angry which could mean nasty, it meant back away now, "listen, I've always known girls who did it. I bet you know people who do it, but you just don't even know that they do."

"Yeah. Yes. I guess I do." The waitress had come out onto the patio and was bending, clearing a table in her little black skirt. She had white running shoes on like Cathy Heilbrunner's. And tattoos on her ankles. He couldn't see the back of her neck, under her ponytail, to see what secret was written there.

Jenna said, "Maybe my potential is to do this. Really well."

"Huh," he said. "That's what Deenie said."

"I know she did. Good line, eh?"

"So I guess," he said, "I guess you did it before. Before this place."

"Yes," she said quietly. "I wasn't doing it when I met you. I was honest about that. But yes, I have done it before. It's always there."

"Okay."

"It's always been around me," she said. "It's just something I always thought was normal. And it is."

"Okay," he said. He waved his hand at the waitress, pointed at his coffee. "Okay then. Maybe I'll run into you then, somewhere."

"Sure, maybe you will."

"Maybe," he said, "we can have a coffee some time."

"Maybe in a while, yes."

And this was like a small yellow light in the redness, buried under that raw fleshy mass, and it would soften to orange if he dug it out and held on to it. "Okay," he said. And he forced himself to say goodbye.

Genevieve was there when he arrived; they had given her a lousy table in the corner and she was looking around half-smiling, as if determined to have a good time. She was wearing her cream turtleneck, which was a little silly for the heat, but it was rather sexy because it was thin and tight; she probably knew this.

He apologized for being late but she didn't make a thing of it, as she once would have.

"What are you wearing?" she said.

"This? It's just a shirt."

"Wow. Is it like a soccer thing?"

"It's Sporting Lisbon. I just got it this afternoon. I guess you don't like it."

"Wow. No, no, it's just. It's kind of bright for you."

It was long-sleeved, which he thought was cool, mostly bright red, with white stripes and corporate logos. It had not been cheap. It went well with the quite baggy dark blue jeans.

"What's all the writing on it?" she said.

"*Parmalat,*" he said in his best Portuguese accent. "I love that word. It sounds like a Turkish capital, doesn't it. Tartars, Tartar hordes from the land of Parmalat. But I think it's actually dairy products. Which isn't very manly, is it? I've always found it funny that all these macho guys are really proud of their yoghurt."

"What's it made of? It's something synthetic."

"I guess. I'm trying something new."

"It's kind of tight, too. Wow, you have lost weight."

"No I haven't. I just never wear tight things."

"You are, you are so skinny." And she put on her worried face, which was irritating.

"Sinewy," he said. "I'm a tough motherfucker in this shirt. How are you?"

"How is work?" she said, as he had known she would, and so he had things prepared to tell her. Good things: he told her that he had made demands of Mike and that Mike seemed prepared to accept them. He was pretty confident that on Monday Mike was going to make him a new salary offer, and he was prepared to talk about some new courses, too.

She was predictably ecstatic about this. She told him she was proud of him, and that she had always known that Mike recognized Justin's abilities, really; she had always known that it would be a matter of time. She had always known Mike wasn't so bad, that his experience in the corporate world was actually useful at a college. Justin had been a bit snobby about this, he had to admit.

So, thus relieved, she began to talk about her own career, which was going unsurprisingly well. She was working on another eco-thing, a project that involved corporations buying credits to offset their carbon emissions. Justin had to ask her to explain it several times, but it was complicated.

You could see her bra outlined quite clearly under the tight turtleneck. It was cutting into her side a little bit. He tried to make out, without staring too obviously, which bra it was; he knew most of them. This one appeared to be slightly padded, which would probably make it a new one. He disliked padded bras because they made it impossible to discern the shape of the breast. And her nipples would never pop out no matter how air-conditioned an environment she entered. The fact that they were worn deliberately to prevent this embarrassment made them even more irritating; they said something about their wearers, something not good. Although Janice, at work, Janice had good reason to wear them: that was a work environment and she was surrounded by leering teenagers all day long. He felt sympathetic to that. But this was a bar on a Saturday evening. He wondered how Janice's weekend was going, if she was still with the fireman, and what his body was like.

"Hello," said Genevieve, "you're not even listening."

"Sorry," he said, "I still don't get it." He dropped his eyes again, quickly, to her breasts. She had always had nice breasts, if perhaps a little floppy. He couldn't tell the colour of the bra, which meant it was probably flesh-coloured, to be invisible, which was also irritating, although he knew it shouldn't be.

"Okay, let me try again. Say you run a factory, or say you decide to drive a car with lower emissions. You go to the agency and you say okay, here I am, and—"

"Hey," said Justin, "you know you can see your bra right through your shirt."

"What?"

"I can see every single line and strap. I can see the curves of the cups. Is that deliberate?"

"Whoa," she said, and she was turning red. "Does it look silly?" She looked down at her chest.

"No, not at all. I bring it up because it's kind of sexy, and I'd rather talk about that than about carbon emissions." He was looking unabashedly at her breasts now. It was possible that all this talk about them might cause the nipples to stand up and be visible. It was worth a try anyway.

She put her hands over her chest. "What is with you?"

"I'm trying to get your nipples to stand up," he said matter-of-factly. "If I talk about them long enough, it might happen. Or is that just guys with hard-ons?"

"Justin, I don't believe you. Stop it."

"What are you worried about? It would be fun." And it was true; he was stiffening as he said this. He leaned forward. "Listen, do this. Don't think about it, just do it. Go into the bathroom, lock yourself into a cubicle, take off your bra, I mean take off your shirt, then take off your bra, then put your shirt back on. Stuff your bra in your pocket. Then come out again and sit down with me."

"*What* are you *talking* about?" She was looking around, pink-faced, as if Justin might be causing a disturbance that would get them ejected.

"Okay." He sat back, sighing. "Don't then."

She sipped from her white wine. She stared at the table and then up behind his head. She didn't know where to look.

"Sorry," he said. "Just an idea."

"Is that your best effort at seduction?" she said.

"Not really. Forget it. Hey, don't you have even the faintest exhibitionistic tendencies?"

"How did we suddenly get here? We were talking about environmental credits."

"Yeah, it was boring."

"Well, I'm so sorry about that." Now she was white, not red, and her lips were pressed tight together.

"Ope," he said. "Sorry."

"What is the matter with you? Did you just ask me out here to make fun of me?"

"Actually," he said, "I think it was you who wanted to get together."

"I wanted to connect with you. Really. Not just be silly."

"Ah," he said. "Silly. Of course. *Silly.* How silly of me."

She was silent for a second. She had her arms folded across her chest now.

"Sorry," he said, "to make you self-conscious. You weren't thinking about your boobs before. It's like that Peanuts cartoon where Linus says to Lucy that he's aware of his tongue, and she says that's ridiculous, and the next thing you see her—"

"Were you really coming on to me just then?"

"I guess. Sure I was." He looked at his watch.

"Well," she said, leaning forwards a little, "do you want to talk about that? Is that something we should talk about?"

"Nope, not really. If it's not going to happen then it's not going to happen."

She leaned back again. "Oh, I see. You just wanted a booty call."

"Not really. But the idea just occurred to me."

"Because you were bored with what I was saying."

"Pretty much, yeah."

"You're disgusting." She laid her hands flat on the table as if to get up.

"What's so disgusting about . . . about wanting to . . . about desiring you, about feeling desire?"

"Wow." She stared at him now, her nose pointed slightly upwards, her mouth set. "You can be so cruel. You always had that."

"Cruel? Why is making a pass at you cruel? I guess I've never understood that, that's true."

"Well, I'm not flattered, if that's what you're saying."

"Yes, I can see that. Well, wasn't this a good idea?" He looked around for the waitress, and the bill.

He walked for a long time. It was a hot evening. He walked through the café crowds, and then south through a housing complex towards downtown. He ended up on a roaring street full of nightclub queues. It was Saturday night, after all. There was a place called The Secret or something; it was an expensive one. He knew he had just been going there all along. He hoped there wasn't a dress code.

The black guy with the bow tie and the headset opened the door for him without so much as a glance, so he was okay.

This one was much more crowded than the Manor had been. There were girls everywhere; crowds of them at the bar, in their bikinis and white mesh wraps, and wandering the floor in their schoolgirl kilts and knotted white blouses. There were some fantastic ones, too: goth girls with tattoos and the black bangs, nurses in white dresses and white stockings. There were groups of guys in suits, mostly, not many guys alone. He scanned the whole main floor, and the fleshy orange-skinned girl dancing under the purple lights on stage, to make sure Jenna was not among them, before he moved to the staircase leading to the second level.

"VIP lounge, sir," said the skinhead with the black bowtie at the foot of the stairs. "Ten-dollar cover."

"Okay," said Justin, reaching for his wallet.

"It will be added to your bar tab," said the guy. "Enjoy yourself."

Justin walked up the velvet-carpeted stairs, which were seeded with tiny lights, not quite Christmas lights; more like the emergency lights along an airplane aisle, the lights that come on when you're going down.

The upstairs lounge looked out over the stage, and there was a bar up there. There were just a lot of deep leather sofas. Guys in suits were sitting on them and girls were sitting on the guys, and writhing and moaning against them. There were hands and mouths on nipples, hands cupping cellulited buttocks and stroking the inside of thighs.

A number of the girls at the bar smiled at him and said hi.

He found an unoccupied sofa in a corner, facing away from the stage. It was fairly dark there.

A girl came and sat down beside him even before the waitress did. She was tall with glossy black hair, and skinny, super skinny, a little bony even. Her name was Rosanna or something, her accent eastern European. She leaned in to him and stroked the back of his neck and asked him how his evening was going.

He was watching a pale one at the bar though, a redhead with freckles. She was milky, fleshier.

He told Rosanna he wasn't going to need a dance right then. "But," he said, "would it be terribly rude of me to ask you to ask that girl over there over here? The one in white? I had my eye on her when I came in."

"Not at all," smiled Rosanna, "here, you can have anything you want." She got up and sent the other girl over.

The waitress arrived along with the redhead. Justin ordered himself a beer and the girl—Chantal, she was French, from Quebec, with an alarming accent—asked for a Southern Comfort and ginger, which was a drink he had never heard of before. But then he knew they were supposed to ask for expensive drinks, as expensive as they could, and they got the waitresses to make their drinks without booze, so the girls could stay sober, and charge the client full price. He knew this and he didn't care. He ate up Chantal's full breasts and round little belly with his eyes.

She kissed him on the cheek as the drinks came and put her hand on his thigh. Gingerly, he put his palm onto her knee, but he wasn't sure how far he could slide it around. He wanted to put his arm around her shoulders and have her breathe into his ear; he had seen other guys do that. You probably had to pay for a dance first. And this was what he was going to do, after this drink.

He had a hundred bucks in his pocket, which probably wasn't going to go far. But they probably took credit cards, at least for the drinks. He guzzled his beer.

He told Chantal he was a teacher and she loved that, that was so sweet, and she told him she had only been in town for around six months or so and that she was twenty, although he suspected her of exaggerating upwards. She smelled of candy, like Jenna.

Her English wasn't perfect and he tried some French but couldn't understand her when she spoke; her French sounded more like Hungarian. She said she was from the countryside.

After his beer he ordered a bourbon, straight up, and she finally asked him if he'd like a dance. He nodded, although he wasn't quite ready. He wanted to finish the bourbon first.

She stood up and turned her back towards him, then slowly sat down on him, stretching out so her head rolled next to his. He put his hands on her cool thighs, then gingerly on her waist. She shook her head so her straight red hair was in his eyes and mouth. He breathed in. He was getting hard already.

She breathed in his ear, rubbed her cheek against his. Then she peeled the straps from her shoulders and shook her breasts loose.

With his chin on her shoulder, his face was a foot from them. The nipples were pink and erect and beautiful.

She arched her back, ground her ass against his crotch. He wanted her to not do that so much. He wanted her to not do any of it, actually, as he knew he would be thinking of Jenna doing the same thing when he left, but he wanted her to go on, too.

She stroked her own nipples for a while and made little moaning noises in his ear, as if she was really excited.

It was embarrassing, too, to be sitting there so helplessly with this silly grin on one's face. Justin imagined he looked rather childlike. He glanced around briefly at the other sofas, the men on them, the women at the bar. Nobody was looking at him.

The music was sickly dance pop, but soft, like bad jazz; it didn't have the thumping beat of dance music. It was the kind of music he imagined fourteen-year-old girls listened to in suburbs. He had never known one of these girls. And here were all these thick-wristed men in charcoal suits and big metal watches, breathing in the girl music with these sheepish smiles. There was something emasculating about the whole thing.

Now she slid off him. "Want another?" she said. The song had ended, of course.

"Sure," he said.

She waited a second, beside him on the couch in her stretchy green thong, for the first notes of the next song to begin. Then she quickly pulled the thong down, lifting her pelvis off the sofa, her hip bones jabbing upwards in little exclamation marks, and sliding it down her thighs. It wasn't sensual, it was efficient.

Then she swivelled towards him and spread her legs. She stretched one leg over his, the weight of it on his thigh. She squirmed towards him, bringing her crotch right up to his body, and leaning back, so he could not but stare right into her parted lips. She was completely shaved, of course, or waxed, more likely, there was not a trace of stubble.

Nor was there a trace of moisture between the folds. It was smooth and dry like a model of a person.

She stroked herself there with her pink-clawed fingers, parting the flesh and moaning a little.

Justin was blushing red, for it was embarrassing to be staring with such fascination into her vulva, and yet he couldn't not, for he was excited and inflamed and disgusted at himself.

After a little of this—just enough, just enough before the complicated folds lost their mystery—she sat back on him, completely naked now, his cock protected only by his jeans against her aggressive rubbing.

He began to stroke her more confidently now, moving his hands around to cup her breasts, and she let him. She let him brush his lips against her ear, too, and her neck, which was thrilling.

At the end of this song he asked her if she took credit cards and she said sure, so he said okay, one more then.

During this one she slid down on her knees in front of him and actually laid her head on his lap. Then she looked up at him, threw her hair back and giggled, for she knew she had frightened him. But then she pushed her palm all the way up his thigh and brushed the bulge of his cock with the back of her hand. She glanced over her shoulder and back again. She had positioned herself so that no one could see, from behind her, what she was doing with her hand. And you would have to be very close to Justin, perhaps leaning right over his shoulder, to see from behind him.

There was a horror and pain in this, of course, because he could only see Jenna doing it, and yet it was an incredible thing to be happening for only twenty dollars. So he let her stroke him gently for a minute, wondering how it would end, and then the song ended and she stood up and pulled her thong on again, and her bra top, while Justin sat there deflated and wondering if he should pay for another song in case she was actually going to get him off there, in public, in his jeans. This was the plan, of course, to get him to wonder that, and he was at least sober enough to realize that she would keep you going all night like that. And the music was sad now, just melancholy and embarrassing, and he was an idiot, and the whole sweetness of the place, the poignancy of that saccharine music, its childlike vulnerability, made him sick with pity.

It was strange to feel such fierce desire and pity so insepar-able but then he supposed he always had, even when pudgy thirteen-year-old Anne-Marie Doucet had let him put his hands up her shirt and feel the heavenly weight of her breasts, and then even up her skirt to feel the rubbery mound through her underwear, when he was twelve or thirteen too, somewhere around there, although she was a year ahead of him. That had been exciting and humiliating too, for she was so ugly he would not have wanted anyone to know about it, and he felt terrible about it.

Sometimes the memory of that first touch of warm cottony pad between the humid thighs would still arouse him, even now, and he would masturbate to it at night.

There was some awkward waiting together for the waitress to come and take away his card and then bring it back to him with the drinks and the dances and the cover charge all on it, $140 before tax and her tip and maybe a tip he should be leaving for Chantal, too, he didn't know, so he wrote $180 and signed it with the feeling you have when a roller coaster starts to plummet. She kissed him on the cheek and told him he was sweet and she would love to see him again and he should come back soon.

Even when he looked back at her from the top of the stairs, she smiled sweetly at him from her perch at the bar and waved him goodbye.

Outside, on the street, his cellphone rang. It said "blocked number." He answered it quickly.

"Hey," said a male voice. "It's Danny."

"Danny." He stood there for a second, blinking.

"Danny, from the bar."

Justin was cold, standing out there, although it was still warm. The hair on his arms was standing up. Danny was the little ponytailed drug dealer he had spoken to. "Danny, Danny, yes. How are you?"

"I got a line on that thing you wanted."

He tried to say, "Excellent," but coughed.

"You want it?"

"Ah." He looked around at the people getting out of taxis, shouting, little women tottering on skinny legs. Everybody was drunk. They were all in groups. He took a breath. "Yes. Yes I do."

"All right, it has to be tonight, a'ight?"

"All right. A'ight."

"So you're going to meet a guy called Tommy. I'm going to tell you where. And you bring eight hundred bucks cash."

"Eight hundred. Jesus Christ."

"You don't got it?"

"Yeah. Yeah, I got it. I just didn't think it would . . ."

"Well, you can try talking to the guy if you want. It's between you two."

"All right. Where do I go?"

He didn't have a pen, of course, so he just had to remember an intersection and a building and a buzzer code. It was eastwards, in a public housing complex, but not too far.

He went to a bank machine and took out a cash advance on his credit card. He didn't know what people did without credit cards. Ask him to do them favours, he supposed. He was a powerful guy with his credit card.

He got on a streetcar with his money. His heart was knocking against his chest and he felt as if he might throw up. This was the first time he had actually felt very scared of something. He had to try to slow his breathing down.

But he couldn't turn back, because if he did he was a wimp and he would never have this thing he wanted to have, and you could have whatever you wanted to have. And this tingling, this tight skin and mouth and the nausea, was a great deal better than crying, or than marking papers, and the sensation was not unlike the feeling he had when he first peeled Jenna's clingy top down over her popping little breasts, or when he noticed the way the guys on the street looked at him when he was walking the dog, with her, or, come to think of it, not unlike the expanding-head feeling he had had when raking those chips in at the poker game, or the clear vision he had had when leaving that place at dawn, those fizzy perceptions that had probably come from taking those drugs, that energy. So he stayed on the streetcar, wishing that he had some water and that this meeting was over.

26.

The next day, the Sunday, was torpid, an eventless day of sludgy rain, rain that was almost hot. It swept the apartment roof and the iron fire escape in waves. Justin slept for as long as he could, got up and wept a bit, and then went again to his knapsack and opened it and contemplated taking the thing out. He had looked at it for a while last night but had put it back in fright.

The bag was heavy. The thing was inside a cloth bag, a shoe bag that said Aldo. It was grey, not a flashy silver as he had feared, and the grey metal had a bluish hue. The metal was slightly pocked or pitted. It felt a little oily, although there were some flecks of rust on the barrel and around the trigger guard. It looked rather old. Perhaps it was some sort of antique. The stock had scored wood panels on either side for grip, abrasive like a cheese grater. There was one big screw on either side of the stock. And coming out of the bottom was a small metal appendage or spur. He had no idea what that was for. There was almost no barrel at all, the whole thing was stubby, so it could be easily hidden. He could easily get his hand around the grip and the trigger. He raised it to shoulder level, closed one eye and tried sighting down the barrel at his fridge. It was hard to keep it steady. He remembered Armando standing there. Then his arm quivered and he had to put it down.

He had no instruction manual, and had never fired such a thing, but he imagined there would be lessons on the web. He had had to pay extra for a small box of bullets. There was a cocking hammer you could presumably pull back with your thumb the way they did in Westerns, but he was afraid to touch it. The guy had assured him it was not loaded, and he had even pushed out the magazine to show him. And he had showed him where the safety button was.

He put it back in the bag. He would have to read some kind of manual. He found a shoebox and put it inside it and then put it under his bed, aghast at his idiocy for doing such a thing. It was completely useless. And then he would take it out fifteen minutes later and study it again.

He tried lifting it and sighting again. He stood in front of the bathroom mirror and pointed it at himself, aiming it steadily right between his eyes.

He waited for the day to end. It took a long time: he went out with an umbrella in the afternoon to buy a sandwich and it felt as if he had been in the apartment for a week, and it was only halfway through, as if time had stuck. He still had the evening.

He spent that reading news stories. And then on gun sites.

There were very many models and variants of PPK, and he didn't know what year or series this was. The bullets he had were .32 calibre, which was a little disappointing as there were models that fired .38s available. He had an idea that the local police had .38s and he didn't want to feel like a wimp. Not that he would ever be firing at police, or at anyone, but if asked he would have liked to be able to say, quietly and knowledge-ably, "Thirty-eight." He should perhaps have done a bit more research before buying. But then this thing was the only one available anyway.

He would have liked to talk to Andrew about this toy, it would have been something, if it had in fact been a toy, they would have loved playing with together. And Andrew always loved the technical stuff, horsepower and tensile strength and amps and watts. It was sad that he couldn't talk to him, Andrew. He didn't know why, but he couldn't. He could call him and Andrew would love to see it and if he was just calm about it they could look at an operating manual together, but he wouldn't be calm about it. He would have to know why Justin had it, and that would be just too hard to explain. He was too far away from Andrew now. He missed him then, and felt sad about that.

Somewhere in the world on some computer there was an operating manual and an exploded view which he saved and printed.

It turned out to be quite easy to load. He did it with shaking fingers, but the rounds slid in neatly and the magazine clicked shut.

There was still an hour or so before he could go to bed. He resisted calling Jenna by looking at naked women and repulsive spurting sex on the computer.

The humid morning was a relief. He didn't have to be in to the college till the afternoon, and he left early; he was eager to face whatever it was that awaited him there. He really didn't know what it would be; it might be a contract or a fist fight or perhaps the police. Whatever it was, he wanted it.

It wasn't until he was out of the subway and onto the airless bus, heaving and sinking along the eight-lane road to nowhere, that he gave in, just pulled out his phone without thinking about it and dialled her number, the way smokers trying to quit will light up suddenly and feverishly, with gluttony.

She did not answer, of course, so he folded his phone and dialled again and again, hanging on to the greasy metal pole with one hand as the bus dipped and shuddered. He dialled five times.

"What?" she said.

"Okay," he said, "I'm sorry to bother you. And I'm not going to keep bothering you. I just . . . hang on. There's a seat." She was silent while he inserted himself between two white robed men with intriguing hats, possibly religious, and swung into a seat that had appeared. This was a good omen. He turned his face to the window and said as quietly as he could, "I just really need to know if you are, in fact, seeing someone else."

There was a silence, which was chilling, because it gave him his answer.

"So I guess you are," he said.

"Justin, I—"

"It's okay. It's your right. I guess I'll be seeing people too. I just need to know."

She sighed. "There is someone, I guess, yes."

"You guess. Okay." They were passing the factory that made plastic bubble windows and it was itself studded with plastic bubble windows that looked endearingly unfashionable; they looked like houses from the future in the past, like the sets for

1960s space dramas. And they were all clouded now, too. It was beginning to rain again. "This is none of my business, but I can't help asking, did you meet him at the place, the place where you work?"

"Justin. You are just torturing yourself."

He said, "I figure that's the only possibility, since you're not exactly sociable. I figure that's where you would meet anybody. Through clients. It must be weird though, after a guy has paid for—"

"It's not like that," she said.

"Well, it doesn't matter. It makes sense. More sense than I did, with you."

"What are you talking about?"

"I mean I guess we never would have worked out. I guess one of your clients is more your type."

"More my type? Oh, you mean like a low life?"

He was silent.

"You mean someone not like you. Right. You've never been to a strip club in your life, have you Justin? You're completely different, aren't you, Justin?"

He thought about this. "No, you're right. I'm not. That's true."

"Are you okay?"

"Yeah. I'm sad, but I'm okay."

"You need to calm down," she said.

"Yeah, I know, I will. Okay, Jenna. I'll go now. Okay?"

"Okay." Her voice was soft and beautiful again.

"Good luck then," he said. "Call me some time and we'll have a coffee. Okay?"

"Okay."

He didn't have an umbrella and so was damp by the time he made it to the campus. He walked into the building through the main entrance, not underground; he wanted to be seen. Nobody looked at him strangely, or at all. (What had he expected? That they would throw garlands on him, or bow down before this conqueror, this tyrant?)

Janice was up and moving about the office, filing things, watering plants. Grey-haired Erna was at the front desk. Mike's office door was closed, the light not on.

Justin stared over Erna's head at Janice's buttocks as she moved. She wore a rather dull outfit today, the usual tight trousers, grey this time, and a loose white cotton top that was almost like a sweatshirt. It was below her usual standard; it must have been because she was sad.

He waited until she turned and looked at him and—indeed, she wasn't wearing her usual perfect makeup—raised his eyebrows at her as if to ask what was wrong, and she smiled and shrugged. He was not sure, exactly, if this communication had taken place—if she had understood it as he had—but it was possible, indeed he thought it likely, that they already shared this kind of code, without knowing each other.

"Hey," he called to her. "Hello, Erna."

"How was your weekend?" said Erna.

"Tiring," said Justin.

"You look tired."

"Ah," he said, "those bags under my eyes are something else. I fell. They're black eyes."

Janice turned to peer at his face. "Really?"

"Small altercation," said Justin.

"Right," said Janice. "You're such a brawler."

"You never know. How are you?"

"Oh, you know."

"Trouble in love," said Justin.

"I guess," said Janice.

"Mike in?"

"He called in sick," she said sadly, as if this were evidence of some societal decline. "He left an envelope for you."

The women pretended not to watch Justin as he opened it. He pulled out the letter and read it below the level of the reception barrier so they couldn't read it.

Pursuant to their negotiations, Mike was delighted to offer him the position of . . . at a salary of . . . as agreed.

He looked up smiling. "Janice," he said, "I can tell you need some advice about something. Why don't you come and have a coffee with me. My class isn't for another hour. Erna, can you spare Janice for ten minutes?"

"I think I can manage that," said Erna, and she turned and smiled at Janice in a way that made Janice blush.

He walked slightly ahead of her to the cafeteria. For once he wished it wasn't quite so public. They sat in a central pod, one with no fried rice or sauce on its surface. In the sick light she looked younger, like one of the students.

"Relationships suck, don't they," said Justin.

"Why do you say that?"

"Well, I was in one, I guess, until recently, and it ended."

"You know, I knew it. I could so tell. You were all excited and happy for a while. I heard you talking on the phone to her. I am so sorry to hear that."

"Yeah, thanks, and also I figure things aren't going so well with, ah, Brian?"

"Listen," she said, "Linda called this morning."

"Linda?"

"Knelman."

"Oh yes."

"She wanted me to tell you she got your note and she was really happy about it. She said she would have contacted you but you didn't write a phone number or anything."

"Oh right." He drank his coffee quickly.

"She said she was really touched. She said it was really beautiful, what you wrote."

"Oh. Ha." He felt the blood flooding his face. He must have looked like a russet potato.

"So, I thought I would tell you. That was nice of you."

"Thanks." He drummed his fingers on the plastic.

"You weren't all that close to her, were you, I mean when she was here?"

"No, not really. But I guess I always, I don't know, respected her, I guess." He had to stop talking about this or he would cry again. He had never thought about respecting Linda Knelman before, but now he actually did feel that he had always liked her. And he really did feel sorry for her, real sorrow, anguish even, which he now had to control before it spilled.

She said, "Well, anyway, I wanted you to know too that I was really impressed. That you wrote to her. I'm not sure if everyone has."

"Hah. Funny thing if *I'm* the nicest guy," he said.

"What?"

"Nothing."

"Well, it means a lot, these things. Little things."

He said, quickly, "So, breakups, eh? You and Brian. I figured things hadn't been going so well."

"Well, for a while, no. We did break up."

"That's what I thought. Listen, I wanted to ask you—"

"But things are okay again. We're back—"

"Would you like to come out with me some time?" He was staring straight at her. He could allow her to pretend to think that he hadn't heard what she had just said. It would enable her to pretend that she hadn't said it.

She sipped her coffee and looked around. "Out where?"

"Anywhere. Dinner. Or just a drink. I know some cool bars downtown you might like."

"Wow," she said. "That's a surprise."

"That I know sick bars?"

She laughed. She was red, too. "No. None of the professors have ever asked me out before."

"Well, that's okay then, I'm not a professor. I'm just a con-tract . . . no, wait a second. I am now. I'm a full-time instructor now. Mike just promoted me."

"Really? Is that what was in your envelope? That's amazing. Congratulations."

"So now here I am. A real professor, asking you out."

She sighed. "That's a nice idea, and thank you so much, but—"

"You know the area around Lansdowne? Downtown, in the west end?"

She shook her head.

"There are a lot of new bars and boutiques there. There was a whole spread about it in that magazine, that one with the octopus on the cover?"

"Oh right."

"I've been to a couple of these places. You read the article?"

"I guess. I think so."

"There's that place Meme. It's more an after-hours. A little bar called Hex Key. Full of musicians. Rock guys mostly, but DJs too." Justin suspected she was more of a club girl than a fancy restaurant one. She would be afraid of the food at a place like Blacktable, and he would be happy to avoid it. It was bad enough he was going to have to go back to Hex Key.

"Really." She was frowning now, looking down. He almost had her.

"There's a fantastic dance club. You like to dance?"

"I *love* to dance. That's one of the things that always came between—"

"Persimmon. It's called. This is a kind of fashiony place. Like you'll see models."

"Oh, Persimmon. I've heard of that."

"We should go dancing. At Persimmon."

"Wow," she said. "I haven't been dancing in like a year."

He opened his knapsack, found a pen. He pushed a napkin across the table at her. "Write down your number," he said. "Monday is a good night for there, actually."

"Monday?"

"Yeah. I hear. It's like their industry night. We could go tonight."

"Tonight." She hadn't picked up the pen yet.

"Maybe a weekend is easier."

"No," she said. "That sounds great. Let's just go."

"Tonight?"

"Yes, sure, tonight. I'd love to see it." She wrote a number on the paper and handed it to him.

"Cool," he said.

They walked slightly closer together back to the office. He knew she was feeling guilty. He wondered how that felt. It probably felt delicious.

There was a feminine silhouette, a tight and curvy one, erected on spikes, ahead of him, before he perceived that it was Annette the PR idiot, waiting outside Mike's office. She frowned a little as she saw Justin and Janice coming towards her. Then she put on her concrete smile. It was probably her only smile; she probably used it when she was firing people or making her kind of desperate love.

"Hello," she said, and her smile dropped again. She took in Janice and then Justin and then Janice again and she looked a little tired.

"He's not in today," said Janice.

They stood there for a second, Justin smiling at Annette the PR idiot and wondering if she remembered him. Janice waited too, perhaps to see how well Justin knew Annette.

"Okay then," said Janice. "I'd better get back to work."

"I'm going to sit in my classroom for a bit," said Justin. "Before it starts."

Janice went through the door, looking back at him once.

Justin waited until she was well inside and said quietly to Annette, "I think he's sick. He won't be in for a couple of days."

"Oh," said Annette. "That's too bad."

Justin moved a few steps towards his own classroom door and she followed him, a bit aimlessly. Or perhaps he was just magnetic today.

"It's Justin," he said.

"Of course. I remember you, Justin."

He turned and leaned against the wall abruptly and she had to stop quite close to him. "How are you?" he said. "We never did have that meeting."

"Were we going to have a meeting?" she said.

"I thought we were going to connect. Discuss things."

"Well, we still should."

Justin looked her up and down and was not afraid for her to notice this. She was wearing a suit, as usual, with a tight skirt in a thin material, and no stockings, and fantastically tall black shoes, matte black leather. Her jacket was cut low enough to show a white tank top, and through that the outlines of some kind of baroque bra, lace in curlicues like a wrought-iron balustrade. He said, "You look very . . . elegant, as usual. You are always well dressed."

"Well, thank you." She looked at him with what could only have been curiosity.

"Actually," he said, "this is probably totally inappropriate for me to say, but you look incredibly sexy today. You look hot."

She laughed and blushed and said, "That is not inappropriate of you at all. Nobody minds hearing that."

He took another step towards her—too close, really, for politeness—and leaned against the wall to make it seem more natural and casual. "Okay then," he said, "it's really forward of me to say this, but I can see that this bra—not that I'm staring at your chest, but there is a bit of edge showing, so I guess I can't help but notice, that is a very expensive bra. I know something about these things."

"Ha!" She was looking over her shoulder, down the corridor, her face bright. "A straight guy who knows about bras. That's exciting. Well, you are right. It's a fantastic bra. I got it in Vegas."

"Vegas?" He blinked. He saw poker tables, guys in cowboy hats—images he had only seen in movies, really—and was stunned by it for a second, by the incongruity of the word and this fish-fry-scented concrete underground corridor. Vegas was a place where people got drunk and had hookers for a thousand bucks a night. But then he had never been to Vegas, he had no idea what it was like, whether Annette was the kind of person one might find there, renting hookers for a thousand bucks a night. Perhaps Vegas was just like this place, which was like any place. Was Vegas known for its bra-shopping? Did they have special bras there? He said, "That doesn't surprise me. You are always dressed in a way that I find . . ."

"Yes? Careful now," she said sternly. She was playing at being scolding, but her eyes were darting behind him, behind her, looking for Mike, as if he might loom in ghostly or holographed form even when not there.

"Very elegant," he said. "And very sensual. Sensual, I guess."

"Well, thank you." She looked up the hallway one more time. Staring over his shoulder, she said, "You're not so bad yourself."

And he knew in that second, and only for a second, really, that if he actually tried to touch her then—and he was so close, he could—she would respond, right there in the hallway; he could drag her into a computer lab, whatever, and she would follow him, let him do whatever he wanted. Women were not so foreign, really, not so unlike him, or whoever Jenna was seeing; people were all alike, really.

He knew he should leave her there too, at this moment; his instinct—an instinct for keeping the upper hand, he supposed—told him that.

"Well," he said, "I'll be seeing you around." He hoisted his heavy knapsack. "And I'll be noticing your bras." He leaned in and kissed her cheek, then walked away, the powdery touch of her face burning on his like a light.

He walked down the tunnel, away from his classroom, no idea of where he was going, and the end of the hall was narrow like the perspective in a video game, and at the end of it there was nothing but another white wall and more corridors, and it was quickly a lonely space. It reminded him of Jenna and of not having her, because there was nothing in it but painted concrete rushing past; it was a whitewater rapids of nothing, of anguish, but there was a difference to the anguish now: he was observing it. Even in thinking of it this way he was making something of it, directing it like a stream of fire on everything around him, and that was making those things more beautiful, for them to be illuminated by pain in this way.

He stuck his hand under his shirt to feel his belly, which was stretched taut and churning as usual—it was like touching the rubber seal over a hot tub. He swung his knapsack around to his front and felt the reassuring metal weight in it. He opened it as he walked, reached inside it and grasped the stock and the trigger guard, as if he was going to draw it out there in the hallway. The metal was warm from being against his back.

He went back to his classroom, his shoulders squared. He

went into it as if he owned it. He released his grip on the gun and lowered his knapsack onto the front desk gently and still it made a heavy thud.

There was a chair, one of those chairs with half a desk surface attached to it, and the writing board was loose. He went and wiggled the board. It just needed a screw. And then he brought his elbow down hard on it to smash it completely. He hit it this way twice, three times and he heard the splintering of particle board and it fell loose on the floor, spraying screws. With a rush of pleasure, he kicked the board across the floor and it slammed into the radiator with the bang of hollow tin.

He took his bag and strode down the hall and towards the first stairwell that would take him up from that basement to ground level, out to the air, to the world out there. He had a loaded gun in his bag. His whole body felt hard.

THANKS

Richard Bingham
Shaughnessy Bishop-Stall
Jowita Bydlowska
Christa Conway
Doris Cowan
Jennifer Lambert
Martha Magor
Douglas Manuel
Anne McDermid
Canada Council for the Arts